Samuel Silas Curry

The Province of Expression

Samuel Silas Curry

The Province of Expression

ISBN/EAN: 9783337375379

Printed in Europe, USA, Canada, Australia, Japan

Cover: Foto ©Andreas Hilbeck / pixelio.de

More available books at **www.hansebooks.com**

THE

PROVINCE OF EXPRESSION

A SEARCH FOR PRINCIPLES

UNDERLYING ADEQUATE METHODS OF DEVELOPING

DRAMATIC AND ORATORIC DELIVERY

S. S. CURRY, Ph. D.

Dean, School of Expression ; Instructor of Elocution, Harvard College ; Acting Davis Professor of Elocution, Newton Theol. Inst. ; formerly Snow Professor of Oratory, Boston University, etc.

" What hand and brain went ever paired?
What heart alike conceived and dared ?
What act proved all its thought had been ?
What will but felt the fleshy screen ? "
— *Browning.*

𝕭oston

SCHOOL OF EXPRESSION

FREEMAN PLACE, BEACON ST.

1891

To A. M. P.

Amice, alter ipse.

The waves still murmur to the listening shore,
   A star comes forth to meet the rising moon,
   Again the breezes dance with leafy June;
But one, the long-loved comer, comes no more.
Oh! dost thou see a boatman's single oar
   That toils alone 'mong rocks to find the way?
   Oh! from those peaceful shores of trustful day
Return, once more a faltering heart restore!
A sheet toil-worn and blotted here is spread
   For thee its lines more full and clear to trace;
Alas! I cannot hear thy kindly tread,
   And all is dark, I cannot see thy face.
So to the winds the scribbled lines I throw,
To roam, and find a heart its word shall know.

AIMS AND RELATIONS.

" For us and for our Tragedy,
Here stooping to your clemency,
We beg your hearing patiently."

DURING the last twelve or fifteen years, as I have met different classes in various institutions, I have endeavored at the very beginning of each course to give a general conception of the purpose and nature of the work to be undertaken. As the students have come together, strange to each other, strange to their teacher, and unacquainted with the subject, it seemed best thus to introduce them to the work. It was found necessary to do this also because many had absolutely false ideas of the department, and others such vague notions as to furnish no foundation for a beginning. Before this method was adopted, the simplest exercises would fail to accomplish any satisfactory results through mere misconception, not so much of the specific exercises, as of the general nature and aim of all work for the development of expression. Out of such efforts this book has grown. Of course it is not meant that all the principles here discussed were considered before students began to work. Only about one half the first hour could be devoted to such a definition, but, though only a few ideas could be awakened, it was the endeavor to state the fundamental elements, and to suggest lines of thinking, so that in the future practice and study the students would be led naturally into a comprehensive grasp of the nature and aim of such work and its relations to other departments of education.

From the loose notes and jottings-down of the various phases of the problem, I conceived, many years ago, the idea of writing a small pamphlet as a general definition of the work, that not only misconceptions might be removed from such classes, but also from the minds of all students, and even from many who were thoroughly posted in reference to other departments of education. It was written, but never published, because it seemed so inadequate to meet the great need. It continued to grow, and although it has been retained more than the nine years prescribed by Horace, it is still very inadequate to accomplish the purpose for which it was conceived. There are, however, some things to be considered. Little has ever been said upon this general subject. Books upon elocution exist by the score, but where can be found a work which exactly defines its province, which shows distinctly its relations to universal education and to universal art? So that the work is practically an endeavor in a new field.

Many of the principles can only be seen in their completeness after a more definite discussion of each particular phase of the problem, so that many of the points discussed would be far clearer and more in place at the close of a complete unfoldment of the methods for the development of each specific phase of expression. For example, among the most fundamental ideas of the work is the necessity of specific study of mental action in relation to expression, or the co-ordination of the conscious and the unconscious; but these can only be fully realized after a discussion of vocal expression.

Again, the proof that expression can only be improved by training can only be seen after a thorough discussion of the principles in accordance with which the voice and body can be developed so as to become more plastic and more adequate agents in every respect for the manifestation of the mind. And yet, as this work is the introduction to a series of works which are meant to unfold the fundamental principles of more natural and adequate methods for the development of all forms of delivery, it has been thought best to endeavor to give a comprehensive general conception of the whole field, that each specific part may be made clearer and more definite, and not be misconceived from lack of a true idea of the whole, or the relation of the parts to each other.

It may make the matter clearer to outline the whole under-taking. This, possibly, ought to be concealed, as it may seem too great for any hard-working teacher to accomplish. But if this is so, it is still well, possibly, to record the intention, that the place which this work is meant to fill in relation to the whole may be seen by the reader. The materials for all the other works are being gathered in exactly the same way as they have been gathered for this, and in fact, some of the others could have been produced more adequately than the present work, because they are more intimately connected with the practical work of teaching.

The whole series of works, as conceived and planned, include the following :

It can be seen that the department of pantomime is here omitted. The reason for this is that another has long been working upon this department and it is but just that it should be left to him to complete. This does not imply, however, that there is any agreement between us that one should take one department and the other another, or that our opinions are the same, for they are not; it is my own feeling of honor, and after the publication of his work another work will be pub-lished showing the peculiar views held by me in regard to that special department, and to show its connection and con-sistency with the principles unfolded in the investigation of other departments.

It seems of vital moment that at the present hour there should be an adequate understanding of the great problem of expression. Every science is making advancement. The whole problem of education is being discussed, and is it possible that this most vital and most practical relationship between conception and manifestation should be entirely ignored?

In manual training, in physical training, and indeed, in every phase of education there are wonderful advances, but is it conceivable that our public school teachers should have instruction in so many branches, and yet in relation to the voice that not one word of instruction should be given? The benevolent ladies of Boston who have given teachers such opportunities for studying these various subjects, have done a great service to the cause of education, but it is only a beginning. All over our country our teachers are suffering from sore throats, and pupils, on account of a mismanagement of the voice of teachers, and a failure to understand the problem of expression, are having their voices made hard, their bodies made awkward, and are being given power to conceive ideas but no power to manifest these ideas to their fellow-men.

A free people must not only be an educated people. Freedom and oratory have ever gone hand in hand. The vital interests of our nation and of religion have ever been made dependent upon powers of expression, and upon this power must depend the growth of individual character.

It is to aid in this cause that this book has been written — to call attention to the subject, to endeavor to show its connection with modern thought, art and education, and to strive to give leaders in education a clearer conception of its possibilities.

It is also sent forth as an endeavor to help, in a small measure, directly or indirectly, the few who are laboring hard to make their work an art and not a trade, and are struggling under widespread misconception of the nature of their work, even on the part of college presidents and principals of schools; and yet who, despite all, are struggling toward an ideal, striving ever to rise to a higher plane and a broader view.

The book is issued with the same motive that the School of Expression was founded. Without the School of Expression these methods could not have been applied and tested, as no other institution offered opportunities for the evolution and perfection of such advanced views in all the different phases. The greatest debt is therefore due to the earnest students who have attended that school, who have furnished the enthusiasm, the perseverance, and patient application that has rendered this series of books possible; and also to the public-spirited citizens upon its committees who have encouraged the struggles of the humble school to higher attainments and nobler ideas.

While the author has studied with over forty different teachers in different parts of the world, except in general suggestions, he is not conscious of having borrowed anything directly for the work without giving credit, so that no other must be held responsible for the views adopted.

No one can be more alive to the imperfect and inadequate presentation of the· subjects discussed in this work than the writer himself. When it is remembered that from five to eight hours a day, six days in a week, have been devoted to teaching, it can be seen how little leisure and strength are left to discuss subjects needing such careful investigation.

This statement, however, can be taken either as an apology or as a claim. As an apology for the imperfect form in which the ideas are conveyed; or on the other hand, as a proof that it is no mere study-room theorizing, but that every idea has been born in the actual work of teaching. The illustrations are such as have often been used in answering questions asked by earnest and inquiring students. So that if any one should think that on account of this lack of time for preparation and more adequate illustration, the ideas, principles and methods in every department, not only in this particular book, but in all the others, have not been maturely considered, these very facts abundantly disprove it. Everything has been conceived and born from actual experience, and every method has been tested with every variety of students as to age and nationality, habit, normal and abnormal, general education and professional aim.

Mr. Pater has said that all art is the removal of rubbish. The reader will no doubt wish that there had been a greater application of this principle to the present work. For his comfort, however, it may be said that much has been written which has not been printed. It also may be said in excuse that the author has hoped to get a year of advanced and additional study separate from teaching in order to more carefully and accurately arrange the ideas and give finish to the book, but this opportunity has never come and will doubtless fail to come in the future. Hence, on account of the urgent need, it is sent forth with all its imperfections on its head, in the hope that "the incomplete," if not "more than completness," yet may, in some sense, "match the immense."

School of Expression,
Freeman Pl., Beacon St., Boston.
    June 19th, 1891.

SOME OF THE GENERAL IDEAS.

" Art was given for that ;
God uses us to help each other so,
Lending our minds out."
— Browning.

I. THE PROBLEM.

I.   The NATURE OF EXPRESSION is found from a study of all its phases
to be a process of revelation.   Expression implies mystic activity causing
action manifest to the senses.   The apprehending mind does not attend to
words, forms or motions for their own sake, but taking these as mere signs
constructs the thing signified.

II.   MISCONCEPTIONS OF EXPRESSION arise chiefly from confusing it
with appearance.   Expression is the result not of physical but of psychic
action at the moment of utterance.   The physical actions are directly
caused by mental action.   Thinking before an audience to awaken thought
in others is not the same as thinking alone, but it is not primarily a physical act.

III.   There are three KINDS OF EXPRESSION, one belonging both to the
eye and ear, one to the ear alone and one to the eye alone.   Each of these
reveals a different phase of experience — experience which can only be adequately revealed by its own inherited language.   Their essential nature is
complementary to each other; and they are only in perfection when
properly united.

IV.   EXPRESSION AND PERSONALITY are intimately related.   Though
unconsciously and indirectly, the peculiar character of the man affects his
modes of utterance.   As all forms of art unconsciously reveal the characteristics of the artist, so delivery being more intimately related to the man
is more essentially revelatory than any form of art.   Hence development
of expression must be more or less dependent on the development of the
experience and soul of the man.

V.   The EMOTION IN EXPRESSION, according to a majority of the best
masters of expression, is genuine.   One-sided views making expression
entirely a product of intellect, or of will, or of emotion, completely violate
its character.   As the faculties of the soul are in unity, so expression
demands their united co-operation and complementary action.

VI. It is important to study EXPRESSION IN ART because all the arts are one, and the study of expression in any one of them will throw light on that of another. The elements of expression are found to be representation and manifestation; one of these elements being more intellectual, the other more emotional; one more dramatic, the other more lyric; one more reproductive, the other more representative; one more objective, the other more subjective. Every work of art must have both of these elements, which are borrowed from the expressions of the human body.

VII. Studying EXPRESSION AS A FORM OF ART we find that it is usually considered to be a representative art. But this is an error, as it is essentially subjective and manifestive, and while both elements must ever be present the essential greatness of all lyric and dramatic expression consists in the transcendence of the manifestive over the representative elements.

VIII. Comparing EXPRESSION AND HISTORY we find that there has been ever a gradual progress from objective imitation to a greater degree of manifestation. This is found to be especially true in prose composition, and must be true in delivery. Hence, as the character of expression has greatly changed, methods for its development must also change, and the great advance in science, the greater understanding of the human body in relation to the human being, and the greater advance in art — especially in music — furnish a lesson as to the reforms in methods of developing histrionic and oratoric expression.

II. SEARCH FOR METHOD.

IX. Turning to the FUNDAMENTAL PROCESSES OF NATURE for light as to general principles regarding a method, we find that nature always expresses from within out. She begins from a center for the unfoldment of forces at this center which unfold in all directions according to the openness of the channel. This is a fundamental characteristic of naturalness. Nature everywhere shows freedom and unity.

X. IS ARTISTIC SPONTANEITY the same as animal spontaneity? Man has an element of conscious volition not common with the animal. Spontaneity refers to the whole nature acting, so spontaneity with man means co-operation and co-ordination of all the faculties. Essentially it shows an union of the conscious with the unconscious, the voluntary with the involuntary elements. The great danger in developing expression is that deliberation and conscious obedience to rule should usurp the place of spontaneous impulses. The deliberative and conscious action of the man is rather for regulation and direction than for complete domination. The union of spontaneous to deliberative actions without destroying the fundamental nature of the former is the highest characteristic of art. The development of expression must more than all other forms of art require the development of spontaneity and a mystic co-ordination of it with deliberation.

XI. The DEVELOPMENT OF EXPRESSION can be accomplished by developing the cause or psychic action, by securing control of the voice and body as a means, and by securing such a technical skill in the use and application of these as will effectually accomplish the result. The only way to improve expression is by affecting the causes and the means, as expression is an effect.

XII. As MENTAL ACTION is the cause, it must first be developed. Mental action is often considered as having nothing to do with expression, but all faults of voice, all faults of delivery, can be traced directly or indirectly to wrong action of the mind. One faculty especially to be trained is the imagination. This stimulates emotion. The proper succession of the mind in thinking must also be trained and a harmonious balance secured of thought and emotion.

XIII. To fulfill the requirements of the problem special attention is needed to the subject of TRAINING. Training is a stimulation of nature's processes. The two great processes in nature are, progression and retrogression. Training can correct evil habit and can develop along the line of nature's intention. It is a conscious and deliberative evolution.

XIV. Every art has its special TECHNICAL TRAINING, so in expression there are right and wrong ways to accomplish results. Special skill has to be acquired in education for expression.

XV. The great importance of the development of expression is dependent upon CRITICISM. Criticism is a comparison of the actual with an inherent ideal. All literature is a "criticism of life". Criticism in expression is absolutely necessary. The possibilities, mistakes and failures must be shown to the student, and he must be made to realize his possibilities. The application of remedies for abnormal action and the right stimulus to restore and develop is dependent upon critical insight. The greatest danger is flattery and the greatest difficulty is to inspire with the true artistic spirit of enthusiasm and self-sacrifice.

III. TRADITION.

XVI. Every method of investigation must recognize an historical element. There is a use as well as an abuse of history. Slavish following of tradition is the bane of all elocution and even art; but having investigated nature and the principles of general art, comparison with some of the leading traditions is very important.

XVII. IMITATION is the earliest method and has been almost universally practised. The arguments for this school are that expression is essentially an imitative thing, that it requires example, and that this is the only way of reaching the great subtleties and difficulties of the problem, which can not be analyzed. The objections to it are: that men are naturally different from each other as to pitch of voice, nature of voice, temperament and mode of action.

XVIII. The universal sense of the inadequacy of imitation led to the MECHANICAL SCHOOL. Speech has been analyzed and its peculiar characteristics found to be stresses and inflections, and rules have been prescribed for the proper use of these as signs of emotion. The arguments against the school are: that it has overlooked the most subtle and many of the most essential elements of vocal expression, and has especially ignored the spontaneous and tried to make all deliberative and obedient to rule. The whole tendency has been to turn expression into a mechanical art.

XIX. The reaction against the mechanical gave rise to the IMPULSIVE. Since the mechanical method worked to get the natural signs of emotion, some said, then if emotion produces these things why not try to get the emotion rather than the signs, and entirely forget the signs. The result was almost a complete lack of attention to delivery. The arguments against the school are: that man is abnormal, a creature of bad habit, and must be trained and made normal, must know the right from wrong way of expression. He needs also to acquire a gamut of passions and a gamut of languages for their manifestation, otherwise he will drift. Many of the ablest speakers have but one emotion, and hence a monotonous form of expression. That all phases of human nature appear to need special training. Man is a creature of education and especially in any form of art is education more necessary. A price has to be paid for any skill or greatness in art.

XX. Dissatisfaction with all current methods has led to the importation of a SPECULATIVE one, which in its own country had been completely discarded. The so-called Delsarte system is founded upon Swedenborg's Correspondences. Everything is essentially a trinity, beginning with God and coming through all nature and the life of man. All his powers are arranged in trinities and all his agents of manifestation and all their actions. It is contended that this gives a philosophic basis for work in expression. The best things in the original method, such as the element of training, have been entirely ignored for the speculative and artificial division of man's mind and body and their languages.

XXI. In all these methods there can be traced many truths; but everywhere there can be seen a recognized need for ADVANCE. There must be a more careful study of science, the laws of life and development, study of the underlying principles of all art, since all the arts if not derived from expression, at least borrow terms from it. Art is more and more regarded as an intervention of personality. Its underlying principles must be related to the art which shows itself through the primary languages. There must also be advance in studying the real function of expression as an art.

IV. APPLICATION.

XXII. The importance of expression is seen in its FUNCTION IN EDUCATION; it is not merely professional, it belongs to all education. It shows the practical side of education, as education has two sides, the reception of truth and the manifestation of truth. These two processes are mutually necessary for the development of character, the aim of education. A knowledge of expression enables a teacher to secure harmony, enables a teacher to test assimilation and originality. Reforms in education have all tended to practical results which are shown in expression.

XXIII. The FUNCTION of a TEACHER shows the need of special training on account of the neglect of the work, and its great difficulties. Traditions need to be fostered and the work encouraged and emphasized till it occupies its proper place.

XXIV. A proper elevation of expression is important on account of its relation to SPECIAL ARTS. Oratory and public speaking must be cultivated by all free peoples. "Agitation means liberty." Dramatic art in some form will always exist. When neglected it becomes a curse, but when elevated and arraigned by thorough dramatic criticism and when it is used for the cultivation of taste, it is a great means for the development of the human being. A newer and later phase, if not a more important one, which is more subjective and that meets the higher artistic requirements of the age, is the rendering of the Monologue and Public Reading.

I.

The Problem.

" .   .   .   . Art remains the one way possible
Of speaking truth, to mouths like mine, at least.
How look a brother in the face and say
'Thy right is wrong, eyes hast thou yet art blind,
Thine ears are stuffed and stopped despite their length,
And, oh, the foolishness thou countest faith!'   .   .   .   .
The shrug, the disappointed eyes of him
Are not so bad to bear — but here's the plague,
That all this trouble comes of telling truth,
Which truth, by when it reaches him, looks false.   .   .   .   .
But Art — wherein man nowise speaks to men,
Only to mankind — Art may tell a truth
Obliquely, do the thing shall breed the thought
Nor wrong the thought, missing the mediate word."
                                                            — *Browning.*

I.

NATURE OF EXPRESSION.

"Inalienable, the arch-prerogative
Which turns thought, act—conceives, expresses, too."
— *Browning.*

BEFORE we can understand a part of a plant, the entire organism must be brought before the mind. Had we never seen anything belonging to an elm except a fragment of a limb, it would hardly be possible for us to conceive the grace and beauty, or even form an outline, of that beautiful tree; for before we can understand a part of an object, we must have a conception of the whole. The mind can proceed from the whole organic structure to its parts in a perfectly natural order of conception, but it requires the most penetrating intelligence, with many years of thorough training, to conceive a fish belonging to an extinct species, from one of its bones.

Hence, as a wise traveler, before he visits a foreign land, feels it necessary to consult those who have gone before him, and to seek every means of becoming acquainted with the places he expects to visit, that he may carefully lay out his course, in order not to overlook places and objects of the greatest interest; so it is necessary in undertaking any study to understand as thoroughly as possible its essential nature, and its general bearings, so as to secure an adequate conception of the extent and limits of the field of investigation.

To define accurately any science or to indicate the exact ground to be covered by any form of investigation, is a most fundamental requisite to progress. Till this is done all search will be aimless, all results chaotic.

Cicero's statement that everything must proceed from a definition has been taken in the fullest and most literal sense regarding all scientific investigations; but, unfortunately, the principle has not always been obeyed in investigations regarding any department of art. The best art writers are so afraid of having an artificial system, so anxious to consider art in direct harmony with nature, so desirous to be like art herself, suggestive, that they proceed from almost any point of view. Hence, many works upon art are simply called "talks" or "conversations."

But if we are to have clear ideas and adequate conceptions, a definition is just as necessary in our endeavors to investigate any field of art as any department of science. This is especially true when the purpose of the investigation is to find the fundamental elements of a specific phase of art, the cause, means and instruments employed, in order to establish such methods of instruction as will be most helpful to its advancement. For art always presupposes science, and in such investigations, study must not only be devoted to the art itself, but to the scientific aspects of the department of nature upon which the art is founded.

Besides, in art, it is not a mere definition that is needed, not a mere statement of limitations, but more than this, it is a presentation of the ideal, a statement of the province, the subject matter, the means of manifestation, the possibilities and the end the art especially aims to accomplish. Every man feels the importance of an ideal in life, and we all respond in a measure to Browning when he says that the ideal of the worst man in the world is higher than the actual attainment of the best man in the world. No man in life ever grows greater or advances farther than his ideal. Certainly the same principle holds true in art, which is the image of all human life and activity. An artistic ideal may gradually extend and improve, but it is always ahead of actual attainment. No matter what a man's work may be, if his ideal conception of it is low, soon or late everything relating to it will be degraded. This is especially true in those forms of art where there is a continual tendency to lower the ideal. Here especially "a man's reach must exceed his grasp." Even vast knowledge and perfect technical skill cannot compensate for the lack of a high ideal.

Especially, however, in subjects where numerous misconceptions are scattered abroad is a statement of the fundamental elements of the art important ; because such a definition is the best means of correcting false ideas and bringing thoughtful minds back to a more thorough and definite study of the facts. Thus we find special need for such a method when we come to the study of the nature and relationship of all the living languages of man, with reference to their harmonious development and artistic employment. Here, more than anywhere else, do we find a vast number of loose expressions, incorrect ideas and inadequate opinions.

Writers of every age have recognized the importance of all subjects relating to delivery whether oratoric or dramatic, but, in relation to no subject of education are there such diverse views regarding proper methods of development. Articles and books are to be found upon the subject without end, but most of these hardly get beyond the discussion of the general importance of delivery ; and in none of them do we find the real problem discussed, or any adequate outline of principles underlying proper methods for the education of the orator. The

establishment and endowment of a school of oratory has
been the subject of discussion since the time of Protagoras, but is the problem yet solved, or have adequate
methods been unfolded? We have had during the last
few years in England and America many articles upon
the importance of establishing a school of acting, but
where can we find any discussion of the methods that
should be adopted, or any indication of the real work that
needs to be done in such a school? All that writers
seem to think necessary is that there should be a school
established and endowed, forgetting that a school with
wrong methods would not only do no good, but would do
an infinite amount of harm.

It is, therefore, with much hesitation that the work is
undertaken of making a few suggestions regarding the
solution of such a problem; for in coming to a subject as
broad and general as this, great care and thorough study
are required. A definition must not be a mere opinion,
but must be the result of observation and directly
founded upon facts. An adequate method for the accomplishment of such an important work as the development
of human delivery must not be a result of mere theory,
but of careful observation and long-continued experience.
In all scientific investigation, even the necessary hypothesis must be founded upon facts. A working hypothesis
in science must be the best apparent explanation of all
facts regarding the subject as far as known, and must be
proved or disproved by a careful comparison with additional facts.

All art tends to be conventional and traditional, so that
the investigation of any subject connected with it has
special difficulties. Reforms of methods in art require
generations for their accomplishment; for almost all men
confound what is customary and conventional with what is

natural, and too often substitute opinion for observation. If in our study of the facts of nature we may seem at first to arrive at conclusions opposed to many traditions, let it be remembered that all scientific investigation, before there can be any progress, must break away from mere traditional opinion and be directly concerned with nature herself. Opinions, however old, are not necessarily facts. If what is old is true, then it will not be harmed, but strengthened and confirmed by a fresh and rigid comparison with the phenomena of nature. Besides, opinions which are thoroughly sound, and originally discovered from careful observation of nature, become narrow, superficial and one-sided when there is not a constant comparison with nature. In art, more possibly than anywhere else, do we find that "the letter killeth but the spirit giveth life." Hence we can see a great necessity for renewed study of the nature of human expression.

So universal are the misconceptions and so various are the opinions regarding the whole work of dramatic and oratoric delivery, that we must begin with the subject at the foundation, and must come to it as children, assuming absolute ignorance, lest we lose sight of some of the most important elements of the subject, and so take for granted that which will lead us fundamentally astray at the very beginning of our work.

For of all phases of education, this is the most difficult; nowhere is there so great danger of superficiality, conventionality and one-sidedness of every kind. There are many reasons for this. Expression is subjective as well as objective, and requires no mere study of appearance or even of the philosophy and anatomy of the body, but a close scrutiny of everything most intimately related to the soul and the soul's activities. We do not come to the study of a leaf or plant or stone, but something connected with the fundamental elements of our being. And this is not all. We come to study not only thought, but those mental actions that are involuntary and unconscious. We come to the investigation of the most complex and difficult of problems — the subjective in the objective. So that very soon every student of delivery feels like joining in the prayer of Burns —

> "O wad some power the giftie gie us,
> To see oursels as ithers see us!
> It wad frae monie a blunder free us,
> And foolish notion."

What is meant by expression? If we study a man standing face to face with his fellow-man, wrought up to the highest pitch of excitement, endeavoring to reveal his thoughts and feelings, we find there are many means which he simultaneously employs in making himself understood. So that the term expression is here employed to cover all the living languages of man, natural or artificial, which he uses in speaking face to face with his fellow-man. Sometimes it is used as merely covering the natural languages of motions, actions and tones. Here it is used in a slightly wider sense than this, as including the living language of speech as well as of motions and voice.

The most fundamental element of expression is the idea of revelation of man's psychic nature through his physical organism. What our fellow-being thinks, feels or is, is shown us by what we see of the action of his body or what is heard from his voice. We see that expression is not of the body but through the body; we feel that there is something mystic and hidden, unseen and unheard by our fellow-men and often only vaguely felt by ourselves; but it is made manifest by the motions and actions of the body, and the tones and modulations of the voice. We feel conscious of something which is called emotion, and find this emotion tends to cause something outward which is motion. We are conscious of an inward condition, of indifference for example, or antagonism, and immediately the actions and positions of the body become expressive of the unseen condition, and, through this expression, the psychic state is seen and felt by our fellow-man. Inward emotion causes an outward motion; inward condition, an outward position. Thus expression is, "the motion of emotion," the presentation of a vast complexity of physical actions which are directly caused by psychic activities. The objective phenomena are manifestive of subjective experience.

This conception of expression does not need to be established by argument; it only needs careful observation. The facts can be seen on every side in the most familiar actions of men and animals. Expression is one of the most universal and fundamental characteristics of man; it belongs directly or indirectly to every act, conscious or unconscious, from the first smile in the cradle to the fading away of the wrinkles around the eye after death; and, indeed, if we look deeper, till the bones themselves return to dust.

As we study further, we can see that expression is not peculiar to man. Throughout the universe we find that everything which is revealed to sense is simply an external manifestation of something which is mystic, an outward sign of an inward substance, an outward action of an inward activity. Force is not revealed *per se* to sense, it is only the phenomena of force which are seen, felt or heard. But, though force is not itself revealed to sense, there is nothing manifest without force. Matter itself is but force in a state manifest to sense; it may be called the expression of force. This conception of the

universe is the result of experience common to us all;
all have felt "a presence that disturbs" us

> "with the joy
> Of elevated thoughts, a sense sublime
> Of something far more deeply interfused,
> Whose dwelling is the light of setting suns,
> And the round ocean and the living air
> And the blue sky, and in the mind of man :
> A motion and a spirit that impels
> All thinking things, all objects of all thought,
> And rolls through all things."

Evidences of a half-conscious recognition of this conception of expression are to be found in the familiar words
of every-day speech. The word emotion is formed from
its most salient characteristic, a tendency to produce
motion, or, as some think, to become a motive to will.
Again we say that man "exists," but we do not say
"man is," on the other hand we say "God is," but in the
strict use of language we do not say "God exists."
Existence, derived from the Latin word *sisto*, a redupli-
cation of *sto*, means that which stands out, that which
possesses borrowed essence ; so that we may say existence is the expression of essence. The instincts of the
race, therefore, bear testimony to the relation of force to
matter, of the mystic to the manifest ; and much of the
ablest philosophy and the highest poetry have ever heard
the voice of the Earth Spirit as she sings in Faust —

> "Thus ever at the loom of time I ply,
> And weave for God the garment thou seest him by."

It can be seen at once that expression is most intimately related to language. The term language, originally applied only to speech, is now so generalized as to be
applied to every means of communication between one
man and another. Even all forms of art are recognized
as simply forms of language. Ruskin in his "Modern

Painters" says : "Painting, or art generally as such, with all its technicalities, difficulties and particular ends, is nothing but a noble and expressive language, invaluable as the vehicle of thought, but by itself nothing. Take for instance, the 'Old Shepherd's · Chief-mourner.' Here the exquisite execution of the glossy and crisp hair of the dog, the bright, sharp touching of the green bough beside it, the clear painting of the wood of the coffin and the folds of the blanket, are language — language clear and expressive in the highest degree. But the close pressure of the dog's breast against the wood, the convulsive cling-ing of the paws, which has dragged the blanket off the trestle, the total powerlessness of the head laid, close and motionless, upon its folds, the fixed and tearful fall of the eye in its utter hopelessness, the rigidity of repose which marks that there has been no motion nor change in the trance of agony since the last blow was struck on the coffin lid, the quietness and gloom of the chamber, the spectacles marking the place where the Bible was last. closed, indicating how lonely has been the life, how unwatched the departure of him who is now laid solitary in his sleep ; these are all thoughts — thoughts by which the picture is separated at once from hundreds of equal merit, as far as mere painting goes, by which it ranks as a work of high art, and stamps its author, not as the neat imitator of the texture of a skin or the fold of a drapery, but as the Man of Mind." .

Art itself is but the revelation of man's conceptions, "the intervention of personality." Landseer simply used the spectacles, the open Bible, the shepherd's crook, the coffin and the dog as means of revealing to us cer-tain conceptions of his mind and feelings of his heart. These simple objects are presented to put us in communi-cation with his thinking and feeling soul.

We must not think, however, that language and expression are the same; above all we must not think that expression is simply a form of language; it is really the aim of all language, the aim of all art, the aim of all modes of communicating the thoughts and feelings of man; in short, language is only a means of expression.

Expression, however, belongs specifically and fundamentally to the living man, directly manifesting his feelings and thoughts through his organism. Man's natural languages are the first he employs, and expression belongs primarily to these. So that "the expression of man and animals" is broader and more specific than the language of man and animals. Language implies a more conscious and deliberate use of the means of communication, while expression covers all forms of revelation, conscious or unconscious, voluntary as well as involuntary, belonging to man or animals.

Every form of art is either expression itself or a means of permanently recording and preserving expression. In many forms of art expression is dependent upon the execution in some permanent medium of the fundamental elements of the direct revelation of man's powers. An expressive picture of a man, for instance, is that in which his most significant actions and features are represented and accentuated.

So that there is no doubt that the fundamental application of the word expression applies to the revelation of man by motion and tone. And just as language does not remain confined to speech, so expression is used in a broader sense and is not confined merely to the natural languages. Therefore in the study of methods to develop and to co-ordinate in the living man all means of communicating his thoughts and feelings, his states, conditions and purposes, expression is the most adequate term

that can be found. Better than any other word, it represents all the means which consciously or unconsciously
show simultaneously what man thinks, feels and is, to his
fellow-man.

When we come further to study the actions and modifications of man's body, we find that they are not necessarily expressive. We find that expression is not of the
body, but through the body. "It is the soul that
speaks." Actions of the body may be merely external,
accidental, mechanical or utilitarian. Nothing is ever
expressive which is not the transparent means of manifesting the soul; that is not directly caused by some
thought, emotion or condition of the speaker's psychic
faculties and powers.

Hence the most expressive man does not necessarily
make many motions or a great display of voice. In fact,
whenever motions of the body or tones of the voice call
attention to themselves, they distract the attention of the
auditor from the thought, and in so far destroy expression. The object of training the voice and the body
must always be to make them a better channel for the
manifestation of thought and feeling. The highest perfection in the action of every agent of expression is
always in proportion to the transparency.

However perfect the skill displayed by the circus rider,
the dancer or the performer of any difficult physical feat,
such an exhibition is not expression. Splendid tones in a
singer may display wonderful skill in technique, but sudden leaps and skips of the voice are not necessarily
expressive; for one of the most fundamental of all dis-
tinctions is that expression is not exhibition. But this
distinction is unfortunately often forgotten. Performers
often esteem it the height of their art to be able to make
very beautiful gestures or attractive tones; in fact, elocu-

tion especially has been regarded as mere skill in exhibition. Notice the class of selections which are the chief stock and store of our public readers. The piece which can exhibit technique of voice has been most popular. Medleys mixing up extracts from great authors, so as to pervert absolutely their meaning, selections with low characters so that the face or body can be twisted into abnormal shapes, and the voice constricted into some guttural, husky or nasal quality, or extracts full of oddities and abnormal emotions are the most popular with elocutionists. Rarely do we have selections from the best authors read from our platforms. In fact, our highest authorities in elocution justify abnormal qualities of the voice as essential elements of the art.

One of the best illustrations of this abnormal tendency is the way ordinary elocutionists read Dickens. Too often, his characters are made caricatures of nature, absolutely unlike any thing in existence.

Illustrations of confounding expression with exhibition are infinite. Notice the way some of our teachers and readers hold their hands — placing their fingers in an artificial position, such as would rarely if ever be found in nature. The result may be a very pretty hand, as is of course the object of the performer, but this confounds expression entirely with appearance. Indeed, to "appear" before an audience is often taken in the literal sense of making an appearance, overlooking the real province of expression as the art of revealing the ideals and conceptions, the emotions, experience and character of man. This position of the hands is discussed by Quintillian, and has been practised from his day to this, yet such placing of an agent externally limits its freedom, and as all expression is modulation of the body by emotion, it can be readily seen that hindrance to such modulation must fundamentally hinder expression. If an agent is externally fixed, it must be the same for all conditions and occasions; and sameness is death to all power or truth or beauty in expression of any kind.

Thus we can see that not only is expression not exhibition but that exhibition is the greatest enemy of expression. Whenever a man makes a display of the means of expression for their own sake so that the attention of the mind is called to the execution, there can be little or no communication of thought or feeling. The only emotion awakened is wonder at the skill of the performer. When a speaker, for example, makes a great display of tears, the effect of grief is lost. Men may look at such a display and feel some weak emotion such as pity, but no sympathy can be awakened by such an exhibition. Emotion must ever transcend its sign. Whenever the signs and means of expression are greater than the thought, they cause all attention of the auditor's mind to be concentrated upon the physical action itself; thus most radically perverting and destroying the true nature of expression.

And yet so long as the world is as it is, the public will desire exhibition for entertainment; a show is something the world can see at a glance without making any intellectual effort to comprehend its meaning. Many are governed by what pleases their senses; what fascinates most the eye is taken for highest art. Unfortunately such spectacular exhibitions are considered by many as synonymous with dramatic expression, whereas there is not the least dramatic element in them; for the most essential element of the dramatic is the revelation of human character.

All the arts are one, and the same principles or misconceptions will ever be found at work in each. Unfortunately we have many examples of exhibition in other departments of art. The painting of the present day shows the same evil tendency. An artist endeavors to paint striking pictures so as to be awarded a place in an exhibition. So that it has been said a young painter after working hard to get into the Paris Salon, has to work for several years to overcome the evil effects of his course. In an exhibition some time ago a very large painting occupied a post of honor in one corner of the gallery. The great black prow of an ocean steamer covered one-fourth of the canvas, making a striking picture which every one who came into the room would notice. But it gave no conception of the grandeur of the ocean or of man's power over it. A leading artist said, "A little curling smoke in the distance would give us a better conception of a steamer than that." As the earnest student goes into our exhibitions, he feels that this is one of the curses of our art. So that our best painters often do not send their best work to the exhibitions, and when asked about it by visitors to their studios they make some such answer as this, "If you were a musician you would not like to play a symphony in one corner of a room while a brass band is playing in another corner."

The preponderance of exhibition over expression has been a fundamental characteristic of bad art of every kind in every age. In fact it has been in all time the death of art. "The highest art conceals art." The best art is always expressive rather than decorative. The best art does not exist for the display of technique or the means employed, but for the revelation of that which is hidden. In all great art the impression steals upon us, we scarcely know how. Consciousness of the mere means destroys the perfection of the communication. The greater the art the more transparent the mechanical means of execution. Every great art work seems to bring soul face to face with soul, and causes both to lose sight of the means by which their thoughts cross from one to the other.

All art is an endeavor to tell the truth, and the highest art is the manifestation of those deepest and subtlest truths which are most liable to be lost sight of by the race. Hence the power of expression is dependent on the amount and character of the inner psychic conditions revealed, and upon the transparency of the manifestation. In short the true artist in any form of delivery as in any art, never presents his technique, his voice or body, his gesture or his attitude as an end to the audience, but uses them only as a means of manifesting his thoughts, emotions and convictions — his real manhood. Vocal or gesture training which tries to introduce beautiful tones or graceful movements for their own sake as a means of decoration is absolutely vicious. Mere admiration for voice and skill may result, but no deep, genuine passion is ever awakened. We are very little impressed with that which seems to cause great labor; the most ignorant mind will feel that something is wrong, though unable to give any adequate reason.

There are two ordinary forms of imperfect expression, which seem entirely opposite and yet have one element in common : they both attract attention to the mechanism of the speaker. One of these faults is due to an absolute lack of control over the voice and body, or the misuse of the mechanism in speech, a physical friction, so to speak, which will call the attention of the speaker himself to his mechanical action, and the same effect greater in degree will be produced upon his audience. The opposite fault is affectation. This results from a misconception of art or of delivery, from pride in a graceful body and beautiful voice, or from some kind of aggregation. While this fault seems to be so antithetic to the other, yet it has the same effect; for the speaker's consciousness is centred upon the mechanism, and the mind of the audience always follows that of the speaker.

In one case there is too little voluntary control, and in the other there is nothing but voluntary control. In both cases the action is apt to be conscious. Too much consciousness of manner, of language or of any means adopted in expression is wrong from whatever cause it may arise. Awkwardness is simply too much self-consciousness due to lack of control, while affectation is due to too much consciousness in control, to an over-plus of volition. There can be no great expression without ability to use the means of expression, with little consciousness of the mechanism both on the speaker's part and on the part of the audience.

We must not, however, fall into the great error of supposing that truth is antagonistic to either beauty or grace, or that fidelity to truth must necessarily lead to awkwardness or ugliness; for all true beauty is of the soul, and all true grace, of the spirit; so that artistic fidelity to truth will bring us to the very highest beauty. For though the statement that "beauty is the splendor of the true" may not have been written by Plato, yet it is an aphoristic expression of the soundest philosophy of æsthetics.

Not only is this true, but we find that when we come to study the aim of expression, whether that aim be to please or to win men to the truth, there is fundamentally implied the necessity of expressing charmingly. It is love of truth, love of our kind, that leads man to expression. Therefore fidelity to truth itself demands that it shall be put in the best possible way, that it shall be so rendered that no antagonism may be awakened, but on the contrary a disposition to receive it. In fact, it is the deeper, more delicate and beautiful, the more subtle and spiritual elements that are most apt to be lost sight of in ordinary expression; so that fidelity to truth demands freedom from all sham and restoration to the simplicity, the plenitude, the beauty and charm of nature.

It is strange that the lesson is so difficult to learn, that there is no antagonism between truth and beauty, and that affectation for the sake of a misconceived decoration is not only a violation of the truth but is fundamentally hostile to all laws of beauty.

As an illustration, take what seems to be a very important exception to the principle. In the expression of anger or any ignoble emotion, truth seems to demand that everything should be made as ugly as possible, while beauty demands that the ugly element be softened and toned down and only suggested if not eliminated. Both of these facts are true of abnormal emotions and characters; but granting them to be universal principles, the exception is only a seeming one, for both beauty and truth demand a contrast between the normal and abnormal, and the abnormal is chiefly of worth in expression to show the departures from the normal; because whether in truth or beauty, the abnormal indirectly suggests the normal, and sometimes the normal can be more effectively suggested by presenting the abnormal; but to present the abnormal merely for its own sake, violates all the laws of truth as well as beauty.

Thus we find that expression is not a mere physical thing, that it is not a quality of the body, but the result of the manifestation of the soul through the body; the revelation of the subjective through the objective. We find that it is not a mere appearance or display, but a revelation through outward signs of inward and otherwise hidden substance; in short, that exhibition is the worst enemy to true expression. We have also found that what is within must ever transcend that which is without, and that the test of true power in expression is not the appearance or the beauty of the sign, but its significance and suggestiveness, not in the skill displayed or exhibition that is made, but in the degree of revelation. In other words, the fundamental test must be truth and never prettiness for its own sake, or mere beauty or grace which attracts attention to itself as an end instead of serving as a truthful revelation of the corresponding quality of the soul. We find that affectation is not only wrong in itself, but that its action is the direct reverse of nature's method, and must therefore essentially hinder nature's process and supplant her causes.

Thus we make one step in our search for a method of developing expression. The result of all work done must be to enable man to "tell the truth, the whole truth and nothing but the truth." It must not be an art giving a man the power to seem to be what he is not, to cause him to try to create thought in other minds which is not in his own mind, and never merely to give a display of graceful actions or pleasant qualities for their own sake. In short, that while it is necessary to speak as beautifully as possible and to bring grace into every phase of expression, yet the highest delivery must be a result of the revelation of the deepest elements of the soul.

II.

MISCONCEPTIONS OF EXPRESSION.

" Style is the man himself." — Buffon.

SOMETIMES we realize better what a thing is by studying what it is not. Truth is often more adequately comprehended when contrasted with its opposite, falsehood. There are always near every great truth many errors which seem identical with it. This is due to the fact that every great truth is fundamental; it is deeply hidden from our eyes, and to find it requires searching beneath the surface. It is below all appearance although it may be revealed through appearance. Men are apt to dwell upon that which first arrests attention, and what appears to be true at first sight is often accepted as a fundamental principle. Nearly all falsehoods and misconceptions rise from mistaking accidental appearances for fundamental causes. And as expression has to do with appearance we can see why such a great number of misconceptions arise in connection with this subject.

Not only does this give rise to the fundamental misconception that expression is the same as exhibition already discussed, but to the mistake so long and so widely prevalent in the distinction between matter and manner in public speaking. This distinction as commonly understood is ridiculous and impossible ; for it is implied by it and asserted by many, that work in the study of a subject and the embodiment of the thought in words is a mental act, while delivery is a physical act.

It is true that in delivery there is an added physical element which is not present in the preparation of the thought. In expression there must not only be thought and the feeling such thought awakens, but this thought and feeling must not exist vaguely in the soul. They must be thought and felt, so to speak, into and through the body. But though different, the chief, the fundamental action in delivery, is psychic; so that expression is an action of the mind fully as much as composition is. The true orator must have great power of thinking, not only while composing, but at the moment he speaks. Preparation can only be general, can only secure an outline of the thought, can only make him familiar with the road; but however definitely he may mark out this road, the path must be re-traveled in the act of speaking.

Many great scientists who are good thinkers, cannot speak in public, but this is rarely due to physical conditions. Their voices are frequently very strong and many of them have magnificent physiques. It is simply because they have not developed the action of the mind in speaking as they have in making investigations, or in arranging and expressing ideas in written words. The writer, the musician or the painter has trained his mind to use a certain tool for the expression of his thought and feeling. Hence, although he has used his voice and body all his life, he cannot effectually think and feel, so to speak, into his own voice and body. Ole Bull, it is said, could speak best to his fellow-men and even pray best through his violin.

A bad ear does not refer to physical defects as to size or structure; its possessor can hear sound as far away as his musical friend; the imperfection exists because the mind has not been trained to use the ear for the apprehension of intervals. All who have ever trained poor ears have realized the necessity of securing attention through the ear. So the fundamental problem for the development of a speaker must ever be to bring his voice and body under the domination of his soul.

Not only is delivery a result of mental actions but of actions different from composition. The action of the mind in creating, in thinking out a subject, does not have such direct relation to other minds; while the act of thinking in delivery is the endeavor so to think and feel as to lead other minds and hearts simultaneously to follow us. The one is more creative, the other is more reproductive; the one is merely to comprehend, to understand, to get possession; the other is to realize and manifest, to make the thought clear to other minds or to awaken in other souls a response to the importance of the truth at the moment of utterance.

Almost all the faculties of the mind are concerned in the act of expression. They do not act so analytically or individually as in production. They act more spontaneously, more harmoniously, more synthetically. A greater number of the faculties in more complex co-ordinations and combinations must be awakened. The whole man, in short, must act; even those powers which are more unconscious, more akin to instinct and intuition, must especially be awake. These must ever furnish the fundamental impulse. The writer arranges his ideas and endeavors to embody thought in words, while the speaker not only endeavors to embody his ideas in words, but to reveal all the phases of experience arising from these ideas or associated with them through a co-ordination of all the living languages of his personality. Not only must he have "words that burn," but tones and inflections, motions and actions, which breathe and live with the deepest life of his soul.

If this is true we can see that there are certain extemporaneous elements in all true delivery. Even though the speaker's ideas may be put into words, and the words be read or given from memory, still, all great oratory requires that the ideas be re-created. The thought must not only be reproduced by symbols, but the process of its creation must be reproduced and manifested. The powers of the man must act at the time he speaks, no matter what his preparation may have been, or he is not an orator. The idea that a man in speaking is a mere physical machine is the fundamental cause of the bad delivery so prevalent at the present time. Whenever a man thinks that he is simply *doing* something that will awaken thought in others, without thought in his own mind, not merely a day or a week or a year before, but at the moment he endeavors to convey the thought — or who thinks he can awaken feeling in another's breast when his own is cold — is trying to accomplish an end without legitimate cause or means, and is acting in direct violation of nature's fundamental laws. It is only by a vivid realization of an idea or situation that genuine emotion is stimulated in the speaker's breast. Emotional conditions can be prepared; but the feeling itself can only be a spontaneous realization of the pictorial conception in the mind of the speaker at the moment he speaks. There is nothing so ineffective and unnatural as stale emotion; one of the most fundamental instincts of the human soul requires that emotion shall be extemporaneous and spontaneous.

Thus, all effective delivery in speaking is due to the direct possession and realization of ideas at the moment they are spoken. Mere possession of the idea yesterday will help, but will not enable one to express it to-day, without re-thinking it, re-seeing it, re-feeling it, inspired by contact with other souls. There is no true living expression without a realization of every idea in succession as the cause. Even correct technical and physical actions in delivery result from this realization of the successive ideas and successive situations.

Whenever a man says that all his care and study is for the matter of his speech, that all oratory depends solely on what is said, he confounds the function of the orator with the function of the essayist. What is to be read in an easy-chair by the fireside is one thing, what is to be the immediate revelation of the living soul, the living thought and passion of the living man face to face with his fellow-men, is a different thing. Literary composition is a very great art and so is oratory, but they are not the same. One is a representation of thought and truth in verbal language, the other is "the presentation of truth by personality," and the revelation of all phases of this personality in connection with truth by a co-ordination of the living languages of the man. The orator not only conveys truth clearly by means of words, but shows its vital relation to the human soul through the co-operation of the living languages.

Not only is this true, but the style of the words is different. That which is written for an essay rarely makes a good speech. This fact may not be realized in our modern oratory, for modern sermons and speeches are not always written spontaneously or extemporaneously. In many cases they are mere patch-work, in most instances possibly they are more like essays. There is an endeavor to say everything in words. It was not so with the Greek orators. Many men have contended that what has come down to us as the orations of Demosthenes are merely abstracts, because they are too concise for public oratory. But this is the modern, perverted, abnormal idea of oratory. Looked at from an ideal point of view the literary style of perfect oratory must be more concise than the style of what is simply to be read. There are many things which the tone of the voice can say better than words. A motion of the hand, an action of the eye or of the face, can supply an ellipsis which the essayist or novelist must give in words.

One of the most familiar illustrations of this is the difference between the drama and the novel. All will probably agree that the amount of thought is as great in Hamlet as in a great novel — as for example, in David Copperfield, though Hamlet covers only a few pages and David Copperfield takes several volumes. This difference is due to the fact that the drama is to be presented through the living languages of man and be both seen and heard, while the novel is only intended to be read in an easy-chair.

This principle is shown by Dickens himself. In a fac-simile of a page from the readings as arranged by him from his novels for his public recitations, I counted the words which were erased. In the original novel there were one hundred and ninety-three words, and of these one hundred and nineteen were marked out; yet no important idea was omitted that Dickens could not readily supply by a look or a tone or some use of the natural languages in combination with the words.

Thus we see that a man face to face with his fellow-men, in full possession of his personality, with power to reveal the action, emotion or condition of his whole nature, must express differently from the writer at his desk. Each breathes his personality into his work, but the speaker has the advantage of all his natural languages as well as words, and can reveal simultaneously any phase of his personality when his body is in a state thoroughly prepared and attuned to his being with all the channels of expression free from any constriction or hindrance. So that all ideal oratory must be concise, or at least its style must differ from the essay as the drama does from the novel, or the poem from history.

This tendency to conceive all expression as a mere physical thing, the result of some tact, entirely independent of the mind and soul, as in the case of misconceiving expression as exhibition, is not confined to elocution. There is a widely prevalent tendency now to consider all art work as something separate from the real man, the result of technical skill. Some one has said that Gustave Doré did not read the Bible until he read it to illustrate it. His illustrations certainly hint at this.

Some time ago a large painting of Christ on Calvary was exhibited in different cities. The faces of the Jews and Roman soldiers, according to their different types and the coarse and vulgar thoughts animating them, were carefully and accurately portrayed. The ideal characters of the piece were placed at the foot of the cross, with their faces hidden. The Master himself was represented merely as a physical body emaciated by suffering. It sold for a very high price and was evidently painted for this end — painted as a striking picture that would impress strongly an ordinary observer; but as a picture, except as a mere study of technique, it was a failure. It showed the worldly side and that only, and gave no hint of the significance in history of the great tragedy of Calvary. If it had been painted by an honest disbeliever in Christ, it could not have been painted so, if the painter had been a true artist, because he could see the significance in history, and the power over thousands of lives of that death, and would have honestly tried to portray Mary the Magdalene and John as well as Judas, the

Romans and the Pharisees.   Such a picture as this could
only have been painted by one blind to spiritual facts, one
who merely painted from his models.   He evidently was
not in sympathy with that great scene, and Calvary to
him was simply a weak man dying in the midst of coarse
and villainous men.   Certainly there were those that
realized more what it meant.   While they could not
appreciate completely the spiritual element of the Christ,
and the reason for his death, yet there were those at the
foot of that cross who "kept all these things in their
hearts."   These are merely prostrated with grief and
their faces hidden, and no yearning eyes look up to him
with a vague, instinctive faith.   Above all, no repose
rests upon the brow of the Christ, or is inspired in the
faces that look upon him.   Such a picture is a sad com-
ment upon the technical exhibition falsely called art,
which is so common at the present day.

In the same way delivery is now regarded merely as
the art side, by which most people mean merely the
technical manner, merely the polish.   Frequently those
who come to study delivery tell the teachers that they
have done sufficient work upon the matter, and they now
wish to work merely upon the manner, as if manner were
something separate from personality, separate from the
action of the mind and soul of the man, and could be put
on or off like a coat.

Yet this common distinction between matter and manner, making one physical and the other psychic, naturally
leads to such conclusions.   There is no doubt that a
man's mode of presentation may directly reverse the most
essential elements of his thought, and though they may
be logically distinguished from each other, the one is not
a physical thing and the other a mental thing.   The
trouble with bad delivery nine-tenths of the time is a

failure to use the faculties of the mind, or a misuse of them in the act of speaking; and one reason why delivery has not been made better is this very fact that it has been considered merely a physical thing, separate from personality; for such a view causes the speaker to try to develop delivery by aggregation, rather than by seeking such methods as will train his powers and agents to manifest his personality simultaneously with his thought.

Teachers, too, have been led to seek for the causes of imperfect delivery in the body only, and so have unconsciously been prevented from tracing faults to their true causes.

Again, it is often said of a speaker that he is too dramatic. When we see and hear him we find that he is not dramatic at all. He simply has a labored, aggregated delivery, foreign to his own personality. The nature of the man and his delivery are so disconnected that the most ignorant can feel that there is something wrong; and so for lack of a word ignorance calls it "too dramatic."

Of all faults in expression the worst is for a man not to be himself. It is not only the worst fault, it is the most common. But what is the cause of it? It is often simply the idea that delivery is a physical thing, separate from thought, something a man can join to himself by some process of aggregation. The young speaker gets the idea that in order to express well he must add something to himself greater and better than he really is, must try to be somebody else, like the toad in the fable must endeavor to expand to the size of some real or imaginary ox. The result is, that the man becomes stilted and artificial. He cannot be natural, for he is uncentred. His powers cannot act effectively, for they are unpoised and out of harmony.

Abnormal, however, as this may seem, it arises more naturally than we would first think. Every man's ideal transcends his actual. His power of conception surpasses his power of performance or execution, or at any rate the power of conception is first in the natural order and much easier. Few are willing to do the hard work of training necessary to attain power of execution, and it is just at the point of carrying conception into execution that the mind is most readily led astray.

Besides this, the young speaker gets a conception of the wonderful power of expression from observing the delivery of another man, and thus is very liable, consciously or unconsciously, to imitate him or endeavor to aggregate his peculiarities. The same is true of the young actor. He observes the wonderful power of Irving or Booth for example, and tries to execute the same passages. But he begins at the wrong end. He endeavors merely to reproduce results, to aggregate, but does not go to the cause. So he loses the simplicity and power, and merely aggregates the outside. Therefore the expression is felt at once to be an adjunct and not the evolution of the man's mind.

There is still another cause of all this. In most of our systems of education everything man learns has to be gathered by instruction. The aim of education in modern times has been too much a mere matter of acquiring information. The highest type of a scholar has been and still is in many quarters, one who has the greatest knowledge of the greatest variety of subjects. All the great reforms in education for the past two hundred years have been endeavors to correct such an inadequate conception. The aims of the "new education" in every age from Commenius, Rousseau, Pestalozzi and Froebel, down to the innumerable educational reformers of our day, with their endeavors to establish natural methods of teaching languages and to apply in every department advanced methods of education, have this in common : that they have endeavored to educate or unfold the man's powers rather than to merely cram him full of facts, to stimulate him from within, and not merely to fill him from without.

But although there are many widespread reforms in all departments of education at the present time, and these reforms have affected almost all classes of schools and professions, strange to say, it has reached last that department of education, or at least has made no great advance in that department of education where we would naturally think it would have the first effect, namely : the work of elocution or expression. Many of the reforms of education, especially in the study of English, were advocated and initiated by an elocutionist one hundred and fifty years ago. But, notwithstanding that, and the fact that we have had several great advocates and workers in this department, still, either on account of the lack of encouragement or on account of a lack of co-operation on the part of a great number of thinkers, public reading, recitation and speaking in our schools is taught in violation of the most fundamental laws of true education. We still have in our public schools the small boy trying to expand himself into Webster; we still see in most places the young man standing up for his declamation as stiff as a soldier on parade, and making gestures which any man of common sense knows to be unnatural, that could only have been aggregated from without. If the expression of the man had been drawn out from his real nature he could not possibly have made such movements.

All our professional schools, and especially such as schools of Law or Theology, where young men are placed to be trained for public speaking, are behind in methods of education. This is one very important reason why the work of expression or the education of public speakers has not made greater progress ; in all that pertains to the speaking, the methods do not yet deal, as a rule, with the fundamental condition of the problem. Students for the ministry are still taught in many places to write essays, and have rules laid down for them which are purely external and artificial. All that is given in delivery is a few general suggestions and criticisms, with little or no training. The same is true of the colleges. While very wonderful progress has been made in the study of English in many schools, yet the progress has been very slow, and in reality little has been done for the improvement of anything more than mere verbal expression. The problem of improving men in practical expression in all its branches has received little attention.

Several years ago, a young man who has since become a popular preacher and has been pastor of many of our best churches, came to me with his commencement oration for assistance in its delivery. After he had read it through to me I called his attention to the fact that it was not at all prepared for delivery, but was a mere essay; and, as an illustration, I took one sentence, composed of twenty or thirty words, and put it into four or five, and asked him if that was what he meant. He said "yes, but that was the way anybody would say it." I told him he must speak his speech as anybody would speak it if he expected anybody to listen. It was with great difficulty, however, that I persuaded him to go to work all over again and write his speech with his audience before him and his purpose in mind, and endeavor to express simply what he had to say. With such a use of language good delivery is impossible.

I know Emerson said that those parts of a speech not well written must be covered over with good elocution, but he must have meant this as a joke. It hardly seems possible that our great reformer should have had such a misconception of the real work of delivery. It is rather to be taken as an indirect rebuke to this universal misconception of delivery as an aggregation to conceal superficiality of thought; not a truthful and adequate revelation of profound thought and feeling, but a substitute for them.

It seems strange that it has taken the world so long to see that aggregation in all art, and especially delivery, is affectation; that the fundamental nature of expression requires the human being to be self-centred and all truth assimilated; that all expression must be simply the evolution and revelation of the conditions and actions of the soul; that the aim must not be to seem, but simply to show what we are; that of all phases of education the work for the development of expression in any form needs most of all to proceed according to the fundamental laws and principles of nature.

III.

KINDS OF EXPRESSION.

"Blest pair of Sirens, pledges of Heaven's joy,
Sphere-born harmonious sisters, voice and verse,
Wed your divine sounds and mixed power employ,
Dead things with unbreathed sense able to pierce."
— *Milton.*

WHEN we come to study expression still more closely we find that man's entire organism is linguistic; that every part of the body is concerned in the manifestation of the conditions and actions of the mind ; that the whole body breathes and thrills with the activity of the soul.

And not only is the whole body linguistic, but every part of the body plays a distinct role in expression. The feet, for example, can manifest certain conditions of the man which cannot be indicated by any other agent in the body.

Nature shows everywhere an intention that all parts of the body should co-operate with each other for the accomplishment of one end. The language of the hand is entirely distinct from the language of the face, though the two are capable of the greatest unity and consistency. The language of the torso is entirely distinct from the language of the arm. The language of inflection discharges a different function from that of tone-color, so that one can never be translated into the other, but both are meant by nature to be present at the same time, as the co-ordinate revelation of different phases of the soul's conditions and activity.

We find that the languages of the body, while composed of many diverse elements, can be divided into three classes, each of which is given by means of a separate mechanism : verbal expression, vocal expression and pantomimic expression.

Verbal language, including all words or speech forms, is a language of conventional or artificial symbols. It is the language, however originating, that is most dependent upon education, and has been more completely developed by custom than any other; for while the tendency to words may be innate, yet, in all cases, education has shaped their peculiar form. A child born of English parents, removed in its earliest infancy from an English to a German family, for instance, will show very few traces in speech of its English origin. A brogue is not so much an inheritance, as the result of the speech the child hears from its parents during early childhood. The earliest speech the child hears, is of course the most important in determining the verbal language of the man.

Verbal language being a symbolic form of expression, that is, words being equivalent symbols of ideas, can be recorded; though Humboldt, the father of philology, held that only a spoken word could be considered a real word. "It is," said he, "only by the spoken word that the speaker breathes, as it were, his inner soul into the soul of his hearers. Written language is only the imperfect and mummy-like embalming, of which the highest use is that it may serve as a means of reproducing the living utterances." Yet universal custom regards written and spoken language as the same. That they contain elements entirely distinct from each other is shown by many facts. It is only verbal expression that can be written in artificial signs so as to be the common property of the race. Vocal expression cannot be recorded or expressed in symbols so as to be reproduced by another voice. The discovery of the phonograph enables us to record by means of a mechanical instrument certain peculiarities and modulations of the voice, but it is only a mechanical process, and gives no key by which living effects can be reproduced by another voice.

Again, verbal expression may be partially separated from vocal expression if spoken in a whisper. This does not wholly separate them, for a whisper, though tone-color may be eliminated, can be modulated and show changes of pitch and inflection, and is often very expressive. Still, we can feel something of the significance of mere words as a language, distinct from vocal expression. We find that in a whisper a man may manifest his thoughts, but that he cannot reveal feelings such as love or joy. Thus the peculiar province of verbal expression is primarily to manifest human thought and reason, and is the most complete and adequate means of revealing ideas.

One of our ablest writers very beautifully and poetically says that words are fossilized poetry. His figure is not only beautiful, but correct. We must remember, however, that the fossil is not the living animal. The spoken word comes from the heart of the speaker, living and breathing with his life, full of the warmth of his heart. The written word, on the contrary, is the fossil remains of this living word. Thus, written language, though the most important record of thought, is not a complete or perfect language of itself. There are elements of expression revealing important phases of experience that cannot possibly be recorded. No symbol can manifest adequately the inflection, the color, the pitch or any of the modulations of the voice which so clearly manifest the emotional conditions and the motives of the speaker.

The exaggerated attention paid to verbal expression is due to the fact that it is the most conscious form of expression, also to the fact that it is a language that can be recorded so as to be seen by the eye, and is the means of preserving the great ideas of the past. Besides, it is the most definite language and primarily the most necessary for adequate communion with our kind; the others are normally intended to be its adjuncts.

Vocal expression appeals only to the ear. Verbal expression when spoken also appeals to the ear; when written, to the eye. But as has been said, there never has been discovered any adequate means of recording the phenomena of vocal expression so as to appeal to the eye, either because it is so completely passing, or because its phenomena are so wonderfully complex and subtle. Even in our own day such a careful observer as Herbert Spencer says that "cadence is the running commentary of the emotions upon the propositions of the intellect." This is true when said of all vocal expression, all modulations of the voice; but is not so true of cadence as it is of tone-color. Such vague and inadequate remarks as this reveal the fact that the speaking voice has received very little attention from scientists. Writers differ in regard to the range of the speaking voice, some contending that it has only a range of two or three notes, while others contend that the voice in speaking has a range of more than an octave, still others say fully two octaves. Science has not given us exact statements regarding most of the phenomena of the voice in speech. The voice in singing has received more attention, probably because singing is an artificial art, and a tone can be prolonged and partly recorded, and so studied independent of words, and also because the phenomena of vocal expression, though essentially music, are more complex than song, and facts regarding it more difficult to obtain.

Vocal expression is especially liable to be lost sight of on account of its connection with verbal expression.

Voice is usually considered as the mere material of speech, and men do not think of it as being a language of itself. But it is distinct from words in many aspects. For instance, it is distinct in respect to the organs that produce it. Voice is moulded into speech wholly in the oral chamber, and there is no modification of the elementary sounds of the language lower than the soft palate; while the language of tone is produced more especially back of this, the inflections and changes of pitch being produced in the larynx, and the tone-color and the qualities of voice being produced primarily in the pharynx, but really also modified by the whole body.

Again, it is distinct in significance. While words are manifestive of the thought, it takes the tones and inflections of the voice to manifest the emotions of the man, and the relation of his experience to his thought. Inflection manifests intellectual belief, conviction and earnestness, sincerity of motive and the like, while the color of the voice manifests the deepest emotional conditions of the man — his joy or sorrow, his love or hate.

In fact, the elements of vocal expression are not only distinct from those of verbal expression, but have power to completely reverse the spirit of the thought that is embodied in the words. It is impossible to put into words the function and subjective relationship which can be so delicately and exactly revealed by the color and various modifications of the tone. Falsehood can be easily told by words, but it is very difficult to hide the false ring when there is an endeavor to express an untruth through tones and inflections.

Another proof that the function of vocal expression is distinct from words, is found in the fact that it is often separated from verbal expression in nature. In the little child vocal expression is very effective before a single word can be articulated. The tones, inflections and modulations of the voice reveal the feelings of the child. Again, birds and animals have vocal expression in a crude form, but no verbal expression. Parrots and a few other birds are taught to imitate a few words which are repeated without much reference to their meaning, but this does not disprove the principle.

Now, if all this is true, how false is the ordinary conception of vocal expression! Most people pretend to look upon a beautiful voice, beautiful tone-color, soft and beautiful intonations, definite attack, good inflections and well-developed form in speech, as merely so much decoration, something to add to the beauty of speech, but with no distinct function in manifesting truth. This fearful error has its root in ignorance; for while the tones and inflections of the voice do very materially add to the auditor's delight and pleasure, still all forms of vocal expression supplement the verbal and manifest the emotional elements, while verbal expression can only symbolize the outline of the thought; and it is the co-ordination of the two that is the glory of human speech.

The importance of this vocal part of language to the truthful presentation of thought cannot be overestimated. Man's inflections and tones will be believed more readily than words. The reason for this is that verbal expression is more manifestive of conscious mental action, while vocal expression manifests not only the conscious feelings, but also the unconscious emotions and conditions of the speaker's character and soul, and is recognized and read by the instincts of man.

The third form of expression may be called pantomimic. This word is used as the most convenient term to express all forms of language which appeal to the eye. This meaning is indicated by the etymology of the wor.!

rather than by its usage. All the attitudes and motions of the body which manifest emotions and conditions of the soul, the permanent bearings which indicate character, belong to this form of expression. Pantomime is similar in significance to vocal expression, and also belongs to the realm of what is called natural language. Like vocal expression it is read and apprehended by the instincts of men. It is a language which is very generic, and belongs also in some form to most animals. It manifests the character and conditions of the man, but does not directly symbolize his thought, and its most important elements are almost wholly unconscious.

There is of course a conventional form of pantomimic expression, the sign language of deaf mutes and that of the Indians. This form can represent ideas, but for the most part in all civilized countries of the world pantomime is more interpretive, more suggestive as a language than a symbolic representation of thought.

There is a tendency on the part of many to belittle pantomimic expression, but linguistic action in some form is never absent. Vocal expression is not separated from words in ordinary speech, but pantomime is more independent. A look of the eye, a grasp of the hand may speak what many sentences would fail to convey. In the stir of deep feeling, when the tongue is dumb with inadequacy to express the depths of the soul of man, the lip trembles, the eye flashes, the body expands, the hand is held out and gives a gentle pressure, and all is clear; the soul at once feels the links of sympathy, the appreciation of the whole situation. In the manifestation of feeling, the revelation of the relations and real character of the man, pantomime is far more effective than words.

It is evidently the intention of nature that the language of each part should bear witness in its proper sphere to the truth expressed by the others, and thus "in the mouth of two or three witnesses every word be established." Without this harmonious co-ordination of languages, without this harmony of all nature's intended agents of expression, perfect truthfulness and adequacy of expression are impossible.

Thus when we come to study expression we find that a normal man has these three languages. It is never fair to compare one of these with another, for nature evidently intended that they should complement each other, and that no one of them should ever be substituted for the others. All the objection that has been urged against pantomime has been due to the endeavor to make pantomime discharge the function of words, and the same is true of vocal expression. Pantomime, vocal expression or the representation of ideas by words, must each be judged according to its appropriate function, its own peculiar action and character, but not in respect to the substitution of one form for another; for the meaning of one can hardly be translated into that of another. They stand in organic unity and one can no more be compared with another than the function of the head can be compared with that of the hand. One can as well be substituted for another in expression, as the arm can be substituted for the leg in walking.

Thus oratory is meant to be the co-ordination of all the living languages of man; bringing the character of the soul to witness the truth uttered by the tongue. It is meant to be a living presentation of thought in all its aspects, in all its relations to human character, by the co-ordination of many languages; and not a presentation of everything through one language — that of words.

No skillful lawyer in conducting his case calls witnesses that will contradict each other. The great artist in any department will seek the best means of conveying his conception. The material employed, the drawing, the purpose of the work, the place it is to occupy, he knows very well must be carefully considered. So the true orator despises nothing. He knows that every language natural to man is intended to perform a certain function in his great work of speaking, and that unless all these languages are brought into co-ordination, unless the testi-mony of each is made to bear out the same purpose, he knows that one will contradict another, and his expression thus be weakened. He realizes that his whole manner must be a transparency through which his thoughts and feelings can be seen; that one is the candle, the other the blaze, without which there can be no light.

Supposing for the sake of argument, we grant that vocal and pantomimic expression have simply to do with manner, and that verbal expression has to do with the matter of the speech, then, as has been shown, the manner has power to reverse the matter, and oratorical truthfulness absolutely requires the two to be consistent with each other. Both are absolutely necessary to a complete and adequate manifestation of the thought and soul of the man.

A man who says it makes no difference how a speech is delivered, that all depends merely upon the thought, overlooks the fundamental characteristic of unity in nature. Every form of expression manifests a different phase of the man; yet all in unison with each other form a transparency of character. It is only by the use of these three languages as co-ordinate witnesses that any truth can be revealed or established by man.

On the other hand, the man who says it does not make any difference what he says, that all depends upon the manner of his speech, is much farther from the truth.

He seeks to accomplish an effect without nature's appointed means. The proper cause will tend of itself to find adequate means, but the most adequate means without cause is dead.

Here we see some of the causes of the decline of the art of oratory. Such one-sidedness of view as these and others that could be mentioned, would be the death of any art. As can be seen, the real province of oratory has been lost sight of. It has become a mere language of words, all rhetoric of modern times having passed over to the mere recording of ideas in symbols. Oratory has lost its original and fundamental character of revealing the many phases of the experience of the soul, through nature's well-appointed and manifold means of manifestation. Oratory is no longer the simultaneous manifestation of truth and experience as realized by the whole soul, but the mere communication of ideas through words; no longer the co-ordination of nature's manifold languages by the simultaneous revelation of the many phases of human experience for their mutual interpretation, but the mere use of one language to the exclusion of all others.

This change is no doubt due to the invention of printing, and to the fact that a part of the function of ancient oratory is now discharged by the press, so that men now study rhetoric simply to become writers. But it will be the endeavor to show in the course of this work that this divorce has hurt the art of writing itself, because a true writer must have an instinctive and a vivid consciousness of the relation of language to his own and to other minds. Hence, some study of the intention of nature to combine diverse elements of revelation is necessary to enable the student to grasp a special form of language. It is a well-known fact that a dramatic writer absolutely requires some such experience; but it is not only true of him, it is true of the novel writer, and every writer who wishes to move effectively the soul of man. For the speaker to neglect such work is absolute folly.

From all this discussion we can see something of the many-sided character of expression, but when we come to look at the experience of men, we find the same complexity. Man is just as capable of emotion as he is of thought. In fact, some able masters of psychology contend that no thought is complete without its proper complement of emotion. If this is true in nature, it must be true in expression, and no mere verbal expression manifesting the thought can be complete without its vocal accompaniment manifesting the emotion. Every truth we find has associated experience. This experience is not a mere adjunct, is not a mere associate of the truth, but it is the very life and soul of the truth. One of the most fundamental characteristics of all great poets and artists is what has been called by Dowden "consentaneity of thought and feeling."

An important distinction has been made between fact and truth. Fact is the mere external body, truth implies the soul. Ordinary histories give us the facts regarding the heroes of Scotland for example, but the real spirit that animates these heroes is only presented to us in works of art like the novels of Sir Walter Scott. The mere facts of English history are given in the ordinary historical books, but the spirit, the truth of Richard III, of Henry IV, of King John, has never been so well presented as by Shakespeare. The Duke of Marlborough said he had read no English history but that written by Shakespeare. The highest art uses few facts and these in such a way as to awaken the co-ordinate experience. Writing is great in proportion as there is such a suggestion as will rouse the experience which is the hidden soul of the truth uttered. So in delivery, verbal expression, of course, deals more with facts, the other forms of expression with experience. When all three of the languages combine as nature intended, then only, can man reveal the depths of his soul. Emotion arises in obedience to the stimulation of an idea or situation, and there is a tendency with every idea or phantasm, as Aristotle called it, for emotion to respond. Facts can be given by words alone, but when an idea stirs feeling and experience as it does in nature, the other languages of man must reveal these, if they are revealed at all.

A man may read the words, "The Lord is my Shepherd, I shall not want," in such a way as to clearly convey the thought, but at the same time give the impression that it is a very disagreeable and painful experience that has led him to speak. Thus one of the most beautiful compositions ever penned can be read in such a way as to convey the impression of dry facts, or of a struggle to get them. Of course when so read the real truth is not told, for the essential idea of the psalm is one of experience. It is simply a record of experience. It is the verbal embodiment, or using the figure of Humboldt, it is an endeavor by the author to verbally embalm his experience. If the reader does not assimilate and bring to life again that experience through imagination and sympathy, he is not possessed of the real truth of the poem, and of course cannot manifest it. And if he kills out, from false ideas of language or evil training, all the natural means of manifesting such experience, what wonder if all is cold and dead. A still worse fault is of course introducing the wrong experience, but repressing the right experience is the quickest road to such perversion.

To secure the highest possible expression, the whole nature of the man must be aroused, and all his languages

must be brought into use in order to convey the whole
truth. The presentation of the truth must ever be the
aim of expression; not merely the abstract facts, which
may be regarded as the external body of the truth, but
the spirit must be brought back to life. He must not
only convey a correct impression of the truth itself, but a
correct impression of the relationship of that truth to the
human soul. Otherwise, in the most important sense, he
is untrue, for the worst falsehood is often a half truth.
It is better that men should not have truth conveyed to
them than that it should be conveyed in such a way as to
inspire contempt and hatred. When an orator speaks of
some infinite danger in a tone of indifference, not only is
no one awakened to the danger, but actual indifference is
induced in his audience. It would have been far better
for his hearers and for his cause, had he never spoken at
all, for he has dulled every susceptibility to truth.

Possibly to tell men a part of the truth, to give an
abstract, or a mere outline of the facts, without giving
any of their relations to the human soul, may answer
many of the purposes of science and scientific instruction, but in the great practical work of instructing the
untaught, of awakening man to rescue his brother in
danger, of inspiring man to a higher life, it is powerless.
Oratory goes farther than mere instruction. It seeks to
rouse the latent energies of men, it seeks to make men
realize the outcome of a certain course of action, it seeks
to give men phases of experience belonging to the higher
faculties of the soul, so as to awake nobler motives and
dispositions.

Art is the interpretive presentation of nature, and the
great characteristic of nature is its plenitude. Nature
does not do things one-sidedly or abstractly. One-sidedness in art is the worst of falsehoods, and this is espe-

cially true in oratory. The aim of all oratory is to incarnate truth, to translate the mystic into something manifest, to translate the abstract into such a concrete form as will cause it to be felt in all its relations to human thought and human activity. It is to present truth in all its relations to the experience of personality. Such a province can never be fulfilled by confounding art with science, oratory with mere instruction, or without meeting every need and every requirement for the perfect manifestation not only of the truth, but of the complement of truth in experience, and thus awaken the disposition to receive the truth. If truth absolutely requires a complement of experience, expression of that truth requires that its embodiment should be complemented by a vocal and a pantomimic language manifesting the experience.

Thus we see that expression is complex and belongs to the whole man, and that its complexity is in correspondence with the complexity of the experience of the soul. We see also, that the complex elements of language have normally as complete and perfect unity as the psychic conditions which they are intended to manifest. We also find that without complete co-ordination and co-operation of these various languages an adequate and truthful manifestation of the experience of the soul is not possible. Thus we can draw an inference as to what is the end of all work for improving expression. It must in some way develop and bring into unity all the faculties concerned in expression, and must train the individual power, and bring into co-operation all the languages of man according to their intended functions, in order to reveal truthfully and adequately the possessions of the soul, so as to cause them to be truthfully realized by others.

IV.

EXPRESSION AND PERSONALITY.

"Man can give nothing to his fellow-man but himself."
— *Schlegel.*

IF such is the character of expression, if it is not the result of any process of aggregation, not a matter of mere manner, if it is a manifestation of the subjective, if it is manifold and complex, and its complexity corresponds with the nature and complexity of the faculties and powers of the mind, then there must be a very intimate relation between expression and the real nature of man. If we look again at some of the most common misconceptions of the nature of expression we shall find many of them take their rise from some misconception of the relationship between expression and personality.

Let us take the two greatest faults in delivery. In one of these the man may be really in earnest, may feel to the depths of his soul the importance of the thought in relation to others, but from a misconception he may polish down his delivery — his mode of presenting his truth — until nothing but the smooth, delicate finish is manifest to his fellow-men. The real character of the man, the depth and intensity of his nature, even the impression produced upon his own soul by the truth, is not revealed in the delivery. All that can be seen and noted is the skillful use of certain actions, vocal or physical, and in general an endeavor not to do anything to offend the taste of his audience. His delivery is fault-less, his elocution perfect, but still you feel that its very perfection conceals the personality of the man. When a great occasion arises you prefer to see him make some mistake, if such a blunder can show that the activities of the soul transcend the activities of the body, for mere mechanical perfection is inconsistent with life.

On the other hand a man may be genuinely in earnest, may have a real love for his fellow-men, a deep appreciation of the truth, but on account of the misuse of the means of expression, he may manifest it in such a hard tone, or with such abnormal movements that these intervene between his own character and the truth and the audience, in such a way as to call the whole attention of his hearers to his delivery. If a man tries to manifest love with clenched fists pounding on the desk, or sympathy in a tone of anger, or affectionate pleading in an attitude of antagonism, his delivery is fundamentally untruthful. It hinders rather than bears witness to the truth, if indeed it does not absolutely deny the spirit of the truth which is uttered. The bad habit of the man stands out before his audience more prominently than anything else, and his real character and feeling on the occasion is not revealed.

In both of these cases it is taken for granted that the man really feels and has a proper possession of the truth; but actually this is rarely the case, for misuse of any of the languages soon or late perverts the pure fountain of ideas and feeling from which they flow.

While these two faults seem to be directly in opposition to each other, really they have something of kinship. In each case the revelation of the thought and feeling of the speaker is hindered. The attention of the audience is distracted and more or less drawn from the truth itself and obstructed by, if not centred upon, something which should be transparent. The perfection of all expression must be due to the transparency of person-

ality.   There must be a perfect manifestation of the
conditions and activities of the spirit and character of
the man, and whatever really improves delivery more
intimately unites delivery to the soul.

The fundamental cause of nearly all faults in delivery
is a failure to properly assimilate truth.   One of the most
common forms of this difficulty is that the thought is
merely aggregated and does not enter into the system
and become a vital part of the man.   What the speaker
says seems to come merely from the head.   It seems to
have been merely acquired for the occasion.   We feel
that the man is merely performing, though he is unconscious of it. , He has felt that he must speak and has
prepared something to say.   But this something is the
mere thought of his mind and has no vital relationship to
the deep emotions and conditions of his being.   Rarely
do we feel that the man himself really speaks.   How
frequently do we hear a speaker whom we know to be
good and what he says to be true, yet we feel that in his
delivery the two do not come together; that they do not
co-ordinate in expression as nature intended.   Sometimes
a man's words seem to be merely his creed or the doctrine of his church, or to be acquired from books, so that
all he says seem only intellectual abstractions.   Sometimes we feel that what is said is merely for party purposes and is not the living presentation of the experience
underlying the whole structure of his character and manhood, and which has been awakened by the ideas he reveals.

The real problem of delivery, therefore, is how to
reveal thought and experience, not how to make this little
inflection or that little gesture; not how to polish most
beautifully our manner so as not in the least to offend
the most conventional audience; not how to please and
entertain nor how to soothe gently into slumber; not how

to acquire such skill as will enable us to stir feeling without having any ourselves; but how to reveal the real character of the man with what is said; how to show truthfully the life of the soul. No external coaching, no mere study about what the man has to do with his voice and his body, can furnish a substitute for that which can only be produced by the direct impulse of a living soul.

Men have always spoken of artistic instinct and of dramatic instinct. From time immemorial the artist has been considered to be inspired. Homer and the poets since his day have invoked their muse. The truth of this old idea of the muse is, that when anything artistic is done it always seems to be given to the artist. It seems to come to him. In the old days the muse seemed to stand at his side and whisper in his ear. Here is a great truth put into the form of poetry. For the goddess that sings to the artist is his subjective soul — the artistic semiconscious instinct, awakening and realizing and revealing the mystic side of truth.

This artistic instinct is a response in the harmonious co-ordination of all the faculties of our nature toward the production of one whole. The greatest hindrance in the world to expression is one-sidedness. A man whose intellect alone responds to truth can never make an orator, because he never can have any oratoric instinct. On the other hand, one whose feelings alone respond, independent of intellect, can never become an orator, because blind feeling will lead him completely astray and make him ridiculous. It is only when thought and emotion, balanced by will, simultaneously respond to the truth so as to bring directly all the languages of man into unity, that true oratory is possible.

Unity is the fundamental law of all art, and in oratory it never can be obtained except through co-ordination of impulse, reason, feeling and volition, of the conscious and the unconscious in one simultaneous outflow through all the natural as well as artificial languages of man.

It will aid us in tracing this subject more adequately to its fundamental elements to return once more to the misconceptions of art, and to look at the relation of all art to personality.

We have had in all ages and in every department of art two schools. One of these believes that poetry is mere rhythm; that its beauty is primarily a beauty of sound and only secondarily of sense. The other believes that poetry is primarily sense, and that sound and rhythm are only means of manifestation. The one regards art as a matter of technique; the other regards art as a means of revealing the fundamental impressions and conditions of the soul. One says the most stormy passages of music may be written when the composer is in a mood of complete indifference; and on the other hand we find Beethoven walking around Vienna with a soul on fire catching the mystic undertone of all he heard. In short, we find one who believes that art is only technical skill, and the farther the art from human experience and character the better — that he is the greatest artist who can produce the greatest effect with the least possible feeling himself; and we find another who says that there can be no great impersonal art, that art is in its very nature the embodiment of man's understanding of the mystic problems of the universe, the revelation of the impressions which have been made upon his soul.

There is a growing tendency at the present time in all departments of art to trace the connections between the character of the artist and his work. A striking instance of this tendency is the thorough study that has been made of the life of Shakespeare. The great desire of the world for facts regarding his life has caused the lovers of his art to search into every nook and corner for vague hints regarding the influences that moulded the man and his art; but as few facts could be found, great critics during the past fifty years have examined more thoroughly than ever into the depths of his plays, establishing as far as possible the dates at which they were written. They have studied his whole life in connection with these plays and out of this has also come a more thorough study of the nature of his art.

Shakespeare's career as an artist lasts over a period of twenty years, usually divided by critics into four periods, which have been called by Dowden: "In the Work Shop," "In the World," "Out of the Depths," "On the Heights." In the first period Shakespeare is found not to be complete master of his art; he seems to fear his art. In this period he is struggling and is, no doubt, uncertain of success; his plays are the exact mirror of such conditions of life. In his second period Shakespeare is filled with patriotism and ambition, and his plays are more melodramatic. In this period Shakespeare has won great friends, is successful and happy, and we have the great comedies written. In the third period he passes into the depths of gloom. He suffers evidently, either for his own sins or the sins of others. In this period were written the tragedies which are the highest productions of human genius — Macbeth, King Lear, Othello and Hamlet. His period of greatest suffering is, according to most critics, the period of his greatest art. But in this condition of sorrow. Shakespeare does not remain. In his last period we have the peacefulness of age. "The Tempest," "Cymbeline" and the "Winter's Tale," his last plays, breathe with forgiveness and love. They have romantic subjects; he seems to rise to a more ideal world. Even the villain Iachimo is reclaimed; and Shakespeare with his own Prospero lays aside the magic cloak of his art at peace with all mankind. Another illustration is the correspondence of Prince Henry, afterward Henry V., to Shakespeare himself. Some contend that but for the experience of his own struggles and efforts, Shakespeare could never have painted this wonderful character. There are some critics who are still skeptical upon sundry points, but the majority are agreed, and the discussion affords one of the most wonderful of all illustrations of the connection between personality and art. It proves that the art of Shakespeare, the greatest of all time, is no external show, no objective exhibition entirely independent of himself. Though he is according to Browning, our most objective poet, yet in this greatest artist through all his plays we come closest to the soul, we feel his convictions, his earnestness, as well as his great insight into the human heart. As Professor Corson has said, "We know Shakespeare — or he can be known, if the requisite conditions are met — better, perhaps, than any other great author that ever lived — know, in the deepest sense of the word, in a sense other than that which we know Dr. Johnson, through Boswell's Biography. The moral proportion which is so signal a characteristic of his plays could not have been imparted to them by the conscious intellect. It was *shed* from his spiritual constitution." Why? Because his power in expression was as perfect as has yet been accorded to man. For this reason, though Johnson had a most painstaking Boswell, who lived with him, understood him thoroughly, and wrote a biography which has been one of the books of the greatest interest in modern times, yet to-day we know Shakespeare, even as a man, better than we know Johnson. We do not know, of course, the facts of Shakespeare's life so well, we do not know quite so well how he was esteemed by those who lived with him. All the facts we know about him might be placed upon a few pages, but his personality shines through his work, even through his plays. We feel the moral grandeur of the man, his insight into human nature, his grand moral proportions, his intuitions, impulses and ideals; and these are the greatest part of the man and form the foundation of his character.

Some oppose this idea and ask why we should not regard Shelley's or Browning's villains as expressive of the personal character of their authors. To which it can be answered that the character of these authors is shown more clearly in the way they paint villains than in any other way. Shakespeare in Falstaff shows his moral rectitude as well as in Henry V. He could have treated Falstaff with cant and bigotry or with sympathy with his sin. Like many modern French authors, or even English dramatists of his age, he might have justified Falstaff's sin. But such degradation is never found in Shakespeare. The immoral, when treated by him is given with moral truthfulness, thus showing the essential rectitude and nobility of his own character.

Again others answer in another way, and consider that they have proved that art has connection wholly with imagination and not with character, by asking the question "Was the personality of Shelley noble?" Shelley is the best illustration of the fact that art is more intimately related to the character of the artist than any other mode of expression. Shelley in his essays has been shown by many critics to be a different man from what he is in his poetry. In his Defence of Atheism or Essay upon Christianity, we see his intellectual views, his prejudices. We see that phase of his character which

was the result of circumstances, persecutions and misconceptions.   In his Prometheus Unbound, we feel what he
desired the world to be.   Here we meet his faith and
hope; the beautiful soul that was revealed otherwise only
to a few sympathetic friends is made manifest to the
world.   Here the real man is revealed truthfully though
unconsciously and indirectly through his art.

True art does not reveal a man's opinions so much as
it does the man himself.   When men speak frankly and
directly through words, there is a one-sided expression of
the mere opinions of the man; the deeper motives, conditions, aspirations and faith which are the real soul
of the man cannot be manifested except through co-
ordinate modes of revelation — that is, through art.

The common idea is, that dramatic poetry is an objective form of art; that the dramatic poet completely
buries his personality, simply talks through another character, and hence his own character is entirely distinct
from his art. · While there is an element of truth in this,
yet the revelation of the author's real feeling, though
indirect and possibly unconscious, is the more effective.
Browning deliberately chooses the dramatic monologue
as the highest means of manifesting the deepest feelings
and experiences of the soul.   He hides himself as much
as possible, but this hiding of his direct opinions causes
a truer revelation of the deeper dispositions and spirit of
the man.

And this principle applies to all the arts.   Painting is
said to be one of the most tell-tale of all arts, and there is
no form of art, however objective it may be, that does not
reveal the subjective character of him who executes it.

Mr. Enneking when he went to study in Munich found
the class which he desired to enter full, but he was
allowed to stand behind the students and look on.   While

waiting for a vacancy he fell to studying the work of the class as they were drawing from the same model. While doing so he discovered that all the tall members of the class were drawing the figure tall, while the short members of the class were drawing the figure short. Those with long noses made a long nose in their drawing. In every case the physical peculiarities of each artist were reflected in his drawing from the same model, though all were striving to be accurate.

This fact in art has been attested by many observers; and this physical reflection is merely an indication of a deeper one. The emotions, experience and character of the artist mould his work far more than his physical traits and peculiarities.

There is still another important confirmation of the relation of art to character. We find in history that the degradation of art of all kinds, in every age, has started with a tendency toward mere technique, toward the separation of art from its revelation of the subjective activities of the soul. The pupils of Raphael descended merely to copying his delicacy of color and the peculiarities of his technique. In their study of the master's tone and beauty, they lost the thought and the depth of soul which he struggled to manifest.

In many departments of art at the present time we note a similar tendency. Then very careful should the young student be who begins the study of any art. But especially ought there to be caution in the study of oratory or dramatic art. For evil tendencies in art have always shown themselves in histrionic art first of all. In this field evil seed has ever seemed to fall first, and to produce here the quickest and most abundant harvest.

Students of dramatic art only wish to know "the business" of a part or of a play. How little there is of deep meditation, absorbing thought, despairing efforts for new conceptions, for inspiration, for the noble "accident" which comes seemingly of itself, yet only comes after long-continued and oft-repeated effort!

Again, the higher a work of art the more intimately is it connected with human character and experience. A play of Shakespeare brings us far nearer, not only to the personality of the writer, but also to the personalities of history, than any other record. Hamlet is not a history, it is a work of art, and hence it is a revelation of the conceptions of one human soul regarding other human souls, struggling amid the problems of life. There is a distinction between the history of the times of Henry V. and Shakespeare's revelation of that character. We have more facts in one, but we have more truth in the other. We have more external relations in one, but we have more soul and life in the other. Without art it may well be said that the greatest depths of personality cannot be revealed to our fellow-men. A great work of art may enable a man to conceal the facts of his life, but all the more it reveals the character and depths of his experience. A reader of Robertson's sermons never finds a word regarding the mere events of his life or regarding the peculiar trials through which he, as an individual, was passing, but the great experiences of his life are felt everywhere. We do not read the mere facts, these are given in his letters; but we do find the truth and character of the man.

Now if all this is true in such arts as painting and poetry, how much more must it be true in delivery. The artist must depend upon artificial means, and it may seem plausible that his art should be entirely independent of his soul. But there ought to be no doubt in the case of a speaker or a reader, who must do all through his own organism. There is no external brush, there are no pigments and combinations of color which can be scientific- ally applied. That art which is most intimately associ- ated with nature must show the most intimate connection between personality and art. Oratory has been defined as a "presentation of truth by personality," and from even the artificial Quintillian, who said that an orator was "a good man speaking well," to the greatest orators of our own times, this truth has ever been recognized.

It will make clearer the relation of personality to deliv- ery if we study some views of art as given us by its greatest interpreter in modern times. Browning regards art as the only adequate way of telling the truth. One soul can never reveal adequately to another its concep- tion of the highest ideals except by suggesting them through the medium of art. "Our human speech is naught, our human testimony false," he says, but art, in which man does not speak to men but to mankind, may teach a truth obliquely, may "do the thing shall breed the thought." In ordinary speech, though we may tell the truth it appears false to the one to whom we speak it; and it is only by art that the spirit that reveals the impression can be awakened in the breast of another.

Through the study of art, men have found that each sees something different in the world. As some one has said, "men see nothing but what they are." According to Browning, art not only expresses the thought or the truth, but discharges a still more important office, it awakens the disposition to receive that truth.

To explain this more clearly, let us examine an extract from one of his earlier works:

> " Truth is within ourselves; it takes no rise
> From outward things, ... and 'to know'
> Rather consists in opening out a way

> Whence the imprisoned splendour may escape,
> Than in effecting entry for a light
> Supposed to be without.   Watch narrowly.
> The demonstration of a truth, its birth,
> And you trace back the effluence to its spring
> And source within us, where broods radiance vast,
> To be elicited ray by ray, as chance shall favour."

If all truth comes from within, true expression must do more than give mere bare external facts. There must be some suggestion to awaken activity within. For one soul to convey truth to another adequately, requires a complex co-ordination and suggestion, in order to quicken the subjective activity in many directions. Thus, and thus only, the soul of man can be awakened to truth. Art is the only power given to a human being to awaken the conscious and unconscious impulses of another soul, and to cause it to create and realize truth from within. Unless the thing can be done that shall "breed the thought," shall cause the thought to germinate in the depths of the soul, the truth is not felt and realized, in fact it is not understood. Unless this process is stimulated even the greatest truth presented to man will appear like falsehood.

Thus art is a necessity of human nature. It is not only intimately connected with personality, but is absolutely necessary to the growth of personality. Without the endeavor to execute, without the endeavor to embody the good beyond him, man cannot grow toward that good, and reveal the apprehensions and experiences of his soul to others. Thus art is no mere skill in technique, no mere superficial polish, no mere amusement, but is most deeply intertwined with the human soul and is its only means of manifestation. It is that which shows man to be made in the image of his God, without which he cannot grow nor his nature achieve its ideal.

Now all this especially explains the function and the nature of true delivery. The aim of all expression, the aim of all delivery, is to "do the thing shall breed the thought." Thought uttered merely by one language, or through its symbols, appears false, appears cold and lifeless, but when the associated experience is simultaneously manifested through the natural languages, when the emotions, the earnestness, the sympathy and all phases of personality bearing any relation to the truth are simultaneously revealed, then the proper attitude for the reception of the truth is engendered in the heart of the hearer. At the same moment that the intellect and understanding become awake to the ideas of the mystic, the unconscious activities of the soul are awakened to the living reception of the spirit, which lies deeper than the ideas. Only when this requirement is fulfilled do we have presented to us a true example of a powerful delivery — one in accord with nature's intentions.

True the speaker's character may be concealed by a certain kind of work in expression. Mere polish may hide the depths of his soul and call attention merely to the outside, thus hiding his real nature. But such art is false — false to the soul and to truth. It is worse than sounding brass and tinkling cymbal, nor has it ever, nor can it ever stir the depths of the human heart. To any one with an eye to see or ear to hear, the first impression received will be that of affectation. Nor can it, in fact, ever be characteristic of a strong man. Such work soon or late will enervate and dwarf the power of the greatest soul.

If we believe that there is an element of art that is "shed from personality," as the light from the sun, how much more must this be true of delivery. Certainly man's living languages in their complex relationship, each discharging a specific function, yet all working together in perfect unity, reveal the character and soul of the man, though more transiently yet more directly and more adequately than any form of human art.

Of course some one will say, all this applies to oratoric delivery but it has nothing to do with public reading or acting. But the same principle holds true. All who have looked into the kindly eyes of Henry Irving — the inspiration of vast numbers of his fellow-artists — enjoy his representation of the arch hypocrite, Louis XI. the more intensely because they know the character he portrays is entirely foreign to his own. His intuitive insight enables him to understand the subtlety and greatness of Louis, and his own noble character enables him to accentuate more strongly the powerful elements of the royal murderer. A man who is in daily practise of a sin can not artistically present a character in correspondence with his own, because we know ourselves less than we know any one else. He would be unconscious of the real perversion in the character. Such perversion must be seen and appreciated with respect to an ideal before there can be true expression. An artist must be deeply conscious of the right and the wrong, or he can accent neither. This is why one who has been thoroughly tempted and has conquered is enabled to express more effectively a wider range of characters.

A bad man is limited to one type of characters. A man may do bad deeds occasionally, but have continual struggles and aspirations after what is right and be enabled to manifest noble characters at times; but this only proves the principle.

It has been plainly shown that there is not one Hamlet, but as many Hamlets as there have been actors who have played the part well. If Hamlet were given alike by all actors the art would be absolutely false. When we see the same character taken by two actors it is a most effective revelation of the characters of the two men. The difference is chiefly a difference of personality.

In the light of such principles how utterly frivolous appears the widespread notion that a speaker who has good delivery must have poor thought ; that an elocution-ist, a reader or an actor need not be an educated man ; that expression is the product of special "aptitude, the result of birth and not of training," and which may be present with a high degree of efficiency while in other respects the mind may be very weak. In fact, that an actor or a public reader is necessarily a man of low men-tal calibre. How such an absolutely false conception should be so widely diffused is a wonder. As a matter of fact all histrionic art at the present time is in a low con-dition. There are few educated men who have real intuition, few who have a real culture of their artistic nature, and an adequate conception of the dignity of their work, so that possibly the idea is due to observation.

Of all uninteresting performances in this world, the mere repetition or recitation of words is absolutely the tamest. To bring out a truth in poetry there must be insight. Lovers of true poetry are dissatisfied with the histrionic art of our day. It is only an Irving that can bring an educated audience to the theatre. Our public readers choose, as a rule, to feed the lower tastes and appeal with their imitative modulations to the ignorant. All who love true literature feel sympathy with a certain teacher who went home sorrowfully after spending an evening at an entertainment given by one of the leading elocutionists of this country, saying that it was a great grief to him that a man of such talents should degrade his art by rendering such selections.

If all this is true, how deeply must all feel that in all expression that is to do more than merely tickle the fancy, the soul must act.   It is the activities of the deepest and most fundamental powers of human nature which interest men most deeply, and which stir them most effectively.   Expression is not a mere vocal jugglery; it is not a mere feat of the articulating organs; not a display of beautiful tones; it is essentially a mental act — an act of the deepest forces of the soul, truthfully manifested through the natural languages of the body.   It is the soul held up as a mirror to nature, and a mirror also to that in nature which is the deepest and grandest of all its phases — human experience and human character.

Is delivery the mere acquirement of a few external rules and a few superficial graces of manner, and above all can it do this merely as some adjunct, independent of greatness of character?   If this is not true of the objective arts, how can it be true of a subjective one?   Expression unites music — the highest art, according to Hegel — and sculpture and painting.   If it is not a union of all the arts, it brings into action their most fundamental modes for the revelation of living character.   If art is an agency of personality, this which brings into co-ordination all man's fundamental languages cannot occupy a low place. And if oratory is the most direct conscious and unconscious revelation of soul to soul, there must necessarily be behind it a great artist — a soul broad enough and deep enough to "speak not merely to men but also to mankind."

Thus we see that oratory can not be separated from character.   But on the other hand when it is represented as being wholly a matter of character a great mistake is made.   For as the personality of the artist determines the treatment of his subject in art, but does not necessitate that his art shall truthfully manifest that personality, so, though the character of the orator gives the cause of the oration, this does not necessitate that his delivery shall truthfully manifest his character. A man's character may be belied by his delivery. We have found that expression is an artistic, sympathetic co-ordination of all the languages belonging to man, so as to simultaneously reveal, not only what he thinks, but what he feels, and what he is; that "in the mouth of two or three witnesses every word should be established." The character of the man depends for its most effective revelation upon the testimony of these various witnesses, and if any one of them bears false witness there is not only confusion but untruthfulness in the expression. The character should be revealed and not concealed or belied by the delivery. The character must not only exist in the man, but his auditor must feel and see it in his tones and actions. His delivery must spring spontaneously from this character and be an intrinsic part of the oration.

V.

EXPRESSION AND EMOTION.

. . . . Si vis me flere dolendum est
Primum ipsi tibi.   —*Horace.*

THE intimate relation of personality to expression brings us to another question often discussed during the last few years. How far does the speaker, the reader or the actor really feel the emotion and experience which he is called upon to manifest? How much of his nature and what sets of faculties are active? Is expression the product of reason, of will or of emotion, or of all the faculties and powers of the soul?

The most important misconception of the relation of experience to expression may be called the mechanical or intellectual view. This view was formulated and advocated by Diderot in his famous Paradox published about one hundred years ago. He was the first, as far as known, to contend that sensibility and passion are enemies to expression; that the possession of real passion is ridiculous; that all great oratory and acting is simply an act of the intellect and reason; the less feeling the better. "Sensibility," he says, "cripples the intellect at the very time when the man needs all his self-possession." "Feeling is the disposition which accompanies organic weakness." He held that the orator can never produce any effect except from direct and careful calculation beforehand, and without allowing himself to be trammeled by feeling at the time he speaks. Some modern writers on the subject say that a man cannot afford to have genuine emotion, that it would wear him out, that he must be entirely concerned with giving the "signs of emotion," that he is an artist in proportion as he can give these without having feeling, and that he can only have "symptomatic emotion," or the effect produced upon his nervous system by the assumption of such signs. This discussion has been revived during the last few years by M. Coquelin and by Mr. Henry Irving. Mr. Archer, in his "Masks or Faces," has gathered the testimony and experience of the greatest living artists, and with few exceptions all have agreed with Mr. Irving against Coquelin and the Paradox.

It is necessary to give some attention to this subject here, because this view has taken deep hold of the elocutionary methods of our times. Stated in its baldest form few elocutionists would probably acknowledge it, yet as a matter of fact, nearly all the methods for the development of delivery are influenced by it, if they are not in conscious accord with its teaching. Many teachers boldly avow that feeling is none of their business. "We are only concerned," they say, "with the signs of emotion, the modulation of the voice, and the actions of the body, their development and proper use." The firm though unconscious hold which the Diderot view has upon this age is shown in the fact that many teachers of literature condemn all manifestation of emotion. "Bring out the thought" is continually heard, "have nothing to do with feeling." It is considered by many unscholarly to show feeling, as if thought were separate from emotion. Strange to say the discussion of the subject connected with acting is in advance of that in relation to public speaking and the rendering of literature.

It would seem that of all artists in the world public speakers would be the least affected by the mechanical view of Diderot. Yet, strange to say, it is in relation to public speaking, in America at least, that the theory seems to have the firmest hold; at least, the only book published in English to justify a similar theory is a work by Nathan Sheppard, entitled "Before an Audience." The views of this book have been advocated by many speakers. It is a very inconsistent work, the author sneering at elocution as well as at feeling. He out-diderots Diderot, as he holds that the whole secret of delivery is will. Feeling is nothing, abandonment is the greatest folly. This view professes to be founded on personal experience; he says, "If I had taken the common advice and 'forgotten myself,' I would have lost myself and my bread and butter." To him "delivery may be natural and yet be wrong," he has no faith in nature. He does not of course say that intellect is a hinderance, as Diderot says of feeling; but he implies it, for to him all is will. In the baldest form he says, "If you wish to move your audience simply do it." Practically he says, thought is nothing, feeling is nothing, simply have an intention and execute it by the direct force of will, that is the whole secret.

A third misconception makes emotion the sole cause of expression. The ranter rises before his audience with no thought, and endeavors to force himself into a state of feeling which will carry all before him. An American actress works herself up into a state of almost hysterical emotion strong enough to carry her through the performance of her part with all the real force of nature. The emotion according to this view must not only be genuine, but must be of sufficient force to compel expression as it does in life. The whole situation must be as real to the person as if it were actually happening. The speaker must be driven by uncontrollable emotion to the proper modes of expression.

All these three views are incorrect, because they are one-sided. They overlook the nature of the human mind and its relation to the various languages. Nearly all that Diderot has said about the intellect as intellect may be accepted, but when he tries to make intellect a substitute for emotion he violates a universal principle of nature. He advocates an error which has been a curse to all modern histrionic art and oratoric delivery; directly or indirectly it is this view which has poisoned all our elocutionary methods. It is no doubt very important that the will should be active in speaking, and here and there in Mr. Sheppard's book there is a grain of good sense. The error, as before, is the one-sided, exaggerated emphasis of one phase of human nature in delivery. Man is not mere will. Of all weak men, of all men who are unattractive, the man who has no feeling, no thought, but only a stubborn will, is the worst. Yet this seems to be Mr. Sheppard's highest ideal. To him such an abnormal phenomenon makes a histrionic artist and especially an orator. The emotional theory is more ridiculous than the others and so corrects itself; besides few believe in it. It also is abnormal because it is one-sided. Expression if it is normal and effective must be the revelation of the whole mind; the thought and the emotion must both be genuine and balanced by will, and while each may be separated in analysis, yet all are so thoroughly united in consciousness that it is not always possible for the artist himself to distinguish them. The intellect must be so active that there will be self-possession; the head must be cool, but the heart must be warm. As Mr. Irving has so well said, "It is quite possible to feel all the excitement of the situation and yet be perfectly self-possessed. This is art which the actor who loses his head has not mastered. It is necessary to this

art that the mind should have, as it were, a double consciousness, in which all the emotions proper to the
occasion may have full sway, while the actor is all the
time on the alert for every detail of his method."

Since these one-sided views furnish an important element in preventing the adoption of adequate methods for
the development of delivery, it may be well to consider
the subject more carefully and to study something of
the nature of emotion.

From the time of Aristotle emotion has been considered as arising first from nature — that is, from an object
of sense — or secondly, from an idea, or, as Aristotle
called it, a phantasm. When a public speaker relates
a story or describes a scene emotion is the result not
of what he sees before him, but of the images in his
mind. There was an ancient custom still sometimes
resorted to in modern times, to bring the wife and children of a criminal into court in order to awaken the
sympathy of the jury; but in most cases the emotion is
awakened by an imaginary picture or a remembered scene.

What difference is there between emotion arising from
a real scene and the emotion stimulated by an imaginary
situation? The emotion arising from a natural object
may be more intense, may completely dominate the man;
but emotion arising from a mental stimulus can be more
easily controlled and regulated. Delivery, or the proper
expression of emotion, demands control. It is only controlled emotion that stirs an audience. Uncontrolled
sorrow chokes the voice and inspires little sympathetic
response in others. In fact, it often tends to awaken
contempt, although from the standpoint of weakness it
may be natural. It constricts the throat; while controlled sorrow causes activity of the respiratory muscles
and modulates the muscular texture of the whole body.

Uncontrolled sorrow shows only physical effects; controlled sorrow shows activity of the whole soul. Where there is effort to control, the real manhood of the sufferer is revealed, and the noble impulses of other souls are aroused from slumber. This especially marks the difference between pathos and bathos. To endeavor to feel everything just as in nature will lead a man to become impulsive, sentimental and one-sided. The greatest artists and speakers belong to none of these schools. There ought to be another school which may be called the imaginative. In this the emotion is the result of an imaginative conception and picture. Such emotion is genuine, as genuine as emotion in nature, but it is different in kind; it is also more or less different in degree. It has an æsthetic element which is not found in nature, but it is just as natural to the human soul. Emotion in life is often independent of thought and will — artistic emotion, never. Emotion in life is expressed for the relief of an excited sensibility, but emotion in oratory and art is revealed for a purpose. The imagination in its conception of the scene, situation or character, the relation to the audience or the occasion, sympathetically awakens passion which diffuses itself over the body and tends at once to action; but the will resists the action, thus reserving the emotion till it becomes intense and dominates the whole man. Feeling is awakened in others by suggesting a corresponding mental picture. Expression is not an intellectual cataloguing of the physical effects of passion or even of the literal facts regarding the mental image.

Thus emotion generated in the soul in the contemplation of a scene differs in some of its characteristics from the emotion born in rehearsing the same scene to another. The latter is directed, restrained and regulated;

the former is a more passive indulgence. Emotion may
be killed out, or may become motive to will; it may be so
restrained as to become intense and affect the muscular
texture in the action of the whole body; and still be as
genuine, as real, as natural as if allowed to take its own
course. A horse is a horse, when bridled and harnessed
and driven by the hand of man, as well as when running
wild over the plain. The aim of expression is simply to
make others feel what we feel ourselves, and emotion
though stimulated by imagination and regulated by will,
must be genuine.

From this can be seen that the function of the imagination in expression is a very important one, and if we
study the action of the mind carefully we will find that the
imagination is not a mere decorative faculty, but is fundamentally necessary to all mental and to all emotional
action. An act of perception is not an act of the eye but
of the mind. In geometry a point is defined as that
which has neither length, breadth nor thickness. Such a
thing is purely mystic, it cannot be seen by the eye or
conceived by the mind; it has to be embodied, it has to
be converted into an image to be perceived, just as to be
seen it has to be embodied in a dot. Again, the mind
conceives a globe, but we can see only a portion of the
globe with the eye. We can perceive a house, but we
cannot see the whole house; part of it is constructed and
built by the reproductive faculties. We cannot see a
whole room, a part of it has to be constructed by the
imagination. The imagination, even as we look into the
face of a dead mother, is the most active agent in creating emotion. What is there suggests what is not there;
the kindly voice, the gentle look, the loving smile are
perceived by the mind, not by the eye, and the heart is
stirred to its depths.

We can thus see that imagination is really necessary to expression. Power in expression fundamentally depends upon the power of the imagination to call up the scene at will before the mind's eye. Men are taken up with the literal. The function of art is to inspire men with the ideal; not because the ideal is less real, but because it suggests more than is seen. If the soul of the speaker cannot penetrate to the soul of things, if the pictorial faculties of his mind cannot break through the literal walls in which men are placed, if he cannot see and realize the whole from the part seen, he will not move men, but will have to deal with commonplace facts. The aim of art is to lift men out of the commonplace, to open their eyes to see in the individual the universal, to embody in the finite for finite conception that which is infinite and eternal.

We hear it continually said by students, "Oh, if I could only speak some of my own thoughts, or if I could talk about a scene that I saw, I could feel it," but this is a mistake, for the lack of imagination is apparent in speech as well as in recitation. No man living ever saw the cross upon which Christ was crucified or knows the real Calvary. Even if the real spot were known, two thousand years have changed the very stones upon which stepped those feet which "were nailed for our advantage on the bitter cross." What is left must be ideal, even as we stand under the few relics of trees which are called by tradition Gethsemane. To see Gethsemane requires imagination. The Sea of Galilee, without imagination would lack all power to awaken feeling. As a mere sheet of water it would not compare with Lucerne, if feeling must arise from what is seen. "The things that are seen" are transient, it is what is not seen, though forever really there, that moves and stirs the soul.

The highest requisite of a good speaker, a good reader or a good actor, is the power to see what is not visible to the eyes, to realize in imagination every situation, to see the end from the beginning by the imagination, and to realize a unity of purpose in each successive idea. Every artist must be a "maker-see." As we further study emotion we find that it is stimulated by some simple object or situation. Shakespeare shows Antony holding up the mantle in which Cæsar was robed at the battle of the Nervii. This simple token carried the mind of his audience away from the literal scene to one that was national, to an occasion that was the glory of every Roman. It is while looking at this simple robe, and not at Cæsar's body itself, that the fatal stab is painted, possibly the most imaginative picture in English poetry.

> "Through this the well-beloved Brutus stabbed;
> And, as he plucked his cursed steel away,
> Mark how the blood of Cæsar followed it —
> As rushing out of doors, to be resolved
> If Brutus so unkindly knocked or no."

The mind is sometimes dazed as it stands beside a dying father or a dead mother, but long afterward a vacant chair or a hat hung away, may stir the heart more deeply than the real presence. It is a little pair of shoes come upon suddenly, that moves the soul of the mother. It is the delicate suggestion that awakens the imagination and touches the fountain of feeling. Not only does the speaker's own feeling depend upon imagination; it is necessary to awaken the imagination of his auditors. A speaker cannot give his emotion to his fellow-men, but he can awaken their own. There is a certain transmission of emotion; when we see some one laughing heartily, we laugh too; but this is rather sympathy, it is rather due to contemplation of the person than to a direct transmission of emotion. The blind or deaf would receive no impression of feeling. The artist, whether public speaker, reader or actor, must not become a spectacle. We have all seen a speaker shed tears himself, while his audience were moved only to pity him, if not to laugh at him. He shed tears enough for the whole audience; and became a spectacle, a mere object before the eye. The great speaker treasures his tears and paints their cause. This rouses imagination, awakens kindred souls, and tears are shed from other eyes. It is the amount of feeling stimulated by imagination controlled by the will for a purpose, which stirs the soul. He who merely plays with signs without having this delicate imaginative feeling permeating his being, will soon or late become superficial, and his art weak and ungenuine.

As we analyze, however, even a purely intellectual process, we find that there is a volitional and an emotional element. According to the philosophers, the difference between musing and thinking is that in musing there is merely a drifting current of ideas. The mind, in other words, simply drifts from idea to idea, these ideas flowing through the mind by the passive action of the laws of association, but in thinking there is a conscious critique of this current of ideas; there is a self-direction and self-determination of the mind. This, of course, is a co-ordination of volition with intellect. There is also here a species of double consciousness. Consciousness in musing is not exactly the same as it is in definite thinking.

And not only so, but interest must be awakened in the mind. Admiration and emotion quicken attention. That is to say, thinking is impossible in its highest sense without simultaneous intellectual, volitional and emotional activity. Mere dry, cold, intellectual attention cannot be secured in a child's mind. Ideas must be awakened, the mind directed to a specific object, and a responsive interest awakened in the breast. So that the fundamental intellectual processes of the soul are due to the co-ordination of the elemental powers of being. And this is especially true in expression. By long discipline the mind can separate and engage in abstract thinking with a minimum of emotion, but this is not the kind of thinking that makes a man an orator.

Now from this analysis we can see that the normal process of expression requires first, an intellectual element. The mind sees the idea, grasps the situation, and then the feelings normally respond to this idea. Emotions awakened by the successive objects and situations upon which the attention is focussed are regulated and often restrained by will, and these diffuse themselves through the whole body and cause a response in the very texture of the muscles; so that the color of the voice and all the subtle actions of the body are awakened by these internal impulses.

Face to face with this conception, as old, if not older, than Aristotle, we can see the special errors of the one-sided views. They all violate this normal process of nature. Diderot holds that expression must result from thought alone; Mr. Sheppard, that it must result from will alone. The latter view must be very similar to the first, for it is inconceivable that any one should advocate that emotion could be forced by volition. The most ridiculous of all things is a man trying to pump up emotion by mere force of will. Emotion can only be awakened by a mental grasp of an idea or situation. Accordingly these views may be regarded as essentially the same. In fact, Mr. Sheppard's view, though on a lower plane, is evidently derived from that of Diderot. The emotional view hardly needs to be discussed at all.

This also is one-sided. It implies that only one power of man's nature has to do with expression. Wild, uncontrolled emotion, emotion entirely independent of thought, is worthy of what Diderot said of all feeling ; but a normal man never has such emotion. A disciplined soul shows itself most of all in relation to emotion. The thought, the will, the emotion are in perfect unity.

The first two views imply that emotion is necessarily wild ; that it can never be trusted. But every true artist knows that when thought, emotion and will are simultaneously aroused, in an unconscious, spontaneous way, that emotion is a law unto itself. The greatest artist can hardly tell how or why, but he knows that he acts as he is taught by his own soul. In a great crisis of emotion, as in the famous potion scene in Romeo and Juliet, the explosions, the reactions, the rhythmic surgings of passion come in accordance with natural impulses of the soul, stirred by ideas and imaginative situations. Consciousness or even a course of reasoning will never awaken the great force of passion except through such ideas. Reason and will are only used to regulate, to guide, to restrain, to secure a proper diffusion through the whole man, but the impulse itself is mystic in its origin and in many of its modes of action.

The development of the power of abstract thought with the repression and killing out of all emotional response, is death to all oratory, to all art, if not to all happiness in human life. The normal process of the soul is a picture — an idea, ideal, or a situation — an emotional response to which becomes the motive to will. With the intellect cool, the heart warm, the will active, we have the strong and active human being. If art is man's reproduction in his degree of the universal processes of nature, then art demands that these three co-essential elements of his nature shall be developed and brought into co-operation. If delivery or histrionic art is that form of art which is nearest to personality, more than any other form it demands harmonious development and co-ordination of the elemental powers of the soul.

These one-sided and superficial views overlook another peculiarity of the human mind. There seem to be several planes of consciousness, so that while one object, or part of an object, may be in the focus of consciousness, many other objects can be held in the background. Perspective in painting is an objective embodiment of this characteristic of the human mind. The mechanical school teaches virtually that genuine feeling is entirely inconsistent with proper self-possession and self-control, that there is but one plane of consciousness, and that the mind is a little narrow vessel which cannot contain thought if it contains emotion, or emotion if it contains thought. This school seems to lose sight of the fact that the head can be cool and the heart warm simultaneously.

No better example of the complexity of the mind can be found than in the act of public speaking. In a good extemporaneous speaker there is a conscious purpose, a conscious arrangement of thoughts and a conscious selection of words. There is a consciousness of the effect the thoughts are producing upon the audience; a consciousness as to whether he is saying the right thing or not. "The true orator must not only have the power to say the right thing; he must also perceive that he is saying the right thing." The orator is also more or less conscious of the action of his voice and of his body. He is not necessarily controlling this deliberatively by direct action of the will or by rule. Consciousness merely recognizes what is going on. Though the speaker may be entirely unconscious of the sources of his emotion, even of the time when it comes to him, being, in fact, often surprised himself at the action of his own soul, yet in some degree he is always conscious of the effect of his ideas, of the emotion as it comes, and of the effect of these upon his organism. He is also more or less conscious of the modulations of his voice and the positions and attitudes of his limbs and body, although their actions may be spontaneously determined by emotion.

This complexity is perfectly natural. When a man is in great grief, he will attend to the simplest details of life. He will brush his hat and comb his hair to attend his mother's funeral. Some one has mentioned the fact that a lady almost prostrated with grief gave directions to prevent the top of a mahogany table from being scratched by the casket which was to contain the body more precious to her than all the world.

The best public readers or actors never try to study a poem or a part according to the conception of another, or merely with a process of reasoning as to what is to be done. The true artist studies carefully and thoroughly, gets his mind full of the ideas and then endeavors to execute this conception, all the time observing carefully the effects of the emotion that arises in his mind upon his voice and body. He struggles in every way to abandon himself to his conception of the situation and continually studies the effect of the unconscious impulses, the spontaneous outflow from his own soul upon his voice and body. These ever afford him his best instruction. It is a teacher's function to stimulate these, and to lead the student to study himself. He must show the student wherein he does not abandon himself, where the unconscious impulses of his nature are not awakened, or his whole nature does not speak and where mechanical determination has usurped the place of spontaneous outflow.

The teacher must awaken and co-ordinate the impulses from the student's whole nature. He must see that one faculty is not cultivated more than another, but that all are equally strong. The highest aim in teaching delivery, as Froebel said of all education, must be "to bring such objects before the mind as will stimulate spontaneous activity."

The truth of these principles is further proved by the fact that the advocates of the mechanical school are generally comedians. In France, where the mechanical school has its special home, there is no such thing as tragedy. The artists there who have approached most nearly to tragedy believe in genuine emotion. To bring forth tragedy requires seriousness. Even a Shakespeare only produced his great tragedies in the period of his life, when he was undergoing great sorrow. The best comedians, however, such as Jefferson, Toole and Clarke, believe in genuine emotion.

Again, the arguments for the mechanical school are specious. For example, it is contended that a man cannot speak to a large audience as he does to an individual man or in a parlor; that the voice has to be modulated according to the hall. This can only be done by direct action of will, says Mr. Sheppard. It can only be done, according to Diderot, by mere deliberation. It will be granted by all that no man feels, in trying to move a thousand men, as he does when in conversation with one. The situation is different. The emotions will be different, and expression correspondingly different, but how can any one say that they are any less genuine? A man stirred by great patriotism, trying to arouse a thousand men, has as genuine emotion, has even a greater degree of emotion. So every gesture must be expanded and every inflection extended according to the measure of the intensity of his thought and feeling. Besides, the sympathy of the audience affects the speaker, and it is very difficult for him to feel exactly the same before different audiences. Indeed, every true artist has to discipline himself to secure his emotion as the response to his imagination, and not be dependent upon the sympathy of his audience in order at all times to carry out his ideals. Artistic emotion must be controlled, but this is no argument whatever for the adoption of the views of the mechanical school, whether of the will or intellect, in delivery. It proves rather, the importance of the view here advocated, that true delivery, like every noble act of man, calls for the activity of his whole nature, the co-ordination of intellect, sensibility and will.

These one-sided views, therefore, are all inadequate. The human being was evidently given the power to reveal all the three elemental phases of his nature simultaneously. Language of the intellect is symbolic. This symbolic language can only vaguely suggest emotion. Each power of man's nature has a peculiar language by which alone it can be adequately revealed. The highest language is only suggestive, and must never be too literal. It must ever be sympathetic, and must aim to stimulate a corresponding activity in another soul. Otherwise true communion is impossible. If this is true, and only one of these powers is active in speech, expression must be, in the nature of the case, imperfect. Adequate expression not only instinctively demands words but tones and motions to reveal experience, and nature evidently intended the experience to be genuine, as she gave languages for the revelation of its every phase.

If Diderot's Paradox, or the volitional theory be true, the problem of developing expression must be the mere study of the signs of emotion, a perfect knowledge of these and the power to deliberately produce them. In fact, this is the view taken by the mechanical school of elocution. The most advanced methods founded on these views, requires a careful study of the expression of every part of the body and such a thorough practice of all these expressions, that the man can have a vocabulary of pantomimic and vocal actions, which he is to use deliberatively as in the case of words. Nearly all our elocution has been taken up with this view.

But on the other hand if the view here advocated is correct, then the development of expression is an entirely different problem. The proper co-ordination of the faculties of the soul in expression must be studied, and while the voice and the body will call for as thorough training as the mechanical view, nay, even more, and while there must be as careful study into the expression of all the parts of the body and practice upon the vocabulary belonging to every agent, yet all this is done as a means and not as an end. All training aims to open the channels of expression and to develop the genuine action of every faculty and power, spontaneous as well as deliberative. In short, effective delivery can only be developed as all the powers of the soul are made to act in unity through a normal body with all its agents acting in harmony according to their intended functions. Thus alone can there be a simultaneous manifestation of thought and experience, and the expression of the human being have power to move effectively his fellow-man.

VI.

EXPRESSION IN ART.

" The sight never beheld it, nor has the hand expressed it; it is an idea residing in the breast of the artist, which he is always laboring to impart, and which he dies at last without imparting."—Sir Joshua Reynolds.

THE highest authorities consider all the arts as one in fundamental principles, if not in aim. Phidias, Giotto, Leonardo da Vinci, Michael Angelo and the greatest artists of all time were not specialists in one art, but students of every form of art. They were painters, architects, sculptors, musicians and poets.

The arts reflect each other; the terms which are applied to the arts are borrowed from each other. We speak of the tone of a picture, and the color of a piece of music. The sculptor must have a sense of color and music, or his work will be cold. Each art may definitely require a special set of faculties to be trained, but these are co-relative and must be brought into harmony for power in any one art. Hence a certain amount of training in different arts develops the art capacities, and enables the mind to grasp the elements that are fundamental to all art.

In a study of any phase of art, to secure an advance, there must be a comparison of its work, its methods, its modes of procedure and even its technique, with other arts. Such a comparative method is in accordance with one of the fundamental requisites of all progress. A principle must be studied from different points of view, before it can be thoroughly apprehended and tested. Without such a comparative study, there is danger of superficiality and conventionality — of taking mere rules for laws of nature. When a worker in any one line of art merely studies his own phase of the problem, he is apt to become one-sided and technical; and so losing the fundamental grasp of what art really is, he can only gain a superficial mastery of his own art. Accordingly there must be many points of view, if not execution in different arts, in order to secure the highest development and efficiency of the art capacity.

This comparative study is especially important in all phases of delivery, and all forms of histrionic art, on account of the fact that these cannot be recorded and are so completely passing, that we are very apt to miss the universal principles of true art upon which greatness depends. Besides, these arts are so near nature that some doubt whether they should be regarded as arts at all. Hence there is a special necessity, if we are to discover any fundamental principles governing expression, to bring all its phases into comparison with nature and the elemental principles dominating all art. Light may be found from those arts which can be recorded and thus preserved, and whose essential characteristics on this account have been more carefully studied and whose laws have been more definitely formulated.

When we verge thus upon the study of the essential nature of art, we come to a problem which has puzzled the greatest philosophers of all time. But however great the question it can not be ignored; for our ideas of the nature of delivery and expression will be closely connected, if not identical with our views of art.

What are the fundamental elements of a work of art? Without entering into the question as to the origin of art or the philosophy of art, we can see at once that one essential characteristic of art is expression. Art is a necessity of man's nature. It is deeper than language, yet it is the highest mode the soul can secure to reveal itself. Expression is a term universally applied to all forms of art. It is true, art is sometimes divided into decorative and expressive, according as the aim is mere beauty or to manifest the human soul. Decorative art deals with that which is upon the surface, while expressive art belongs essentially to the revelation of the nature of man. But as has been said, "The growth of art has been in all times toward expression," and the greatest art of all ages has been expressive art. In fact, when we come to look carefully at the best decorative art, we find that it, too, is expressive. The division between decorative art and expressive art has regard to the use of the art rather than to its essential nature.

Looking then at art from the simplest point of view, we find two things. First, a subjective, imaginative conception, or emotion, and this subjective idea or feeling, embodied so as to become an object of sense, perception. The transcendentalist and the realist both agree to the great fundamental fact that all art is the revelation of subjective impression into some kind of objective body. This, as we have seen, is expression.

That expression is the essential element of all art is abundantly justified by every discussion of the subject. We read everywhere of expression in painting, expression in song, expression in music, expression in architecture, expression in sculpture, expression in poetry. While occasionally men look at a work of art merely for the skill with which it is executed, yet all art is born in instinct, and appeals to the instinct of the observer; and that which makes the most universal appeal to instinct in the race is expression.

If expression is thus a fundamental characteristic of art, all art must primarily bring us to the study of the human being. We are thus brought to agree with Thoré that "all art must be as human as possible." In it are the peculiar characteristics of man's nature; it is simply the reflection of man's soul evolved by a process as natural to him as the growth of his own body. We will also find that the brightest light to be thrown upon art, the best means of understanding and developing the art capacity in man, is a study of human expression. Accordingly, not only is there an advantage to expression in the study of the elements of art, but we also find an advantage to art in the study of the elements of expression.

Starting from the idea that expression is an essential characteristic of all great art, and that all the arts are one, we find that a work of art reveals its subjective ideal or conception through organic form in one of two ways: by representation, or by manifestation. These modes may exist simultaneously; but the difference between them can be accurately determined, and one or the other necessarily predominates in any work of art.

In representation man communicates his ideas by a symbolic or objective presentation of their forms, qualities, actions or relations. By such means can be shown the size, the length, the height, the form, the distance, the color, the action of the objects, the uses to which they may be put, and like characteristics. There are many phases of representation. One is purely conventional. The word *horse*, for example, represents to the mind, by agreement, a certain animal to which the symbol has no relation whatever, being designed merely to awaken in the mind an image of the animal. A whole nation uses *cheval* to represent the same idea. Again, we have another form which is imitative in character. For example, a man may use the word bell for a certain idea, and in addition imitate with his voice in speaking the word the sound of the bell, or he may imitate the sound with mere tones. Again, a photograph is a mere copy or imitative representation of outside appearance. This is the lowest form of representation. Again, the representation may be only suggestive, there may be little imitation, little of the mere copying of the object, but a general suggestion of its character, of its size, form or shape. For example, in a picture, the general impression of the artist may be intimated rather than the more literal outside facts of the scene. Browning's poem, " As I ride," delicately suggests the motion of the horse. Some one has said that the words, "as I ride," suggest a shape exactly like a horse's back. A good painting intimates the idea to the imagination, does not literally present it to the eye. This is artistic representation and its principal form ; its appeal is not to the eye, but to the imagination. But all these various presentations of the object or subject from the lowest reproduction to the most delicate suggestion, have certain characteristics in common. They are all objective and are used to aid in creating an image. Conventional symbols alone can directly stand for anything subjective.

Manifestation in art, on the contrary, does not deal in those things that stand in the place of something else ; it does not deal in symbols but in signs. Signs or the external actions or effects of hidden causes are found everywhere in nature. Nature rarely expresses symbolically, but reveals manifestively. The bird's song is not a symbol of its life and joy, but it is none the less expressive. Only occasionally do we have representation in nature, as in the song of the mocking-bird. In manifestation the endeavor is not to exhibit one objective part through another, but to reveal thought and feeling directly through natural, significant actions. These are present everywhere in nature and are read by animals as well as by man.

Thus, the difference between what is symbolic and what is significant is this: when one thing stands in place of another it is symbolic and representative; when some phenomenon, motion, action or sound is the direct effect of a mystic cause, it is significant and manifestive. A laugh represents no idea, but it does manifest a state of feeling; the word *mountain*, on the contrary, stands as the representation of an idea in the mind.

The difference between representation and manifestation will be clearer from an illustration. It is said that Schumann, in the composition of one of his works, was haunted by a butterfly floating upon a leaf down a small stream. Does his music represent to us the butterfly that was in his mind? Of course not, because music is not a representative art. A painting, a poem or some form of symbolic or representative art could adequately tell the story and suggest the picture that was in the mind of Schumann. The same picture cannot be exactly represented to another mind, because representative art, especially when it is a revelation of the mind, is inadequate and must necessarily be indefinite. All, however, would be made to see a butterfly, a leaf and a brook of some kind. But the music of Schumann is expressive; though it cannot represent the picture, all agree there is a revelation of the greatest tenderness and delicacy. The music awakens beautiful and delicate pictures in the listener; not necessarily the same as those of the author; but a feeling is stimulated similar to that which stirred the heart of the composer while the specific pictures are left to the imagination. The spirit though not the body is conveyed by manifestation. Painting or poetry could represent the image in Schumann's mind; but music can only manifest the feeling. Noble music reveals the emotion awakened, rouses the soul to see visions, but can not represent images.

Representation is more rational, and can symbolize ideas; manifestation is more emotional, and can reveal states of feeling. The one is more objective, the other is more subjective. One deals with external forms, colors and actions, the other deals with the essential conditions and dispositions awakened in the heart by the contemplation of objects, scenes, situations or actions.

It can be seen at once that it is through the representative mode that intellectual definiteness and clearness is given to expression. Without this all forms of art would be vague, because this appeals to the understanding, and awakens definite pictures in the mind which are necessary to the understanding and more or less to the imagination. But as we have found, motive, disposition and emotion are just as important subjects for expression as ideas. These have as great or even greater influence over our fellow-men, than any representation of facts. All art is the revelation of the subjective into the objective. The ideas and images of the mind, being in correspondence with objective things, can be represented; but experience belongs to the human soul and can only be manifested. Ideas cause experience and representation may indirectly suggest experience, but it is only in music, in vocal or pantomimic expression, or some form of manifestation that feeling, disposition and motive can be directly revealed.

So fundamental are these elements, that the arts may possibly be divided into representative and manifestive.

Sculpture would be the most representative, music the most manifestive art. Like all divisions of the arts, however, this is unsatisfactory. It must be understood as showing only the preponderance of one or the other of these modes of expression, as both belong to all art. This is similar to Gurney's division of the arts into Representative and Presentative. He calls poetry, sculpture and painting, representative, because they "represent things outside of themselves," while he classes architecture and music as presentative, because they "present things which cannot be imagined." This contains a truth, yet such statements as, that there is absolutely no such thing in nature as architecture or music, is strained, to say the least. The word representation here refers to that which stands for something else. Representation is used to cause a mind to conceive an objective thing; while manifestation is the process of direct revelation of some experience of the soul. The first is intellectual, the second is more emotional. One uses symbols, the other, signs. Hence this is a different classification from that of Gurney. The reference here is not to the relation of the subject of art to nature, but to the modes of the soul's revelation. This classification, however, is not meant as a division of the arts, but as an analysis of the elements of expression in art.

The terms representation and manifestation have a relation to the common terms, idealism and realism. It is found in art that idealism and realism are simply two phases of art. When art becomes too ideal it becomes vague and indefinite. When it is simply realistic it becomes merely a literal copy and is not art at all. "Without the spiritual," as Mrs. Browning has said, "the natural is impossible; without sensuous, spiritual is inappreciable." Every true artist "holds firmly by the natural to reach the spiritual," endeavors to fix "the type with mortal vision, to pierce through with eyes immortal to the antitype some call the ideal—better called the real." Representation of course tends to realism, and manifestation tends more to idealism. But the terms are not synonymous because manifestation may be real as well as ideal, while representative art may be necessary to the expression of the highest ideal. Blake, though very ideal, is quite representative, especially in his illustrations. These terms regard art from another point of view. All this shows how impossible it is to make a satisfactory division of so complex a subject as art. The chief advantage is to secure clearer views of its elements.

In the study of these two elements some curious facts are brought to our attention. One is that while manifestation in art is first in the order of nature, yet representation is brought to perfection earlier. For example, sculpture reached perfection before painting, which is more manifestive, and both these arts are brought to perfection before music, which is still more manifestive than either. Although rhythm is the "first-born of the imagination," the symphony is one of the last.

The value of the representative mode of expression has been greatly exaggerated. The cause of this is its relation to speech and utterance. Representation appeals more to the mind, and can be more quickly understood. Again, as it deals with the outside rather than the inside, it appeals to the eye as well as to the mind. In proportion as anything is representative it can be seen at once; in proportion as it is manifestive, it can only be realized imaginatively, mystically. Representation is expressive more of human reason, and outside the realm of art the products of the reason are rated higher than those of the imagination and feeling. Another reason for this over-valuation of the representative mode in expression is that given for the greater attention paid to verbal expression, namely, it can be recorded. A statue may come down to us from an otherwise unknown period and show us a conception of a master mind of that age. In fact, the statues of Greece show the ideal and the real spirit of the times more perfectly than any historical or philosophical treatise. But her oratory, histrionic art and music, these could not be recorded, hence we can only vaguely apprehend how the Greeks spoke or sang, how the Athenians felt or acted.

Which of these modes is the higher? This depends upon the point from which we view art. If the aim is the revelation of ideas and thought, representation by symbols, artificial or natural, is the most definite and adequate means of communicating the thought of one human being to another. But if the object is the revelation of the highest ideal, of that which is deepest in the soul, which can hardly be shown by representation — the manifestive element must be considered higher. The manifestive mode of expression is most powerful in its direct influence upon the living, acting, thinking, feeling human soul. It tends to broader culture and to refine and spiritualize the sensibilities of man.

Some philosophers have gone deep into the nature of music. Schopenhauer has shown that while painting can reveal ideas, yet ideas belong to the realm of phenomena, and are hence themselves expressions; that painting is the expression of an expression, but that music is the direct manifestation of the *noumenon* or the great soul of the world. Hegel and nearly all of the philosophers since his day have held that music is one of the highest arts. In the difference between Greek art and Christian art as unfolded by him there is something of the same thought. Greek art was physical; it simply represented the physical body. There was little facial expression through which the deeper and more subtle emotions of the soul are manifested. It is only in Christian or Romantic art that facial expression and the more manifestive art of painting are brought to perfection. Greek art was the perfection of representative art, and had its highest expression in sculpture. Sculpture uses the three dimensions of space, painting uses only two. While sculpture is one of the greatest arts, while "it shows the innocent and unshamed child awaking to a consciousness of itself," yet painting has been able to reveal impressions of the soul never possible to sculpture. It has a wider variety of subjects, and reveals greater depths of the soul. The revelation of the human face, of the great and powerful passions that flash through the eyes and features, could hardly be revealed in sculpture. Facial expression is not a representative but a manifestive form of pantomime. It is painting that can be made to breathe with the very life of the soul.

When we pass to music, every dimension of space is obliterated. Music becomes the direct revelation of the man, a revelation of his life and soul often entirely independent of any representative element. The musician from one, two or three sounds which are everywhere in nature can "make not a fourth but a star." The architect may build a Solomon's temple, the musician may build a temple for a minute as he breathes out his music, revealing all the emotions of his soul.

A novel is more representative than a poem, than a drama, but it is not so high a work of art. In fact, in poetry it is only the words that are representative, and the higher the poetry, the more does the manifestive predominate. Poetry is no more mere words than painting is pigment. The great power of Hamlet, as a work of art, is because words are few and suggestive, and all representation is transcended by manifestation. A man who merely deals in representation may be upon the plane of science, upon the plane of facts, but he is not in the realm of art at all until he rises into the realm of manifestation.

Art, whether it lasts for five minutes or for a thousand years, is the unfolding of personality. When the impression of some great event in man's life, or in the experience of the world, can be so revealed or manifested for others that all the race can feel it, then we have art. The ideal everywhere tends to be buried beneath the literal. The eyes of men become blinded by prosaic detail, and it is the province of art to manifest the ideal, to reveal the soul which lies everywhere in nature, hidden in the folds of a literal body. Of course, the more permanent the art is, the better; but sometimes a long life of objectivity must be sacrificed for one vivid glance of the invisible. If only what is permanent be art, there is no art in oratory. But if art is the revelation of the human soul, then the most direct and powerful manifestation through the living voice, the living body, of the most profound experience is art though it die the moment it is born. The instinct of the race has ever held it to be art, for more than all others it has been the means adopted by the noblest men to inspire their fellow-men to nobler ideals.

So that when we come to study the importance of these two modes in their relation to each other, we find that in any great work of art, the manifestive must be present. It is the transcendence of the manifestive element that is a chief difference between poetry and prose, or between good poetry and bad poetry, or between high art and low art. The mere mechanical structure is of very little importance, except in so far as it is made a scaffolding for that which manifests and reveals the subjective conditions and emotions of man.

As a proof of this let us look at the arts which are more especially representative. Let us consider some great painting for example. The universal judgment of the masters is that when a painting merely copies, merely photographs a scene, it is low art. Even the realistic school of painting holds this more or less. It holds that while nature must be truthfully represented, yet there must be selection, and that not everything can be represented even in the simplest flower. Now what is the principle of this selection? Is it not that those parts which are most manifestive, most significant, which most serve as signs of the real character of the objects, must be represented?

One writer has said that painting is the most tell-tale of arts; that you can tell the character of a man as you look at his work. Thus even an objective artist, such as the painter, must breathe into his art his deepest experience. If he merely represents literal facts he is cold, and his spirit is lost. A great painting, therefore, is great because it is manifestive.

Thus all that art can do is to give the impression made upon the soul, and whenever there is too great representation of detail, then the great general impression which can only be suggested or manifested, is lost.

In one of the pictures of Holman Hunt, The Shadow of Death, commonly called The Shadow of the Cross, we have beautifully painted shavings, and an exact reproduction of a carpenter's shop. Several years of study were given to the kinds of tools used, and these tools are all carefully represented. We have a young worker of the time, weary with his work, standing up, stretching out his arms. Behind him a shadow thrown upon the shavings is seen by his mother, whose back is turned to us, with the color of her dress, and the texture of the cloth, and even the boxes in which she is searching accurately and definitely imitated, with every detail perfectly copied. But the Christ is hardly seen there. The aim of the representative element in art is to aid in showing the impression in the artist's soul, and that impression, if it was a true impression of the scene, was not a mere impression of shavings, of a saw that was pulled upward and not pulled backward and forward. It was the impression of one in history who humbled himself, took upon himself the burdens of the world, who labored at his trade, and who developed his personality in the midst of human environments, and whose mother was not a simple bundle of clothes and textures, but a woman who "pondered all these things in her heart," who, if she caught sight of the shadow of the cross, would have so revealed it as to give us a unity of impression, and not a mere descriptive representation of a few objective things. In the face of the tired young man, no satisfactory conception is given of the future, or of the real nature of the youth. The work is so representative that all the impression we receive is of various literal details. These are represented, but the spirit of the scene is not shown. The representative elements transcend the manifestive, reversing the great law of art. The representative is thus limited. The higher art is, the more suggestive it must be.

Novel-writing may be considered the most definite form of representative art; but how inadequate this is to give an exact picture of the mind, is shown in the illustrations of the ablest novels by the best artists. Each artist will give a picture of a character entirely different from any other. However vividly portrayed in words, there are as many Micawbers and Ethel Newcomes as readers.

Programme or descriptive music is largely representative; the lower forms are more representative, while the higher forms are more manifestive. Beethoven's Eroica and pastoral symphonies are very representative. "The Storm" passage in the latter is vividly descriptive. Beethoven, however, placed upon the programme when this symphony was produced, *Mehr ausdruck der empfindung als malerei,* "more expression of emotion than portraiture," that is, more manifestation than representation. Here we see the idea of the greatest of musicians as to the relation of these elements.

Thus, we must not compare these two modes; for both are essential elements of every great work of art. The representative element in some degree is necessary in all forms of art, because the idea must be shown, a pictorial conception conceived, and these must be embodied in some kind of external form. The idea must be apprehended, and hence must be represented in familiar objects of sense, otherwise there can be no adequate conception formed of the definite meaning and purpose. But the manifestive must also be present, for "art is the intervention of personality." Not only must the truth be shown, but there must be a revelation of the soul that awoke to it, and the love that embraced it. Even in poetry and the artistic use of verbal expression, this is true. Macbeth manifests the deepest truths regarding the human conscience and the human soul, as well as represents to us certain scenes, characters and ideas.

But it is in artistic delivery where all the languages of man are brought into harmonious action, that we realize fully the co-ordinate relationship of manifestation and representation to each other.

Does not this explain more adequately the application of Browning's idea of art, which was applied to delivery in Chapter IV? "Art remains the one way possible of speaking truth," because art is a union of manifestation and representation. True expression not only represents the ideas, but can simultaneously manifest the spirit of the soul that speaks. It not only symbolizes the thought or meaning, but is able as well to reveal the conditions of the personality that speaks. Thus all the powers of the hearer's soul will be awakened to action. Not only will thought be made clear to the intellect, but dispositions favorable to the reception of this truth will also be quickened. The artist will be enabled to tell the truth "obliquely," suggestively, indirectly, adequately, "do the thing shall breed the thought, nor wrong the thought missing the mediate word," and thus "paint his picture and save the soul beside."

This explanation of the elements of art has a most forcible illustration in the modern conflict which has gone on in relation to music. Many think that the chief object of the life-long discussions of Richard Wagner was to show that the highest art is the proper co-ordination and unity of the elements of all art. Whatever may be our opinions regarding him, his ideas about art are worthy of our most serious attention. All his views regarding "the art of the future" do not concern us, but one or two points illustrate the principles here discussed.

The special point in Wagner, that is of interest in the study of expression, is the bringing of words and music into harmony. The old idea regarded words and music as antagonistic to each other, the view was something like Dogberry's, "if two ride of a horse one must ride behind"; and the one to ride behind, according to the old musicians, must be the poet. It was shown by Wagner conclusively that neither need ride behind, that on the contrary, they could ride abreast upon two equal chargers, and could mutually assist each other in accomplishing the great end. The importance of this in art has not been appreciated. It is beginning to dawn upon the world that he was right when he said that the growth of art must be dependent upon the co-ordination of the various forms of art, bringing them into harmonious co-operation for the conveyance of one impression.

As an æsthetic principle, Wagner contended that it is the true nature of music not to be the end, but a medium, of dramatic expression. The dominating principle of his work seems to be that poetry, music, pantomime, painting and the plastic arts, in fact every form of art, can be made to co-operate toward one end, that they can be so interwoven as to be completely interdependent, by all being made subservient to the one great aim of dramatic expression. The reason there are so few singers who can sing in Wagner's operas, is because the singer must think and feel as well as display vocal execution.

Wagner introduces characteristic musical phrases as exponents of emotional or scenic complications. These are called the "theme" or "Leit Motif." This is used by Wagner more freely than by any composer. He employs such a "theme" for every character, and not only so, but for every prominent feature in the scenery or action of the play, and he even indicates the change of the passions of his principal characters by distinct phrases.

Now it can be seen at once that this melodic form becomes in his hands a representative symbol. As we hear it, a distinct picture is conveyed to the mind by

these phrases.   Sometimes he interweaves these so as to
tell the whole story of a life in a single scene, as in
Siegfried's "Trauer Marsch."

Thus, whether Wagner would approve the terms here
employed or not, to me his best work is the harmonious
co-operation of what has been here called the representative and manifestive elements of expression in music.
This idea did not originate with him ; Sebastian Bach,
Beethoven and others show examples in their music, but
he first contended for it as a doctrine — though of course
not in the terms here used — and not only contended for
it but practiced it in his own art.

As an illustration, let us note in the "Götterdämmerung" the parting of the lovers.   As Siegfried leaves
Brunhilde in the opening of this play, he winds a parting
strain upon his horn, and as we linger over the tender
scene the orchestra takes up the parting note of the
horn, and as the sound grows fainter and fainter in the
distance, the illusion is kept up in the mind and we feel
the gradual passing away of Siegfried over the hills and
far through the forest.   At the same time, the manifestive elements in the music are revealing the emotion of
the lovers and the tenderness of the separation.   The
representative element helps the manifestive because
it sustains and intensifies the imaginative picture.   The
listener's heart goes out to Siegfried wandering afar in
the depth of the forest, as we hear the faint echo of his
horn, while the whole orchestra pours forth the feeling
of the two lovers.   These two elements are intimately
intertwined in the music, as the pictorial conception
which is the creation of the imagination is co-ordinated
in the human heart with corresponding feeling.   This
representative element is very delicate — only one instrument is concerned with its production — and its effect is

transcended of course, by the manifestive elements of all the other instruments.

Take another illustration of the co-ordination of representative and manifestive elements from Siegfried. In the noted anvil song, while Siegfried is hammering upon his sword the strokes of his hammer and the blowing of bellows are brought in co-operatively and rhythmatically with the music of the orchestra. Even his filing upon the iron which is regarded as among the most disagreeable noises in the world, is woven by Wagner into such music that it is not discord. It intensifies, when not over done, the pictorial conception of the reality, and aids in producing the illusion. It gives a kind of frame-work, so to speak, to uphold the manifestive elements which reveal feeling, as good drawing aids and is necessary to color in painting. Of course it is a very daring piece of work, and when done badly the noise can easily be made to destroy the music of the orchestra and the voice of the singer, and to make all ridiculous. Whether or not he was entirely successful in this and in other cases, the thought was a great one in art, and will aid men to see how the most diverse elements may be brought into co-operation to produce an artistic effect.

Better illustrations of the principle are afforded by Wagner's failures. In the Götterdämmerung a steed is brought upon and across the stage. The writer carefully noted the effect upon the people, especially the remarks they were making. All of them were able to pick out flaws in the horse. Some said he must be an old cart horse with the hair worn off the side by the shaft. This of course was not true, yet the horse was insignificant. He could not be brought into harmony with the other stage effects. This proves the fact that representation is a dangerous thing. Representative elements must always

be transcended by the manifestive.   Only so much representation can be introduced as will aid the mind to conceive the situation.   It cannot be literal or imitative, but
only suggestive.   In this case the representative became
so strong as to appeal only to the eye and not to the
mind.   The horse was not a suggestion to the imagination but a literal presentation, and the attention of many
was so absorbed in the horse that they wholly lost the
effect of the music.   Herein lies the weakness of
Wagner's art, as well as its strength.   He was so
strongly impressed with the importance of representation
in music that he has sometimes gone too far.   The horse
was a discord in music, and not an element of harmony.
Whatever appeals merely to the eye is not art.   It is
only art when it appeals to the mind.   The representative, when it appeals only to the eye, becomes
merely imitation, and is the death of art.   So long as
the manifestive transcends the representative the co-ordination of the two will produce the greatest artistic effect.

Of course there is no attempt here either to defend or
to criticise Wagner.   The only aim is to illustrate the
points here made regarding the nature of expression in
art, to show that the highest expression is that which
reveals both of these elements, and to open the way to
prove that delivery can only be improved by developing
both its representative and manifestive elements.

There is an additional and more weighty reason for
all this discussion regarding expression as the fundamental element of all art.   Schiller, Herbert Spencer and
others have held that all art is derived from the play
instinct.   Leading writers of almost every school of
æsthetics, have held that art is innate.   If these are
correct, the origin of art must be very intimately associated with the original and innate or natural languages.   In

fact, when the origin of art is more carefully studied, this relation may prove to be more intimate still, and art be found to spring directly from the natural languages. For before art there was expression, since expression is in some form as universal as life. In the lowest forms of life we begin to see certain external signs of internal conditions. Even the plant manifests its life in obedience to the same law. The leaves of the tree are an outward sign of an inward force. So it is in infinite degrees up to man. As the human being gradually develops we begin to find a desire to record his feelings, but before this record there is the expression, the presentation directly to his fellow-men of the many phases of feeling. The earliest games are associated with the natural languages. One of the most elemental and instinctive impulses in the human heart, the earliest to show itself in the child, is the dramatic. In his earliest play he begins to act his part, and so it was in the childhood of the race. Here we have the earliest unfolding of artistic instinct. And the primitive play, and the mimic dance, and the rude song must necessarily antedate the more permanent arts; that is to say, histrionic art in some form precedes all other forms of art. Songs were sung before they were written. Childhood, whether of the race or of the individual, acts and speaks before it draws. Art for its highest subjects, its most definite terms, constantly refers to the natural languages of man.

Hence in this work the word· *expression is used in its elemental sense as applied to the human being using his own natural languages in their natural unity;* and all *other uses* of the word, in painting, sculpture, music and poetry are considered *figurative.* These arts borrow the term naturally, as the aim of all art is revelation, and the fundamental conception of expression is found in the relation of man's soul to his own body and its natural modes of manifestation. There is one original form of expression which is the father of all expression in art.

We see proof of this in the influence of dramatic or histrionic art of different forms upon the other arts. Dramatic art flourished in Greece before the greatest period of sculpture and painting. Before a Phidias was an Æschylus, before a Homer was oratory and the singer of Homeric hymns, before Albert Dürer was a long line of Minnesingers, before Hamlet were the miracle plays, before Walter Scott and the modern novel was Shakespeare. Thus dramatic art has ever led the way. Histrionic art is the most direct means of expressing the emotions and conditions of the human soul, while painting and sculpture are rather records of such expression. The fundamental elements of expression that we find in works of art can all be traced back to a beginning in the natural languages. The living manifestation of the man through the living body, the living face, the living voice, directly to his kind, an expression that does not require physical matter or any instrument or means except his own organism, must be connected with the beginning of all artistic ideas. It is primarily from the exercise of the human voice that reason and imagination grow, and that the whole human being expands and unfolds his higher powers. The art of music is born when sound is used as the means of revealing the deepest emotions and the highest ideals of the human soul. It was only after observing the repose and strength that are revealed through the human body, and after seeing the expansion and modulation of the human form under the influence of emotion that man grasped the clay and moulded a Theseus and a Niobe. The conscious possession of his own body by emotion awakened man as

his conceptions widened and his feelings deepened to
mould matter as a new embodiment of the expanding soul.
Expression in his own body led him to realize that he

> "May so project his surplusage of soul
> In search of body, so add self to self
> By owning what lay ownerless before —
> So find, so fill full, so appropriate forms —
> That although nothing which had never life
> Shall get life from him, be not having been,
> Yet something dead may get to live again,
> Something with too much life or not enough,
> Which, either way imperfect, ended once;
> An end whereat man's impulse intervenes,
> Makes new beginning, starts the dead alive,
> Completes the incomplete, and saves the thing."

Oratory may be sneered at, but public speaking in
some form will last as long as the race, because it is the
most direct and natural combination of the two fundamental modes of revealing the soul, representation and
manifestation. All the clearness and definiteness of
thought can be given by the one, and all the fullness of
life and all the depth of experience possible to the soul,
can be revealed by the other.

Whatever a man may write and however perfectly and
adequately he may present it, there is a desire on his part
when roused by noble thought, high purposes and strong
convictions, to meet his fellow-men face to face; and not
only to embody his conceptions in words but to manifest
every shade of his experience by means of voice and
body. However clearly truth may be presented through
words, the fundamental instinct of the race demands this
co-ordination of all human languages as the most direct
and complete manifestation of his spirit.

When histrionic art in any form is degraded it is a
curse to all morals and to all art, for all other forms of
art soon or late follow in its train. A realistic actress

like Bernhardt must have a play like La Tosca written for her, in which four or five people are killed for no other reason than to give her occasions for exhibiting the physical effects of emotional excitement. Thus is caused to be written a most degraded play — a play without any moral, social or artistic purpose. Then a host of imitators arise, and public taste is vitiated, to say nothing of the moral effects of such realistic pessimism. On the other hand when histrionic art, whether in public reading, recitations or any other form of art, is elevated to the highest standard, universal art is ennobled and refined; for this is the most direct means of stimulating the imagination and awakening artistic ideals in the mass of the people, thus developing taste and appreciation of the best art of every form.

Hence to improve expression man has to be developed as an artistic being, for expression and art in many phases are essentially one. The instincts and intuitions are to be educated. The eyes are to be opened to the province of art in the revelation of the soul; and though we may not go so far as Schelling, and say that art furnishes the highest solution of the most fundamental problems of philosophy, at any rate we must realize the fact that art is the highest mode of adequately manifesting the soul of man, of revealing his highest conceptions and deepest emotions. Hence if oratory or any other form of expression is to be improved, it must be considered a part of artistic training and must be accountable to its laws. Every art, and especially expression, must not only be developed according to its own peculiarities as an art but must be compared with the fundamental principles which underlie all art, for only by comparison of such principles can departures from nature's elemental modes be tested and any canons worthy of regard be obtained.

VII.

ART IN EXPRESSION.

"The letter killeth but the spirit giveth life."

HAVING thus examined the relation of expression to art, we are prepared to study the artistic use of the natural languages, or the relation of art to expression. According to the ordinary conception, so widely diffused that it is almost universal, all elocution is a form of representative art. In fact, it is regarded as something upon the lowest plane of the representative, a mere imitative art. The highest excellence in elocution is often called imitative modulation. He is apt to be considered the greatest elocutionist who is the most skillful imitator, who can represent the beat of a drum, the thunder of rolling waves, the tolling of a bell, or the singing of a bird. So that elocution has come to be regarded as a synonym of all that is empty and superficial in art. Words have been too much regarded by the elocutionist merely as "sound echoing the sense," and not as representative symbols through which he can reproduce or suggest ideas. While both ideas and their symbols must be given carefully, yet the peculiar province of his own art is to manifest feeling by the modulation of the tones that are the material of words.

While there is a small class of words which have this imitative or representative character, such as the buzzing of the bee, the murmuring of the waves, and the like, it has been conclusively shown that though onamatapoeia, or mere sound echoing the sense, has played a part in certain instances, yet it is only one of the many elements which have brought forth language. But though this should be granted, yet language is employed so figuratively, words are used in such secondary senses, that if we take the word thunder, for instance, the feeling and the idea which it is called upon primarily to manifest, may be entirely foreign to the sound of the thunder.

Take, for example, an expression from one of Cunningham's lyrics, "But give to me the snoring breeze"; by taking the word "snoring" here, and endeavoring to represent the idea of snoring, the whole spirit of the lyric is lost. Some editors print "roaring," others "snorting," but the same principle holds true. Again, in one of Whittier's poems, the noble Mexican woman who finds her dead husband, as she ministers to the dying soldiers, sees upon a youth's breast the eagle of the North, and turns away in horror as from her husband's murderer. "But she heard the youth's low moaning," etc. Now if in reading this line the moaning of the youth is represented, the whole spirit of the poem is lost. The fundamental expression required is the manifestation of her passion, of her sympathy and of our admiration for her noble deed. Here is an illustration also of the fact that representation tends to carry us to mere accidents. The moaning of the youth is a mere accident, not the highest expression of pain. The reader has always several situations and emotions any one of which he may choose as the cause of expression. If he has the conception that his art is a representative one, and chooses, as is so often done, every opportunity for representation, the spirit of the best poetry is destroyed.

Mere words can never determine expression. When we speak of the moaning of the waves and the sighing of the winds, a rhetorical figure is employed, and to represent the sighing and the moaning would be to turn figurative language into literal, which is indeed often done in elocutionary rendering. This, we can see, violates the principle so long governing the use of figures. They must not be made to go upon "all-fours." In fact, when the reader brings out the buzzing of the bee, the moaning of the waves, the thunder of the cataract, the sigh of the wind, the attention of the mind is called to a kind of vocal jugglery and the emotion excited is not unlike that aroused in one who looks at the tricks performed by one skillful in sleight of hand. Men are called upon to listen to and recognize mere accidents in nature. The body is shown rather than the soul. Who has not heard a beautiful poem utterly ruined by bad recitation? Many mistake the cause, and say that such poems are not capable of recitation. Our elocutionary art has been brought so low that every thing in a delicate poem of Shelley or Keats is made literal. The poetic spirit is often perverted and ruined, because it is not appreciated. The conception of the art is to imitate accidents, referred to often very remotely, and not to reveal the soul that listens; to give the sound of the cataract and not the emotion of him who looks upon it. This, it can be seen, is a false conception of art, causing the representative to transcend the manifestive, if indeed there are, in such work, any manifestive elements at all. True poetry of all kinds can be recited, and its dignity increased with the right kind of manifestive reading or artistic rendering.*

If one will take up the simplest lyric, for example, "The Daisy," by Wordsworth, and read it free from any artificial system, the fundamental emotion felt is admiration, and of course, this ought to be revealed by the voice. In examining an elocutionist of some prominence once, who

---

*The extent to which imitative elocution is carried is shown by an advertisement in which a lady mentions as special accomplishments "bobolink tones and baby cries taught."

wished to study, I gave her one of these beautiful lyrics; but she could not read it with any expression at all, said she could not see "any thing to it." The reason was, she had been taught only the lower kind of elocution, and simply looked for things that could be imitated; but, of course, there were no such elements in so delicate and beautiful a poem. She was looking along the lines to find "something to do." Her mind saw no picture, and of course her heart felt no response to the beautiful ideas. Words symbolize the image, but the voice manifests the response to it. Vocal expression is primarily manifestive, like music. In fact there are more subjective elements in vocal expression than in music.

Let us take for example, Bryant's beautiful little poem "The Bobolink." As it is usually rendered, we have chiefly an endeavor to represent the bird's song. When we examine the poem we find four lines of each stanza manifestive of the emotion which rises in the heart of the poet or of the reader, in response to the sight of the bird and the green meadows, or to the song which ever lives in the heart of one who has heard it. There is not a particle of imitation; all is manifestive. Then we come to the endeavor to manifest the spirit of joy which dominates the bird itself, and last of all we come to representative syllables which only delicately suggest — they cannot imitate — the wonderful song. The voice here, of course, becomes representative. The endeavor is to picture objectively or to hint to the imagination some faint· echo of the song itself; but this element, as can be seen at once, is delicately introduced in the poem, and the manifestive elements, even in the last lines, completely transcend the mere imitation of the song. This poem is taken advisedly because it contains more representative elements than almost any one in the language. But even here the representative element is only introduced in connection with the manifestive. The imaginative picture is first seen and felt, the verbal or legitimately representative language is made to suggest what is seen, and the heart speaks its joy at the sight. Carried on by feeling we endeavor to assimilate the bird's spirit by sympathy to our own hearts, to manifest the awakened experience, and finally at the close of each stanza to rise to a delicate objective embodiment, which can only faintly suggest the inimitable song.

If art is merely imitative, merely skill to tickle the fancy, then the best elocutionary art would be simply the imitation of this bird's song. But all art, as has been shown, is chiefly the revelation of man's soul, and if so it is not to represent the sound of the bird except so far as to suggest the spirit of that song, because the words which are the legitimate symbolic representations, will convey the idea without literal representation or imitation. The function of art here is to reveal directly the feelings of the soul of the one who listens to the song; but as usually read, all the energy and attention is given to the imitation of the song, to the neglect of the more important element of manifestation. The effect of such work is to call all attention to the skill of the performer. A true union of representative and manifestive elements awakens the imagination and carries the hearer away to the green meadows and summer breeze. The fundamental aim of the writer is to reveal the spirit not the letter of the song of the bobolink, and the aim of the reader should be the same. In fact, no human voice, however perfectly trained, has ever been able to give more than a crude suggestion. Introduced delicately it helps to carry on the illusion and gives a union of the conscious and the unconscious, the objective and the subjective, the

body with the soul. But the soul must transcend the
body. Besides, if only the objective elements were introduced, the performance often becomes a subject for ridicule rather than for admiration. In all representative
work, there is a rich comical element. Comedy deals
more with the objective, more with accidentals than with
essentials, and for this reason there are more representative elements in comedy and the humorous.

The prolonged struggle among those who are trying to
elevate dramatic art is shown in the many criticisms,
especially in England, upon the famous speech of Mer-
cutio in "Romeo and Juliet." His description of Queen
Mab driving over the parson's nose and the lawyer's
fingers and the soldier's neck, furnish such great temptation for representation in order to raise a laugh in the
audience, that it has become notorious as an example of
the tendency to obscure the real poetry for the sake of
the external imitation of accidents. All was on the
plane of farce as it was given formerly, before the critics
and better artists fought against the degradation of the
spirit for the letter.

One aim of art is to secure an objective body for a
subjective ideal. This is the reason why manifestive
elements in art are so despised and so overlooked. The
desire is to make all objective, but this is impossible in
many cases, and the objective embodiment, to be art at
all, must be united to the subjective. The objective
must simply form a kind of body, that the soul may be
manifested. If the objective only is present, every thing
is dead, for only the body can be represented; life and
soul can only be manifested. Some one has said that
wax-works, the most lifelike art, is the most lifeless.

Some one may say the illustrations here are lyrics, and
ask why not use the word lyric for manifestive and dra-

matic for representative. It is true that in all lyric art manifestation predominates ; and in dramatic art there is more of representation. The lyric certainly was the beginning of all vocal expression. True dramatic art, however, is a union of both elements. It is even doubtful if the representative ever transcends the manifestive in the best dramatic work. Note, for example, Hamlet's soliloquy upon death. Observe how little there is here of representation. Our impression is not of what he did, and the person who renders it is not primarily concerned with what he did — if he is he makes it ridiculous — but with the assimilation of what Hamlet thought and felt. In short, the legitimate presentation of it requires manifestation rather than representation. Of course, there is a small representative element, but the assimilation of the true spirit of the passage calls for a predominance of manifestation.

Again, take an illustration of the same principle from pantomime. If we study a man in conversation, his hands, his face, his body, as well as his voice, are all manifesting subjective emotions and conditions while his words are representing his ideas. If two men who do not know each other's language meet in a desert and endeavor to communicate with each other, then the hands and body deal in signs as substitutes for words. One can tell the other the road, he can show that he wishes a drink of water; but no one will contend that this is nature's intended artistic use of pantomime. One will tell the other of a foe before him by showing his fright or antagonism, but here is only a poor substitute for words. When we come to the use of words we note occasionally representative actions by the body. As examples, when one man says to another "there is the door," or when old Polonius says "take this from this,"

his hand becomes necessary for the clearer representation of the words. But such use is rare; it is only indicative, only points out objective things. It is only in the school-boy period, and only there because of false methods of education, that a boy looks for a subject with something to point to — the north or the south, the mountains, the sun, moon or stars — because such actions of the body are only occasionally introduced in life and merely supplement words. The highest function of pantomime is manifestation. The simplest words, as "good-night," can be rendered by manifestive vocal expression and pantomime in a hundred ways. Representation confines it to one. Take a simple phrase like, "he fell." Representative pantomime becomes ridiculous and can only indicate vaguely and indifferently the direction or location of the fall. But manifestive pantomime can reveal the feelings of the man who contemplates the fall. It can show that the fall was comical, was dangerous, that it was a moral fall, a literal fall, a fall to be regretted or to be rejoiced over, a fall that caused surprise or awakened anger, a fall that brought ruin or escape to the innocent.

Besides, the element of manifestation is always present. The positions of a man manifest, they do not represent the conditions of his soul. The actions of the face manifest the feelings of the mind. This manifestative element is never absent, the representative is only there occasionally and only in descriptive passages. Again, representation only belongs to the hand and arm, while manifestation belongs to the face and the whole body. Great oratory has little or no representative element in voice or pantomime. A great poem requires the simplest and most delicate manifestation.

Some years ago a graduate from a prominent Western college recited an extract from Longfellow's "Building of the Ship." The last part contains the well-known apostrophe to the ship of state:

> "Thou, too, sail on, O Ship of State;
> Sail on, O Union, strong and great;
> Humanity, with all its fears,
> With all its hopes of future years,
> Is hanging breathless on thy fate;
> We know what master laid thy keel,
> What workmen wrought thy ribs of steel," etc.

Instead of feeling the spirit of patriotism; instead of rising to the grand emotional condition which dominated the poet, and which must dominate the man who reads it, unless he is imbued with the basest perversion of art; he marked out with his arms the direction and outline of the keel; held up his arms to represent the ribs of steel; made one hand an anvil and beat upon it with the other to represent "what hammers beat"; drew his arm down as if his hand grasped the handle of the bellows, to represent the forge, and so on. A more ridiculous performance can hardly be imagined, yet the mode of delivery had been given him as the best means of interpreting the poem, by a leading elocutionist of this country.

Take another case. A young man gave a recitation once of a part of Tell's apostrophe to his native mountains, from the play by Sheridan Knowles:

> "Ye crags and peaks, I'm with you once again;
> I hold to you the hands you first beheld,
> 'To show they still are free. Methinks I hear
> A spirit in your echoes answer me,
> And bid your tenant welcome home again."

Here, instead of seeing the grand pictures rise before his mind, and feeling the thrill in his soul by the assimilation of the patriotic spirit, he showed us where the hills were. When he expressed his joy at their freedom, he held his hands as if handcuffed and broke the handcuffs.

When he endeavored to represent the effect of his feeling their welcome to him, he took one hand and shook the other as if they literally shook hands with him.

It may be said that these are extreme cases. And so they are ; but these students had been taught, I am sorry to say, by elocutionists of prominence. However, let us study the art of a leading elocutionist. One of the leading readers of this country, who has been around the world, comes to my mind. In giving Shylock, he does not have any internal sympathetic assimilation of character, but he adjusts his head, his limbs, his throat; every thing is aggregated and adjusted, nothing is unfolded. There is no internal link of unity. The voice as it comes out is the result of an elocutionary trick in the throat. It is mere throatiness, a mere mechanical effect without any psychic cause. Any actor who went upon the stage with such a tricky use of his voice would be hissed off, or should be. Such work may serve as an exhibition for people who merely want to see what a man can do with himself, but there is not a particle of art in it. It is not even representative, it is a miserable substitution of a trick for genuine expression. Hundreds of illustrations could be given of the same kind. One of the saddest things regarding public recitation is that ordinary audiences rarely see the difference. They have little conception of the violation of the fundamental principles of art as applied to interpretative reading.

Then again, note the difference between good acting and bad acting. Booth, our most artistic American actor, brings out a psychic link of unity so that one always feels that the acting is a real manifestation. He does not assume the character by any external trick. He does not bring a great labored grasp of the muscles of the throat such as elocutionists have so long taught as necessary for characters like Shylock. There is not the least hint of merely an exhibition of "doing things." We feel that there is an instinctive and intuitive assimilation of a character, and no mere external mechanical aggregation or trickery. There is representation, but it is always transcended by manifestation.

Here, on the contrary, is one of our elocutionarily-trained hopefuls, taking for example, old Gobbo. Legs are stiffened, knees are bent, back is humped over, hands hung out, the voice artificially thrown into a piping sound. Any one can see that all is mechanical. There is no link of sympathy, no inner union of all these external signs, no evolution from within, but all is aggregated and mechanically adjusted.

Representation and manifestation must go together, and the highest representation is not imitation. When every thing is objectively aggregated the art is low, unsatisfactory and hollow. There must be, if there is to be any expression at all, the objective manifestation of something subjective. There must be subjective assimilation, not objective aggregation. When this character of old Gobbo is properly rendered there is an instinctive, intuitive conception of the character. There is a subjective assimilation of the feeling of the old man. The textures of the muscles, having been thoroughly trained, are responsive to the sympathetic assimilation of the character, every movement of the whole man is the harmonious evolution of the conception, so vividly realized that every thing seems to come from within outward. The voice may not be so sharp and piping but it is true to nature. It suggests far more than any thin, artificial, mechanical piping which has no relation to the mind. The one method is by external imitation, the other is by sympathetic and instinctive assimilation revealed by the harmo-

nious co-ordination of artistic manifestation and representation. One is the lowest form of art, if in fact it
can be called art at all, for there can be no art without
unity; the other is the rendering of the spirit of nature
in accordance with nature's own processes and laws.

One of the greatest and most artistic performances
ever produced upon any stage is Mr. Henry Irving's
Louis XI. Here all is unity, the hands, the face, the
feet, the voice and every part completely correspond;
there is a consentaneity of the whole man. The process
by which the character is adequately and correctly represented is essentially a union of the manifestive with the
representative, the manifestive transcending at all times.
The same is true of his most powerful and artistic per-
sonation of Dr. Primrose. There is absolutely no trick.
All is so harmoniously blended that every thing seems a
part of an organic body of which his imaginative conception is the soul. At no point does he make an exaggerated aggregation or extravagant motion for the sake of
exhibition. All is in harmonious co-ordination; it is not
an exhibition, it is the revelation of a soul at every step
and in every motion.

This principle is shown us by Ellen Terry in Olivia,
a part which never seems to have received due praise.
An elocutionary student commenting on the action when
the terrible revelation is made to Olivia, was heard to
remark, "she does hardly any thing at all," "any body
could do that." In fact, the actress becomes absolutely
still; she does not moan and groan, but is stricken down
just as a woman of such a beautiful character would be.
There is no tearing explosion of passion; Olivia is too
deep and lovely a character for that. But alas, an artist-
ically-perverted public wanted to see a display of the
wringing of hands and the tearing of hair, or exhibition of

groans. Those whose hearts were open were thrilled by the unparalleled repose, the force and struggle of a great soul in its realization of an awful fact. The greatest passion in nature does not make the greatest display. Just before the revelation is made, she is carried away by an exuberance of joy; and in such a demonstrative mood there is a great deal of movement; but in either case there is little or no representation. In fact, this artist among those of our time, uses the greatest amount of manifestive and the least number of representative elements. Contrast this wonderful artist with a realistic actress like Sara Bernhardt. Ellen Terry manifests the depths of the soul, Bernhardt merely represents the literal details and accidents of excitement. The one appeals to the imagination, and makes us *think* and *feel;* the other appeals only to the eye and makes us *stare.*

Another illustration may be found in Mrs. Kendall's rendering of the wife of the iron master. Notwithstanding her voice, in the scene where the perfidy of her lover is revealed to her, the powerful pent-up and controlled passion escaping only by the subtlest movements produces a great effect upon the audience. Every act appeals to the mind and soul.

Now if all this is true of the stage and of public reading, how much more must it be true of the delivery of the public speaker. Of all things in the world an aggregated delivery is the worst, and most foreign to true oratory. Yet in much of our public speaking the law seems to be, the more earnest the speaker or the greater the passion, the more must there be of loudness and muscular energy. Never was any thing more false to nature. The more intense the passion, the more hushed the voice, is nearer the truth. So long as a passion keeps its demonstrative character, it may increase in loudness, but the very

moment the element of control enters, that very moment
range of voice increases rather than volume. Loudness
increases as passion tends to destroy control, while the
resonance of the voice increases with diffusion of passion
under retention. In short we can see, after this analysis,
a further explanation of the severance of personality from
delivery. When delivery is poor, nearly all will be found
to be representative. The speaker has worked upon his
execution from this point of view; and his real personality is not shown because this can only be revealed by
manifestation. The idea of the mind may be represented
by words; objective actions outside of us can be represented occasionally by motions and tones, but the soul
with its deepest and most mystic experiences can only
be manifested; and it is precisely this experience which
has power over our fellow-men, and which is needed for
the interpretation of truth.

There is a difference in the degree of representation
and manifestation, in the different forms of expression.
Acting has essentially most of representation; while oratory, so far as emotional expression and delivery are
concerned, has most of manifestation. Public reading is
mixed, containing at one moment almost as much representation as acting, and again it is fully as manifestive as
oratory. Neither form is ever found entirely alone. It
is the union of the two that makes art. Again, there are
different modes of representation — dramatic, verbal and
others. Oratory has more of verbal representation, while
acting has more dramatic representation. There can be
no mechanical division of oratory from acting. Good
story tellers are always dramatic; and good orators nearly
always belong to this class. The most dramatic men of
our times have not been actors. Few actors, if any, can
compare with John B. Gough, Henry Ward Beecher and

Abraham Lincoln. Even the most successful teachers and business men have this instinct strongly developed. It is absolutely necessary to any one who must see a truth from many sides, or as different men see it. It is fully as much an oratoric as it is a mimetic instinct. The mechanical methods of acting in modern times tend to destroy it, so that often we see little of it on the stage.

One of the most advanced forms of dramatic writing is the monologue. Not only has all Browning's work been written in this form, but a vast number of other authors, not only in this country and England, but also in France, have adopted it. The monologue can only be rendered by means of public reading; it cannot be acted. If the monologue, as many think, is an advance over the drama, then public reading must be in advance of acting as a form of histrionic art. The difference between public reading and acting as arts, is that acting is more representative and reading more manifestive. A monologue is more suggestive to the imagination, more manifestive of feeling, and there is less "business." There is a greater call for all the subtleties of facial expression and less call for mere adjuncts. It is thus more subjective, more suggestive, appeals rather to the imagination than to the eye and affords a far more subtle study of character, in many respects; and the wonderful possibilities before it as a form of dramatic art are incalculable.

Good acting, however, has a manifestive element as well as a representative, but as has been shown, the tendency of modern art is toward the subjective, toward greater manifestation of feeling. If this is true it will be natural to look for a greater emphasis of public reading. There was a report abroad that Henry Irving and Ellen Terry would take the play of Macbeth and travel with it, reading and acting only the special scenes between Mac-

beth and Lady Macbeth. Had they done this, or if they
do it yet, it will mark what I consider a great advance,
and will not only reach a greater number of people, but
will stir the imagination far more affectively than any
stage representation.

Some one will ask, how reproductive art can have a
manifestive element. According to the common opinion,
a reproductive art is a mere mechanical process; and, if
there is any expression in it, it is not at all due to the
reproduction which is simply the result of a copying
process. But when we come to think of it, can there not
be an artistic wood-cut? Can there not, in other words,
be an artistic reproduction of an artistic work? Note,
for example, the reproduction of George Fuller's paint-
ings by Mr. W. B. Closson. Take his wood-cut of the
Winnifred Dysart, for which he received a medal at the
Paris Salon. Did Mr. Closson simply represent or simply
copy the painting of Mr. Fuller? Certainly not. Of all
works of art, a copy is the poorest. The traveler finds
in the Pitti and the Ufizzi, and in all the great galleries, a
vast number of painted copies of Raphael and the old
masters. Every little detail is copied out accurately so
far as mere externals go. But who is satisfied with such
a copy? It is a correct copy, but the spirit is entirely
lost. It is a mere representation of the external. That
in fact is all that can be represented. The manifestive
elements of the work are always the elements that are
lost by the mere copyist. He has no soul to see the manifestive elements. An artistic engraver's reproduction of
a painting may not be a mere copy, because the same
colors are not used. The reproduction of a painting by
a wood engraver is a reproduction in black and white of
the same spirit in a different sphere. Thus the artistic
engraver studies carefully his work of art. He gets into

its spirit. He realizes in his imagination what the original artist saw and felt, and from the thorough and sympathetic insight into the work of art, feels and sees a conception which is as near the original as his personality will admit; and this conception, which is essentially the engraver's own, enables him to interpret the painting. All true reproductive art must be interpretative. To be interpretative there must be more than mere representation. There must be a manifestive element. This artistic instinct is fundamentally necessary to artistic reproduction. Without it the work will be merely an external shell whose soul is gone.

This is the reason why even the best photographic process is imperfect. Photography is a great art, and we prefer the photograph of a great picture to a mechanical copy; but still, these reproductive processes are always mechanical. They lose something of the spirit, although they suggest much of the fundamental feeling. We feel that there is a getting away from personality. As some one has remarked, the difference between a photograph and a painting may be clearly shown by taking figures and draping them exactly like Raphael's Sistine Madonna; the original effect will be absolutely lost. There is a manifestive spirit pervading all such work, which can never be attained by mechanical processes. The artist's soul must intuitively and instinctively feel its way toward a revelation "from within out." No photograph of the Dysart could ever produce the effect which Mr. Closson has produced in his wonderful wood-cut. Nor can a photograph ever give us the interpretation of Rembrandt's portrait of his mother, as given by Mr. Closson in his new art. The reproductive artist must be true to his original, as the so-called creative artist is true to nature. He must give the spirit and not the letter.

But expression is not wholly a reproductive art; the true oration is written for delivery, and not to be read upon a sofa. A true drama is written to be presented by histrionic expression, and much is left unsaid, for the histrionic artist can give it more adequately than is possible for words. Delivery is the most subjective form of art. Here, above all places in the world, a man must speak "not merely to men but only to mankind," and it is the subjective element that enables him to speak to mankind. He who recites a great poem is not merely a reproductive artist, he must create again the poem; many things must be his alone. The emotion, the experience, even the pictorial images, must, to a great extent, be his own. Often a great actor has revealed new beauties in a work, to the author himself.

This may be illustrated from Bible reading. When a clergyman reads the Scriptures objectively, every thing appears dictatorial, or at least dogmatic or didactic; it seems as if he said to men "This truth is for you, not necessarily for me." One of the greatest teachers I ever knew once said in regard to reading the Scriptures, "You must enjoin the truth upon yourself and upon other men." Whenever the Scriptures are read without first being enjoined upon the speaker himself, whenever they are read as an intellectual lesson, merely as something for men to know, or as so many words, the performance becomes tame and flat. It inspires no realization of worship. No conception is awakened that it comes from God. Above all things it is worst when read representatively. No affectation is worse than this. But when the Bible is read as if the reader's heart and soul were talking with God, listening to God and feeding upon his truth, how different the effect! And yet Bible reading requires the utmost reverence for the letter of its original.

Thus it can be seen that delivery involves both representative and manifestive elements; that the representative elements are more intellectual, the manifestive
elements more emotional in character, and that the representative element is chiefly the work of the writer, so
that delivery itself is chiefly manifestive. And as the
highest art-work is a union of manifestive and representative elements, so in delivery the chief aim is simultaneously to represent ideas of the mind, and to manifest
emotions and conditions of the soul. A writer can
embody his thoughts by mere representative symbols,
but the subjective realization of the soul, the intuitive
unfolding, the germination of the truth, its consequence
to human character, the experience it awakens, can only
be given manifestively. Subjective experience can only
be signified and suggested; it cannot be symbolized.
Experience can be manifested through voice and action
in connection with the representation of words. Many
able men are often heard to say, "Truthfulness is more
important than truth." And yet how often do these very
men who see the bearing of this in life, fail to see the
application of it to expression. Truth is general and
apprehended by the intellect, and is expressed by representation; while truthfulness is a quality of individual
character. It cannot be represented, it can only be
manifested. If a man speaks and professes truthfulness
directly in words, this causes doubt to spring up in
others' minds. It must be shown indirectly, unconsciously, manifestively by voice and action; not the
narrow artificial use of these according to rules, but the
true noble spontaneous union of these with words as
nature intended. Thus the great problem of delivery
is to unite the manifestive elements to the representative,
to realize the depths of experience in relation to truth,

and to manifest these with that truth so as to interpret it and to lead to its adoption. Words alone are not adequate to convey a correct impression and secure a deep realization of the situation. This can only be done through manifestation.

From this we can see the importance of the work of training the delivery of public speakers. The true aim of the education of the public reader, the professional artist, or the orator, must be to enable him, not merely to represent, but to realize the profounder elements of truth and emotion, and to manifest this experience so as to interpret and impress more strongly the truth objectively represented.

Notwithstanding these facts, we find in the present methods of educating speakers, that all work is devoted to thought. There is no work for the imagination or for the development of emotion. The lawyer is taught a knowledge of law, the preacher is given a knowledge of Hebrew, Greek and Theology, and an understanding of the framework of sermons. But what work is done for the development of those faculties of the soul, upon the action of which speaking absolutely depends? The little that is done for delivery is in the way of external criticism of faults, and endeavors to make the man conscious of these, with mechanical rules for conscious obedience. There is no work for the training of the real man for the development of his nature by inspiration and training, so that these faults will be thrown off unconsciously. Nor is there any where any known recognition that all delivery is previously manifestive, or subjective rather than representative or objective.

Expression does not fill men from without; it draws out from within. No man can give feeling to his fellow-men, he can only awaken it. The highest expression is showing to others what we possess. The greatest manifestation is simply the revelation of the finite soul endeavoring to comprehend the infinite. By a link of sympathy, by an intuitive appreciation of the situation we can realize the many phases of experience; and one soul is able to represent to another the ground of its convictions, and to manifest simultaneously, consciously and unconsciously, the motive dominating the life, the feeling and the passion inspiring the whole man.

Verbal expression is necessarily representative; and the education of delivery must consist in the development of the natural languages, so as to co-ordinate their manifestive power with the representative character of words. Here we see the most important relationship of expression to art. We have found that the union of the manifestive and the representative is the highest characteristic of great art in any form. And if all art is the projection of the human, the soul's appropriation of matter for self-revelation, a domination of man over things, we can see the fundamental root of this principle. So that in educating delivery, we can come back with these elements of art and re-apply them to make that delivery perfect, art itself becoming a mirror to show us what is needed.

VIII.

HISTORY AND EXPRESSION.

The unimagined good of men
Is yearning at the birth.
— *Emerson.*

HAS expression any history? or is it some fixed and eternal thing, not affected by "the development of the collective spirit"? To enter into a full discussion of the historical changes through which expression has passed, would be to attempt what has never been undertaken, and would require a volume. Yet it is too important a phase of the problem of delivery to be wholly omitted.

Hegel's discussion regarding the development of art may possibly throw some indirect light upon the subject. He divides the arts into periods. The first is Symbolic, where matter transcends the idea, the idea not being clearly manifested or even able to permeate its material fully. The second is called the Classic period. Here the idea finds its form, permeates its material, and there is a perfect balance between them. The third period is the Romantic or Christian, where the idea transcends its form. Here the artist feels that the idea he wishes to express cannot be completely embodied, that it belongs to the spiritual and eternal and can only be suggested. The chief classic art is sculpture, while the chief Christian arts are painting, music and poetry. Sculpture occupies the three dimensions of space, painting requires two, while music passes entirely beyond all limitations of space. While some may doubt whether all art must necessarily follow these steps, and that this furnishes a true philosophy of the development of all art ; yet all acknowledge that this is true of Egyptian, Greek and Christian art, and their relation to each other.

Has there been in oratoric delivery a correspondence between its successive changes and this histrionic or philosophic unfoldment of art ? Let us look only at one phase, and this rather as an illustration of the principles already laid down, and as a preparation for our further investigation, than as a discussion as full as such an important subject demands.

The difference between Greek and Christian art, in respect to the elements of representation and manifestation, explained in Chapter VI, must be seen at once. Greek art was perfect as far as it went, but it attempted little more than to reproduce characteristics chiefly physical and objective, separate from the personality of the artist. Hence sculpture was its favorite and highest form. But Christian art deals with the deepest emotions and conditions of the human soul. One treats of man's physical life, of physical beauty ; the other of his spiritual life, of truth and beauty of soul. One deals with time, the other with eternity. One was a perfect balance between the ideal and its material embodiment ; in the other the ideal rises above all balance with physical matter. The depths of the human heart came more into consciousness, and facial expression was studied and embodied in art. Suggestion is an essential law of all Christian, or as Hegel calls it, Romantic art ; because there is an endeavor to reveal that which is too deep, too infinite, to be more than hinted at. The art of expression is simply an art of intimation. Hence we see that Christian art must necessarily be manifestive and more or less imperfect when judged by the old representative standards. For "to express the infinite we must suggest infinitely more than we express." And even in the technical execution there must be a decided suggestion of its inadequacy.

The difference between Greek and Christian art was never more clearly defined than by Browning in Old Pictures in Florence.

> Growth came when, looking your last on them all,
> You turned your eyes inwardly one fine day
> And cried with a start — What if we so small
> Be greater and grander the while than they?
> Are they perfect of lineament, perfect of stature?
> In both, of such lower types are we
> Precisely because of our wider nature;
> For time, theirs — ours, for eternity.
> To-day's brief passion limits their range;
> It seethes with the morrow for us and more.
> They are perfect — how else? they shall never change:
> We are faulty — why not? we have time in store.
> The Artificer's hand is not arrested
> With us; we are rough-hewn, nowise polished.
> They stand for our copy, and, once invested
> With all they can teach, we shall see them abolished.
> 'Tis a life-long toil till our lump be leaven —
> The better! What's come to perfection perishes.
> Things learned on earth, we shall practice in heaven:
> Works done least rapidly Art most cherishes.
> Thyself shalt afford the example, Giotto!
> Thy one work not to decrease or diminish,
> Done at a stroke, was just (was it not?) "O"
> Thy great Campanile is still to finish.
> Is it true that we are now, and shall be hereafter —
> But what and where depend on life's minute?
> Hails Heavenly cheer or infernal laughter
> Our first step out of the gulf or in it?
> Shall Man, such step within his endeavor,
> Man's face, have no more play and action
> Than joy which is crystalized forever,
> Or grief, an eternal petrifaction?
> On which I conclude, that the early painters,
> To cries of "Greek Art and what more wish you?"
> Replied, "To become now self-acquainters,
> And paint man, man, whatever the issue;

Make new hopes shine through the flesh they fray,
New fears aggrandize the rags and tatters:
To bring the invisible full into play,
Let the visible go to the dogs — what matters ? "

Professor Jebb, in a comparison between Demosthenes and Burke, in his Attic Orators, has shown that this same difference exists between Greek prose and modern prose, especially in oratory. "No speaker, probably, of modern times has come nearer to the classical type than Burke; and this because his reasoning, his passion, his imagery, are sustained by a consummate and unfailing beauty of language. The passage in which he describes the descent of Hyder Ali upon the Carnatic is supposed to owe the suggestion of its great image, not to Demosthenes, but to Livy's picture of Fabius hovering over Hannibal:

"'He drew from every quarter whatever a savage ferocity could add to his new rudiments in the arts of destruction; and compounding all the materials of fury, havoc and desolation into one black cloud, he hung for a while on the declivity of the mountains. Whilst the authors of all these evils were idly and stupidly gazing on the menacing meteor, which darkened all their horizon, it suddenly burst, and poured down the whole of its contents upon the plains of the Carnatic. Then ensued a scene of woe, the like of which no eye had seen, no heart conceived, and which no tongue can adequately tell.'"

"Brougham contrasts this passage with that in which Demosthenes says that a danger 'went by like a cloud,' with that where he says, 'If the Thebans had not joined us, all this trouble would have rushed like a mountain-torrent on the city,' and with that where he asks, 'If the thunder-bolt which has fallen has overpowered, not us alone, but all the Greeks, what is to be done?' Brougham contends that Burke has marred the sublimity of the 'black cloud' and the 'whirlwind of cavalry' by developing and amplifying both. This surely, is to confound the plastic with the picturesque. Demosthenes is a sculptor, Burke a painter. 'The most memorable triumphs of modern oratory are connected with the tradition of thrills, of electrical shocks, given to the hearers at the moment by bursts which were extemporary, not necessarily as regards the thought, but necessarily as regards the form.   It was for such bursts that the eloquence of the elder Pitt was famous; that of Mirabeau and of Patrick Henry owed its renown to the same cause.   Now these sudden bursts and the shock or the transport which they may cause, were forbidden to ancient oratory by the principal law of its being.   In nothing is the contrast more striking than in this — that the greatest oratorical reputations of the ancient world were chiefly made, and those of the modern world have sometimes been endangered, by prepared works of art."

It seems very unfortunate to me that one so well versed in all that pertains to Greek art and literature as Professor Jebb, should have omitted entirely any discussion of the difference in delivery between Greek oratory and that of our day.   But though there is no mention of delivery by such a thorough writer there is abundant evidence to prove that there was the same difference in delivery as in writing.   In fact, the difference must have been more marked, for delivery and histrionic art are nearer to subjective conditions and the real spirit of a man or of an age than prose composition or any art.   Differences of style can be traced by the scholar, but differences of delivery are far greater and are seen at once by all.

As an illustration and confirmation of this, let us take the greatest of all Christian or Romantic artists — Shakespeare, and compare him with either of the great Greek dramatists.   There is a wordiness or externality about the expression of emotion among the Greeks, which is as different from the suggestiveness and the depth of subjective revelation in Shakespeare as can be conceived.   In

arranging a Greek play for modern performance the long
speeches have to be severely cut to avoid tameness. And
yet Shakespeare does not possess the external correctness,
the absolute verbal perfection, of either Æschylus, Sophocles or even Euripides. The Greek plays are as perfect
as a Greek temple or a Greek statue, but their very
perfection limits them to the finite. But Shakespeare
touches deeper chords, suggests the infinity of the human
soul, and gives his auditor a look into the eternity beyond.
The peculiar polish of Greek art is foreign to such intensity and infinity.

No doubt the difference was far more marked in acting
and histrionic expression than in verbal expression and
structure of the plays. There could not be any more
subtle expression in the Greek actor's face through his
mask than "joy which is crystalized forever, or grief an
eternal petrifaction." Some of our greatest critics contended that the Greeks were as superior to us as we are
to the wildest African tribe. But if these could be carried
back to a Greek theater, and should see an actor come
striding upon the stage with his feet many inches above
the floor and a monstrous mask upon his head, they would
be as astonished as a country audience was said to have
been at one of the leading Greek actors while making
his provincial tour; and if he should open his mouth and
roar out his big voice, bringing to bear all the artificial
resonators arranged in his immense mask, there is little
doubt that these fastidious classicists, as was reported of
the ancient audience, would run for their lives from
disgust if not from fear.

This is the special point which concerns us in this
investigation; for if the delivery in oratory and all histrionic expression has changed, the methods for its development must change, and Quintillian can no longer furnish

the model for the development of the modern orator. We have also possibly in this one reason for the odium against elocutionary training, which, as is well known, is more intensely felt by those most completely dominated by the highest modern artistic ideas. That there must be some change no one can deny. The modern orator no longer has two or three years to prepare his oration. No such opportunity comes to him as came to Demosthenes when all the patriots and scholars of Greece journeyed to Athens to hear his immortal oration, On the Crown. Has, then, the art of oratory been supplanted by printing, and was oratory an art belonging only to a period of general ignorance? There can be nothing more after Greek art, has been the cry in sculpture, in painting, in poetry, in oratory, by those who only look backward in all ages. But we know when we come to study art that there has been an advance. There was a time when a comparison of the art of Shakespeare with the art of Sophocles would have provoked a smile, but that time has passed. There was a time when a comparison of Raphael or Michael Angelo with Greek painters would have been received with the same sneer, but that time was so long ago that it is almost forgotten. What an outcry would have gone up at one time at a comparison of a Gothic cathedral with a Greek temple, but the sneer has long been hushed. Only in sculpture do the Greeks remain supreme and unsurpassed.

A change in one form has always caused a change in others, and in fact we find that while there have been very few changes in the elocutionary method of developing delivery, yet delivery itself has changed gradually with the changes in literature and art. Not only all oratory, but every form of histrionic art has undergone a like transformation. Often the bad habits of expression have been directly or indirectly due to the incongruity between the methods of developing delivery and the artistic spirit of the age. Antiquated methods, when followed, lead to artificiality, while those who condemn such methods are led to the opposite extreme of rejecting all training, allowing their expression to be born of impulse or random caprice. It is a recognized fact that many of our best orators have corrected serious faults and developed their delivery by observation of nature and a careful study of themselves, independent of conventional elocutionary systems.

Modern oratory especially differs from ancient oratory, in possessing greater subjectivity. Christian oratory must have greater intensity, and therefore must necessarily have less external perfection. It must deal with truths more spiritual and internal, and can no longer, as was the case with Greek and Roman orators, aim for grace as a definite object for its own sake. This same principle must govern public reading and every form of histrionic art, for the aim of the highest Romantic art is expression and not exhibition. The problem which weighs heaviest upon the human mind is the interpretation of the infinite in the human soul, and the infinite of eternity. Whatever is related to these is of most profound interest to every human being. Soon or late, all art will be judged directly or indirectly from its relation to human life and character.

Again, modern speaking is more extemporaneous and more spontaneous; extemporaneous not as to subject, but as to manner and delivery, and intense embodiment of the human soul. It must be less deliberative in the use of the natural languages, because a more direct embodiment of the activity of the human soul. The spirit of Romantic art absolutely disproves the dictum which still has its advocates, that nothing is artistic unless it is brought into the realm of deliberation. That no gesture, for example, is artistic unless we know exactly why we make it and when we make it.

Even in the acting of the present time one hears of the "Old School." Some of the best of the older actors have a style of acting which is absolutely different from the best actors among the younger men. In fact, since Talma the whole declamation of the stage has changed, and the change is in exact accordance with the change in other forms of art. It is a change, though less in degree, that corresponds with the difference between Greek art and Christian art. It is not a mere difference of individuals, but of styles caused by the spirit of the age. The same differences are seen in public speaking. As one compares the speaking in the largest cities, with that in a district remote from the most advanced centres of culture, the same difference is noticed. The man who has not come into contact with the spirit of the time especially manifests in his delivery the method of the past, while those most advanced in culture, who have come in contact with the artistic and scientific spirit of the time, show greater simplicity and subtlety, more intensity and variety, more manifestation and less representation.

Part of this difference may be due to the difference in degree of education, but not all; for often the one far from the metropolis has greater ability and is as fine a scholar. The difference must be because one has the methods of the books and the past; the other evolves his method from contact with the world, from a more intimate connection with the artistic spirit of the age. Science can be gained from books and observation, but the artistic spirit of an age can only be gained by contact with art. This cannot be transported. The "carriers of art" are always feeble. A man may become educated alone with his books ; but culture, while calling for this requires also a direct observation of art and a direct contact with the most advanced minds of his age. Oratoric delivery mirrors the man and the effect upon him of his time.

Thus we see that the various changes in expression and the history of art bear a direct relation to the historical development of the character of the race. Expression in the art and oratory of Greece was different from expression in the art and oratory of to-day, and it should be so from the nature of the case. Greek expression was right for that period ; it was the truthful manifestation of Greek life and character. Greek art was more representative, more plastic, more like sculpture ; ours is more manifestative, more like painting and music. The reason for this is that the life of the Greeks was more objective, more physical ; ours is more subjective, more spiritualized, more intense, because of contact with the Christian religion and the stimulation of the subjective forces by two thousand years of development since their day. They were taken up with beauty, and the moral man among the Greeks was one whose outward acts were well balanced and proportioned ; while we are concerned with character, and a good man with us is not one of external morality merely, but one who is upright in motive. Accordingly it is very natural, in fact, inevitable, that modern expression should be different. Each age and nation must produce its own type of expression. History corroborates these conclusions, and we find in Roman art one of the best examples of weakness of the art spirit, and we are not surprised, because Roman art was borrowed from Greece. A borrowed art cannot be great.

What must we expect, then, if Greek and Roman art be engrafted upon Christian times, and Quintillian's

Institutes of Oratory be accepted as a standard for the development of oratoric delivery to-day? This work was prepared with great scholarship and was written in finest Latin and the most beautiful style. It contains a great number of references to the Greek and Roman orators and the opinions of earlier writers. Thus for the purpose of history the book is of great value; but for the purpose of instruction it is absolutely wrong. It was written in the days of the decline of oratory and art, and can not give us the best methods of the greatest teachers. It looks at everything from the standpoint of appearance. All that is said regarding delivery is upon the mere out-side of the subject. So that granting it represents ade-quately the methods of the Greeks in developing delivery, and no doubt it hints at their conceptions of this work, in the nature of the case it is inadequate for modern times, because it is too objective, too representative for our age. A complete change has come over the spirit of the world; and all forms of vocal delivery, more than any other art, because more intimately connected with the soul, must show that change. If this is true, methods of developing expression must recognize the difference.

The human soul and the human body are better under-stood. Everything is now traced to a cause. All kinds of education have been reformed. The world has been brought to realize that the highest education results from stimulating nature's processes and not from observing arbitrary rules. The scientific spirit of the age is making itself felt everywhere. It is not possible that delivery can be developed in the old artificial way.

In that Quintillian's "Institutes" are accepted as the highest authority in methods of delivery, we find a partial explanation of the great difficulties to be overcome to emancipate oratory from stilted declamation. Austin's

Chironomia, published in 1805, is still considered a standard work upon elocution. Hundreds of authors, in fact nearly all, especially in the realm of gesture, have followed Austin as an absolute authority. The work simply consists of a gathering together of the precepts of Quintillian and the Greeks and Romans so far as known. Different positions and gestures are illustrated with minuteness. To show how far the world has grown during this century, if one of the poems he illustrates should be given according to illustrations by any good reader to a critical audience, it would appear very ridiculous. Unfortunately, however, we can still see similar exhibitions in all our schools. The gestures of the students are coached and given according to the same method, and are pure aggregations in all cases, or to call them by their right name, affectations. They have no inherent connection with the impulses, instincts and psychic action of the student.

The great error of the book is, that it considers Greek and Roman art as the absolute standard, which we are to imitate under all circumstances. We have already seen that Greek and Roman art was chiefly concerned with the limbs. Of course the same was true of oratory. So far as pantomime is concerned, it was chiefly concerned with gesture. How to hold the toga was one of the characteristic questions discussed by Quintillian. Every thing is a matter of general appearance. But Christian art is chiefly concerned with the deeper conditions and emotions of the mind, which are revealed, not so much by motions of the limbs as by the positions of all parts of the body, especially by the expression of the face. The face is the absolute centre of all modern manifestation. The subtle play of the fingers in co-ordination with the face, and the expansions and actions of the torso, the positions of all parts of the body, are the most important means in modern histrionic expression. Hence, Christian oratory is more simple and less declamatory than that of Cicero.

There seems to have been a tendency after Demosthenes, who marked the highest period of ancient oratory, to an exaggeration and perversion of the real truth and beauty of Greek delivery. We especially ought to remember that the age of Quintillian was not an age of great orators. Oratory as an art, was dying. It is a beautiful shell with the life gone. Very beautiful it is, gleaming with signs of a long-past glory, but to follow it slavishly has had a pernicious influence upon oratoric delivery for over a thousand years. What was genuinely expressive in the Greek period, when translated and aggregated by the Romans, had an element of pomposity, an element of empty declamation in it. But when these ideas had a second transplanting, and above all, when that second transplanting was from the classic age of art to the Christian age of art, the absolute untruthfulness of it, the empty declamation and affectation, can easily be imagined without looking at the facts. And this is exactly what Austin tried to do, and what, unfortunately, he has done. What may have been the natural evolution of the Greek, and possibly of the Roman, to the expression of emotion by great, "magnificent" motion of the limbs, can not be the evolution of genuine emotion in the modern period. In fact, Austin hardly does them justice; but this of course is natural, for art can never be transplanted. Hence, elocution has been an endeavor to aggregate what is not genuinely expressive. The study of delivery is an entirely different thing from the study of the thought, and after the thought and the speech have been prepared, the youth carefully avoids making a gesture of his own, for fear it may be wrong, and stands up to be taught what gesture to make and where to put it in. Can there be a more false principle in art? Has there ever been in any age of the world more ridiculous sham than has resulted from such a method?

We can see that such a method violates the fundamental nature of expression. It must be genuinely manifestive. It must not be an aggregation. For one nation to try to act like another nation is ridiculous affectation. Peoples two thousand years apart, entirely different in their genius, their education and the experiences by which their characters have been moulded, can not be alike in expression. An artist begins to be an artist when he begins to be himself, and delivery especially requires all action to be centred in the real spirit of the man. It is the most simple and direct manifestation of the soul, and must be free from all aggregation, from all endeavors to be like the Greek or like the Roman. The inspiration must be received from our own time, broadened and deepened by the study of all other times.

Still another illustration may be taken of the mistake or the failure to apprehend the difference between Christian art and classic art. Sheridan, one hundred and fifty years ago, contended that the English ought to have accents like the Greek, and that all inflections and modes of delivery should be uniform, forgetting entirely the fact that Greek accents were placed upon the language in the period of the grammarians, long after the golden age of oratory and histrionic art, which had brought the language to such perfection.

The great difficulty of getting free from the shackles of declamation has arisen again and again in the history of the world. In one of Fielding's novels, the worthy Partridge is made to say regarding Garrick's performance of Hamlet: "Nay, you may call me a coward if you will; but if that little man there upon the stage is not frightened, I never saw any man frightened in my life. He the best player; why, I could act as well as he myself. I am sure, if I had seen a ghost, I should have looked in the very same manner and done just as he did. The king for my money: he speaks all his words distinctly, half as loud again as the other. Any body may see he is an actor."

We can see differences even at the present time. For example, French oratory is in advance of English. French delivery is more simple, more direct and more animated. The whole body speaks continually, in the greatest variety of movement. English oratory is peculiar in that it has almost completely ignored pantomime and has become very one-sided, as may also be said of speaking in America. But the one point which stands out prominently before us is the difference between the oratory and the instruction in oratory. There is a widely diffused feeling that the oratory taught is not in accord with the spirit of the age.

Is not the cause here hinted at the true one? It is only the school boy, and a few readers and old-school orators that speak according to the elocutionary standards. The best speakers and actors break away from these methods, though taught them ever so thoroughly. This can only be because such methods are wrong or at least out of harmony with the modern spirit of man.

Does not this give us an explanation of the stiltedness of elocution? Has there not been an endeavor to place the rules of Quintillian and the style of Cicero upon boys who are imbued with the spirit of subjectivity and simplicity of Christian art and times? The congruity is about equal to draping a boy in his great-great-grandfather's garments and sending him in such an antiquated costume to a public school.

Expression, thus, like every thing else belonging to man, has a history. It changes with every age, and true methods for the development of its power must also change. We find that the difference between Greek art and Christian art is that the latter is more subjective, more intense, more subtle and spiritual. We find, also, a corresponding difference in the modes of expression. Greek and Roman art were chiefly concerned with the limbs; Christian art has more facial expression. Greek art was plastic; Christian art is pictorial and suggestive. Greek art was more physical and representative; Christian art is more manifestive. While the highest art in Greece was sculpture and architecture, the highest art in Christian times is painting and music. And, as has been shown, the style of oratory, so far as words are concerned, is affected by this change. Hence, above all, the style of delivery must also have changed, so that Christian oratory is more extemporaneous, more simple, more subtle and varied; one was more objective, the other more subjective; while one calls for a greater volume of voice, the other calls for more inflections and greater varieties of pitch and tone color.

Hence, we can see a new phase of our problem. We must come back to nature. Each age and each individual presents new problems. We can have no superficial and external standard of uniformity for nations and ages. We must find general characteristics, general methods broad enough to include all nature. It is only the method that is uniform; the manifestation is infinite and varied. The causes from within must dictate and mould, as the influences from without draw forth and shape the manifestations.

We can see the necessity of studying this problem in relation to the instinct and intuition of the time. We can see also that in order to secure a new criterion for criticism, in order to become free from the shackles of tradition, there must be historical study of the different phases of expression. Above all, there must be a study of the universal principles governing expression in all art, that the artistic use of the natural languages of man may be so unfolded as to manifest truthfully and adequately the experience deep and intense, in all its phases, which stirs the human soul at the present hour.

We have thus looked at the more immediate phases of delivery and histrionic expression. We have found that expression does not consist merely in something done, but in something revealed, not in something aggregated from without, but in something unfolded from within. The chief falsehood opposed to expression, is exhibition. Expression has been found not to be mere manner, but a revelation of the activities of the soul, a transparency of character. It does not consist in multitudinous actions or modulations of the body, except in so far as these are significant or revelatory. Hence, the first principle that must govern the development of true delivery, is that there must be a removal of affectation of every kind.

All modulations of the body must be more immediately connected with the soul, and made in some way more significant. Endeavors to acquire mere grace and manner for their own sake, to assume merely the signs of expression, or to appeal to the eye and ear for their own sake, are fundamentally antagonistic to the essential nature of expression.

Again, we have found that expression is complex and belongs to every part of the body, each discharging a distinct function. It is composed of many languages which are different in nature from each other, so that one can not be translated into any other, and yet all these languages co-operate together, and their distinctive differences cause possibilities of greater unity; in fact, we find in the reconciliation of these opposites, the highest example of harmony. We find, also, that in their completeness, they simultaneously appeal to the two leading senses, eye and ear, to which all art is addressed; and that they show the elements of all the arts.

As we study the nature of man's being, we find that these complexities of the different forms of expression correspond with the complexity of the soul; not only does each part of the body have a distinct language, but this language is capable of manifesting some phase of experience which is not possible to any other means of manifestation. The voice vibrates with emotion, as the tongue and lips mould the sound into symbols of thought; the eye beams with the intensity of purpose, as the torso expands with the earnestness of excitement; and the hand unfolds the intention of the man and the relationship of the truth to the hearer. Thus, as we study the nature of man in relation to expression, we find it was nature's intention that he should reveal all the phases of the soul's realization of truth; that not only is man to convey truth but truthfulness, not only thought but experience; not only is the fact conveyed by the symbol, but the affection and emotion stirred in connection with it, are revealed by other forms of expression, so as to cause adequate and perfect conception of the truth and the soul. All training for the development of expression must unify and develop all the languages of man; in some way the repressed modes of manifestation must be restored, and the whole soul and body be brought into harmonious activity. All mistaken suppositions regarding the superiority of one language over another or **any** exaggerated use **of** one must be corrected, and a true apprehension of the particular use of each in its own peculiar sphere must be secured. Nature's ideal intention must ever be man's fundamental aim. All development requires that there shall be no separation or killing out of any of the natural means of manifesting truth; such a method must necessarily result in perversion and one-sidedness. True development in expression of any kind must ever secure harmony of the faculties of being and the agents of body.

Expression is intimately intertwined with personality: it must grow with its growth, strengthen with its strength and change with every change. Character itself is the most elemental expression, and directly or indirectly affects that which is the most immediate revelation of the soul.

The improvement of expression must be connected with the development of the man. The faculties and powers must be strengthened and brought into harmony. All expression must result from genuine thought and genuine emotion. Its fundamental law must be sincerity. One-sided views are especially hurtful.

To prevent mistakes, the meaning of expression in art has been studied. All great art is an endeavor to embody and manifest what is mystically perceived in the soul; to show not merely the body of nature, but the soul that animates this body; so that a manifestive element is fundamentally necessary to every phase of art. Great painting, sculpture or music reaches the depth of the soul. The two essential elements in art are found to be manifestation and representation; but it is found that the higher the work of art the more must the manifestive elements transcend the representative. Tracing the application of this to delivery, we find the same principles; while expression has been found to be both manifestive and representative, yet all great orators, great readers and great actors have not been characterized by mere skill in representation, but by their power of manifestation. Just as the great artist always shows the greatest power in combining the two elements and making the manifestive transcend the representative, so has it ever been in oratory.

To clear the way for the justification of the departure from tradition and the artificial aggregation of the past, it has been shown that expression varies with every age and every nation; that the histrionic expression of the Greek must have been different from the expression of the modern Christian; that while the great underlying principles were the same, yet, just as it is seen at the present time that the French differ from the English in expression, so still greater differences must mark the oratory of the modern from the Roman. Hence, methods of development must also necessarily vary.

It is incredible that such great progress should be made in all other directions, and that oratory and histrionic delivery should remain the same; that methods of developing them should not change after more thorough understanding of physiology and the human soul. If so great a difference between the art of Æschylus and Browning exists, the delivery of Pericles and Gladstone cannot be the same. The greater subjectivity of man must cause a corresponding change in the subjectivity of delivery; true expression must be less and less decorative or external, and more and more expressive and manifestive.

Expression must be developed by the direct study of the facts and principles of nature; artificial methods which violate the true nature of expression can only produce superficial mechanical results; it cannot be developed by any trick or by sleight of hand, however skillful.

There seems no rational way except by developing the proper action of the mind and the soul, by bringing thought and feeling into greater activity and union, and by developing the particular power and function of each agency and bringing all under control. Emotion must be developed according to nature's intention. All hindrances, psychic and physical, must be removed; in short, there must be harmony of all man's faculties, co-ordination of every agency of expression, and all must be brought into that unity and consentaneity which were evidently intended by nature.

II.

Search for Method.

"Man knows partly but conceives beside,
  Creeps ever on from fancies to the fact,
  And in this striving, this converting air
  Into a solid he may grasp and use,
  Finds progress, man's distinctive mark alone,
  Not God's, and not the beasts'; God is, they are,
  Man partly is and wholly hopes to be. . . . .
  God's gift was that man should conceive of truth
  And yearn to gain it, catching at mistakes
  As midway help till he reach fact indeed. . . . .
  If ye demur, this judgment on your head,
  Never to reach the ultimate, angels' law,
  Indulging every instinct of the soul
  There where law, life, joy, impulse are one thing!"
                                        —*Browning.*

IX.

FUNDAMENTAL MODES OF NATURE.

All nature is but art unknown to thee. — *Pope*.

THE problem of delivery has been studied from different points of view, in order to apprehend some of the essential elements of its nature. We have found that it is not a superficial or simple problem that we have to meet, but one that is as deep as the soul of man and as broad as universal education. But though the problem may be partially recognized, it is not at all solved. How can expression be developed? This is the great question before us. All the investigations into the nature of expression, its complex character and the various difficulties associated with it, have been undertaken simply to prepare us to answer this question. In order to secure an adequate method, such a study of the nature and relations of the subject was necessary, to anticipate dangers and avoid misconceptions. But we come now to a different phase of our problem; we must investigate expression more definitely as to its processes. All human observation begins with the most immediate and most apparent phenomena; so men usually study nature merely from her external forms, and objective results, rather than from her modes of procedure. Accordingly the latest discoveries in science have ever been in relation to nature's processes.

It is a maxim in every body's mouth, that all art is founded upon nature. But what do we mean by this phrase? With some it merely means that there must be external conformity, or likeness to results of nature. In a painting, for example, the drawing must be in exact accordance with nature's forms and adjustment of parts. But this can only apply to some forms of art; and even in these departments this phrase cannot be literal, otherwise all art would be merely copying, or photographing. A higher view of the relation of art to nature, is that there seems to be a correspondence in the processes of production. Like an organism, all the parts of an art product must inhere. A work of art must seem to have grown, must seem to have been developed out of a center.

In the particular phase of art we are studying, there is a still more important aspect in which art must be founded upon nature. In all oratory or histrionic art, the artist's tools, or the instrumental means employed, are the voice and body; and these form a part of nature herself. Organism can only be attuned or developed in accordance with nature's own modes of growth. The voice and body cannot be built; they can be trained, can be placed under greater control, or stimulated to higher development, by careful exercises or modes of stimulating them in accordance with the intention of nature. So that the study of methods for such development, more than any other phase of art or education, demands careful, patient and direct study of nature.

It is therefore essential to know some of the characteristics of nature's methods of expression. No art can be founded on any mere hypothesis or theory. No worse misfortune could happen to any art, than that every teacher should have his individual system built upon a narrow theory, or one-sided conception of some single phase of the work, and should devote his energies to the promulgation of this, rather than to a careful and conscientious study of nature. Such a course is especially harmful in expression, for nature must furnish, not only the tools, but also the method of procedure itself.

Not only must we find nature's modes of procedure, but we must find nature's fundamental processes. Every thing in nature is built upon a very few simple elements. The varied structure of the physical world, we know from the science of chemistry, is due to combinations of a very few substances. Everywhere nature is governed by law, and a law is only an elemental fact common to a whole group of phenomena. Accordingly, if we study nature's modes of procedure, nature's method of growth and development, we find also a few fundamental characteristics which belong to every organism, and to all life.

In the study of the processes of nature, especially of nature's fundamental methods, we have to deal with more complex problems than we meet in the investigation of mere forms and products. If a painter is to paint a picture of some scene, his study of nature is very important; all the modes by which nature distinguishes object from object, the colors, especially the lights and shades, and the fundamental elements of form, must be observed. But when we come to study, not nature's products, but modes of producing results, we are far more liable to make mistakes; for then we have to study modes of action, and in nearly all cases, especially in all the aspects of expression, we must observe that which is rapidly passing, and which can not be stayed. It is for this reason that the phenomena of the voice in speaking have been so long unexplained. In the use of the voice in singing, the note can be sustained so as to afford opportunity for more careful study, but an inflection is gone the moment it is uttered, to prolong it is to change its character. Rarely can it be isolated or even repeated, or kept before the mind for more careful analysis.

But if this is true of all forms of histrionic art itself, how much more is it true of the art of developing expres-

sion, for the reason that people usually do not distinguish
the results of training from the man himself. Nor do
men distinguish a speaker's lack of training from the
speaker himself. When a public reader does poorly, men
think he is not capable of doing better; they do not distinguish his bad art from his possibilities. On the contrary, when a man does well, it is looked upon as an
inborn characteristic of the man himself, in no way
dependent upon education. We often hear the remark,
"Such results as that can never be accomplished by training." Even many educated men can not, from what they
see a man actually do, conceive of his doing better; they
are unable to distinguish the possibility and power of the
man, from his actual performances. Above all, they can
not perceive the hinderances arising from a misuse of the
faculties and the agents of expression.

Again, there are no recognized styles in delivery and
public reading, and almost none in acting. So that while
there are schools of art in painting, specifically and accurately defined, and though the same differences are presented in all our public reading and oratoric delivery, yet
rarely, if ever, do people think of different schools of
histrionic art. Again, as regards methods of developing
delivery, is there any well-defined, or even poorly-defined
account of the various methods, with their specific differences, by which oratory and histrionic art have been
developed? There has never been a specific method
thoroughly worked out, which has presented adequate
methods for all phases of the problem. All that has ever
been done, has been the production of certain methods
or so-called systems, each of which merely regards one
phase of the problem.

From all this, we can see that great care is needed in
our investigations, for we can not make comparisons of

art with nature in the different phases of expression, as easily as we can in a statue or painting. And great care is needed when we seek to invade nature's own realm, and endeavor to stimulate her own processes and develop her own organisms to a higher state of efficiency. Any one can see the great difficulty of such a task.

But however difficult the task, however many mistakes may be made, however inadequate may be the results accomplished, still the work must be undertaken, if methods for developing delivery are to be shown to have any scientific basis.

We have already found that expression is a universal characteristic of nature. Let us study the expression of organic life, among the most familiar objects around us. The leaves of the tree express the life of the tree. The blooming of the flower is the manifestation of the life of the plant. The song of the bird is the expression of its life and feeling. The swift curves of the bobolink are manifestations of its spirit. The leap of the lamb, and gambols of the kitten, reveal the inner plenitude of life.

But what are the characteristics of these expressions? One point we specially note is, that they all come *from within outward.* All outside actions are the manifestations of inner life, and are produced spontaneously, not deliberatively. The force that directly causes the rose to bloom is in the heart of the parent stem. There is no blooming flower without a store of life in the root of the plant. The bird's song is simply an overflow of its life and joy. Nothing ever grows, blooms, sings or acts in nature, independent of such inner impulse. Here we find at least one fundamental characteristic of nature's mode of procedure. Nature does not build; no organism has ever been constructed by aggregation. There must ever be internal assimilation. Every thing has its "seed in itself"; such a process of unfoldment is everywhere present as a characteristic of life. The more nature is studied, the more universal do we find this law. From the evolution of a planetary system to the blooming of the smallest flower, every thing is from a center, from within, outward. If we take the leaves of a flower, and pull them apart by a mechanical process, we do not hasten growth but destroy life. We can increase growth only by stimulating the root. Nature's action is from mystic forces to manifest phenomena.

All growth in nature, then, is simply the manifestation of internal energy. It is true there can be no growth without external elements and forces, without light and heat, moisture and soil; but without a center around which these can play and by means of which they can be brought into co-ordination, all will be dead. All life seems an emanation from a mystic center.

This characteristic of expression in nature may be illustrated by the difference between an animal and a machine. The animal moves by means of some hidden force in the depth of its own being, while a machine moves from an external application of force. The life and strength by which the bird sings and flies, comes from its own heart. But a machine moves according to fixed mechanical laws, and the application of the force is definite, and is almost as manifest as the action itself.

Man by some forms of training may apply force to the agents of expression, exactly as force is applied to a machine; but the result can never be other than mechanical and artificial. All true, noble expression must be in accord with this universal law of life; it must result from impulses originating in the depths of the soul.

All great art is dependent upon the intuitive impulses of the artist's nature. Without artistic instinct no mechanical dexterity, however skillful, can make an artist. Hence, the great point in training an artist is to so co-ordinate the development of all the faculties of the man as to stimulate the artistic impulse and make it stronger and nobler. A development of these characteristics of nature to act from within outward, is therefore an essential principle ever to be obeyed; for every true artist seems to be dominated and inspired; that which he manifests seems to be given him, and its very method of production must seem to be the spontaneous action of nature. And expression closest to nature as an element or form of art is no exception. Expression must be the external manifestation of internal plenitude of force and life. It must be the outward revelation of the whole being, with all its faculties and powers as agents acting in unity and co-ordination, according to nature's intention.

Wordsworth's criticism of Goethe was an illustration of this principle. He said that the poems of Goethe did not seem to be sufficiently inevitable. That is, a great poem must seem to be what it is from an internal necessity; a story must seem to be told in the one inevitable way. Every true work of art must seem to be the inevitable result of an internal cause; the hearer or observer must feel that it could not be otherwise without being degraded.

The art of expression is the least mechanical of all arts. As has been shown, there is no mechanical instrument like the piano or violin of the musician, the brush of the painter or the chisel of the sculptor; the instrument is the man's own organism, itself a part of nature. Hence, this law of nature must apply universally and absolutely to all phases of expression in every form of art. So that all true work for the development of delivery of whatever form must recognize that expression is simply an effect and that its cause must not be wholly deliberative. That the deliberative part of the work must be to get the man into the proper condition, to direct attention to the idea, or to sustain the conception of the situation, until the proper emotion is stimulated; but the impulse itself must be spontaneous. It is a fundamental error to endeavor to get an effect independent of the natural cause. In this respect, the art of expression differs from an art like painting, sculpture or music. The musician must patiently work until he is a perfect master of an instrument which is no part of himself. The artist, after his instrument has become part of him, can so play that his music seems the extemporaneous and spontaneous effect of the emotions of his soul. The deliberative element has become so hidden beneath the spontaneous element that it is not perceived. But in expression the instrument is a part of the artist's own organism, and while there must be patient work to secure control, it is still more necessary that technique must be concealed than in other arts.

An illustration often adopted by those who are arguing for the importance of improving delivery, is that elocutionary training is the same as musical training. As the musician must secure control over his instrument, so must the speaker secure control over his voice and his body. And some go so far as to claim that just as the artist always chooses deliberately the note of the piano which he is to strike, so the man must choose the inflection, the gesture and every modulation of his organism in expression. There is a sense in which this is true, but it is not wholly true, because the piano is an external instrument, while the voice and the face and the whole body are parts of man's organism, and their movements are so various and complex that it is not possible to choose all of the means of expression. Besides, there are some subtle expressions of the face, and tone color which can not be deliberatively called out. Man is not wholly conscious of the action and process by which they are produced. Hence, the reader has an element of spontaneity which is different from the spontaneity of the musician. And the speaker having a more complex instrument, has something co-ordinate by which his work is produced which cannot be found in a mechanical instrument. So that his expression must be more directly the effect of emotions which are stimulated by his ideas.

Again, expression is not quite the same in speech as in song; for, although in song the instrument is a part of man's organism, still the voice is made to follow an objective score just as a musical instrument; and men forgive apparent effort which in a speaker, a reader or an actor would be intolerable. In the case of the orator especially, there is also a process of thinking simultaneous with execution; the ideas must be originated as well as expressed in words. In the case of the public reader, the thought is to be reproduced and carried before the mind, so as to stimulate emotion. Thus, in either case, the consciousness is not focused on mere external form, or the mere means of presenting the truth, but must primarily be centered upon the fundamental action of the mind.

That men have such terrible faults in expression is due to the lack of this preparatory training. The various languages have not been specifically developed, and all parts brought into proper co-ordination and unity. When all the faculties and powers of a man are so developed as to act in normal co-ordination and unity, and all the agents of the body so as to respond to these impulses, then the impulse toward expression is not mere will, but comes from all the powers of the man, because it is part of his personality, and his whole personality acts in his delivery. His art is not an external acquirement, and his training has not tended to make it so, but has simply unfolded the natural possibilities of the man, and brought all his faculties and powers, and all their agents and methods of manifestation into closer unity with the spontaneous revelation of his personality.

Of course, in all speech there is a mechanical side. Pronunciation and accent have been acquired from a long, deliberate and volitional struggle. These must be so mastered that what was at first deliberative becomes unconscious. But there is little of such struggle in the acquirement of inflection. Children, before they can speak a word, have very expressive inflections.

As a further proof that all expression must be spontaneous, note the fact that great actors rarely undertake to act in any but their own language. Salvini, although he speaks a little English, never acts in English. The deliberate work, the conscious struggle with verbal language, would interfere too much with the emotional actions and conditions which are manifesting themselves through the natural languages.

But, whatever may be our view regarding the degree of spontaneity, there are many violations of these principles of nature in the teaching of vocal expression. One of these is imitation. Imitation is considered by the best writers upon æsthetics the test of low art. Whatever in art is imitative is necessarily low or bad; for only objects of a low order can be imitated. A stick or a flower can be imitated, but the ocean or a mountain never. But there are far greater objections than these to imitation in the work of expression. Imitation is the external copying of what is merely accidental and superficial, and must dwarf the personality of the imitator. No two persons look upon any subject exactly alike, and whenever there is an endeavor to make the expression of any two people alike, a result which imitation ever produces, the principle of originality in nature is violated. There will be hinderance to the direct action of cause in producing its normal effect.

Every work of art is original. Two coins may be made alike because they are produced by a mechanical process. But there are no two leaves alike in all the world. There are no two faces alike, no two voices alike; nature is ever original, and so must it always be with true art. Every great work of art must therefore be an original embodiment. The worst of all modes of interfering with this process of nature is imitation. In expression above all things, every man must be developed according to his own individual nature. Again, no two voices are alike in pitch, and for one to teach another by imitation may ruin the pupil's voice. Many instances of this have been known. What is natural to one man is not natural to another. One man moves rapidly, another moves slowly. To endeavor to make all move by a uniform standard, is to destroy their nature.

But it may be said, it is easy enough to see that nature is inevitable and original. But how can you test spontaneity in expression? One way is that whenever expression is spontaneous, the whole nature acts. Whatever is spontaneous seems to come from the depth of the man's nature. His whole nature seems to be responsive. All the powers of his being are directly, or indirectly, present in the manifestations. Whenever spontaneity is violated there is a one-sidedness, and lack of unity and harmony among the agents producing the expression. The genuineness of expression is always shown by subtleties, so the spontaneity of expression is especially indicated by the expression of the face and the color of the voice. Where there is no spontaneity, these subtleties are always lacking; spontaneity in expression is another word for genuineness and sincerity.

Another characteristic of expression in nature is *unity*. Not only has nature an impulse from within out, but this impulse comes from a center, and subordinates all parts to this center. That is, nature's expression acts from a center, in all directions. There is no such thing in nature as absolute isolation. Nothing stands alone. Everywhere we find mutual dependence. No life or growth exists without a co-ordination of many elements. There is every where a "reconciliation of opposites." Clover was transplanted to New Zealand, but it was not a success because humble-bees were not also transported. Every new discovery in nature has been the further realization of this principle. Every law discovered, from Newton's law of gravitation to the latest phase of evolution, has revealed more and more the unity of nature. But if this is true of objects in nature which seem isolated from each other, how much more is it true of the different parts of an organism. The tree puts forth its leaves upon all its branches at the same time, for there is a vital and absolute union between the different parts of every organism. Death in one part means death in all.

Everywhere, also, there is consistency. We never find the willow leaf on the oak-tree. Each branch upon the elm is similar to the whole tree. The rugged form of the oak leaf is in harmony with the rugged and crooked form of the limb. This relationship existing between all parts, is one of the most fundamental elements of beauty. In art nothing is so bad as patchwork, or any hint at mere aggregation. Unity is a fundamental law of all art. Every great work of art seems like an organism. **Its** unity must seem to be the unity of co-ordination. It must not be merely mechanical proportion, or consistency, for unity implies diversity resulting from a central impulse of life. It must seem to have grown.

But what is the application of this to expression? Not only must expression seem to come from within out, but the whole man must speak; it must seem to be the result and co-ordination of all the faculties and powers of the soul, speaking through all its languages. There never can be true expression without this unity of all the powers of the man. With only the intellect active, there can be no great expression, nor can there be great expression with only the emotions active, or with only the will active. Any one-sidedness in the action of man's psychic nature betrays itself at once in expression. As the mind is a unity, so is expression a unity. Expression must ever be the speaking of the whole being through the whole body. The whole action of the man must be concentrated. All the action of his faculties must center upon the idea. Emotion must be a genuine response to the idea in the mind at the time, or the whole expression is weak and abnormal. Unity has never been secured by mechanical or one-sided methods. It can only result from emotional activity springing from the depths of the soul and diffusing itself through the whole nervous organism of the man. This principle applies to the action of the body, the faculties of the mind, and to the relation of the various languages to each other. It applies, also, to training; for a machine can be built a part at a time, but man's voice can not be built. It can be made to grow; it can be trained and disciplined, and brought under control, but all true training must obey the law of growth.

Another important characteristic of nature is *freedom*. Not only does the impulse come from the center, but we find that nature furnishes an opportunity to every object to fulfill the impulses and intent of its nature. The flower has an impulse to bloom, and no string is found around the bud to prevent the unfolding; we may find a sheath that clasps and prevents the premature unfoldment of the delicate leaves, but this is a help, and not a hinderance to the unfolding flower. The life of the tree has opportunity for a development and realization of its form. Not only does the bird have an impulse of joy, but it has means and opportunity to manifest this joy. However we may regard nature, we find that freedom is one of her most salient characteristics. To find repression, we must come to the realm of man.

Freedom is opportunity to act in accordance with law. Freedom does not mean license. In fact, it implies an element of limitation. The oak can unfold its life only in oak leaves. We never find the lily upon the rose-bush. But the limitations are internal, not external. There is no impulse in the elm to produce poplar leaves. There is no impulse in the willow to produce walnuts. There is ever correspondence in nature between impulse and mode of manifestation, between emotion and motion, activity and action, force and form. Freedom is possibility of acting in accordance with law; license is unbridled disobedience of law, and sooner or later destroys freedom. A grain of corn can grow into a stalk; for it is granted the privilege of unfolding the intention of its nature. It is the very law of the rose-bud to bloom into a rose. Freedom is the opportunity granted to any object to fulfill the ends of its existence; to unfold its implanted forces in its own implanted way. Whatever interferes with the implanted impulses will fetter or defeat nature's normal intention. There can be no growth without freedom. To tie up the plant, to draw a cord around the rose - bud, is to kill it. To put external limits of an extreme kind over the child's nature, is to dwarf the development of its character.

Looking at the work of man we find that there can be no true art without freedom. Every artist is original. Every great artist in all time has acted in accordance with law, but has disobeyed rules. There is a great difference between a rule and law. A rule is an external direction established by authority, or in some way applied externally to the object. A law, on the contrary, is founded in the nature of things. Freedom is not only possibility of obedience to law, but true obedience to law produces freedom, while obedience to rule brings slavery. There are some rules which are formal statements of law, but in such cases they are no longer mere rules.

The opposite of freedom in art is conventionality. There has been in all ages antagonism between nature and conventionality. Man on the one hand has deep, strong impulses in his nature, and on the other he endeavors by direct volition, to conform himself to the established standard of others. The artist who never rises above the mere technicalities of his art is always superficial. The man who lives merely in the rules that have been laid down, however important these rules may be, will be artificial and constricted.

Thus no great art has ever been produced by a mere observance of rule. The great artist has always been one who has broken through rules, and laid hold of the principles of nature. He has ever broken the shackles of conventional authority, and obeyed nature herself. Demosthenes rose above the conventional rules of Isocrates and the other rhetoricians of his day. Giotto broke through the narrow conventional precepts of Byzantine art, which were universally obeyed in his day. Shakespeare broke all the conventional rules, the unities of time and place, which had governed the drama from the time of the Greeks. He obeyed his own instincts, and expressed nature as she really appeared to him.

All the arts have had their conventional periods. In the infancy of an art, rules are more apt to be present. All mechanical art is governed by rules; but as art progresses, and as the artist himself rises, he is guided more and more by his own instincts, and a direct, careful study of nature herself binding the righteous law upon his own arm. As we study the history of art we see the effect of conventionality. Sameness has always resulted from mere slavish obedience to custom or authority.

As we come to study that art which we have found to be most akin to nature, we find mechanical rules laid down about inflection, which are direct violations of nature. We find rules which have been transmitted from book to book for two hundred years, and some for fifteen hundred years. In some of our schools it is still taught that a question which can be answered by yes or no, must have the rising inflection. But no one who will open his ears, or who has given the slightest attention to the fundamental principles of nature as manifested in speech, will contend that this rule is true even one-half the time. There is, of course, an element of truth in it, but a half-truth is the worst kind of falsehood. In fact, such a rule is a mere conventional arrangement to suit somebody's system. If it is founded upon nature at all it is based merely upon the most superficial observation. When a teacher takes a long time to explain to students that they must always stand on both feet in speaking, though he may give physiological arguments, any one who has ever studied an Egyptian statue will not fail to see that the art of elocution is in its Egyptian period.

Many other characteristics of nature could be enumerated, such as ease, simplicity, repose; but these are sufficient to prove that if we are to have a method of developing expression, we must study nature's modes. If nature is spontaneous, free and harmonious, all training in expression must seek, directly or indirectly, to develop the instincts and intuitions of the man. The impulses of his soul must be made true — true to nature in her simplicity, in her ease and in her repose. All art requires education, but this education must not be merely one of technicalities. In an art which is so related to nature as expression, there must be a direct stimulation of nature's impulses, and a removal of all obstructions to nature's processes. There must not be a leaning to artificial modes of execution, nor a mere study of the outside; not a mere seeking to do things in a conventional way, but an endeavor to arouse all the faculties and powers of the man to normal activity and co-ordination, and to set free all the channels of expression. If nature tends to do right, we must strengthen that tendency, and open the .avenues of harmonious manifestation.

These modes of nature's growth are really fundamental laws, and must dominate all the methods which may be adopted to stimulate development. If they are universal modes of nature's action, they must be recognized in all education. These characteristics of expression in nature show that human expression must come from impulses within the breast of the man, that there must be no external hindrance to the outflow of these through the whole linguistic organism. Expression must be the manifestation of the whole being through all the actions of voice and body.

X.

ARTISTIC SPONTANEITY.

O'er that art,
Which you say adds to nature, is an art
That nature makes.

—*Shakespeare.*

In the study of all these principles it has been taken for granted that human expression is governed by the same laws as the plant or the animal. But ordinary views regard artistic action as entirely different, so that it is necessary to study further into the processes of the soul in expression.

In man we meet with elements which are not found in the plant or animal. One of these is conscious adaptation of means to an end, or the power to be guided by experience and perception of the most proper means to accomplish an end. The animal has instinct, man has reason. The carrier pigeon may be carried in darkness by winding ways for hundreds of miles, yet when released it will steer a straight course for its home. The honey-bee that has wandered far, when it has gathered its load strikes a "bee line" for its hive. "A species of wasp stores up food of a kind which it never uses for itself and carefully deposits it in a fit receptacle which is not its own abode, for the use of its young whose birth it will not live to witness." The common view is that there is the greatest amount of instinct in the lower animals, and that it decreases as reason increases until there is no instinct and all reason in the highest man.

Another difference is volition. The plant has no control over its environment. The animal has little if any, while man can change or dominate his surroundings, whether subjective or objective. He can control the attention of his mind, direct it to a new object, or he can call up a new idea or situation, and thus dominate his feeling by changing his mental picture. He can also by deliberate choice select one of many possible modes of expression and adapt it to the exclusion of others. He may by will accentuate that mode, make it salient and all others subordinate.

Hence, there must be certain differences between the spontaneity of the opening flower and that of the orator. In the case of the plant there is only an impulse, modulated or stimulated by environment, without any conscious direction. The central force unfolds along the line which is most open, or most in the direction of the stimulus from without. A vine in a dark cellar will grow toward the light. In the animal there is the same impulse with something higher. Most animals can move from place to place. The bird can choose the branch of the tree upon which it sings, but there is very little choice as to its song, and its expression is the immediate result of reflex action or the unconscious, almost involuntary unfoldment of impulses. But man accomplishes his highest results, consciously, rationally and by choice.

As we study human expression, however, we find on the one hand that it may be as spontaneous as that of the bird, it may be involuntary or even unconscious, or on the other hand, it may be entirely the result of conscious choice, and as artificial as the product of a machine. Man has not only the power to adopt deliberatively words and symbols as the representatives of his ideas; he can also take the natural signs of passion and to some extent deliberatively execute them without emotion. He can, for example, by securing control of the muscles by which

the subtlest expressions of the eye or mouth are manifested, execute these actions by simple acts of will. In
direct opposition to this, man can abandon himself to the
impulses of his heart ; he can laugh from overflow of joy,
or he can shed his tears and abandon his voice to the
dictates of grief.

Which form of expression is natural? Should expression be as spontaneous with man as with the animal?
Should it be entirely the result of conscious deliberation
and choice, or can these elements in any way be united?
Any method for developing expression will be colored by
the answer given to this question.

The ordinary view is that spontaneity belongs naturally
to animals alone or if found in man is the same as wild
impulsiveness, and to be artistic it is held that every
thing must be conscious and deliberative ; and that it is
the province of education, and especially of artistic training, to lift man out of animal impulsiveness to a rational,
conscious and deliberative direction of every emotion and
action. This view practically claims that man is at first
only vaguely conscious of the faculties of his mind and
the agents of his body and has little or no consciousness
of their use. In this condition he is ignorant and
awkward, an untrained, untutored savage. The course
recommended for the correction of this, is first to make
the man conscious of his faculties and agents and their
languages, and his faults in their use. He must thus
pass into a period of great self-consciousness and discouragement, but he slowly wakens to his possibilities on
the one hand and to the fact on the other hand that he
is a creature of habit. Thus he is made to attend to
himself deliberatively until he corrects by conscious
action the misuse of his faculties and their agents of
expression. His conscious attention to himself is con-

tinued until he acquires such facility as that he can consciously use all his faculties and powers with ease. In short, he is given a conception of what to do and how to do it, and is set to work and kept at work until there is little friction in the use of his agents ; and his faculties and powers are under the control of conscious will.

This is generally considered an adequate solution of the great problem of education, especially for delivery. According to this view the artist is the man who has conscious control over every muscle and movement of his body and over every faculty and power of his soul, and can perform every action from the tread of his foot to the flash of his eye, under the direct control of will. So that by having perfect control of the signs of emotion he can "by a mere movement without any emotion himself cause emotion to rise in the spectator that will lift the hair upon his head." On the other hand he who acts spontaneously and unconsciously from the dictates of imagination or emotion is considered only a creature of wild impulse. According to this view spontaneity is a characteristic of nature, but must be replaced in man by mechanical expertness, and the process of developing this must simply be to find the expression and action of each agent, to bring these into consciousness and to remove friction by continued practice, until all parts can be employed deliberatively and at will. But such a method can never meet the necessities of the problem as already unfolded. It entirely ignores some of the most important facts in relation to expression.

It overlooks the complex character of the human being, whether viewed physiologically or psychologically. No man can swallow by force of will. He can push the back of his tongue against the fauces and swallowing follows spontaneously, but without this swallowing is impossible.

All human action in some degree is a union of conscious
and unconscious, of voluntary and involuntary elements.
Many philosophers have conclusively shown how small is
the realm of will and of consciousness in the simplest
actions.   The simple lifting of the arm has but few conscious elements.   Man is conscious of the volitional intention and of the result, but of the process by which the
arm is lifted the man is wholly unconscious.   "It is not
always," says Herman Lotze, "that movements proceed
from our will; they take place as the expression of passionate excitement in our features and in all parts of our
bodies, frequently without, nay, against volition; they
take place in forms whose meaning or use for the expression or relief of this mental excitement we do not understand; we weep and laugh without knowing why the one
should necessarily be an expression of joy, the other of
grief; the fluctuation of our emotion is betrayed in a
thousand variations of our breathing, and we can not
explain either by what means or to what end these corpo-
real agitations associate themselves with those which we
feel within.   Evidently in this way many psychic states,
not only voluntary resolutions but also non-voluntary feelings and ideas have been made by the all-embracing course
of Nature determining starting-points — starting-points
which the soul, at least in part, spontaneously evolves
from its own inner being, but which, after they have been
evolved, call forth their correspondent movements with
the blind certainty of mechanism, without our ordering
and guiding co-operation, nay, without our knowledge
of the possibility of such a process.   The soul is not
directly cognizant of the means of motion — muscles and
nerves — nor of the manner in which they may be
made use of — the nature of the propelling force to be
communicated to the nerves or the contractility of the

muscles. It can do nothing more than bring about certain states in itself, in the expectation that the connection of the organism will attach to these the initiation of a particular movement. The process by which all voluntary movements are executed is concealed from consciousness; the image of the new position to be affected, and the remembrance of the peculiar modifications of our general sense by which on former occasions its execution was accompanied, are the sole two points appearing in consciousness, to which the carrying out of the movement itself is subsequently attached by means of an unconscious and automatically-working mechanism." ·

Again, such a view overlooks the number and complexity of the elements of expression. The twinkling of the eye, the subtle motions of the face, the positions of the body, the modulations of the textures of the muscles, the motions and attitudes of the hand, the positions of the body, the color, the modulations and the inflections of the voice, and a hundred unnamable actions, all spring spontaneously from the diffusion over the body of emotional activity springing from the depths of the soul. But they can never be produced by deliberative, conscious action of will in all the plenitude of nature. To endeavor to do so has always made them artificial and unnatural, and the expression mechanical.

Such a view also overlooks the nature of emotion. It is always spontaneous. Kant first distinguished the nature of emotion from cognition; but the misconceptions of the nature of spontaneity in expression show a failure still to recognize some of the most essential elements or processes of the human soul.

Again, some of the worst faults in delivery cannot be corrected directly. They must be corrected indirectly. As a physician does not lecture his patient upon his disease, but gives medicine according to careful diagnoses, so a teacher thoroughly penetrating to the underlying needs of the man, by correcting these may remove a hundred little external imperfections. When the sense of balance is developed in the human body, when the breathing is rendered normal, a vast number of imperfections disappear without having been brought to the consciousness of the student. Endeavors to correct faults entirely by the deliberate and conscious method cause students to be artificial. We are most conscious of that which is external, so the attention of the mind by such a method will be concentrated upon the outside, upon external and accidental actions.

The view that expression must be improved by bringing all powers and agents into consciousness and under direct control, overlooks the nature of consciousness. Consciousness may be compared to the eye. The most powerful eye in the world can see but little without being focalized, and the field of perfect vision is extremely narrow. If one tree of the forest is seen definitely by the human eye, the other trees of the forest are placed in a dim background. Man can draw still nearer and bring one limb definitely into the focus of his mind, but the forest is lost and the tree is but dimly perceived. On the other hand the man can withdraw himself to a distance and can look at the whole forest, and can go still further away and the whole mountain upon which the forest stands is perceived, but the greater the extension the less vivid the perception. The same is true of the human consciousness, which is in direct correspondence with the human eye. When all consciousness is focalized upon one idea, it tends to become what Leibnitz calls clear, distinct and adequate; but if the mind endeavors to extend itself over a great number of things at once, ideas become obscure, indistinct or inadequate. It is a law of logic that as extension increases intension diminishes. Accordingly, to extend the human consciousness to every action of the feet, the torso, the mouth, the eye, the head, the arm and hand, the inflections and modulations of the voice, will destroy the power of the mind to concentrate itself adequately upon any thing. The normal center of consciousness must be upon the ideas as they pass through the mind. All else should be a background to this. To endeavor to bring all the acts of expression equally into consciousness and under direct control of will would confuse the mind, make the ideas vague and indefinite and render all delivery superficial and mechanical. Besides, so infinitely complex is the whole product of expression, the languages are so numerous, and belong to such diverse agents, that it is not possible for them to be used consciously or voluntarily. The few that have tried have become superficial. A few points have been exaggerated more than others, and all has become one-sided and affected. The auditors have felt a lack of depth in the artist's soul. They have seen through the artificiality of the art as clearly as Scrooge looked through the ghost of Morley and saw the two buttons on the back of his coat.

But let us look carefully at the difference between human expression that is mechanical and that which is spontaneous. As a man speaks to his fellow-men he has two classes of ideas. First, the successive ideas in the story he is telling, or the argument he is making; second, ideas as to the manner in which he is to express these. Each of these classes may give rise to expression, but the mode by which each class causes modulations of the voice and body is different. One is deliberative, the other spontaneous. In one case expression will always be mechanical, one-sided. In the other case the ideas and pictures of the story itself coming before the mind give vivid conceptions of situations stimulating the imagination and emotions, and arousing the spontaneous impulses of the man. In this case, he does not act from determination alone, but from the stimulation of the deepest impulses of his nature, impulses which are deeper than consciousness, deeper than will. The will is still present, but it is blended with intellectual and emotional actions in absolute unity. The man is conscious of what he is doing, but the conscious volition simply directs, restrains and guides, holds each idea till it has more effectively accomplished its work upon the man's own nature, and restrains the impulses until they diffuse themselves through the whole organism. It serves to change the action of the mind from one idea to another and to hold it there. Consciousness and will act at the initiation and at the climax, but between the great spontaneous impulses of the soul are aroused and dominant. Only ideas of things can awaken emotion, ideas of how to do things, mere knowledge of modes of expression, however important, can never furnish a substitute for sincere earnestness or genuine realization of truth. The one causes expression by awakening motives, the other by mere mechanical determination and resolution.

When expression is the normal response to the promptings of an idea or situation grasped by the mind, then the will merely acts toward the other powers of the soul as an engineer does toward his engine. He starts or stops the action, and regulates its speed and its force, but the power comes from the steam and not from the arm of the engineer. So the will is ever present. It holds the mind upon the idea, it retains the impulses which otherwise would fly off too quickly and nervously, until they diffuse themselves through the whole man. Certain great salient modes of execution are adopted, others are restrained and regulated, but no impulse to expression is supplied by will. It never steps down and usurps the place of thought, imagination or emotion, any more than the engineer endeavors to start the locomotive by the strength of his own arm. The impulse to expression must be deeper than will, must furnish a motive to will or all the results will be limited and superficial. Great power in expression is dependent upon power in thought and power of passion. Nothing makes so bad an effect or is felt so quickly as the mere assumption of the appearance of emotion or the mere resolution to be earnest. Earnestness must ever be the spontaneous result of thought and emotion. By long and patient work a man may make mechanical action very like spontaneous action; but it will never accomplish the complete results normally inspired by nature herself. Such a method always omits the more subtle forms of expression. The color of the voice, the expression of the eyes and face can not be brought into the field of consciousness. When it is attempted, the subtle, spontaneous actions are made artificial and mechanical. As we look upon a man stirred by great ideas which are so vivid as to stimulate and co-ordinate the experiences of the soul, the eyes twinkle and flash, the face glows, the very textures of the muscles of the man are modulated so that the voice vibrates with emotion in ways that physiology and the science of sound have never been able to fathom. The whole man is expanded and exalted; and from the crown of his head to the soles of his feet every part of the body is speaking.

We can thus see that the true action of consciousness must neither mean its obliteration nor undue extension, but its proper centralization. The fundamental center or focus for consciousness in normal delivery must ever be upon the successive ideas, the imaginative situation must ever be in the foreground; but this does not forbid in the normal action of the human mind the subordinate consciousness which recognizes the effect of emotion upon the voice and body, the whole relationship of the speaker to his audience. He abandons himself not to mere nervous impulses, but to the impulses that come from the life of his soul, too deep for his own consciousness to fathom. He forgets himself, only in the sense that he gives himself up to a great idea of which he is definitely and completely conscious. He leaves the great fountain-head of feeling free to pour forth its flood into his voice and body. He becomes, so to speak, two beings —becomes a great channel of thought and emotion, great impulses come to him and are given to him, the very ideas themselves that rise so vividly come out of the dim unknown, although his consciousness holds them and dominates them and lets them pass away as others rise, while the voice and body, though restrained and directed in part, are ever kept in the background of consciousness and never displace the fundamental focus of the mind upon one great central idea or situation. It is the vividness of the central idea that stimulates the conscious actions, colors the voice, illuminates the face, dominates the whole body, and brings that unity, freedom, variety and spontaneity which are the universal characteristics of nature.

All this is seen still more definitely when we come to study the faults which are related to consciousness. What is meant by self-consciousness? It is simply the displacement of consciousness. Consciousness is wrongly centered. The man is thinking about his audience, about his own inflections, about the modulations of his own voice, the action of his own body. Consciousness is primarily fixed upon the modes of expression rather than upon the successive ideas.

What are some of the causes of this fault? There are two leading causes which are entirely different from each other. In the one case self-consciousness rises from embarrassment. The speaker may be conscious of great power, and the importance of his thought, but from the fact that he feels that his mode of expression is inadequate his consciousness becomes confused. He is conscious of the impulses of his nature, he is really and genuinely in earnest, but he feels that there is not a co-ordination of the impulses. The channels are not open. He can not unite the spontaneous impulses in his nature to the deliberative elements. Hence, he begins to think of his body, the imperfections of his voice, and the inadequate modes of expressing his ideas. The other form of self-consciousness, though seemingly in direct opposition, is very similar. The man who holds the mechanical view of delivery having prepared every movement, being conscious that he has a very graceful body and a very beautiful voice, rises to speak. The audience feels that his consciousness is upon himself, as in the other case the consciousness is upon the voice and body. Though he is perfectly at ease and unembarrassed, yet a sense of inadequacy, a sense of superficiality, is felt by the audience. The man has self-consciousness in a worse form than the other. The first by practice, by looking his audience in the face may rise above his doubt, may in some way secure co-ordination of the impulses, and may come to know the use of his organs and agents, and his awkwardness and stiffness may wear away. The more faithful the practice, the more this is apt to be the case, though there is danger of bad habits being formed, from the lack of true control.

In the other case, the more practice the greater is the tendency to develop self-consciousness. The point of view of the mind is wrong, the method of expression vicious; it is only remedied when greater earnestness of purpose or power of conception lays hold of him, and he forgets the machinery of his art.

The true remedy for chaotic consciousness is the proper centralization of consciousness upon the ideas. There is not so much in either case too great consciousness as there is consciousness of self rather than of thought and purpose. A noble unconsciousness of self in art as in life demands that it be fixed upon ideas rather than upon effects of ideas, upon the aim and purpose, upon that which is to be done for others, while the manner of doing it, the modes of execution and the impulse, must in part, at least, be spontaneous.

Thus while education may extend consciousness, it also develops the specific field in which ideas can be focused, and where they can be more vividly realized. This great true center of consciousness was fixed by nature, and can never be displaced by art. Consciousness must be deepened, as well as extended. In the development of delivery, everything must be genuine as in nature. There must ever be present both the conscious and unconscious elements. Education develops nature's processes, stimulates her impulses and brings them into stronger unity and co-ordination.

The most rapid driver upon the road, when seemingly letting out his steed most freely, is most alive. He takes a firmer grasp of the rein, is more on the lookout to guide the horse correctly than when he is passing along in a simple walk. So in expression, powerful passion intensifies impulses, but also makes consciousness and volition as well as emotion more alive, and all are co-ordinated into greater unity. The driver does not leap down and push his vehicle, the impulse comes from the animal, but the reason is also active to guide and direct. By skillful use of the processes of education, by the great law of co-ordination in the relation of the conscious to the unconscious, with a thorough understanding of the proper center, even unconscious impulses may be corrected and made normal without making them directly conscious or voluntary. Education is the process of stimulating and developing all the normal processes of the soul and bringing them into greater unity and harmony. This must be done, or expression can never be developed.

That something more than mere mechanical expertness is required, is indicated by the universal instinct of the race, which regards the highest and best expression as full of life, and the worst expression as lifeless. The most common characteristic of life is hidden and mystic. The leaves upon a tree express the life, but without inner plenitude of life diffused through the whole organism, the leaves would be dead. So that what is really meant by living expression is that the emotion must come from within, that the center of the being shall be roused and the forces and emotional activities diffused into every part, just as the life is diffused in a tree or in an animal. When expression is mechanical, the voice can be made louder, there can be greater rapidity, there can be greater enlargement, but these are not life. All such modifications can be performed by a machine. Life is ever spontaneous. No mechanical force, no amount of will, no amount of consciousness, no mere deliberative employment of means to an end, can furnish a substitute for spontaneous diffusion of energy through the whole man. True life is not manifested by loudness or by mechanical exaggeration, nor by one-sided exaggeration of one form of expression, but by the diffusion of emotion into every part of the body or the co-ordinate union of all the psychological impulses, and their manifestation by the most subtle and co-ordinate actions of every part of the body.

Again, artists have ever recognized that all knowledge must be translated into instinct. Every form of information must be so assimilated, and so transformed by the personality of the man, that it is lost in his intuitions. "All knowledge," George Innis said, "must be merely the soil in which instinct is to grow." All great art seems to be inevitable, not only in relation to its parts, which must seem to be incapable of being changed, but it must seem to be an inevitable product of the spontaneous impulses of a great soul. We have abundant proof that the spontaneous element in all delivery and in every phase of histrionic art is a most important one. From time immemorial, the race has used the term "artistic instinct." The great poet, the great painter, the great sculptor has ever felt that something was given to him, something done for him, that his deliberation and skill in execution were merely a carrying out of these fundamental impulses, merely obeying their orders. No orator or artist has failed to feel this in some sense. From Homer to Tennyson, the poet has called upon his muse. The muse in every art is simply the recognition in another way of this same fact, that man, like nature, has mystic impulses in his soul; that he has "unconscious reason." What is done seems to come out of the unconscious, the involuntary part of the man, which is only directed and regulated by volition. The ideal and the forces to carry it out are given to the artist, and he is not a mere mechanical performer.

There are, then, ordinarily considered to be two views of spontaneity. The first regards it as merely animal and in man synonymous with wild impulsiveness, the result of undirected force. The second regards it as synonymous with dexterity or mechanical agility, attained simply by the acquirement of mechanical skill.

Neither of these views can be regarded as true artistic spontaneity. They both imply that spontaneity is a characteristic of some one phase of the man. But nature is never one-sided. A kitten is spontaneous not because it is wild, but because an exuberance of life comes from the center of the animal and dominates its whole body. As we study nature we find that the most complex being has the greatest unity; and if so, the complex impulses of such a being must also have greater unity than the impulses of a cruder animal. Everywhere in nature we find an animal of a low order without great co-ordination and unity of all parts; but when we pass higher in the scale of nature and come to man we find that all parts have more direct specific functions to perform, and more intimate relation with the center. There is every where a greater localization of function and extension in opposition. But this is in proportion to the establishment of a mystic center and to the domination of this center over the parts differentiated from each other. If this is true, then the highest form of spontaneity should be characteristic of the highest form of life.

Spontaneity must be regarded as a co-ordination of all the impulses and forces of human nature into one. Thus only will all the difficulties of the problem be met. All investigations have shown that the whole man must be concerned in expression; and hence, that the unconscious as well as the conscious, the involuntary as well as the voluntary powers of the man, must act in expression. When this is the fact, spontaneity always results This natural spontaneity is found in children who have not

been perverted.   When it is made the object of education
and by careful training is made perfect, the conscious
direction of means to an end being co-ordinated with the
unconscious and involuntary processes in exact accordance
with nature's intention, then and then only have we
artistic spontaneity.   As growth in nature requires development in all directions, so true harmonious development
of the human being requires all the faculties and powers
to be developed according to their own specific nature,
and all to be brought into a more perfect union ; the
faculties meant to be conscious so to act, and the will so
to move the parts of the body which are meant by nature
to be under volitionary control, that by a mysterious
co-ordination the unconscious and involuntary powers and
agents are also brought into action.   Any endeavor to
make an agent or action voluntary, which was never
intended to be so, is to violate nature and to make men
artificial and mechanical.

True spontaneity, therefore, does not mean an absence
of deliberation, but the simultaneous action of the deliberative, the conscious and the spontaneous elements in
their own proper sphere, and a co-ordinate union of them
in any great impulse.   It is a co-ordination of the deliberative with the unconscious that is the glory of human
expression.   It is the foundation of all eloquence and all
poetry.   In all the provinces of art it is this which is the
poetic and real artistic element.   Every artist must have
a long, deliberative, conscious struggle to secure truthful
execution, but if this struggle does not rise above technique and secure and develop the unconscious impulses of
the soul, the man can never become an artist.   The
mechanical work is absolutely necessary, but the mechanical work alone is not sufficient, nor on the other hand,
will the impulses and instincts, however strong and power-

ful, of themselves accomplish the result. There must be a union and co-ordination of the two, just as in nature in the lifting of the arm, there is a co-ordination of the conscious and the unconscious elements.

This further complexity of the human being also shows a correspondence with the fundamental languages of man. As verbal expression is more representative and objective it is more a matter of conscious choice, while vocal and pantomimic expression are more manifestive or presentative, and are therefore more expressive of the spontaneous subjective impulses of the soul.

The neglect of a study of spontaneity in expression is very curious. The cause is no doubt found in the fact that there has been so little study of emotion in psychology. Feeling is mystic; and no satisfactory explanation has yet been given of the elements or even the classification of emotions. The distinction between the action of the soul in feeling and in knowing was not made until Kant. But emotion is still not understood. Many define feeling in such a way as to show that it is confounded with thought. One psychologist says that a study of feeling is difficult, because when the mind turns to analyze it, the spontaneity of feeling is destroyed. Still another reason in respect to delivery is that when a man analyzes his delivery he only observes the conscious elements, and the unconscious spontaneous actions are overlooked. Thus the subject is extremely difficult. But it is the most essential element in improving delivery.

To summarize the conclusions at which we have arrived: Expression must ever be spontaneous — spontaneous as the plant or the bird. But spontaneity in nature not only means from within out, but in all directions; it means the union of the powers and forces of the organism. If a kitten has one leg all tied up and bandaged, or its tail wired out in a straight line or to a specific curve, its movements are not spontaneous.   Hence, spontaneity in expression demands that the whole nature of the man shall act — his intellect, his imagination, his emotional nature, his will.   Voluntary and involuntary, conscious and unconscious elements, must combine in such unity that the man himself can hardly separate them by analysis.   Whatever tends to make expression come from merely one power of his nature, from the emotions alone, or merely from the intellect alone, from mere conscious deliberation without allowing anything to be unconscious or involuntary, is a most fundamental violation of nature.

Nature is never one-sided, is never mechanical, never has a hobby.   She never accomplishes her results by a narrow mechanical system ; her methods are broad and deep and every element plays a part in every result, *in each is all.*   She has no tricks which may unlock in a moment all the secrets of her phenomena.   The development of expression is, thus, as deep and as broad. as universal nature.   Nature when rightly understood furnishes the fundamental laws which must be obeyed, or delivery can not be developed.

XI.

DEVELOPMENT OF EXPRESSION.

Imperfection means perfection hid,
Reserved in part to grace the after time.

— *Browning.*

CAN anything that is spontaneous be developed? Is not education entirely confined to that which is conscious and deliberative? We find an animal does not become any more spontaneous as the result of taming or training. Wild animals in the depths of the forest gambol and play with the same spontaneity that is shown by the kitten or the dog. The squirrel leaps from branch to branch with all the ease, grace and spontaneity that it has after it has been trained to eat from the hand of man, or perch upon his shoulder. The rose grows under culture by the same law as its crude ancestor. A more delicate and possibly a more varied result is produced, but nature's process is exactly the same. All education is necessarily limited. The central pitch of the voice can not be changed by training without injury. All education must act in accord with nature's principles; but cannot violate or change them with impunity.

To those that hold that spontaneous actions are simply the result of reflex actions of the nervous system, and are dependent upon health and vital conditions, and so can only be improved by securing greater vitality, and are not directly capable of education; to those who contend that all man's movements must be made deliberative by education, and that the absence of spontaneity shows man's chief superiority over the animal; to all such persons, the development of man's powers of expression is a very simple problem. It simply means bringing into conscious control all the modulations of the body or voice that are expressive, so as to enable the speaker to use them by direct choice. On the other hand to those who believe that delivery of all kinds is a mysterious co-ordination of mind and body, of the spontaneous and the deliberative, of conscious and unconscious elements, the problem is far more complex and difficult. To such persons this long discussion of the processes of nature will not seem out of place.

Many years ago I was staggered by a question from one whom I consider to be the leading clergyman of this country, and who has inspired me with more courage and enthusiasm in some directions than any one else in the world. He suddenly asked me, "Can you teach Elocution?" and probably noticing my embarrassment, he added, "Can any one teach Elocution?" I know not whether my answer was adequate or satisfactory, I cannot remember now what I said, but the great, earnest face looked more kindly, and the voice spoke more gently to the youthful enthusiast as the subject was changed. Through all these years I have struggled with that problem, and in fact, this work is an endeavor to answer his second question.

Such a question hints at the doubt which exists in the minds of many of our best thinkers as to whether or not delivery can ever be a subject of education. There is unfortunately no philosophic or well-defined statement of the doubt; but after pondering the subject for many years, and trying to weigh the causes of such doubt, I think that it must be touched, at any rate, by this discussion. It seems to me that the doubt arises from the fact that such speakers feel that somehow the spontaneous element must ever be the chief one in all true oratory, and knowing that the ordinary methods of elocution neglect this fact, they have thus been led to condemn all elocutionary training and to believe that the highest oratory must simply result from nature, that it may be slightly improved from growth in other departments of knowledge, and from practice, but can not be directly developed. But whether this objection has ever been made or not, it will be admitted at the beginning that unless methods for the development of expression stimulate and aid the spontaneous element in delivery they will fail to accomplish any results really beneficial. Thus the aim here is to accept the highest and most extreme objection to all work upon delivery and to endeavor to go to the depths of the problem and show that such objection is rather against the mechanical methods of meeting the needs than against the need itself. If any such doubter has followed the steps unfolded, he must feel that not only can every phase of delivery be developed, but that the principle involved in such development lies at the foundation of all the most advanced methods of education.

The subject is not a new one, nor is it confined to oratoric and dramatic delivery. It is a question which concerns all human art and all human education. There is ever a tendency on the part of man to become conventional, a mere machine on the one hand or, on the other to become a mere wild creature of impulse. It was the discussion of this problem in Rousseau's "Emile" that started the investigations out of which have arisen all the advanced methods of education in modern times. The education of Rousseau's age consisted in every form of mechanical and external manipulation. Man must be completely transformed and moulded from the outside. For nearly a thousand years a degraded view of humanity had been almost universal. Man must be made better by killing out the impulses of his nature. They were at variance with the intentions of his Creator, and must be completely transformed by education. Rousseau contended that nature was always right; that man must grow as the tree grows, and that in all true education the impulses must have sway. He contended that all education of his day transformed and perverted nature, hence that all human beliefs and all human conceptions were warped; to reform this everything must return to the instinct of the race and to the free light and atmosphere of nature to grow according to the fundamental impulses from within.

Here we have two extremes, extremes which come out in all art and which we see especially manifested in man's views of the methods of developing delivery. Rousseau went too far in making man merely an outgrowth of impulse. His views were reactions against the current methods which had gone too far in making everything mechanical. And in elocution, and especially in oratory, it is in the co-ordination of art and nature that we have the highest results. The true advanced education does not merely educate the understanding, but awakens the impulses from within.

There is no doubt, however, that the tendency of the majority of humanity is not in the direction of Rousseau, but is in the direction of the conventional regulation. There is a greater tendency to lose faith in the fundamental instincts and impulses, even in the present age, than there is to become too spontaneous or too impulsive. The greatest and most difficult problem in education has been "to bring such objects before the mind of the child as will stimulate the faculties to spontaneous activity." There is ever a tendency to pass more or less to the mechanical. So that all reformers have struggled for the return to nature and the development of nature's impulses and instincts. The co-ordination of the deliberative and the spontaneous has been the work of all reformers in education. Education that proceeds by aggregating or cramming into the man ideas and information is of little worth. Above all, the artist by his education must come into a thorough possession of his knowledge and of his own being. He must not only know how to do better, but the impulse to nobler action must be strengthened and developed. The artist, the orator, must not only secure skill in execution, but must have deeper, stronger and more accurate impulses. So in delivery, that which fundamentally makes the orator, must be the spontaneous life in his whole nature and the co-ordination of this with knowledge of what he can do.

Returning now to the simplest and most direct study of the problem, we find that expression is a product of nature. Every product implies *cause, means* and *effect.* Expression is the effect of rational and emotional activity. It is the effect of the possession of an idea by the mind, or of the mind being possessed or dominated by an idea or passion. Thus we see at once that the *cause* of expression is psychic.

The *means* in expression are physical. The thought and the emotion depend for revelation upon the body and voice of the man. The emotion is directly known only to the subjective consciousness of the man who feels it. It is made known to other men entirely through the medium of expression, or from the effects of feeling upon the actions, positions and texture of the body or the tones and inflections of the voice.

It is regarded as a truism that effect requires both adequate cause and proper means. Without a co-ordination of both of these no effect can follow, so that we can see at once that weakness of effect must be due to inadequacy of cause or to inflexibility or wrong use of the means. Hence, primarily the power of expression must be dependent upon the strength of the cause which is directly due to the intensity of the impression or strength of the passion, that is to say, upon the faculties of the soul; and, secondarily, upon the plasticity and responsiveness of the body and voice as the agents of manifestation. Not only must the faculties be brought into action, and the voice and body be properly adjusted to their work, but there must also be skill in their use.

And since man is a creative being, able consciously to achieve results, there must be a proper conception of the *effect* that is to be produced, and the special means that can be best adopted and will be most adequate to the accomplishment of that effect. In short, there must be an impulse, a responsive body, that will manifest every phase of that impulse, and the conscious and deliberate intelligence more or less separated or "estranged" from the rest of the mind so as to watch the impulse, to direct the out-flowing energy, that everything may be co-ordinated and brought into unity before the mind of the auditor. And this artistic intelligence must be such as not to interfere with the spontaneity of the cause, or the perfect responsiveness of the mechanism.

Thus, to develop the power of expression, these several elements must be educated. If expression can be educated at all, it must in the nature of the case be improved first, by the development of the proper mental action in reading and speaking. Not only must the strength of the creative faculties and those directly concerned in reading and speaking be developed, but greater responsiveness of the sensibilities to the idea, the co-ordination of all the faculties and powers of the soul, and the balance of thought and emotion by will must be secured. So that the whole mind shall act in all its phases, in all its aspects, in unity for the accomplishment of one result. In short, there must be developed unity and harmony in the actions of all the faculties of human nature. Not only must the power of clear thinking be trained, but the power of reproducing and complementing ideas with proper experience.

In the second place, there must be a development or training of the body and the voice. There must be a mental adjustment of all parts of the body according to the intention of nature for the development of the whole and of each part in particular, so as to secure a condition most responsive to the activities of the being.

The voice especially needs training, the whole vocal organism must be developed and brought into conditions most favorable to modulation by the various emotions and states of the man. Every part of this mechanism must be studied and developed according to the intention of nature, and all parts brought into co-ordination with each other and into co-ordination with the action of man's soul.

Plasticity of body and elasticity of voice are found in nature to be co-essential to all expression. Unless body and voice are attuned to their office, they may serve as the prison-house to conceal or fetter the real feelings and spirit of the man, instead of serving as nature's intended means for manifestation. However strong may be the cause, or the fundamental spontaneous impulse, unless the channels of expression are open the results can not follow.

In the third place, there must be a knowledge of the proper technical mode of accomplishing every result, and training to secure skill in execution. Man has many languages by which to convey his thoughts and feelings: these must co-operate, as has been shown, to produce the strongest and most truthful impression upon the minds of his hearers. One soul must adapt the truth and all its impressions to another, so that the universal laws of art must be understood and the best method of accomplishing results must be consciously or unconsciously evolved. The language of weakness must be distinguished from the language of strength, for things natural to a weak man may not be natural to a strong one. There must be a study not only of what actually is, but of what should be. Not only a study of what is habitually natural but of what is ideally natural, what is nature's normal tendency rather than the human perversion. Every art must have a technique.

Not only must the mental action be first, but out of a study of the mental action must come even the proper training of voice and all technique. Take the technique of vocal expression, for instance the elements of melody: these are directly manifestive of the sequence of the mind from idea to idea. Mere mechanical work upon this technique, independent of a study of the causes of proper melody, will not accomplish the end. So that technique in vocal expression must always be directly studied in connection with the action of the mind.

Not only must we have these different forms of training, we must see also the order of application, or at least the order of importance. Nature always proceeds from cause to effect, so that the very first attention must be given in expression to the action of the mind. The faculties and powers individually concerned in taking and giving truth must be so trained as to perfectly discharge individual functions and be brought into harmonious co-operation with each other in the act of expression.

Next must follow the training of the body and the voice, for upon these the first impulse of feeling has immediate effect.   The agitation of the breathing and the body are the very first effects of emotion.   So, that it is first necessary to have a cause, and second to have control of the means.

The third step in training must be a study of the general principles of art, and a knowledge of the best modes of execution ; the development and perfect skill in the use of the technical means for the accomplishment of the end.

Returning now to the difficulty with which we started, is there here no foundation for a solution of the problem ? If expression implies cause, means and effect, and if we can, as has been shown, stimulate the cause, and secure control of the means, do we not in this way help the spontaneous, unconscious and involuntary elements of delivery ?   Instead of such training making men narrow, it will make them broader.   Instead of making them mechanical, it will remove artificiality and even affectation.   Instead of making men imitate somebody else, it will remove even unconscious imitation.   Instead of developing self-consciousness it will remove self-consciousness and make the man free ; because self-consciousness is nearly always the result of some obstruction in the use of the mechanism, some misuse of the organism, or some endeavor to consciously use what was intended in nature to act unconsciously.   In such training as this, the channels of expression are opened ; all constriction and hindrance removed.   The fundamental cause is stimulated, so that there is developed a concentration of consciousness rather than a confusion of consciousness. Consciousness is not made chaotic by being extended over a vast number of conflicting agents into realms where it was never meant to be found, but is centered on the fundamental thought which lies as the cause of the stimulation of emotion and all expression. In this way the man is developed along all the lines of nature's inten- tion, and what was intended in nature to be spontaneous remains spontaneous, even becomes more spontaneous. What was intended by nature to be deliberative is made deliberative, and is brought under immediate control of the will; the volition of the man is strengthened and developed.

This is a very important point, because man can only be trained along the line of nature's intention. We can not in any form of education oppose nature. And the artificial methods of developing delivery by imitation, or by the mechanical or analytic process, so called, act in direct violation of nature's intention by making that which is intended to be spontaneous, deliberative.

But we meet here another objector, the mechanical elocutionist. Why, says he, is it necessary to do all this? As expression is merely an effect, why not simply study how to produce this effect? There are many who think that this is the whole problem of delivery. They say the training of the mind belongs somewhere else and has nothing to do with the work of expression. They agree that the more the mind is trained, the better it may be for expression, but say that expression itself has nothing to do directly with mental activity, or rather that there is no special training of the mind belonging to the distinctive work of developing expression. Much of our elocutionary work proceeds upon this basis. The study is merely a study of effect. Recently there began to be a feeling that the voice and body ought to be developed for the purposes of expression, but up to the present time, as far as I know, there has been no special emphasis of the fact that there is a peculiar and special training of the mind necessary to develop power in expression, no matter what its previous training may have been; that expression is essentially a mental action, and depends primarily upon the proper action of the mind.

The fundamental reason for all these various kinds of training is to reach the spontaneous element in expression. Working upon effect alone is like a physician working upon the symptoms of disease without going to its cause. The most thorough training for expression will often be careless at first as to certain external faults, as the great physician does not directly attend to the headache which is caused by some derangement in the vital organs of the man.

These methods followed faithfully, not merely one side of the mind will be trained, but all faculties will be developed and co-ordinated; especially the unconscious or spontaneous powers and the unconscious actions upon which true delivery most depends, will be properly developed by a proper co-ordination with the powers which are fundamentally and necessarily conscious.

If the views here unfolded are true, delivery must be improved by improving the action of the faculties specially concerned, by securing a greater unity of action in the whole nature of the man; by securing a more perfect control of voice and body as the organism of expression; and skill in execution as well as a higher ideal and conception of the nature and mission of the art, and the legitimate and illegitimate, the right and the wrong, the strong and the weak, in modes of rendering.

Let us enter into a more specific study of these different forms of training, and show that they are all mutually necessary for adequate or effective development of any form of human expression, and that by a proper union of them every demand of the problem can be met.

XII.

DEVELOPMENT OF MENTAL ACTION.

It is the mind that makes the body rich.
—Shakespeare.

In the study of nature we have found not only the kinds of work needed and the steps to be taken, but also the order in which each form of training should receive attention. While nature grows in all directions simultaneously, yet we have first the seed, next the blade and then the full corn. Nature never endeavors to produce an effect without cause. The natural course, therefore, demands that attention must first of all be given to the cause in expression. But here we meet another objector. Delivery, he says, is only a physical thing. The whole process is a mechanical one. Elocution is only an effect; simply find the right rule for accomplishing the effects, that is the whole secret. If a man has a good mind it is better, of course, but delivery has nothing to do with mental action, it is only the technical part. Such objections are so commonly held that such a departure from ordinary views as is here advanced must be in a measure justified.

The first argument for attention to the mind in the training for delivery is the nature of expression. If the problem has been correctly unfolded in the preceding pages then attention to the action of the mind is absolutely necessary. Every fact unfolded regarding the nature of expression is a most effective argument for the need of mental training in the development of delivery. For example, expression is a manifestation of the soul, the body is only an instrument. The great failures in expression are due to the separation of physical actions from the mind that uses them. The kinds of expression correspond to the elemental powers of the soul. So intimate is the relation of the soul to expression, that in the most objective and mechanical forms the character of the soul reveals itself. The fact that the most eminent artists believe in genuine emotion and mental action is a direct proof, and the fact that most of these have lost faith in mechanical elocution is an indirect proof that attention must be given primarily to the action of the mind. Expression has been found to consist of a representative element which is intellectual, and a manifestive element which is more emotional; hence, the proper co-ordination of these can only be developed by studying the causes of these in the soul. The changes in expression from age to age have kept pace with changes in the subjective spirit, and as expression has improved it has always become a more perfect mirror of subjective conditions, and more intimately connected with mental actions.

As we turn to study the processes of expression in nature, we have found that they are always from within out, that all parts co-operate about a center, and that human expression comes from the whole man, that naturalness requires expression to come from all the powers of the soul acting in their unity.

All these facts plainly prove that any adequate development of expression demands special attention to the action of the mind, as the cause of the impulse for expression.

Again, it has been found that many of the actions in delivery are unconscious and involuntary. When the delivery is mechanical and artificial the more important unconscious elements are always absent, but if the mind acts properly, if there is a succession of ideas, if the expression is merely thinking aloud and is not a deliberative conscious·execution of external directions according to rules, these involuntary actions are present as nature intended. Expression in the one case is deliberative, every action is the result of choice, and only the salient and external characteristics or signs of emotion are given. But where the man loses himself in his subject, where his whole soul is absorbed in his thought, each idea rouses all the faculties of his nature and all the subtle and unconscious elements of expression. Here we have naturalness. All the languages are co-ordinated according to the rich plenitude of nature. Therefore it can be seen at once that by securing proper action of the mind these subtle elements which make the genuineness of all expression are developed. If this is true, study of the mental action in the development of delivery can not be omitted with impunity.

One of the most important arguments for attention to the mind in delivery, is that all the faults of expression can be traced, directly or indirectly, to a psychic source. Just as a good physician is known by his skill to trace diseases to their fundamental causes, and his ability to eradicate those causes, so the development of effective and natural delivery is absolutely dependent upon insight into the causes of faults, and skill in the application of training for their removal. Yet nowhere do we find so many temptations to deal with mere temporary expedients, or to treat mere external symptoms. Such a method also violates all the fundamental laws of education, and makes the man artificial and constricted. Temporary improvement sometimes may be seen, yet such a course will in the end be ineffective, and result in making the man more conscious of his faults, and hence, more constricted and nervous. Above all, the action of the mind instead of being improved and strengthened, will be weakened and unbalanced because the consciousness has been misplaced and confused rather than focused as nature intended.

Let us examine, then, a few of the faults which can be traced to mental causes. For the first example, note the hard qualities of the voice so common in our day. Nine-tenths of the time persons whose voices are habitually hard and cold, have very little imaginative or pictorial action of the mind at the time of speaking. There may be thought, but it is a mere outline, or abstract form ; no series of images rises in the soul. At any rate, there is no response to such images, as all feeling and emotional response to such ideas are repressed and kept entirely separate from the thought. There is no co-ordination between thought and emotion, hence feeling, whose natural language is color, has no effect upon the voice. The result, therefore, naturally follows. This fault is very common among the teachers of our public schools. They deal continually with ideas, independent of emotion. Many of them teach in large rooms, and have to strain their voices to make themselves heard. They are continually endeavoring to convey ideas to dull minds and hence are tempted to sharpen and harden the voice to drive the ideas home. Besides, teachers are apt to forget that "truth is within ourselves, and takes no rise from outward things," but must simply be stimulated or evoked from within. They are continually tempted to deal with mere facts, and thus to separate the emotional elements from thought. This naturally, if not necessarily, tends to make the voice cold and hard. As a further proof of this, those teachers who love their work, who teach with imagination and feeling ever active, who patiently and quietly endeavor to stimulate from within the children's souls, rather than to drive information into their heads from without, are more frequently free from this fault. Nature ever tends to tell the truth, and the teacher who is mechanical and cold, must expect the story to be told in the quality of his tones. If there is no color in the mind, how can there be color in the tones of the voice?

Sometimes this fault is considered to be merely a matter of pitch. One of the greatest educators in this country once said to me, "If you could only get our public school teachers to speak upon a lower pitch, it would be the greatest blessing to the children of our public schools." Though this is occasionally true, most frequently a lack of color or resonance in the voice, is mistaken for a high pitch. If one who has control over the voice makes a resonant, open tone, and then in contrast a narrow, constricted, hard tone, upon the same pitch, an uneducated ear always thinks that the pitch has been changed, and will not be convinced till the illustration is repeated with an instrument. Then the error can easily be perceived. It is only a thoroughly practiced ear that can at once detect the difference without such aid.

Again, college students frequently have this fault. With them it is usually due to the fact that they are continually reciting, translating Greek and Latin, or demonstrating problems in mathematics. Nearly all their work consists in conveying thought and mere facts independent of emotion. Feeling in the ordinary class-room is usually considered out of place. Here again, cold, hard tones are a natural result.

Observe the contrast between the voices of the children during recitation, and their voices when at play; between the qualities of their tones in answering questions in the school-room, and in conversation with their playmates on the street or at home: in the one case the voice is often positively painful, in the other it is very pleasant. The cause is simply the fact that, in the one case the faculties of the mind are spontaneous, in the other, deliberative; in the one case there is imagination and feeling, in the other a perfunctory performance and mere conveying of thought. In the one case, there is co-ordination of thought and emotion, a union of all the faculties of the mind, in the other merely the faculties of understanding, or worse still, merely the memory is active. The voice in both instances is simply the mirror of the intellectual processes. In all such cases, there can be no adequate remedy, no mechanical expedient which will be effective until the cause is removed. Of course, when there has been a long neglect of such a fault, a mere change in the cause will not, at once, make a change in the voice, because a habit long continued produces a permanent physical condition which must be eradicated by another kind of training; but this latter can not adequately accomplish the work, without a change in the fundamental conditions, also.

Of course pupils and students frequently acquire such a hard quality of voice from imitation of teachers, but even in this case, habit of mind on the part of the person imitated, is more or less assimilated, so that there are few or no exceptions to the general rule.

Again, note the continual minor inflections, the quivers and various sad modulations of the voice so common among clergymen. These faults are rarely, if ever, due to physical conditions. The causes of such faults are very complex, and are due often to physical weakness, sometimes to unconscious imitation of the denominational tune, for it is a well-known fact that every denomination has a distinct melody.   Still, that their cause is chiefly a psychic one, is proved by the fact that clergymen who have the most cheerful views of life, who are genial in their intercourse with men, are less liable to such faults; while those who have sad and gloomy views of life are far more addicted to them.   Those who usually have such faults tend to drift in emotion; tend to feel their whole sermon, and the whole situation, rather than each distinct idea in the situation; are apt to speak "into the air," and not definitely nor directly to an audience.

In cases where these faults are due to misconception of the office filled, the position occupied, or the solemn themes discussed by clergymen, or in cases where they arise simply on account of a desire to be earnest; even the faults which result from these remote causes can not be eradicated without direct work upon the action of the mind, for in nearly all cases the immediate cause of such qualities of voice, is the emotional condition of the man at the time he speaks, or at least, such an emotional condition was there when the fault was first acquired. Such faults are extremely difficult to eradicate, on account of the fact that the voice no longer definitely responds to each idea and its co-ordinate experience in the mind.   At first it did to some extent, but on account of a continual drifting tendency frequently the form is left without the substance.   But in all cases, to correct such faults, whatever may be their cause, the man must be made to feel the connection between his thought and feeling, and his tone; he must be made to detect the false ring, and distinguish it from the true response of voice to genuine emotion, and in all cases there is needed a study of the successive actions of the mind, the idea, the emotional response, and then the response in the voice and body. A clergyman who has acquired such a mannerism as to give out his notices with a sad and mournful tone, as serious as he uses in prayer, or at a funeral, must not be considered hypocritical, because often he is completely unconscious of the fault; besides, the quality of his tone is a natural consequence of an endeavor on his part to hold a long sermon in his mind at once, and to feel it as a whole. The feelings of the man are prepared beforehand. Such a wholesale dealing with emotion easily destroys the delicate response of his emotional nature to the distinct and definite ideas he has in his mind at the time; and of course his voice will manifest his predominant emotional condition. The whole problem of correcting such defects must center in securing a co-ordination and concentration of the whole nature upon the distinct and definite idea in the mind at the time of delivery. Again, note some of the unnatural melodies so common among all public speakers. In nearly all cases they are due to defects in the relation of the mental action to the emotional action. When we come to study the difference in the expression of thought and emotion, we find that the direct expression of thought is through form, while the direct expression of feeling is more through rhythm and tone color. Just, therefore, as thought is co-ordinated with feeling, so melody, rhythm and tone color are co-ordinated in expression. If thought and feeling are not properly related there will be some external defect in the co-ordination of form and color. Public speakers are frequently emotional without thought, or at least their emotion and thought are not balanced by will. In such cases the emotion dominates the man and expression is merely the result of the emotional drift. Here we have the key to sing-song forms of melody. Thought without emotion hardens the voice, as we have found, but emotion without thought causes a meaningless drift.

But there is also another result of this emotional drift, which has a very deleterious effect upon the voice. Whenever there is a lack of control over the emotion, that is, when thought and emotion are not co-ordinated by will, the emotion flows to the throat and causes muscular constriction there. Where the emotion is properly controlled in expression there is a co-ordinate control of breath. The throat is passive in such cases and the diaphragm is active. Thus even sore throat in ministers has a mental cause. Those preachers who are very emotional, especially those who drift in emotion, who have no control over it, are the very ones who suffer most from minister's sore throat. By proper control over the emotion a co-ordination between the breathing and the throat is established according to nature's intention. Nature is ever consistent; there is ever a tendency to right action. If the seed is properly planted, and the soil, heat and proper conditions are placed around it, growth and development are normal. Give nature cause and adequate means and she will accomplish the effect. So among public speakers, secure a proper action of the mind and a proper co-operation of all the faculties of the soul and co-ordination of thought and emotion by will, with the proper channels open, then the delivery will tend to be natural and right.

Again, if we study speakers, we find that a very common fault is monotony. There is a constant tendency to speak upon one pitch, or in a very limited range. The cause of this is not only a lack of control over the voice, but is really a mental one; that is, the mind does not receive a specific impression from each successive idea; there is no change in the action of the mind, and it is not wonderful that there is no variety in the tones and inflections of the voice. In nature there are no two things alike. Every idea which is created by the imagination will produce an effect entirely different from that of any other idea. The impression produced by each idea has a character of its own, so that the cure of monotony must ever be chiefly effected through the mind.

Again, note the fact that a great many public speakers do not breathe frequently enough. The reason for this is not merely that they do not think about breathing, for no one should think of breathing at the time of speaking, and in order to correct such a defect, merely to tell a man to breath oftener by a deliberative act of the will, is to make the man mechanical, where nature intended him to be spontaneous. He will be conscious where he should be unconscious. The real cause of the fault is the fact that the man does not receive a vivid impression from each successive idea. He unfolds his ideas by wholesale, or in an uninterrupted stream; his ideas are dim and vague on account of the fact that too great a number of ideas are in the mind at the same time. There is no concentration of the mind upon each fundamental idea, such as will be sufficient to cause the man to breathe. Breathing in expression is not only a physical act, but is caused by the nature of the passion, and the vividness of the impression in the mind. The number of times a man breathes when he is natural is dependent upon the successive action of the mind, while the amount of breath is regulated by the passion and control over it. In other words, as the mind takes an idea for the purpose of expression he breathes spontaneously in preparation for the vocalization. This is a spontaneous co-ordination in nature and can be proved by any one who will take the pains to observe men in surprise or in excitement or in calmness when going to speak or call to a distance. Some of the most distinguished speakers weary them-

selves very much in speaking, on account of ignorance
regarding the cause of their breathing too seldom. By
observing such faults, by studying their psychic as well
as their physical cause, and by working upon both, effective results can be accomplished. Without such a method,
when the physical alone is regarded, all will be made
mechanical and the fault will be continually returning.

Not only must such faults of expression be met by
securing proper action of the mind, but unless such a
method is adopted as a part of the work there is always
in correcting one fault danger of introducing another,
often worse than the first; for example, take the almost
universal tendency to have too little breath in speaking.
Whenever this fault is corrected mechanically there is a
tendency to introduce too great muscular work. Sometimes the muscles used in labored breathing are made to
act, sometimes there is too much breath and all is constricted. In nearly every case the natural rhythm is
interfered with, the spontaneous recovery or tendency to
return at every moment to life breathing is destroyed.
By stimulating the proper rhythmic action of thought and
emotion, by co-ordinating control of emotion and control
of breath, all such dangers are avoided.

No fault can be corrected without stimulating the
inherent tendencies of nature, and this can not be done
without studying and developing the proper actions of
the soul.

Note again, the efforts of speakers to force themselves
to be earnest. The result is a mere mechanical, muscular
energy, absolutely foreign to true earnestness. A long
train of faults follows such endeavors. An irritated
throat, a husky quality of the voice, pushing the voice
instead of inflecting it in making emphasis. All endeavors to force emotion, or endeavors to show more emotion

than a man really has, end in abnormal quivers and tremors, which in common speech we would call whining.

These are some of the worst faults of delivery. They are those which lie deepest and are hardest to correct. While such defects are all associated with physical imperfections, such as lack of control over the voice, physical weakness or muscular constriction, yet the fundamental cause is psychic. Even after the lack of control over the voice has been removed by training and the wrong action of the whole body and all imperfect means of expression are corrected, though the man may have a perfect understanding of his fault, yet without correcting the wrong action of the mind and the removal of the cause, either the fault will return or the man will be merely a self-conscious, mechanical puppet.

Thus we can see at once that for thorough eradication of faults in delivery there must ever be specific and adequate attention to the action of the mind as the first and most important work for the development of delivery.

Common faults may be temporarily relieved by merely working upon the technique, but much of the criticism upon elocution is due to the fact that the work is not radical. The man is made affected or to speak by rule, and is not spontaneously right. The aim of all education for delivery must be to develop the spontaneous and unconscious actions of the man as well as the conscious, so that these shall tend to be right without any mechanical or deliberative interference. Still it must be remembered that the point here is not to prove that all faults have a direct mental cause, or that the correction of this mental cause is all that is needed, but that the action of the mind is one of the leading causes, and that the mind is the most important factor of expression; that wrong mental action is always associated with bad delivery, and must necessarily have special attention, or there will be no radical correction of faults or true development.

Still another argument for the necessity of mental training, is found in the use of the term instinct, in relation to all histrionic expression. People speak of dramatic instinct, oratoric instinct and artistic instinct. Whatever definition may be given to instinct, that it is simply a spontaneous action of all the faculties in their unity, or consciousness recognizing the result but not the process, or as "unconscious action toward an unconscious purpose," in any case we have a recognition of the truth of the principle here unfolded.

The use of such a term implies the fact that all true expression is traced to the action of the mind and that there is ever an unconscious element in all true delivery.

The highest and the most necessary quality of all art is unity, and this is more true of expression because it is the product of a living being through its own living organism. So that, it must have the unity of life itself. The only way this unity can be developed is by securing proper action of the mind. It is only in this way that all the psychological and the physiological actions, the voluntary and the involuntary elements, can be brought into unity. It is only thus that all the complex subtleties of expression can be brought into play.

Study, for example, the relation of being to body. Herman Lotze has shown that the control of the body by will is over-estimated. No man can understand the processes of the simplest movement. We initiate the impulse from the depth of the soul and the work is done. Many of the actions of the body are performed by a series of reflex actions over which man's will has no direct control. This is especially true of expression. The great thing that needs to be done is to study how the initiatory impulse can be awakened. If the mind can be stimulated to act right, the voice, other things being equal, will act right. Not that the will directly controls all the actions of the breathing according to the common theory in training, but that the unconscious and involuntary reflex actions are properly initiated. Much of all the work in breathing, many of the nerves and muscles and many of the actions of the throat in tone never were intended to be directly conscious and voluntary; and to endeavor to make them so is simply to pervert nature. All the training for expression must ever regard this distinction. The function of the will is primarily for the initiation of the fundamental impulse in the depths of the soul. There are many of the very highest and most important modes of expression belonging to the voice and the different parts of the body, which will begin at once to follow from a proper development of the mind and a proper restoration of voice and body to normal conditions and actions, but which no volitionary action independent of emotional conditions, independent of simple, normal, psychic action, can ever execute.

We have found how complex and infinitely varied are the languages which are co-ordinated in all expression. Upon the theory that man by direct choice can do all this, we are required to believe that the mind can deliberately choose a hundred things held before the mind at the same time. But if a man has to consciously choose every emotion, every action, every inflection and every modulation and color of the voice, all will be dim and superficial. True unity in nature is ever dependent upon a center and that center in expression is the mind — the idea. Hence, it is impossible for man to act in accordance with theories of mechanical skill, according to which he must simply know what to do and do it. That he must have his emotions and the expression of every part of his body in his mind in the same way as he has the words of a vocabulary, and that he is to call forth emotions and inflections at will in all parts of his body, and that such conscious control makes him an artist. There never has been such an artist. Whenever there has been one who has acted merely upon this theory he has become mechanical, one-sided, artificial and has failed. As we study such a speaker, different parts of his body may seem to perform perfect actions, but they lack that mystic unity which ever must result from the element of spontaneous growth. As some one has said, " Shakespeare's plays grow, while Goethe's seem to be made." So all great expression must have an element of growth, or there is no unity. It is in the unconscious nature of the man, co-ordinated with the conscious, that is found the root from which all activity in every part of the body seems to flow. By securing a proper action of the mind, simple organic unity in nature results from a spontaneous diffusion of the effects of emotion through the nerves and organs.

We must not, however, make the mistake that all is merely impulsive, that there is no conscious and no deliberative work. When we study the trains of ideas in mere musing, we find a confused mass, more or less without order, without method; while in a train of ideas worthy the name of thinking the mind selects and is focused successively upon each central idea and makes this into a vivid image, and by the power of attention deliberatively and consciously holds it before the mind until an effect is produced upon the unconscious nature. Here we have a deliberative element in direct co-ordination with the unconscious element. Man can control his emotions, man can create emotions that will be so powerful as to stir the very depths of his being, but it must be by following such a process.

Thus, unity of expression is dependent upon a unity of impulse, and unity of impulse is dependent upon unity of stimulation. With the voice and body in proper condition of training, with an active imagination, a powerful impulse can be awakened in the depths of the soul that can bring all the actions of the man into definite co-ordination.

We come now to more specific questions. What actions of the mind need to be trained, and how can they be developed? To answer fully these questions would require a volume. Those who desire to see the steps more fully presented are referred to the work on Vocal Expression and the Text Books upon Expression, soon to be published; all that will be attempted here will be a few simple illustrations, showing the necessity for some attention and the possible results that may follow from development of this phase of delivery.

First, let it be noted that something more is needed than indirect work. This, however, is very important. Many faults can be corrected by simply improving the general taste of the man. A study of art may awaken a right conception of delivery without any direct work upon the mind in delivery itself. The most fundamental needs in delivery may at times be met by interesting a student in poetry, in the study of authors that especially stimulate neglected faculties. But there must be more specific work than this.

All expression is simply the manifestation of possession — it is simply thinking aloud. The laws of thinking must be studied and specially developed. As musing is the drifting from idea to idea while thinking is a focusing of the mind successively upon ideas in a natural or determined sequence, so one of the first actions of the mind to be trained in expression is attention. If we take an extract from the best literature, containing vivid ideas or pictures, arranged in a simple and natural order, and read it over silently, that is, rethink it, we find the mind pausing upon one idea and then leaping to another, as has been fully explained and illustrated by Coleridge in his essay upon method. We find, also, that the steps may be made definitely and certainly, or so vaguely and indefinitely, that the mind may end in chaos. The definite sequence, the accentuation of the steps, and the power to hold the mind upon each idea until it stirs the whole man is the fundamental requisite of all vocal expression. This action of the mind must be accentuated for expression. Thinking, to awaken thinking in others, requires an exaggeration of the processes of thinking, for the idea must affect voice and body. It must stimulate an emotional impulse toward expression. Thus the first action of the mind which must be developed is the power to hold all the powers of the mind concentrated upon one object or idea.

Another action of the mind that needs training is the power to create or reproduce vividly these ideas. The successive ideas upon which the mind is focused, are pictures. They are the work of the imagination. They may be apprehended very dimly and vaguely or even abstractly. This pictorial power is very susceptible to training. The right kind of work develops philosophical rather than verbal memory. Not only is there need for the development of the power to see each idea, but there is an imaginative grasp of a situation; an idea does not stimulate emotion, it is an idea in its connections or relations that moves men.

Another action to be developed by training is the emotional response of the soul to these pictures in the mind.

This attention is conscious and deliberative, but the response to the idea contains a spontaneous element. As we call up and hold before the mind a picture, the soul is moved. We do not naturally remain neutral. Emotion of some kind must spring up in the heart.

We must watch this response; but we must not interfere with it. We can take a most beautiful extract and endeavor simply and truthfully to reveal the emotional conditions. The unconscious and the involuntary will thus be awakened and can be studied and co-ordinated. It is very important for the student to be able to distinguish, what he does himself by will and what seems to be done for him, or independent of his will. Let the student take some simple line full of great joy, for example, abandon himself wholly to the emotion and practice faithfully. He will become conscious of the idea and the response to this idea.

Again, contrast a cold, intellectual line with a line full of admiration. The student will come to know very soon what abandon means, what impulses do for him, the stimulation of breathing, the softening of the voice by emotion, and many other effects. Such a study of self in the act of giving what we feel is very important.

The first of all requisites is that the man shall be able to distinguish when every faculty and power of the soul is acting in its own province.

The best method for the development of this power to vividly portray ideas and to feel the response to them, is the study of lyrics.

A lyric is a most fundamental form of art, it contains vivid pictures and noble emotions. By practice upon this simplest form of art, the elemental impulses of the man can be quickened, strengthened and co-ordinated. I once asked Professor Norton, the foremost art critic of this country, how appreciation of art could be developed in men; he said it must be done by cultivating the imagination. "If I had work like yours to do I would take a collection of Lyrics and have students learn them and recite them over and over." From long years of actual experience before and since that time I can bear my testimony to the wonderful results that can be accomplished.

We see here another reason why the writings of the best authors must be chosen. They give ideas the most truthful, the most imaginative and ideal. The greater the author, the simpler the arrangement and the more naturally one idea is made to grow out of another.

Still another action of the mind needs to be developed. This is the logical sequence of ideas. This methodic instinct can be developed by studying the great essayists and orators; but better than all, by speaking. Extemporaneous speaking is the most effective method of developing proper mental action, especially insight and method. Let the teacher ask a student to prepare and give a simple account of a visit to some place or object of interest, or give a simple account of some great event preparing the thought, arranging the ideas; but leaving the words for the moment of delivery.

In my own work I have also found it a great help to assign to each member of a class some great historical speaker and have him thoroughly investigate his life and works so as to be able to present the essential elements of his power. The student becomes inspired by the speaker he is studying. He not only finds something to say, but is inspired to say it. He is studying oratory from the life of an orator; he is also studying himself, and is engaged in the most direct and effective practice of his art. Are not all these facts sufficient to prove that the mind must and can be developed in delivery? Man has no faculty or power in his nature that is not capable of education. The higher the faculty, the more susceptible it is to training. It is only the beating of the heart and certain physiological functions that are not capable of education. So, also, the higher the animal the more capable it is of development. The possibility of education is the highest test of intelligence.

Many are led to think that because the greater portion of all expression is unconscious, it is therefore incapable of education. If the color of the voice is unconscious then they say, any interference with it by the action of the will is dangerous. If much of pantomimic expression is involuntary, any endeavor to regulate it will produce affectation. That there is great danger has already been acknowledged and shown, and the specific danger will be more fully shown hereafter. But if such were consistent, they would say that man's character is an unconscious result and any endeavor to improve it would be the same as trying to act a character before our fellow-men, and that the education of character would be hypocrisy.

The fact that character is reached indirectly, developed unconsciously and involuntarily, and yet is the highest goal of all education, shows us that the legitimate aim of education, its most difficult problem, is to affect that which is unconscious. True education is all-sided and consists ever in stimulating the faculties to spontaneous activity. Whenever we begin to recognize the fact that education is the process of bringing before the mind such objects as will stimulate spontaneous activity, as will awaken the normal processes of growth, it can be seen at once that action of the mind as cause in expression is one of the highest aims of education. The old misconception of education, that its aim is merely to acquire knowledge, has led naturally to the neglect of all work for true expression.

Many elocutionists honestly think that if delivery is dependent upon the action of the mind "Othello's occupation is gone." Macready is said to have given up the teaching of elocution because "no one could teach feeling." Was he right in this statement? If feeling is not an object of education, then taste is not an object of education; love of music can not be developed; a love of beauty, a love of poetry, can not be educated. If Macready did make the remark, he must have had a poor method as a teacher of elocution. If the development of delivery has reference only to the mechanical signs of emotion, if it is only to develop skill in the use of these signs, then the statement is right. But every faculty and every power in the human soul, directly or indirectly, is susceptible of education.

The imagination, fully as much as any faculty of the mind, can be developed, and with the growth of the imagination, there is growth of feeling. A love of poetry, a love of art, the artistic sense of delivery, must ever be developed through the development of the imagination. By bringing men into contact with literature and art, by stimulating, directly and indirectly, the ideals and purposes, by developing the power of the human mind to conceive situations, to realize the relations and surroundings of different minds in the history of the race, the power of feeling can be wonderfully awakened. I appeal to the experience of every teacher who has labored for years with every class of mind, and who has not tried to do the work in a few days, but who has patiently proceeded, and who has had the co-operation of students — I appeal to such if this is not the case. It sometimes is accomplished indirectly by asking the student what he generally reads, what he habitually studies, and prescribing a course of reading which will remove the mechanical and constricted actions of his mind, which will stimulate his imagination and his emotion from new points of view. Hundreds of men, by merely working upon words or literal facts, lose all appreciation of poetry. Few are willing to acknowledge it, as did Darwin, who said he felt that certain powers of his nature were in an atrophied condition from the one-sided character of his studies.

But the work can also be accomplished directly. It is a problem for direct study and development, for every faculty and power given to man is capable of education, if only its true nature and normal actions are studied. Of course it is not contended that there are no differences of ability in this as in every phase of human life. The possibility of education is not the same, but that possibility exists, and some who are capable of becoming the greatest artists need it most. The spontaneous impulses of human nature can be stimulated. The responsiveness of the voice and body to these impulses can be developed, and the whole expression of the man can become more natural and effective. Certainly if there is no such thing as the development of the imagination and feelings and a co-ordination of thought and emotion to bring these into a better balance by will, if the spontaneous impulses of the soul in their actions can not be developed, then it will be taken for granted that expression can not be developed at all; that it is simply a natural result. In fact it is not even natural, for everything natural has power to grow. It is only a mechanical thing, the result of trickery which can be learned by rule, but is not a legitimate part of education. But in such a view and by such a method, consciousness will be unfocused and nature will be superficialized. There will be a development of greater one-sidedness than before. No external polish can conceal a lack of balance of the elemental powers of the soul.

Thus the work of developing expression must fundamentally depend upon what we may call psychological diagnosis. As the eradication of disease depends upon a skillful insight into the needs and causes, upon careful pathological diagnoses, so must all training for development of delivery be primarily dependent upon a careful consideration of the causes of the faults and of the fundamental needs in delivery. Among these the primary cause must ever be the action of the mind. Such as the action of the reproductive faculties, the logical insight, the method, the progressive action from idea to idea, from thought to thought, the emotional response of each idea and the emotional transition as the mind passes from idea to idea, and the harmonious co-ordination of all the faculties of the intellect and of the emotional powers or sensibilities and of the will in the act of speaking.

XIII.

DEVELOPMENT OF THE ORGANISM.

Nature is made better by no mean,
But nature makes that mean.   —*Shakespeare.*

THE first and chief attention, therefore, in expression, must be given to the action of the mind, but correct action of the mind alone will not secure adequate expression. Many, whose minds are thoroughly trained, who are capable of the greatest thought and most intense feeling, are yet extremely imperfect in expression. While the impulse from the soul may be essentially right yet the body may still not respond to this impulse. The faculties of the soul and its physical agents may not work in unison. Notwithstanding intensity of feeling, notwithstanding earnestness and clearness of thought, in many we find an absolute separation between the soul and the voice, the mind and the body.

Expression depends upon many things; it is first dependent upon the clearness and vividness of the ideas; secondly, upon the responsiveness of the emotional nature, of the unconscious powers to these ideas; and, in the third place, to responsiveness on the part of the voice and body to the spontaneous impulses of the soul. Failure at any of these points will destroy adequate expression. Like an electric current there must be an unbroken line along which the impulse is transmitted; imperfection at only one point will destroy the manifestation. So that, expression not only requires a vivid imagination and responsive emotion, but a responsive body, and a responsive voice. Imperfect expression results from lack of plasticity of body, and inflexibility of the voice, as well as from lack of activity or responsiveness in being. The co-ordination of thought and emotion is no more important than the co-ordination of being and body. An effect in nature is dependent upon appropriate means, as well as upon adequate cause; not only must there be impulse toward expression, but the channels must be open.

Hence we find another form of training necessary. The organic instruments must be prepared for their work. Everything except a few physiological actions needs special training. The more related any function is to art, the more necessary such training becomes. The little child has to learn to use its hands to feed itself; but it requires still more work for the hand to become pliable for the manifestation of the mind. The voice is used in crying as the spontaneous expression of pain, but long and patient effort is required to make the same mechanism perfect as an instrument of speech. The little partridge requires no education to be able to run, but the child must make many despairing efforts before it can walk. Education or training is the law of its being, not only of the mind but of the body. Man from the earliest years of his life has the power to conceive an ideal, and by work to actualize it, and there is no place where this applies more than in the use of his own body.

In order to have perfect musical expression, there must be a musician with music in his soul, and an instrument in tune. The same is true of delivery. While clear ideas, vivid and intense emotions are necessary to expression, the instrument employed for their manifestation, must be perfectly attuned to its work. A good musician will not play upon a piano or violin out of tune, and the speaker who rightly apprehends his office, will not fail to prepare himself in every way, to perfectly discharge the work before him; and he who neglects to bring the body and the voice into harmony with his soul, can no more adequately manifest truth and experience, than a musician can bring perfect music from a piano all out of tune.

But, we must bear in mind, as has been shown, that the body is more than an instrument; it is a living organism. A mechanical instrument can be tuned by a mechanical process, but a living organism can only be tuned by a careful stimulation of nature's processes according to her own laws of growth and development. We can see, also, that in nature, the being and the body are ever united. As man is constituted, a perfect organism is necessary to the mind, as its means of expression.

A proper training of the body, in fact, will aid the training of being, as both are under the laws of development. It has been conclusively shown, that animals of the highest order of mind, have very highly developed tactual organs; man the highest of all has a most flexible hand. Thus body and being are so intimately related that a correct action of the mind tends to bring the body right, and a correct use of the body, tends to render assistance to the psychic action. When the soul is in the prison-house of a constricted and rigid body its feelings cannot be revealed, the emotion which endeavors to transmit itself through tones that are hard and that absolutely belie its nature, will tend to die for lack of room to expand and channels for manifestation. One of the most important steps in the improvement of expression, must ever be to bring the voice and the body into such a plastic condition, that they will always be in perfect harmony and correspondence with being and in subordination to the soul.

Let us look frankly and seriously at the new phase of the problem before us. Is special training for the voice and body in expression necessary?

There are many reasons aside from those already given, why special training for the organism in expression is necessary. One argument is, that the actions of the body and the voice in public speaking and reading are not the ordinary actions of every-day life. The most common actions have had to be learned, and hence, we must natually infer that any new use of the instruments will require new preparation. Every man learns to use the voice in simple conversation about the fireside of home, but when he rises to speak to a large audience so that all can hear, and in a connected discourse, he uses the voice in an unusual way. There is more effort. But frequently this extra effort is applied at the wrong point, and he is soon worn out and his voice so constricted as to make it very unpleasant and entirely unfitted to manifest feeling. Training can prepare the voice by establishing the normal actions and extending them according to nature's own modes until increased effort does not displace them, and power to manifest feeling increases rather than diminishes with excitement and energy. In every part of the body there are certain fundamental actions which need to be firmly established, so that no excitement nor increase of energy will pervert, but rather accentuate them.

Let us further illustrate this principle. When we study men, we find that in some, emotion chokes and smothers the voice, while in others emotion expands, colors and ennobles it. We find further that the man whose voice is made worse by emotion, unconsciously transmits the activity caused by emotion to his throat in the act of speaking, while the other feels this activity in the center of his body, in the region of his diaphragm and respiratory muscles. The emotion in the first case, constricts the throat and voice; in the other, it stimulates the breathing, and develops the proper conditions for voice. But the first man is entirely unconscious of his fault, and whoever thinks that such a one needs only to be told the mistake, has never had any experience in teaching voice. In all such cases the more earnestly the man tries to speak, the more constricted will be his throat, until congestion follows, and we have what is called "minister's sore throat," and the clergyman, the lecturer or the actor must take a long vacation. Many by such a course entirely ruin their voice and even health.

We have already found that there is wrong action of the mind in connection with this fault, that there is a lack of control over the emotion to a certain extent, or, at any rate, a one-sided action in the man's nature, and the correction of this is often necessary for the correction of the fault. But this, alone, will not do the work ; there has been a slow perversion of the nervous system, a wrong use of parts and of muscles, an acquirement of such fixed habits, that definite physical work is absolutely necessary to correct this abnormal action. The breathing must be re-established according to nature's intention ; the nerves, which have become sluggish and incapacitated for the transmission of emotion, must be stimulated, and those muscles upon whose action the normal control of the voice is absolutely dependent must be developed and brought under control. The aim of all such training is to restore nature, to make the man act according to nature's intention regarding his own body and his own being. When this normal action is once perverted by bad habit, it is one of the most difficult things in the world to restore it.

One reason for this difficulty is, that habit so perverts a human being that consciousness makes no distinction between what is normal and what is abnormal. Faults of expression are only vaguely realized in the consciousness of the man. The great struggle of the teacher is to make the man see his fault; but he can not recognize or realize his fault fully, for three-fourths of the actions in normal or abnormal expression are unconscious. There is ever a kind of co-ordination, as has been shown, between the conscious and the unconscious elements, and it is just here that the evil effects of habit are seen. If habit only affected the conscious and voluntary actions and emotions of the man, its effects could be easily and quickly corrected, but, in fact, habit can only be cor-rected by such systematic training, by such careful pre-scribed exercises as will develop the natural co-ordination of conscious and unconscious conditions, until all the nerves and muscles, conscious and unconscious, are developed to act in accordance with nature's normal intention.

Hence, however plausible and however eloquent may seem the arguments of those who say that "all a man needs, to speak well, is to speak well," that all he needs is simply *will;* if he has a fault of voice, he must simply bring his will to bear upon it when he rises to speak to men, such a course can never meet the needs of men. In all such discussions the fundamental problem of the development of delivery is misconceived. For, while there is a great element of truth in this, and while all we have found about the importance of being may seem to prove this statement, we can see at once that it is a most one-sided view of the subject.

Habit is overlooked in such advice. If a man were perfectly normal, if the bridge from thought to emotion and from both to the body were in perfect condition and were never broken down or obstructed, such a view might be correct. But most men are abnormal, all in some particular are one-sided. The emotion that is stimulated by thought does not pass along nature's intended roads to the voice. Instead, therefore, of the emotion transfiguring the voice, it cramps and obstructs it. Where there is not adequate control of the voice according to nature's normal method, the more the will itself is exerted, the more is the voice cramped and constricted. If a man grasps a sword by the handle, the firmer he grasps, the better is the execution; but if his hand grasps the keen edge, the more firmly he grasps it the deeper is the gash in his own hand. When the whole body and voice are so trained that emotion diffuses itself equally to every part, when all parts are normally adjusted to each other and act according to its fundamental function without interfering with any other, then, and then only, can it be said to a student, "all you need is to force yourself to dominate your audience." When once a locomotive is off the track, the more steam is put on, the greater the destruction. Steam can only be safely applied when the locomotive is upon the track along which it was intended, by its construction, to travel. Man's will can do a great deal with his body, but it can not do everything. When a man is abnormal, when he has a bad habit in the use of his breathing, voice or body, while "earnestness covers a multitude of elocutionary sins," yet, without training to place the actions of the man upon the right track, the earnestness may only pervert and destroy.

Again, let us illustrate this principle by a study of awkwardness. Awkwardness is a misuse of the mechanism. There is too much effort at times, there is misplaced effort always. Effort is either directed to the wrong parts, or one part cannot be used without disturbing its neighbor. But to tell a man simply to put more will into his body, to be more earnest, is only to make him more awkward. If the wheels of a machine are ungeared, tremendous force applied will not gear them together. If a man makes awkward movements, certainly it is not lack of force that makes them so; it is misapplication of force, if not application of too much force. It is not fair to say that grace is economy of force, it is as much precision as economy of force, but certainly misdirected will can not make an awkward man graceful. Grace is more particularly dependent upon the principle of centered activity; and no mere amount of force establishes a center. Again, when a man by imitation and aggregation or by merely endeavoring to conform to rule, attempts to make himself graceful, in all that he does he will become more constricted and limited and stiff and affected; and in this case, the amount of energy applied makes the affectation only more manifest.

Again, suppose some one has acquired the bad habit of using minor inflections or has a lack of support in his tone from mere physical weakness, the result of ill-health, or from any cause whatever, suppose he has acquired a manneristic sadness which is present in all his speaking; even in such a case, where we would think that this remedy would directly apply, I have seen men made to drift more by mere endeavors to be more earnest. The mind must be restored, must be led to conceive anew the situation, and in all cases the defect must be eradicated by securing control over the breath, establishing support of tone and normal inflectional action. Training must be applied to restore all to nature's normal condition.

A man when he is acting according to habit, always thinks he is acting according to nature, for, as has been shown, there is no distinction in consciousness, between habit and nature. Some of the most unnatural tones and inflections, some of the most perverted movements and positions, some of the most abnormal actions in breathing

and voice production, have been defended by the possessor of them as being natural to him. However
"throaty" or "nasal" his voice, he feels it is *his* voice,
however constricted his action, he feels it is *his* action,
and, as has been shown, many educated men can not conceive the difference between what habit has made a man,
and what nature intended him to be.

Thus, to develop and make perfect the expression, no
deliberative key is given man. No wonderful explanation
or guide can, in a flash, do the whole work. It can only
be done effectively by a thorough study of men's needs
and habits, and educating them by a thorough training,
such as will restore the subtlest muscles and nerves to
their normal actions.

There is another reason why there should be training
for the organism in expression. We find in the nature of
expression that all the mechanical action must be transparent. Mechanical actions are never seen when expression is perfect. A great orator does not think of his
voice unless there is something wrong with it, nor does
his audience. If he is hoarse, he will think of it himself
and his audience will notice it. If his voice is cramped
and constricted, it will be at once felt as a voice, and if it
is felt merely as a voice, expression is hindered; but if it
is a channel of emotion, the audience loses sight of the
mechanical means, and feels the' thought and emotion
that is conveyed. So it is in pantomime; if gesture
or attitudes are proper, they will not be noticed; if
affected, or over-nice, or labored or merely aggregated,
they will be seen at once.

Thus, the object of all training is to make mechanical
actions transparent; to remove all consciousness of the
action of the mechanism. If all true expression is a manifestation of the mystic, the operation must be such that

the attention of the audience must not be drawn to the organism of the speaker. In proportion as the actions of the organism are concealed will the mystic be manifested. Presenting mere body to men is merely exhibition; as has been shown, entirely foreign to the true aim in expression. We train the body to get it out of consciousness, to make it a perfect channel for expression. A story is told of Peter the Great: That on his way home from church one Sunday morning, he said: "I like to hear this Father preach. After hearing the Court preachers, as I go home I always say 'what a beautiful sermon,' but when I hear this Father I always go home saying to myself, 'what a poor miserable sinner I am.'" So it is ever with true expression; deep feelings are awakened in us, and we almost lose sight of the artist. While in one who makes a mere performance, we think only of the person; we lose sight of his thought, we are not aroused, but only look at his execution, hence we see the force of the saying of Goethe, "It is the highest art to conceal art," for the greatest art conceals the means by which the effect is produced. The means or technique must be lost. The object must be to manifest and reveal the soul.

Again, the necessity or rather a basis for training is seen in the relation of body to being. Note some of the facts which are given us by writers who have studied the relation of the mind to its physical organism. Note, for example, the law of diffusion as stated by Bain: "When an impression is accompanied with feeling, the aroused currents diffuse themselves freely over the brain, leading to a general agitation of the moving organs, as well as affecting the viscera." A vast number of facts "showing that the connection of mind and body is not occasional or partial, but thorough-going and complete," have been gathered by scientists. "It has been noted," says Bain, "in all ages and countries, that the feelings possess a natural language or expression. So constant are the appearances characterizing the different classes of emotions, that we regard them as a part of the emotions themselves. The smile of joy, the puckered features in pain, the stare of astonishment, the quivering of fear, the tones and glance of tenderness, the frown of anger, are united in seemingly inseparable association with the states of feeling that they indicate. If a feeling arises without its appropriate sign or accompaniment, we account for the failure either by voluntary suppression, or by the faintness of the excitement, there being a certain degree or intensity requisite to affect the bodily organs." "Most of our emotions," says Darwin, "are so closely connected with their expression, that they hardly exist if the body remains passive. A man, for instance, may know that his life is in the extremest peril and may strongly desire to save it; yet, as Louis XVI said, when surrounded by a fierce mob, 'Am I afraid? Feel my pulse.' So a man may intensely hate another; but until his bodily frame is affected, he cannot be said to be enraged." Thus we can see that while the body is most intimately connected with being, the transmission, and to a certain extent the character of the emotion, at any rate so far as it appears to others, is dependent upon the condition of the bodily organs. Nothing shows the importance of training to expression so much as the intimacy of soul and body. In fact, true training for expression is as much a mental act as a physical act. It is the putting of mind into the muscles, it is almost a conscious diffusion of emotion through the nervous system. The action of the mind may not be exactly the same as in actual expression. There must be usually a sustained picture in the mind or at least a sustained general emotional condition which shall bring the soul to bear upon the body. Here is the chief difference between this form of training and gymnastics. When the mind is blank in a vocal exercise, as is the case with ordinary gymnastics, poor results will follow. True training for expression demands thought and feeling, even in a mechanical exercise. A purely mechanical action does not affect the deep, unconscious actions of our being.

We are very apt, as these scientists have evidently done, merely to study this intimate connection independent of any possibility of improving it, while to us in our present investigation the great question ever arises, how can the voice and the body be improved as the agents of expression? Thus, if the human body and the human voice were normal, and were not perverted by habit, if they were developed fully from the very beginning, like the legs of a bird, such a course of training would be unnecessary; a little struggle, a little external experiment, and the bird flies to the highest possibilities of its nature. But such is not the case with man; man's gifts are given him in a state of incompleteness and inadequacy. He has to develop all his powers; his gifts are given him in a state of possibility, and he can only enter into possession of them by patient discipline and long, continued struggle. So that the artistic control of body by being is no exception to the general rule.

Is there such a science as a science of training? We look in vain for general principles, and light upon the subject. All the work of our gymnastics is simply empirical; beneath it all there is little or no science of training; there has been in recent years a great study of physiology in relation to exercise. A book very recently issued, on the Physiology of Bodily Exercise, enters most fully and faithfully into the subject; but of the general principles by which the body can be improved for the purposes of expression, little or nothing can be found. While the voice has been trained, and wonderfully trained, for thousands of years, yet the general principles by which it is done, have never yet been placed in a shape which is worthy to be called the science of vocal training. We have had recently a vast amount of explanation of the anatomy and physiology of the voice, just as in other forms of so-called training; but there is no systematic presentation of principles to be found anywhere. And yet, when we consider the vast advance which has been in all biological science, when it is considered how thoroughly every difficulty in anatomy and physiology has been investigated, and how thoroughly the physiological development of all animals, including man, is understood, we feel at once the possibilities of a science as well as an art of training. We feel that all the knowledge of organism can be used to adopt movements and exercises, such as will bring an imperfect organism to perfection; restore abnormal conditions, correct the effects of habit, remove all stiffness and constriction; in short, lift man to such an ideal physical condition that when once he has the proper conception, and the proper impulse and the proper method, the body will properly respond; at any rate, there will be no mere physical hinderance that will prevent the proper co-ordination of the conscious with the unconscious action, and all friction will be removed from the whole body.

The one who objected to the necessity of training the mind in expression will object to the long and patient work required for the preparation of the organism.

Such a one will say, why not simply tell the man how to stand and place his head, his arms, his feet, his body, in the right relations, and that is all there is to do. In other words, why not seek at once for the end? If all expression were deliberative this method would possibly be correct. If the aim of education is to bring all into the conscious sphere, there might be some excuse for this. But training tends to make everything *spontaneously right.* Any other course would not be training, but mere mechanical adjustment. The only method worthy the name of training must be such as will remove the effects of evil habit, and restore nature herself to the normal functioning for all purposes whatever. If a man has to stand in an artificial position, though to all appearances it be mechanically correct, yet until correctness is spontaneous, all will be artificial and constrained. If nature is not centered or normal the spontaneous actions of the speaker's nature will be necessarily perverted. External constriction or mechanical interference is not training. Training restores all parts of the body to their normal relationship, opens all the channels of expression, so that the emotion will normally, diffuse itself in all directions, co-ordinate all parts of the body about their intended center, and develop all in unity and harmony.

There are many other misconceptions of training. One is that all training simply means the acquirement of strength. Men will go to work upon the voice merely making loud noises. In training the body nearly every one will think the ordinary gymnastics is meant, but this is not the case. Ordinary gymnastic work tends to make men awkward and to hinder expression in many ways. It tends to pervert the method of breathing. I have had to have students stop gymnastic work before I could relieve them from sore throats. The only training that will bring the body under control of being is that which will establish its center, develop precision and ease in the action of every part and co-operation of all the agents, such as will develop internal rather than external muscles, the more subtle as well as the larger muscles.

The only point here, however, is to prove the necessity of training, and not to go into the great subject of what is to be done in order to train the voice, and body. These will each require a volume. That there is a science of training must be here assumed.

We can see that all expression presupposes two things. First, a correct action of the faculties of the soul, and secondly, a normal action of the organic means which transmit the action of the soul. Not only must the mind act properly, but there must be in addition, a plastic body, a responsive voice, and all the faculties and agents of the man brought to conscious and unconscious co-ordination by training; these are necessarily presupposed in all great and effective expression.

Men are very apt to think when imperfect action exists in any of these, that there is no remedy; they look upon the action of these as simply the man himself; the power to transform these actions is ever forgotten. A majority of failures in our oratoric delivery and expression in every form, are caused by the mere fact of inadequate development. In all these specific lines, faults of expression can be traced to physical as well as psychic causes. Until all our modern knowledge of the body, and of the soul, and of the relation of each to the other, until all our knowledge of the voice, its structure, its physiology and its use, can be practically applied to form a science and art of training, until methods can be formulated that will correct all abnormal action, and develop voice and body according to nature's normal intention to the very highest efficiency, all work for the improvement of delivery will be external, superficial and inadequate.

XIV.

SPECIAL TECHNICAL TRAINING.

This is an art
Which does mend Nature — change it rather; but
The art itself is Nature. — *Shakespeare*.

THE importance of training the mind in expression has been illustrated. It has also been shown that while the proper conceptive and methodic actions of the mind are the most fundamental and necessary factors, still these alone will not necessarily cause perfect expression. The body may have become so perverted by habit, so established in abnormal action, that though the general cause of this abnormal action be removed, there is still a tendency for the body and the voice to go on in the old way; and the fault will remain. Man's body, and his vocal agents by evil habits may become a cage for the concealment and imprisonment of the emotions of the soul, instead of a living, plastic organism, manifesting its most subtle disposition and activities. Even without such habits, the voice and body are given to man as crude possibilities, which must be disciplined and trained for their work. Accordingly, adequate delivery presupposes a preparatory training of the mind, the voice and body, thus securing control over cause and means; but to secure the effect something else is needed. In order to have perfect musical expression, the musician not only must have music in his soul, and an instrument in tune, but *skill* to play upon that instrument. The same is true in every form of vocal and pantomimic expression. The psychic requisites for perfect delivery, as we have found, are not only thought and feeling in the soul of the man, but proper action of the reproductive faculties, and responsiveness of the whole nature, causing a co-ordinate experience to be revealed simultaneously with the representation of thought. Then the organic instruments, or means to be used, must be perfectly attuned to their work.

But there is something more; the man must have adequate skill in the use of these agents. A speaker may have an emotional responsiveness to thought, and both ideas and emotion co-ordinate under the control of will; and he may have a voice and body perfectly attuned, until all the channels of expression are responsive; but still he may fail to have adequate expression by mere misconception, misuse of the means, or through lack of skill in execution. He may fail through ignorance of what to do and how to do it. The voice and the body must not only be trained properly, but must be used properly. The piano must not only be in tune but the one who plays must be skillful in the manipulation of its keys. The third form of training, therefore, is in respect to the proper use of all agents in expression, and the co-ordination of all the languages given to man for the manifestation of his thoughts, feelings and purposes.

There is a right way and a wrong way of doing everything. Sorrow may be expressed by minor inflections and tremolos in the voice, or it may be expressed by deeper and more intense control of the breathing, or through color of the voice caused by modulating the texture of the muscles by the diffusion of emotion. Though the first way is justified by some of the highest elocutionary standards, yet by an observer of nature, it can be seen at once that one is the language of weakness, while the other is the manifestation of strength. It does not explain the difficulty to say that the one who expresses weakness does not have control over his breath. This is of course true, but by thoroughly training the voice we find there is an additional work to be done. Direct practice in the rendering of emotion is necessary. For there is an almost universal tendency in those who are untrained in expression to either repress all emotion or to express feeling, and especially pathos, so as to give an impression of weakness rather than strength. Besides, the man must be given a higher conception of the function of art and the relation of art to nature.

In our study of the problem of expression we have found that man possesses many languages for the expression of a given idea or emotion. There are an infinite number of ways by which experience can be revealed, and one of the most common faults in expression is the employment of one language or of one part of the body too exclusively. Men fall into the habit of using only one limited phase of natural languages, with a body that can be made flexible and responsive to every phase of experience and capable of a great variety of movements and actions; speakers form the habit of using only one or two gestures. Many speakers use only one agent of the body, all the other parts of the body being practically useless if they are not contradicting the agent acting. Others only use the head, while all the rest of the body, when moving at all, is only in subservience to the head. The same is true of the voice. With a voice capable of a wide range, many speakers use only two or three notes as the utmost limit of the extension of the voice in response to emotion. With a voice capable of an infinite variety of modulation of its textures, an infinite number of qualities, which we may call tone color, we find speakers almost universally obliterating the great plenitude of nature, and using only a neutral quality of voice, cold and lifeless, which irritates the nerves of even the speaker

himself. It not only rasps the sensibilities of his auditors, but fails to reveal the varying shades of experience
upon whose revelation the interpretation of truth depends.

Thus we can see, that in order to bring all the different
languages of the man into unity and harmony, it is not
only necessary that the agents by which they are produced shall be normally adjusted and in proper condition,
but the special meaning of each language, and the special functions it was intended to discharge, must be studied, and skill acquired in the execution of its fundamental
actions.

We can find another illustration of the need of training, if we look again at the person who speaks naturally
and with ease in private life to one or two persons. We
find, when he rises to speak upon a grand theme for a
given length of time, to a thousand people, everything
must be enlarged; not only must there be more energy,
more breath, but longer and more salient inflections,
although the essential elements of the form must remain
the same, or he is unnatural. As in the enlargement of a
photograph, all parts must be enlarged in the same ratio,
so the fundamental inflections, their relations and the
intervals between words must be simply extended in exact
proportions. But this is exactly what the untrained
speaker does not do. His melody reminds one of the
enlargement of the photograph of a face where only the
nose is increased in size. The volume of the voice is
increased, but there is no increase of the inflections and
intervals, hence everything is abnormal. Instead of the
range of the voice being increased, the inflections and the
intervals between words are shorter, and the whole range
of the voice is more limited than in conversation. Here
we find a fundamental characteristic of all declamatory
unnaturalness; there is always a tendency to increase the

volume without extending the range of the voice. The only real prevention of such a fault is the development of the proper flexibility of the voice, a training of the organism to its highest efficiency, and also an understanding of the work to be done, of the essential actions that are the elements of naturalness and effectiveness, and a mastery of these, so as to be able to enlarge and accentuate them and yet preserve their proportion.

Thus it may be seen, that the action of man's organism in oratory must differ from that in private life, and what is meant by naturalness, must refer to the fundamental elements, and not to the degrees of force. If any one who has all his life spoken with ease, but only to a small group, in conversation, should suddenly be called upon to speak to a thousand people, he not only finds himself in a new situation, but face to face with the necessity of doing certain physical things with which he has never been familiar. In endeavoring to do this, he is apt to become mechanical, to merely look at the muscular method of doing his work, and hence to lose all spontaneity. He enlarges his voice mechanically and becomes unnatural and labored, because he has not been trained to enlarge the subtle fundamental elements which make the conversation natural when he tries to speak louder. He speaks often upon a higher pitch, and loses the fundamental elements of inflection, and change of pitch. To illustrate more specifically, there must be an increase in what Dr. Merkle calls "the vocal struggle"; but if this vocal struggle is increased by introducing the action of the muscles used in labored breathing, as is very apt to be done, without increasing the amount of breath in the lungs, the throat will be constricted, and the true quality of the tone will be more or less destroyed. The result in a little while is sore throat, and in many cases failure.

Here we have in a sentence the history of many young clergymen, teachers and speakers.

It is not necessary to carry the illustrations further, as this form of training is more universally recognized than the others. Some points of difference between this and the technique of other arts and some misconceptions, however, should not pass unnoticed.

It can be seen at once that the technical skill to be obtained in expression must be somewhat different from an art like music. For the body is more than an instrument, it is an organism. The mind and the body we have found to be inseparably connected so as to exert continually a very great influence upon each other. Mind, we find, absolutely requires a physical organism as the means of its revelation, and the influence of the one upon the other is direct, and by unconscious co-ordination. So that it can never be the same as the relation between the musician and the piano. In the one case the skill obtained is entirely the result of deliberative acts of will, the result of choice and of long-continued practice; but in the other case, there is a necessary physiological and organic unity.

Still, though different from other forms of art there is as much necessity for technical training. In fact, there is a special necessity for preparatory training, on account of this organic connection and the element of habit. There is a habitual use of the organism from childhood, which may or may not be correct; at any rate, it is inadequate for some of the higher and grander forms of expression demanding a stronger execution, and a more ideal manifestation of the experience of the race. Such technical training is absolutely necessary, not only the preparatory training to remove the effects of habit, which has been discussed, but a training to cause the body and the voice to act according to their normal intention and to accomplish the highest possible results.

There is an old adage which has been applied to every phase of art. "You cannot learn to swim without going into the water." In the discussion here of the proper action of the mind in expression, and the necessity of the preparatory training of the voice and the body, it may be thought by some that we are endeavoring to prove this old adage wrong and that expression is to be improved indirectly, without direct practice in expression itself; that we are first to secure proper action of the mind; secondly, to train the voice and body, and then the man is simply to obey his impulses. But this is not what is here contended for. While the training of the voice and body must be separate and must usually precede technical execution, yet we can see at once that most of the exercises to develop proper action of the mind must consist in the direct work of expression itself.

We can see that all phases of the development of expression are intimately connected with each other. They can not be separated. It has been shown already how intimately connected are mental action and organic training; but mental action is still more intimately intertwined with technical action. In the first place, every technical step must be traced to its mental cause. Mental action is the only safeguard for the highest technique. One reason why Rush made the great mistake of advocating "minor inflections," "semitonic melodies," "intermittent stresses," and the like for the expression of sorrow, was because he found these things in life, and never looked at their mental and emotional cause. He thus failed to note that they are always used in weakness, either in weak men or in cases where emotion is no longer under control. The use of the guttural quality of voice by elo-

cutionists in rendering ideal poetry and noble emotion
is due to the same cause. If the cause of such tones in
character and experience had been examined, such a perversion of art would have been impossible. It was the
failure to compare the actions upon which technique was
founded with the actions of the mind, that caused and
still causes much elocutionary art to be led astray from
strength and truth. Character, thought and emotion
are thus the real foundation of all technique. The power
of the mode of emphasis to reveal the mind and to affect
in the right way another mind must ever furnish the test
of correctness.

We have another fundamental difference so far as the
acquirement of the technical skill is concerned between
expression as an art and an art like music. Though all
true art requires the mind to be centered upon the idea
rather than on modes of execution, still in the practice of
music the mind can be more upon the technique, while in
expression, the attention must primarily be upon the
action of the mind. In fact, technique must not be practice for its own sake, with the exception of a few elemental actions. All technique in delivery must be evolved
from the action of the mind. The necessity for the technique must be found in the nature of experience, for
whatever there is in experience we can find some mode
of revealing ; and true technical work in expression consists in finding the essential forms of experience and the
corresponding fundamental actions, in developing such
actions to the highest efficiency and in bringing them
into harmony with other phases of experience and their
modes of manifestation.

To illustrate further : one of the fundamental technical
points in elocution is phrasing. Now many have taken
this as a mere technical or mechanical point, and estab-

lished rules for its execution; in fact, in one important work on Elocution we have such rules as these laid down for phrasing: We are to pause before prepositions, before relative pronouns, after an extended subject, after every complete phrase, and the like; or, rules which have an element of truth in them, but are founded upon a study of the external form or the grammatical relations of the words. We have found that the mind progresses by a series of pictures, being successively focused upon each. If we study the way this action of the mind is naturally expressed in conversation, we find each picture brings the words belonging to it into a group. Here, then, we have a technical point obtained in the proper way; it is not a mere arbitrary rule, it is founded upon nature's own methods. Technique in an objective art like painting may possibly be the result of an arbitrary rule, but in a subjective natural art like expression, there can be no rule; everything must be the direct action of nature, and the technical training must be founded upon both the psychic and the physiological laws of man's being.

Many illustrations could be given, showing that all principles of expression must be founded on a direct study of the action of the mind, and the effect of such action upon the voice and body in conversation; thus the art of expression is more immediately founded upon the study of nature and the subjective soul than any other art; its very technique must be founded upon the effect of the actions of the mind, extended and developed and trained to their highest efficiency.

Nothing can furnish a substitute for direct and definite practice, persevering struggles and endeavors to reveal every emotion of the soul most effectively. All reformers in education have held that in some form, education must not be the mere acquirement of information; the acquirement of ideas must be ever followed by some kind of practice. While "to know" may be a high aim in education, "to do" and "to be" are still higher. While character or being is the highest aim of all education, "doing" must not be despised, because it is the only mode by which knowledge can be translated into being. "To know what to do and to do it enables a man to become in being what he is in knowledge."

In all education skill in execution must in some way be trained, in every artistic phase of education this is fundamentally necessary. In all modern education men have been filled with information, and this may be one reason why artistic education is so greatly neglected. Still another reason is, that the artistic phase of education is far more difficult; it is a far easier thing to obtain knowledge than to obtain skill in the manifestation and use of that knowledge. The love of truth is inherent in man, and can be easily stimulated and cultivated; but attainment and skill in artistic execution, though equally inherent, requires hard work, patience and long application. Beside, much of the practice called for is mechanical and uninteresting. While in the acquirement of knowledge there is great enjoyment from the first. All this is especially true of vocal expression; there is not much inspiration in work to make a voice flexible, or upon the muscles of the body to make them plastic. Young men studying for a profession can be easily inspired over the great principles of law, or great theories of theology; the whole soul may be awakened in the contemplation of such subjects; but to attain skill in execution speakers must stand upon their feet and practice long hours upon simple vocal exercises or physical movements; and above all, in patient struggles to render the deep phases of human experience.

But there is no other way in any art, and histrionic art, as can be seen, is no exception. A great lawyer is not merely one who possesses great knowledge of the law; a great teacher is not merely one whose head is crammed full of facts; a great preacher is not one who is merely versed in all the great problems of theology; it is not the artist alone who is measured by what he can do; every man who accomplishes great things for the race is so estimated. But above all, in every phase of oratory or expression, the speaker not only needs a knowledge of the true, the beautiful and the good, but there must be worked out an ideal in his soul and body and voice. He must have skill not only to comprehend ideas but to render every idea and phase of experience.

XV.

CRITICISM.

Lorsque nous croyons tenir la verite par un endroit, elle nous ecappe par mille autres.
— *Vauvenargues.*

WE have thus found some facts showing the complex nature of expression, and the still more complex problem of its development. In work which is so complex, so infinitely varied as this, so intimately connected with Nature herself in all its processes, no mechanical rules can be laid down. Nature's own subtle processes must be studied, and her own methods discovered and followed. But even after all our knowledge of the nature of expression, of its causes, its methods and modes of execution, good and bad, we still meet another great difficulty in our work of developing its power. After a thorough understanding of the nature of man, of his mind, of his body and of his voice; after a thorough knowledge of the actions, normal and abnormal, of all the faculties and agents in expression; after a thorough study of the processes of nature, how nature grows or retrogrades; still, deeper than all this knowledge must be a power of intuitive or instinctive insight into the fundamental needs of men. The teacher must have the power to see what a man ought to be, as well as what he is; and he must have insight into methods which are in accordance with nature's fundamental modes, and that can be so applied as to stimulate the man out of his actual condition along the lines of nature's ideal intentions. This new phase of the work may be called criticism.

It is very difficult to find any statement of the canons of criticism, notwithstanding the innumerable works upon the subject. Many think there are no great universal principles, so that it is difficult to find even an adequate definition of the term.

One teacher has endeavored to get several of our dramatic critics to give a talk to students upon the laws of dramatic criticism, to assist them in judging their own and others' work more intelligently. But so far he has failed to find one to appear before a class of students and talk over any of the general principles or reasons upon which he is accustomed to found his opinions.

There are many reasons for this hesitation. The subject is a difficult one, though it seems so simple. The standards of criticism have been changed in every age. In every great era of literature artists have arisen who have broken all the universally accepted rules. Demosthenes broke a principle of the Greek art of oratory at the close of his greatest oration. Shakespeare disobeyed and entirely ignored the unities which had governed the drama with a rod of iron from the time of the Greeks. Consciously or unconsciously, according to one great critic, he rose to a higher unity, to a deeper principle, which includes all that is important in the three, that is, the "unity of character." The greatest critic of Wordsworth's age said, "This will never do," and while he greatly hindered the influence of Wordsworth, and possibly fettered the genius and work of the poet, yet Wordsworth held out against the critic until the world came around to his view. For the last fifty years the critics have been struggling to find some principle by which to criticise the poetry of Robert Browning, until at last, except a few who are behind the times, even those who can not approve his work, are cautious in speaking of him.

As we look over the great criticisms of the past, we find an innumerable number of complete failures. In the diary of Pepys we find eulogy after eulogy pronounced upon dramatists who have long been completely forgotten, while we find many a sneer at the plays of Shakespeare, which are now the admiration of the world.

Even Shakespeare himself was affected by the critical judgment of his time so that he hardly dared to trust his own judgment. He actually thought Ben Jonson a greater artist than himself, and no doubt the critics of his time, though not the general public, were of this view. Hear Shakespeare in one of his sonnets :

> "When in disgrace with fortune and men's eyes,
> I all alone beweep my outcast state,
> And trouble deaf Heaven with my bootless cries,
> And look upon myself, and curse my fate,
> Wishing me like to one more rich in hope,
> Featured like him, like him with friends possessed,
> Desiring this man's art and that man's scope,
> With what I most enjoy, contended least," etc.

It is in the criticism upon the greatest artists that the greatest mistakes have been made. No great original artist has ever lived who did not receive much contemporary criticism that, long years after, has caused the world to smile. Hence, the greatest critics of the present time are extremely cautious in expressing their judgment, while the poorer class of critics conceal their real convictions beneath vague generalities.

Criticism is not merely retrospective. The world's conception of a critic is one who thoroughly understands the past achievements of art, and who judges each new artist by the past. But by such a standard the great artist whose work opens an entirely new field, is ever misconceived and misjudged. Such criticism is ever laughed at by succeeding generations. True criticism is prospective as well as retrospective, is prophetic as well as historical.

But much of our criticism is worse than this, it is merely a comparison by the critic of what he does not like with what he likes. It contains no insight, no sympathy, no dramatic element; he does not see anything from another's point of view, but looks at everything only from his own narrow conception, and thus misses the most fundamental element of its truth and power. The critics upon Wordsworth only compared, consciously or unconsciously, his work with the poetry of Pope, upon which they had fed for many years. Filled with admiration of Pope in criticising poetry, they were only looking for another Pope, and were wholly unprepared for the new departure. Where criticism is merely such a comparison, it is unworthy of the name; it only does harm, it hinders the progress of art, it kills many a sensitive and delicate Keats who has "fished a murex up," which will give color to the poetry of all after time. We can thus see that criticism is a dangerous thing, even in the humblest form. When wrong it limits nature, fetters the spontaneity of genius, kills enthusiasm, and restrains the sympathetic response which springs up in the heart of people for a great artist and causes men to stone the prophet that is sent unto them.

Criticism is not the comparison of one man with another. One button may be compared with another and criticised as to its imperfections, but it is unfair to compare a willow leaf with an oak leaf. Everything in nature is original; everything is made to carry out a specific intention. The folly of this method of criticism was long ago treated of in the old Greek fable of the debate between the stomach and the other members of the body. Criticism must not be an external comparison; it must look to ideal intention; to a deeper relationship; and no man can criticize his fellow-man till he more or less rises to such a height as to see something of the ideals, conscious and unconscious, that have caused the result. Nothing is so great a manifestation of weakness as the appearance of similarity among men. Mere social puppets who are made alike by conventionalities are of no use to the world. The strong man is ever the one who is most himself, most original, who thinks his own thoughts. Criticism, therefore, must not be a comparison of one man with another, or of one man's work with another's. The type may be different, the purposes may be different; the standard of criticism, if standard there be, can not be gained from mere study of one man or of any particular set of men.

Again, criticism is not fault-finding. The greatest fault-finders are always the poorest critics, and the best critics are rarely fault-finders. Mr. W. H. Pater has called one of his books upon criticism "Appreciations," not that he might use, as Mr. Weller would say, "a more tenderer word," but doubtless to emphasize the true or at least the chief function of criticism.

Again, we know that criticism is not always temporary. There are criticisms which have lived forever. The criticism of Shakespeare upon the players of his time is a criticism for the theater of any age. The little critical book sometimes attributed to Aaron Hill, written about a hundred and fifty years ago, is still worthy to be read and studied by every student of histrionic art.

The reason why criticism is temporary, and its laws so inadequate, is because its suggestions are little more than rules. They are not laws, for the laws of nature do not change. All suggestions are more or less upon the surface. The canons which have been formulated in relation to criticism are only the characteristics of one work of art, elevated into a rule for all art.

True criticism is a comparison of the actual with the ideal. This is the only kind of criticism that is worthy the name. That criticism which compares the actual work of art with the ideal of its author and judges of the actual attainments by comparing them with the ideal possibilities, will last forever. Mistakes will be made, but a right path is laid open which will lead out of the mistakes.

Nor is criticism the comparison of one man's ideal with another man's ideal. If one great artist erects a great cathedral in a certain position and another great artist comes along to criticise it, in proportion as he is a great artist will he be slow to find fault. He may at first as he looks at it think what he would have done, but he is very careful to make no comparison in this case. He tries to take in the whole situation and to look at all the phases of the situation, all the difficulties the artist had to encounter. He tries to get into the feeling of the artist's mind, and when he can say to himself, "I know what he tried to do," then he is able to give a just and adequate criticism. Anything short of this is mere fault-finding; it is mere comparative description, but is not true criticism.

The artist Hunt was taken by a sculptor once to see a statue upon which he was at work. The sculptor asked the great artist for a criticism, but Hunt shook his head and said, "I will wait till I know where you are going to place it." He could not criticise till he knew the whole situation and could enter into sympathy with the complete conception of his fellow-artist.

True criticism does not compare Shakespeare with Æschylus and say that Shakespeare was no artist because his work does not possess the same characteristics as that of the Greek poet, but it takes Shakespeare and the age in which he lived, the little province in which he moved, and studies his work and what he has done, ponders his great insight into character, studies him as a Christian poet and not as a Greek poet, as a romantic artist and not as a classic artist, looks at his little Globe Theater and the little narrow stage upon which were unfolded and represented all his mighty creations. The critic stands in the face of the little actual and gazes at the great ideal, at the great results, at the deep insight of the man into his time, and feels the sense of awe which comes from contact with one of the greatest of all earth's artists. If he goes back to the old Greek days and studies Æschylus and the men around him, the art of his time, the things that he endeavored to accomplish, and looks back upon him with sympathetic understanding of the results he tried to accomplish, then and then only, is he prepared to criticise the father of Greek drama, or to compare him with the greatest of the moderns.

The critic may take an ideal conception of what a drama ought to be and compare a special writer's ideal with the universal ideal; or he may compare the work of two dramatists with nature and with their different aims and the different circumstances under which their works were written. There must be frequently in criticism a comparison between two authors, but it is only a comparison of work or a comparison of ideal with ideal in their relationship to the universal ideal, the different methods they employ in reaching this, and the degree of success which has crowned the effort of each, and it never makes the work of one man a standard for that of another.

The requisites, therefore, of great criticism are first of all, insight into character, into poetry, into art, into the profoundest depths of human ideals and human endeavors. Let us illustrate this principle of criticism by the work of the greatest critic of our time. Mr. Matthew Arnold, just before his death, published a criticism upon America which was widely discussed and strongly resented. Now was it a true criticism or not? If on the one hand it was a mere comparison of America with England, it was not a just criticism. Mr. Matthew Arnold was an Englishman and from his childhood had been cradled in English customs. They were no doubt more comfortable to him because he was accustomed to them and was not accustomed to American ways. So that such criticisms would only be fault-finding. Besides, the vocation of England in history is different from the vocation of the United States. This is no disparagement to either nation. America could not, if she should try, become another England. There never can be another England. The historical outgrowth of the thousands of years under the same conditions will never occur again. What folly, then, to find fault with America because it is not like England.

But if on the other hand Mr. Matthew Arnold made a thorough study of our country until he could enter sympathetically into all our customs and into all our needs, and could conceive in his mind what America ought to be, and was able to judge what she might be from what she is, then his criticism was a just one. It was a comparison of a nation's actual with a nation's ideal. No doubt many of his criticisms were of this kind. Some belonged, probably, to the other class and were not criticisms at all.

In Robert Browning's poem on Andrea del Sarto, we have one of the best examples of criticism in the world. Some one has said, "If we should take all the Cyclopedias and all the knowledge which we can gather about Andrea del Sarto, and put them together, all would be

superficial and empty, but here we have a work of art."
Browning penetrates into the real spirit of the man, feels
the greatness of Andrea's ideals and the power of his
execution, makes his ideal, as is the case with every
artist, transcend his actual, and puts the criticism in the
mouth of the artist himself. It is the artist himself who
is realizing all his shortcomings. The penetration is so
deep, the criticism upon his art work lays bare the deepest motives of his soul and character. It reveals what
Andrea felt and realized regarding his own life and his
own art which he would hardly dare speak in words.
The criticism is founded upon the deepest intuitive insight.
We feel, also, the limitations of the man. We see him
writhing under the degradation of his own character and
art. We see one moment his ideal, and the next, his
actual life and actions ; now his endeavor to make himself
content with his actual, now a longing from the depths of
his soul, "Oh, but a man's reach should exceed his grasp."
Andrea compares himself with Raphael and Michael
Angelo, but the comparison is ever the realization of his
own deep needs. In a mere careless evening reverie
and conversation, the whole soul, life and work of the
man is laid bare. We behold the "faultless painter,"
rising on the wing of his own ideal, like an eagle, but we
see the strings that are tied about his feet dragging him
down every moment to the sordid, hypocritical, empty
life he is living. We see him rise, at one moment, on
the wing of what he might and could be under other
circumstances, the next moment, we feel his own semiconscious realization of the cord that drags him down
into the dust. We see him face to face with the painting
of Raphael, criticising Raphael and showing where his
drawing is wrong ; but in a moment we see him drop his
chalk, rub out his line and say, "The soul was right," and

that though the technique might be imperfect and fall to earth, the soul rose to heaven.

Such criticism is an art in itself, and in fact such must be the case with all true criticism. It must be governed by the highest artistic spirit. Mr. R. G. Moulton in his work on Shakespeare as a Dramatic Artist, has endeavored to apply an inductive method to criticism and thus to found what he calls a science of criticism. This is very well when he puts this in opposition to judicial criticism. All criticism must consist at times in gathering facts, and looking at all sides of a work of art. Thus I can agree with all Mr. Moulton has said; but he does not go far enough. Criticism is founded, it may be, upon a scientific method, but it is an art and is amenable to the laws and methods of art. Such criticism does not cover all the ground. It might fully apply to the art of Zola, and it furnishes a great assistance to an introductory study of any author; but induction is an intellectual process. Such criticism covers only the intellectual facts of art. Criticism which stopped there would be almost as cold as mere conventional judicial criticism. True criticism, like all true art, must rise into the realm of appreciation and feeling. There must be imaginative insight as well as sympathetic, dramatic, intuitive assimilation. Mr. Moulton in his interpretive readings of literature, furnishes the best example of the truth of this. He abandons himself to emotions often too much, reading in a swing which is not the true metre or rhythm of the poem, but a mannerism of his own, which appears the same in nearly all his renderings; but he does give the feeling and spirit of the author and his art. Here is where such a method is superior to conventional, authoritative, dogmatic or judicial criticism. While it deals with the intellectual side, it does not fetter emotion.

But in the hands of one not dominated by noble feeling, such an inductive method of criticism would result in carrying science into the realm of art and in trying to measure and control imagination and feeling by reason. Such a course literally followed will kill the artistic spirit. The critic must know where to stop an intellectual process. Not by reasoning, but by an instinct as unerring as that of the creative artist himself. Not only so, but all his intellectual processes are only preparatory to a broader and deeper appreciation, so that the artistic critic can rise to a parallel interpretation, that by two personalities the mystery of art may be felt more effectively by all. The critic must have artistic feeling as well as the artist. The great trouble with criticism is not that it is judicial, but that its judgments are one-sided and premature. It is not subjective but objective. It is not imaginative, not sympathetic, not appreciative, not a harmonious union of science and art, but an invasion of the realm of art by the coldest scientific spirit. True criticism never stands off as any thing separate, much less superior to art; but is itself an art governed by its deepest and most fundamental principles.

In the highest and best sense of the word all criticism must be essentially dramatic. The imaginative insight into another's conception, and the power to feel a situation beyond a man's own soul and life are absolutely demanded before judgment can become any thing but mere fault-finding or flattery. If it is difficult for us to see ourselves as others see us, it is far more difficult to see another as he sees himself, or as he himself sees what he ought to be. But this is absolutely necessary or true criticism is impossible.

One of the fundamental requisites of criticism, therefore, must be insight into character, into motives and habits, and the ability to distinguish habit from nature. There must also be insight into nature's recuperative power, insight into hinderances, insight into the depths of the soul, a sympathetic appreciation of the ideal of another, the motives and possibilities of one often entirely foreign in spirit to ourselves.

But the critical insight is more than dramatic. Dramatic insight enables us to enter into sympathy with the Philip drunk, but critical insight enables us in the Philip drunk to see the Philip sober and to appeal from the one to the other. The true critic not only sees the man as a living personality before him, with all his imperfections on his head, but sees into the struggles, into the guiding ideal, into the inspiring motive of the life, and even catches glimpses of his most latent possibilities.

Of all men in the world, the critic must not be a faultfinder. Above all, he must not be concerned with mere externalities. No critic is a critic until he can criticise from within out. So it was with Lamb, whose depth of imagination could penetrate into the ideal and mission of Wordsworth, into the beauty of his conceptions, the simplicity of his language, the delicacy of his imagination and the profundity of his insight into nature. It was only a Lamb who could free himself from the mechanical perfections of Pope, that had ears to hear the new voice that spoke to the world. The gentle Lamb, whose dramatic criticisms were so wonderful that they are still studied with great care, almost alone of all the critics was able to penetrate into the ideal of Wordsworth. Knowing all the poetry of the past, he had so entered into sympathy with its higher ideals and tendency that he could see and appreciate the new departure.

The same is true of the poetry of Browning. It has taken the world fifty years to get into a sufficient under-

standing of the meaning of the new voice, of its difference from the old, of its meaning to the world, to bring
forth any legitimate criticism.

Most of the criticisms upon Browning have been
merely a comparison of Browning with Tennyson, or
with Wordsworth, or with some other poet. To criticise
Browning we must be able to appreciate his ideal. We
must get at the central word of his prophecy; we must
even get at the conception of his ideas of art; he may
not only have an idea of what he is to do, but an idea of
how he is to do it.

There must also be a recognition of limitations. The
critic must feel that mere external perfection may be the
greatest weakness. True criticism is not merely concerned with external imperfections, but penetrates into
the depths. What flippant criticism can be offered upon
David in the midst of his mistakes and failures! and yet
he is called "The man after God's own heart," a criticism
which three thousand years have not reversed.

We find in every man's heart two desires. The first is
a desire to be judged by his fellow-men, a desire to know
their opinion. There is everywhere by all aspiring souls
a longing for true criticism. The world possibly needs
less fault-finding, but it needs more criticism. Many a
young man, many a young writer, many a young speaker
has looked with longing to an older, and desired advice
and suggestions, but has looked in vain. Side by side
with this longing, a second and seemingly direct contradiction rises up in the breast and says, "I am judged by
no man, it is God who judges me." Both of these are
right. The second is merely a reaction against the dull-
ness of insight. Against the deep insight of true criticism
there is no rebellion in noble souls. These long for those
who can see into the depth of the soul, "the penetrating

stream of tendency that makes for righteousness," the ideal intention of the nature of the man, conscious or unconscious, and nature's power to transform the abnormal into the normal.

Here, then, is the province of criticism. It is the power of the soul of man to go beyond its own egoistic conceptions, and see others as they see themselves, and realize their highest possibilities often unknown to the men themselves. It is insight into an ideal, in the midst of a degraded actual, and into a method by which we can appeal to nature's recuperative power, and transform the actual into the ideal.

Bad criticism is characterized either by fault-finding, or by flattery. The aim of criticism is not to praise, not to compliment, not to condemn, but to inspire. There must be no personal comparison, but the inspiration of a great personality. Bad criticism discourages a man, because it either compares him with another and so gives him no clear insight into his own possibilities, or offers no road to a higher plane, awakens no conception in the student of the connection of his actual and his ideal, gives him a false standard of comparison. Great criticism ever makes a man see better his own ideal, causes him simultaneously to realize his own possibilities, as well as imperfections. There is no comparison with others, but an awakening of a comparison in the student's own breast between what he is and what he can become. True criticism, therefore, sooner or later encourages, awakens hope and enthusiasm; it makes man despise the low and mean, makes men often blame themselves for departures from their ideal, but ever "allures to brighter worlds, and leads the way"; it ever shows the possibilities of the ideal in the actual. It shows man that here in his poor, miserable actual in which he now stands, is the beginning of his ideal. It only discourages and displeases the self-satisfied and indolent — the man without an ideal. Whoever works by an ideal more severely measures his actual by it than any other can, and hence takes courage when another soul with insight into the situation reveals its impressions.

Of the importance of this to the world, no word need be said. The great critic encourages the weak cause, he punctures shams it may be, exposes the hollowness of affectation, and the lack of foundation for all pretension, but he shows the world beauties which its dull eyes would not see, and shows the individual struggling artist a path, unseen before, that leads to higher destinies.

There has been lately, a great deal of sneering at criticism. Men continue to quote Lord Beaconsfield's statements, that critics are simply artists or writers who have failed; and many who have been unwilling to have their imperfections spoken of have endeavored to bring criticism into disrepute. But if criticism is founded upon the insight of one soul into the ideals of another, of the power to see nature's intentions regarding a man, of the man's own ideal, as well as actual attainments and limitations, whether as a writer, an artist or as a man; and if criticism aims to make the man realize all this, we can see at once the necessity of criticism to the world. It has encouraged the faint-hearted, as often as it has discouraged the pretentious.

There is nothing so encouraging as true criticism. A great artist, even like Shakespeare, only vaguely realizes his own ideal, on account of the fact that they are so different from the work about him, and in hours of discouragement often "longs for this man's art, and that man's scope."

An artist ever criticises himself more severely than any one else. He knows more the imperfections of his work.　He sees the shortcomings of his art, and for this reason, every great artist often goes to lay open his work before another, for suggestion and criticism, when he has brought himself seemingly against an impassable barrier. When a great critic endeavors to interpret his work as he conceives it, whether his estimate is quite right or not, it helps the artist to a wider view, leads him to understand certain hinderances, and enables him to remove them.

After an artist has brooded long over his work, at one time he feels its greatness, but often after he has finished a work, sometimes his finest, he says he must try all over again.　Here it is that the critic steps in with a fresh heart, with as high a power of appreciation, and the artist looks at his work through other eyes.　Thus, if the inner life of every great artist could be seen, it would be found that criticism or the endeavors of others to express their appreciation has played a great role in his development.

What a function is this! what breadth of information is required! what spiritual insight is necessary!　Well may it be said, that the great critics of the world have been few.　It is not strange that men have hesitated to unfold the philosophy of such a subject, and that so few of our best critics have endeavored to give an explanation of the principles of their own work.

There are many reasons why the subject should be discussed here.　All true criticism is founded in dramatic instinct.　The stage as "the mirror held up to nature" has ever been one of the chief means for the criticism of life; and hence all histrionic expression is closely connected with, if it is not the fountain-head of all criticism. But the special reason is because expression can never be improved except by the aid of criticism.　Criticism alone is inadequate; but the best method of training can not be applied except by skill in penetrating into the most fundamental needs of men. Hence it has been necessary to unfold the general nature of criticism in order to understand its complex nature in relation to the development of expression. The first requisite, as the man whose powers are to be improved stands before the teacher, is what may be called a psychic diagnosis. Criticism, for the purpose of improving expression, is not the same as that of a mechanical work of art. It is not the criticism of a statue before which we can stand and around which we can walk and upon which we can lay our measuring line. Criticism in expression is not a criticism upon a perfect whole or process, but upon what is imperfect in method and result. The teacher must study a young mind struggling to reveal itself, through an imperfect conception of the nature of expression, through imperfect action of the mind in realizing truth and experience, and through imperfect conditions and improper use of his body and voice.

I once asked a physician very skillful in diagnosis, to give me some of the principles upon which he acted in making up his judgment as to the nature of a disease; but he frankly told me he could not. He said there could be no rule. It had to come to him as he looked the man in the eye. It came from so many directions and diverse ways that it was impossible to formulate a general principle. If this is true of pathological diagnosis, how much more must it be true of diagnosis into the normal and abnormal action of the faculties of the soul and agents of the body in expression. For a diagnosis of a student of expression is not merely physical and vocal, it is psychic. It is, in short, a diagnosis of the whole man, not merely as to character or aim or degree of culture, but as to the normal and abnormal action of all the faculties and agents of man in expression. The character of the student's train of ideas, the responsiveness of feeling to ideas, the responsiveness of his body to emotion; harmonious co-ordination of the whole body; the action of the voice; what nature intended him to be and what he is made by habit; his peculiar temperament and type as a man, his occupation, his health, are but a few of those points which sweep like lightning through the mind of the faithful teacher as he stands face to face with his pupil. The true teacher looks for his beginning not to a system, but to the individual needs before him. He must begin with the pupil where he is. He must have respect for the pupil's conceptions and his ideas as to the nature of expression. But above all he must have respect for the unconscious ideal. He must, in fact, have deeper insight into possibilities and needs, than the student has himself. It is only from such insight that a prescription can be made. Without such a conception all exercises given will be merely experiments.

Then, again, there are subjective difficulties; all work to improve expression must be directed toward the correction of wrong habit and the development of normal actions, and yet a man's consciousness makes no distinction between habit and nature. Whatever a man is habitually, he thinks is normal and natural to him. This habit is called second nature, the aim of the teacher is to correct the "second nature," and bring the man back to fundamental nature. So that criticism must enter into the deepest life of the man, to enable him to distinguish between what is habit and what is nature. The pupil must be led so as to discover this himself, because it can not always be told or even shown.

Again, in making careful estimate and judgment as to what will improve delivery, there must be an accurate conception of the limitations that dwarf the possibilities of pupils, the hinderances that prevent the growth and development of their personalities. The teacher of expression at one time, may make a diagnosis which is so deep and searching that it may take many years to fulfill; at another time he may have to teach some poor minister who comes to him to be corrected, in a few hours, of a sore throat, and yet in each case, like a physician, professional honor demands of him to do his best. Again, if a man is to be a speaker, he must have a different diagnosis from one who is to be an actor, a reader or teacher.

Every danger in all kinds of criticism is found here, such as comparison of one person with another, getting a conception from one great artist, and endeavoring to make every thing conform to this standard. Trying to limit one personality to another, however great the model may be, is wrong. Every soul must be original. The only possibility for growth must be from a free soul, unfolding in its own way. Criticism which violates this, training which does not accomplish this, is false to nature's fundamental law.

Still worse is that criticism which is founded upon the comparison of an individual in respect to his work in expression with an artificial system. A teacher has an idea of certain stresses of voice, and every example, however well rendered and natural, must be made to conform to the system. The first word in the sentence, "Angels and ministers of grace defend us," one author says must be given with a circumflex of an octave. This is absolutely false to the experience many must feel in the situation, but everybody must be governed by this particular artist's mechanical system of giving such and such emotions with such and such inflections of a given mechanical length.

Besides, there are especial dangers such as exist in no other kind of work. In criticisms upon books or art, the whole world stands ready to correct mistakes and the critic himself feels that at any moment he can be arraigned at the bar of public opinion, where his every sentiment will be tested by the ideas and convictions of other men. But the teacher of expression stands face to face with the one he is teaching, and has no such limitation, no such inspiration, no such help to correct mistakes. Hence he is tempted unconsciously to fall back upon his own authority, measure all by his own opinion, to judge everything by his own little system, and to compare the pupil's voice or action with his own, independent of inherent differences of personality.

Here we find the reason why great readers, great speakers and great actors have often been found poor teachers. Working out their own ideals and their own personalities, and becoming strong in their own way of doing things, they are apt to judge all others by themselves. They often set themselves up as examples, rather than seeking to inspire the student to find out for himself. Such a teacher makes himself the model, consciously or unconsciously; thinking of what he can do himself, he is often unable to see differences and the possibilities even in other men. A great teacher must lose his own self and find it in other men. He must bury his own way of doing things, that he may stimulate the ideas and conceptions of another soul. He must, of course, have had such experience himself as to realize his own possibilities, must have, himself gone through the struggles through which his pupil must go. He must be no mean reader, no mean speaker, no mean actor, but the greater portion of his work must be to hide himself and to awaken others.

But some one will say all this is general. How can such a theory be realized? Is not such discussion, after all, mere speculation? The simple aim of criticism is to tell a man his faults. But vast numbers, who are wholly untrained, are able to speak of faults. Their suggestions, however, are hardly worthy the name of criticism. The man himself gets little clew to his fundamental needs. Knowledge of a fault will only discourage a man until he can be conscious of its nature, its cause and some adequate mode of remedying it. True criticism does not deal so much with faults as to awaken a consciousness of the fundamental need lying beneath, and causing faults, and to suggest to the man proper modes of meeting this need. No absolutely perfect leaf can be found on earth.

What good does it do to tell a man his voice is throaty or nasal or hard? In a vast number of instances, such suggestions only make the faults worse, or in making efforts to correct them introduce others still worse. Take one of the worst of all faults, the so-called ministerial tone. Let a man be told that he has this fault, and, in trying to avoid it, he will often try to speak without any emotion at all, and sometimes endeavor to introduce colloquial circumflexes, thus developing abnormal conditions which are fully as bad, in many instances, as the fault he is trying to correct.

How foolish, therefore, is the statement of a great professor in homiletics, made, I have heard, to his class, that it would be well enough for them to invest about a dollar in elocution, and have somebody tell them their faults. Alas, for such a misconception of the great problem of delivery. It is no wonder that our preachers, with such instruction, have such wretched delivery. It is no wonder, with such a conception of training, that

everything belonging to delivery is too often superficialized and degraded.

Hence, to correct a fault like the so-called ministerial
tone, the teacher can lay out a programme of work which
will remove the cause of the difficulty. He can test the
ear of the man, to see whether the seat of the trouble is
there. He can call the attention of the man to the fundamental elements of conversation. He can open his
eyes to the universal normal which men call natural; to
the inflections and forms of speech, wherein they vary
with different people; and wherein they are the same.
The student himself has thus a normal, to which he can
compare himself, and thus bring his need into consciousness; or the teacher may find an inflexible voice, proceed
to work upon this, and develop its normal action.

Do the methods of developing delivery unfolded in this
book furnish a basis for true criticism, and not for mere
fault-finding? The whole problem opens before the
mind, the whole process; the faithful teacher will ever
consider the cause, the means and the effect, in expression. Not merely regard one phase of the problem but
will consider all from a central fundamental standpoint.
Criticism upon delivery tends to be taken up merely with
the outside, merely with the effect; but it is not true
criticism till it can indicate causes and more adequate
use of the proper means.

But he must go deeper still, for the one-sided voice may
be caused by a one-sided mind. The consciousness of the
man must be awakened not by instruction, not by words,
but by being set to work upon great examples of literature, by struggles to express the deeper passions, so that
he can feel the difference between the expression of controlled emotion and the expression of uncontrolled feeling.
Thus the speaker will awake to the fact that his thought

and emotion have not been balanced by will. He can be made to see the cause of his defects. He can be shown, also, that he has not received an impression from the successive ideas passing through the mind, and that the emotion he delivers is only a general ecstatic condition rather than definite feeling caused by the picture in his mind at the time of speaking.

Mere random work with a teacher who has no conception of the fundamental causes of faults often accidentally does good. But too often the student is made self-conscious and mechanical; his real power is fettered or new faults are introduced. The only safe and adequate method is training directed to specific causes.

Thus criticism, like all true art, is only suggestive. It can never be fully communicated in words, especially in so subjective and subtle a work as the development of delivery. The teacher must "do the thing," or rather cause the student to "do the thing shall breed the thought."

Especially is this true of expression, for abuses and bad habits in the use of the voice are more unconscious than any other kind of abnormal action. Hence the necessity of a carefully arranged programme of steps, beginning with that which is most fundamental on the one hand, and on the other, with that in which the student is most normal; and thus the student is set to work until he works out in his own consciousness a conception of his needs. Every true teacher of delivery, after having tried to explain to the student, and after having thought that the student understood his need, has been surprised after some weeks to hear the student come and express the same thing back to him as if it were an original discovery on his part. It makes the teacher realize Browning's words that "the truth is within ourselves." It is the very nature of expression that a consciousness of it can only come through execution. The greatest minds on earth can never adequately explain to another the nature of delivery or the needs for its improvement. All that can be done is a suggestion of the place to begin to work, and the teacher and the pupil working side by side, a consciousness of the need is thus formed.

There must also as a rule, be work in contact with the greatest literature. A low class of literature nearly always demands abnormal modulations of the voice, and tends to degrade the student rather than elevate him. A low order of literature, therefore, rarely shows a man his faults, especially in public speaking, while occasionally something ridiculous or farcical aids in the discovery of affectation and stiltedness, yet there must not be too much practice upon these, as a corresponding fault will be acquired.

In many of our schools and colleges the students elect literature that they may have something easy, but it should be the hardest of all studies. The student who has not been called upon to give expression to that which was in a sense beyond him, or has not struggled with its greatness, has not almost, if not actually, wept over his inadequacy to manifest the vaguely-conceived grandeur, has never realized the power of literature to develop the human soul itself as well as the power of expression.

The great teacher's words are ever few; while his insight must be deep, deeper than that of the student into needs and possibilities; yet his aim is to stir the energies of the man that these may be awakened and all faults thrown off from the energy within. If every imperfect leaf and limb should be taken from any tree, however great and beautiful, nothing would be left but a trunk; and so, if from some artificial standard every specific imperfection by a species of fault-finding, be torn from delivery, all power would be gone. A machine would take the place of a living man. The greatest of all mistakes is to apply a mechanical standard to a living organism. True criticism has to do with the depth and not merely with the surface. It has to do with the root, and only with the leaves through the internal life of the tree. It must ever be profound and severe ; must ever be frank and honest ; but never can be anything more than suggestive, and while external pruning is sometimes necessary, yet criticism must ever be dependent upon and measured by the energy and power it awakens in the depths of the soul.

From our study of the problem of expression and the principles of nature, we have found that expression as a sequence and co-ordination of organic or natural actions, must be developed according to the laws of growth from within out, from center to surface and in all directions. The whole being must be made to act in greater unity, and this not by external manipulation, but by some kind of stimulation of the central impulses. The human being we find to be more complex than any other object in nature. We find that conscious and unconscious, voluntary and involuntary elements are always present in any true natural act of expression, however real and simple. That spontaneity in art has ever resulted from a simultaneous growth in the unconscious or involuntary processes of the human soul, as well as in the conscious and the voluntary, and also in their power to act without interfering with each other. Hence the ordinary method in striving to make every thing conscious or to deal with the conscious and voluntary only, is one-sided and causes artificiality and unnaturalness.

Hence, to improve expression so as to fulfill all the conditions of the problem we must first stimulate the cause, secure proper action and conditions of the organic agents, and lastly there must be skill in execution. All of these are mutually necessary. Other arts have more to do with this skill or the technical work because execution is by a mechanical instrument, but expression is entirely dependent upon organic agents and the execution of actions natural to them.

As a locomotive requires an engine properly adjusted, with fuel and fire and steam, and a track constructed to suit the engine, and lastly, knowledge of the levers and stops that control the movements, and skill in their use, so in expression the soul must be properly roused, the voice and body adequately trained and subordinated, and lastly, knowledge of art and human nature must be acquired and skill to execute the simple fundamental actions necessary to reveal the subjective conditions. Unless the elemental actions of the mind are developed, and unless the voice and body are properly trained, the unconscious and involuntary actions of the soul in expression will not be secured. When all work is upon mere technique, attention is perverted and consciousness rendered abnormal, until even the laws of thinking are violated. Hence speakers often become unable to speak extemporaneously. They must either memorize words and even actions, and give you mere signs, or merely read with motion or modulation. All is made mechanical.

Studying all these forms of training together prevents any one of them from becoming exaggerated. All sides receiving attention, the whole man is developed, and growth is normal from a mystic center and in all directions. As expression is subjective and mystic, it is very difficult for a man to realize his imperfections; hence another must mirror to him, must suggest in some way to the man more clearly his own possibilities and ideals. This is one of the most difficult functions that criticism has to perform. It calls for the greatest care. There must be insight into the ideals and needs of another. There must be sympathetic inspiration and stimulation of neglected impulses, an appeal to higher ideals, and an understanding of all kinds of hindrances and an application of remedies suited to each case.

All this is a mere outline of general principles which characterize true methods for the development of delivery. The specific study of particulars and the far-reaching character and effect of such a method must be left to future investigations.

III.

Tradition.

" Man was made to grow, not stop;
  That help he needed once, and needs no more,
  Having grown up but an inch by, is withdrawn;
  For he hath new needs, and new helps to these,
  This imports solely, man should mount on each
  New height in view; the help whereby he mounts,
  The ladder-rung his foot has left may fall,
  Since all things suffer change, save God the truth.
  Man apprehends Him newly at each stage
  Whereat earth's ladder drops, its service done;
  And nothing 'shall prove twice what once was proved."

— Browning.

XVI.

THE AID OF HISTORY.

"Man must pass from old to new,
From vain to real, from mistake to fact,
From what once seemed good to what now seems best;
How could man have progression otherwise?"

THUS far we have studied face to face with nature some of the aspects of histrionic expression. We have sought especially for hints from nature as to proper modes of developing expression. It has been the endeavor to look directly into nature, as free as possible from all shackles of tradition and conventional views.

Everything human has a history. In the pursuit of any subject, while nothing must come between the mind and nature at the time of investigation, yet after new results are obtained, comparison with results obtained in the past, is one of the safest tests of truth. Without such a comparison there is a continual tendency to run off on a tangent, and to live over again the errors which were exploded centuries ago.

There is a tendency, of course, in a historic method, to become too conservative — to regard the past too highly. The superficial student of history, who has . merely aggregated facts, fears every new discovery and advance as a departure from truth. But in a right study of history there is the greatest inspiration to progress; for the mind becomes imbued with the tendency to advance, which underlies all history from age to age, and hence is not retarded but is rather impelled forward to higher views. The student is made not only more sensitive to errors, more alive to all evil tendencies, but also more confident of every step he takes in advance.

Hence, this work will seem incomplete, if not entirely uncalled for, unless we review in outline the struggles over this problem in the past. So, having now arrived at certain conclusions from an unfettered study of nature, let us return to a study of the leading aspects of expression in the past, and test whether what we have found is progressive· or retrogressive. While even in stage art, which is very apt to be governed by tradition, the greatest merit of the greatest actors has been the breaking away from tradition; yet even these, who have advanced their art by a closer study of nature, among the foremost of whom may be mentioned Mr. Henry Irving, have been themselves most studious of tradition.

The general plan of investigation in this work has been to follow the method which has been most successful in the advance of every department of art. Art, wherever it has gone astray, has done so from a slavish following of tradition, and has always been reformed by fresh, direct study of nature. In fact, the fetters of conventionality have ever been forged by the misuse of tradition, and substitution of authority and example for a direct study of nature. The great use of history is to furnish a light to tell whether we are in her stream of tendency that is ever advancing, or whether we are turning aside into some current that leads us back to methods which have long since been thrown aside as hindrances.

A right study of history serves to impress us more strongly with the necessity of a direct study of nature. It shows us that all the great failures in the study of art have been endeavors to reproduce the effects of some great masters, to elevate accidental remarks into binding rules; or, from a failure to keep in direct sympathy with nature and to follow her methods, in some way to become narrow and one-sided. Tradition teaches indirectly more than it does directly. It shows us how others have followed nature, and how they have failed, and the cause of such failure. In fact, history itself must be studied face to face with nature. The problem must be grasped before history is intelligible. Nature is before our eyes as it was before the eyes of the greatest master. If we study the great master without studying nature, we miss his lesson, as we are apt to look merely at the outside of his work and accept his word as absolute authority. But after we have studied the great problem which he studied as well as his interpretation of it, then we are far less liable to make mistakes. Nay, more, then only can we read his lesson. Even Shakespeare's plays, the greatest studies of nature, can never furnish a substitute for the study of nature herself. In fact, the greatness of Shakespeare can never be appreciated unless there is a direct comparison of all his work with human nature.

One of the greatest needs of elocution is a careful investigation of its history, but no such work has ever been written. Many of the aids to other departments of art are not so applicable to expression, but in methods of development at least, a study of the methods of the past would save men from repeating again and again, age after age, the same errors. While during the last hundred and fifty years, well-defined stages of development can be seen, yet to-day, as we look over the condition of elocution, we find that nearly every one of the methods discarded a hundred years ago is still practiced. This, it seems, could not be, if there were any careful, fundamental study of the history of methods.

One little book, "A Plea for Spoken Language," has discussed some of the topics connected with the history of elocution, but it is professedly a plea for Rush and the mechanical methods of his system. Besides, there are a great many mistakes. For example, Walker is put down as the discoverer of inflection, and Joshua Steele as the one who proved it by further investigation; while the fact is, that Joshua Steele's book was published in 1775, while Walker's book was not published until five or six years later. The author also discusses Walker before Sheridan, although Sheridan's first book was published in 1759, about twenty years before Walker's work. There are, however, many valuable suggestions in Mr. Murdoch's book, but it does not profess to be a history.

The subject is, in fact, extremely difficult for many reasons. First of all, because the art is a completely passing one. What Demosthenes said, we have, or at least enough of it to show his style; but how he spoke it, the modulations of his voice, his action, his whole manner of delivery, are lost. We have the plays of the great dramatists, but we have little or no adequate means of knowing the methods of the actors who "created" the parts. All dramatic art is a mirror held up to nature "to show the very age and body of the time, its form and pressure," but modes of rendering this form and pressure, though they leave so strong an effect upon the world, themselves pass entirely away.

No adequate means have ever been discovered for recording the methods of actors. Many great hopes have been awakened since the wonderful invention or discovery of the phonograph, but while one is able to recognize Mr. Gladstone's voice, for instance, yet much of the color of his tone is lost, and the general action and manner of the man, of course, are entirely absent. So, while the phonograph will do much, at most, it will never be able to record anything but the vocal expression.

If there is great difficulty in recording the effects and modes of expression, the difficulty of recording the methods of developing delivery is far greater. Many of the most illustrious teachers have concealed their methods. Nearly every instructor has some special principle or truth, some peculiar set of exercises, which he uses for the accomplishment of his end, yet these he keeps to himself. There is little or no opportunity of comparing them with the work of other teachers, and with their author they nearly always die.

Again, as has been shown, the work of developing expression is so subjective and intuitive that the teacher himself rarely conveys clearly the methods by which he accomplishes his results. The spirit of criticism — the spirit by which the great teacher helps his pupil — is almost clairvoyant in character. Such an instructor has no rules about the most important parts of his teaching. The statement of his modes and principles of work is even more difficult than the statement of the principles of poetry or the fundamental methods of the great artists in any department.

The history of expression may be considered from many points of view. It is as has been proved, most intimately associated with all forms of art, hence every period and change in the history of art is shown in expression. Thus among our readers we have also the various schools of art. The idealist and the realist are as clearly seen in this form of art as anywhere. But in the present work the only point to bring out is the various methods of teaching delivery, not the history of the various forms of the art.

It was the intention, when this work was first undertaken, to bring out a short history of the methods of developing delivery, but the material became so great that this was found impossible. Besides, there are yet great gaps which the writer has been unable to bridge satisfactorily. Before that phase of the work is published, many years of investigation will be required.

Hence, there will be no endeavor to trace the history of elocutionary methods at present. It will not be possible to touch the work of individual teachers. All that will be undertaken is an outline of the leading methods which have been followed for the past hundred years, and which are still being followed at the present time. Such an outline is very unsatisfactory, but the lesson is so important that it must be undertaken although the treatment may be inadequate.

It must be granted that men do not see things alike. In every department of art, there have always been different schools. Hence, there must be different schools of elocution. There are no rules in such a great art. Every great method must be founded upon Nature herself, and must be consistent, also, with the personality of the man who applies it. The work, too, is many-sided. One man will see it from one point of view, and another from 'nother. To one man every need centers in articulation; to another, every need centers in the voice; to another, every need centers in pantomime. One man will have strong impulses in his heart, and will naturally trust them more in teaching; while another will have little spontaneity, will do everything deliberately, and endeavor to bring all into consciousness. One teacher will be apt to look at his own execution, which has received the approval of the world, and will show a pupil how he himself does a thing to make it effective. He is especially liable to do this if he has worked long, and has come to be a master of expression in his own voice and body. His whole nature has become concentrated in his own modes of execution, and when he comes to teach others, he gauges all by the methods evolved in his own experience.

Again, another teacher will have a very correct ear. This may have been so cultivated that every shade of inflection and melody is clearly revealed to his mind. He has worked hard upon the subtleties of mechanism, peculiar kinds of inflection and stress, and the years of attention devoted to these unconsciously cause him to lift them to the very highest place in the development of delivery. He arranges rules from his mechanical analysis, and endeavors to bring his pupils to the standard of the special action of his own mechanism. Again, another may discover the weakness of such a method, and will fall back upon the mere unguided impulses of his nature. This to him is natural. He sees the impossibility of conforming to an artificial standard without developing self-consciousness and weakness, so he throws overboard every standard, and says that it is only thought, however it may be given, that moulds men. Still another may pass out into the realm of philosophy and even theology, and secure an artificial standard like a trinity, and trace it through the whole universe and apply it to the different aspects of delivery.

Hence, there will ever be different schools. We must recognize that there are more ways than one of doing every thing. Schools of art are more or less of an advantage, as they inspire a broader study of the subject. Even a method which sometimes seems wholly wrong may bring forth results which are not absolutely bad. The reason for this is that the methods for developing the art may be worse than the results. A reader, for example, may read better than the methods by which he was taught seem to warrant. The student, in studying a subject, receives inspiration, and may lay aside or disobey the teaching. His impulses may be followed, and the rule that is given may be disobeyed. The personality of the teacher, being greater than his beloved system, may awaken inspiration in the heart of the pupil that will break the shackles of a narrow system that would otherwise bind him down to artificiality. Some have gone so far as to say that the method makes very little difference. If a teacher will only set his pupil to work, no matter how bad the methods, good will result.

There is an element of truth in all this. Yet, where one student has worked himself free by the inspiration of his own heart and instincts from the effect of bad methods and has risen to success, vast numbers, whose voices are never heard, have been injured, and their natural power destroyed.

The same is true in all great art. The idealist and the realist arise from what men conceive nature to be and what she is capable of becoming. Still, as men pass to too great an extreme in either direction, they pass out of the realm of art ; the realist into the realm of mere facts, the idealist into vague dreams.

Hence, while we must ever be free to study all methods and to find the good in them, we must remember that here, as everywhere, there is a standard of truthfulness which, while it is free to develop various types, possesses certain fundamental conditions which are ever absolute and unchangeable.

The division here followed must, of course, be considered as the opinion of only one, and must not be taken as absolutely complete. Some one must begin, however, and so this attempt is ventured. There will be an endeavor to be perfectly fair, though this will be difficult, as many teachers combine two or three of the methods here presented. Every one of the schools has been studied, not merely from books, but personally, as the writer has been a pupil of teachers of every one of these methods.

XVII.

THE IMITATIVE SCHOOL.

Imitation is suicide. — Emerson.

OF all the methods for the development of delivery, possibly the oldest is the imitative. Many in every age have practiced this method; but the teachers who have practically followed it while not theoretically believing in it, are still more numerous. Even mechanical teachers like Walker and even Sheridan, bewail the fact that they have to adopt imitation. Their method was in violation of their own principles, as they themselves confessed.

Those who believe in this method quote from Aristotle, and contend that all art is founded upon imitation, or at least, must begin in imitation. The writer must begin, they say, by imitating some writer before him. Even Shakespeare began by imitating Marlowe.

Another argument is, that in a mystic art like delivery, where so much is subjective, the only way to get at the subject, they say, is by imitation. All art requires example, and in delivery the only way is for one man to speak a sentence by way of example, and to have the pupil follow by imitation. The art is too subtle for analysis, hence there is no way to improve it except by direct or indirect imitation. By direct imitation the pupil is made to do exactly as the teacher does. By indirect imitation the teacher chiefly imitates the faults of the pupil, imitating and showing what the pupil is to avoid.

Of course it cannot be denied that there are elements of truth in all these arguments. To a certain extent, every great teacher must give illustrations directly through his own voice. A teacher of any method must often illustrate two or three modes of execution to quicken the insight of students into what is true or false to nature; into what suggests weakness or strength.

Another argument for the adoption of this method is the fact, that since methods for the development of delivery can never be given in writing, the traditions regarding the art must ever be of fundamental importance. Hence, a most popular method, especially in studying for the stage, is to give to students the traditions of how leading actors and artists spoke, and have them execute these by imitation.

This method is the one followed at the illustrious School of Declamation for the training of actors in Paris. I have made two journeys for the careful investigation of the methods of this school. My first visit was in the spring of 1880, and my second in the spring of 1882. My knowledge of it came through M. Regnier, who for forty years was the leading actor in the *Comedie Français*, and director and teacher in this school, and who was, unless we except Samson, the greatest teacher that has ever taught in the *Conservatoir*. M. Regnier kindly answered all my questions, and gave me permission to visit the classes. He spent several hours explaining carefully to me, and answering all my inquiries. The school is under the direction of the leading actors of France, so that the students receive inspiration from personal contact with the greatest masters of histrionic expression. In a school supported by the state, and having such teachers, where only about twenty students each year are chosen from over two hundred applicants, even with bad methods, wonderful results ought to follow.

But, when I visited the school the second time, I found some of the same students still working in the class-room. There is simply an endeavor to learn and to copy what the old actors did. Students are sent to the dictionary for a study of faults of speech, but there is little or no training of the kind this book seeks to advocate. There is little study, if any, into the action of the mind in speaking, little study into the fundamental elements of faults and needs, little direct study and development of the voice, so that all students with imperfections in the voice, are simply sent away, and only students who are in a normal condition are set at work on what amounts to little more than dramatic rehearsal.

The school, when it was in the hands of great teachers like Samson and Regnier, produced great results, but, in the hands of weaker men, it is becoming conventional. Everything tends to the mechanical and artificial. There is one occasionally who rises above the methods, and develops himself or herself according to the laws of his own being. Even at the *Theatre Français*, where for over a hundred years the greatest actors of the world have been found, since Regnier, Got and Delauney have retired or passed away, with Coquelin soon to follow, there seem to be none rising to take their places.

Thus has it ever been with imitation in art. Giulio Romano and all the imitators of Raphael became absolutely insipid. Imitation is ever a synonym for weakness in art. The severest criticism that can ever be made upon any artist is a charge of imitation.

The reasons for this are very plain. Every personality is different. To develop a man so as to be powerful in expression, we must develop the fundamental elements of his nature, preserve and train his own personality. Imitation of another always dwarfs personality, can never penetrate into the fundamental depths of a soul, but is ever a copy of outside characteristics. Faults and peculiarities can be imitated, but not excellences. Thus, to develop delivery by imitation is to be taken up with externalities which are ever furthest from the soul of the man.

Besides, imitation is a direct violation of the law of nature, which we have found to demand that all expression must be from within out. Everything in nature is original. No leaf is an imitation of any other leaf; it is the expression and embodiment of its own life, impulses and material. Everything that has life must be evolved from within. Mechanical art can easily make things alike. Two bricks cast in the same mould can hardly be distinguished from each other. But every leaf must depend upon its parent stem and upon its own power and opportunity to assimilate soil and moisture, light and heat. If this is true of the lowest forms of life, how much more must it be true of the highest and most complex. Imitation is an external aggregation of qualities, a manipulation of external parts for external likeness, hence it can never touch the deep and fundamental elements which are to be revealed in human life. It is essentially a violation of the great law of growth.

Many mistake the dramatic instinct of children for imitation. The child simply endeavors under the quickening power of imagination, to enter into sympathy with all life around him. He who carefully watches children, will find them original. They assimilate more than they imitate. They transform objective things to suit their own original conceptions. The plays of children who are left alone are nearly always inventions of their own. At times, children are quick to imitate, but they always mimic the mere accidental and odd characteristics of peculiar people, animals or objects. Their mimicry is concerned with accidentals, as imitation always is. It is only one aspect of Dramatic Instinct, not its highest form. It is an endeavor of the child to get outside of itself, but is more the evolution of the eye than of the mind — the province of understanding objective things, not of true art.

Mr. Ruskin has said regarding art: "These ideas and pleasures" — those received from imitation — "are the most contemptible which can be received from art ; first, because it is necessary to their enjoyment that the mind should reject the impression and address of the thing represented, and fix itself only upon the reflection that it is not what it seems to be. All high or noble emotion or thought is thus rendered physically impossible, while the mind exults in what is very like a strictly sensual pleasure. We may consider tears as a result of agony or of art, whichever we please, but not of both at the same moment. If we are surprised by them as an attainment of the one, it is impossible we can be moved by them as a sign of the other. Ideas of imitation are contemptible in the second place, because not only do they preclude the spectator from enjoying inherent beauty in the subject, but they can only be received from mean and paltry subjects, because it is impossible to imitate anything really great. We can 'paint a cat or a fiddle, so that they look as if we could take them up'; but we can not imitate the ocean, or the Alps. We can imitate fruit, but not a tree; flowers, but not a pasture; cut glass, but not the rainbow. All pictures in which deceptive powers of imitation are displayed, are therefore either of contemptible subjects, or have the imitation shown in contemptible parts of them, bits of dress, jewels, furniture, etc. Thirdly, these ideas are contemptible, because no ideas of power are associated with them; to the ignorant, imitation indeed seems difficult, and its success praiseworthy, but even they can by no possibility see more in the artist than they do in the juggler, who arrives at a strange end by means with which they are unacquainted. To the instructed, the juggler is by far the more respectable artist of the two, for they know . sleight of hand to be an art of immensely more difficult acquirement, and to imply more ingenuity in the artist than a power of deceptive imitation in painting, which requires nothing more for its attainment than a true eye, a steady hand and moderate industry — qualities which in no degree separate the imitative artist from a watch-maker, pin-maker or any other neat-handed artificer."

It is true Ruskin says that the Diorama and the stage are exceptions to the rule, because they are arts which are founded primarily on imitation, but if the principles unfolded in this book are true, the highest principles of art apply to histrionic expression with as much force as they do to painting or sculpture. It is true that much of the ordinary stage representation is imitative in char-acter, and, as Mr. Ruskin says, the pleasure and emo-tions derived from it are much lower than that derived from other arts; but this statement is not true of all stage art. While much of the very lowest art is found upon the stage, there is also occasionally some of the very highest art found there. Dixey's caricature of Mr. Irving belongs to the low realm of imitation; but Mr. Irving's Louis XI is no more imitation than Raphael's Sistine Madonna. It is the result of a creative concep-tion, of long and careful study and imaginative insight.

If imitation does not apply to any but the very lowest forms of the art, still less can it apply to methods of teaching the art. Such a method of teaching alienates histrionic expression from all true art, and deprives it of the inspiration of its noble principles.

But some one will say that the teacher of elocution only begins by a process of imitation, and expects a student to grow out of and away from imitation. But this is not the way even to begin to develop expression, because the action of the mind in imitation is altogether different from the action of the mind in creating. Neither the imagination nor any noble faculty of the mind is awakened; the soul has no conception of the situation; all is taken up with the senses and objective things. If no noble emotion is awakened by a contemplation of imitation, much more does no noble emotion stir the soul of one in the act of imitation. This is the chief objection to imitation, that it makes all expression a mere matter of physical execution, independent of the action of the mind.

There are many other arguments against it. There are no two voices pitched exactly alike. For a teacher with a low voice to teach by imitation a pupil with a high voice, has often constricted and almost ruined the student's voice. Or for a teacher with a very high voice, to make a pupil with a low voice imitate him, can only cause labored action in the throat, limitation of the resonance of the voice, and a perversion of all true expression. The teacher and student may both be completely unconscious of the difference in their voices. The writer speaks from personal experience with his own teachers of this school, and from observing many cases taught by illustrious teachers, who were practicing the method while speaking against it. The teacher would first give the pupil what he would call an example, and the student would, consciously or unconsciously, immediately endeavor to produce the same effects, and would naturally take on the key and endeavor to assume certain modulations, nearly always, of course, with discouragement, because of an endeavor to artificially aggregate the effects of the actions of another voice or body or mind, often consciously foreign to his own conceptions.

Such a method is in absolute violation of the methods of nature, which demand that expression shall be every man's own, that the energies of the soul must be aroused as the direct cause of all the actions of the body. Thus we can see at once that a method by imitation violates the fundamental nature of expression.

Again, the temperaments of men are different. The teacher may naturally read very slowly, and it may be the pupil's nature to read rapidly. A teacher may have a nervous temperament, and would evidently move and speak quickly if he should act in accordance with his own temperament, while for one of an entirely opposite tendency or temperament to read the same way, would be to violate every principle of nature. The first requisite of all expression must ever be for a man to be himself. His own instincts must be trusted. No man has ever become an orator or an artist of any kind who has not done so. Any method of education which does not develop a man's instincts, character and personality, is absolutely false to all true methods of education.

Again, if we look at the results of such a method, we find that those who have been taught in this way have little or no confidence in themselves. When they have a new selection or part to study, they must in every case, be coached. There is little originality, little trust in any thing that is not directly copied. Besides, another result of imitation is to make everybody alike. Instead of the spontaneity and vigor and originality of nature, sooner or later a narrow conventionality is acquired.

Mere imitation in education can never be in accordance with nature's method. It fixes the mind upon the outside, not upon the center. It represses the noble impulses and ideals of the soul. Each character is not developed along the lines of nature's intention, but is more or less warped to become like some other.

There is no need of further discussing the evils of such a method, for they have long been recognized. Professor Alexander Melville Bell, in the preface to his Principles of Elocution, has shown the failure of such methods. "The principle of instruction to which Elocution owes its meanness of reputation may be expressed in one word — Imitation. The teacher presents his pupils with a model or specimen of reading or declamation, and calls on them to stand forth and do likewise. The model may be good, bad or indifferent; it is at all events tinged with the teacher's own peculiarities, and the pupils in their imitative essays, can hardly be expected to distinguish between these accidents of style, and the essentials of good delivery which may be embodied in the model. Thus, becoming accustomed to imitate the former, they naturally confound them with the latter. Each pupil, too, has his own peculiarities, already more or less developed — arising from structural differences in the organs of speech, from temperament, or from habit — the result of previous training or of previous neglect. These fixed idiosyncrasies and tendencies, mingled with the imitated peculiarities, form a compound style which, whatever its qualities, can hardly fail to be unnatural. Besides, as imitation is in a great degree an unconscious act, habits are thus formed of the existence of which the subject of them is entirely ignorant. In no other way can we account for those monstrous perversions of style which are so common, and so patent to all but, apparently, the speakers themselves."

XVIII.

THE MECHANICAL SCHOOL.

A man's reach should exceed his grasp,
Or what's a Heaven for? All is silver-gray,
Placid and perfect with my art — the worse.
— *Browning*.

IT will be impossible here to give anything more than a mere outline of the many methods which may be summarized under the general term "mechanical". The name applies to the great majority of the methods now in use. This section might be appropriately headed "Elocutionary Methods". The general characteristic of almost every mechanical or elocutionary method is to proceed from analysis of the mechanism of speech — from the nature of the modulations of the voice, such as inflection or stress, or the like, and to lay down rules for the proper rendering of thought and passion.

These methods arose chiefly from a realization, on the part of the best teachers, of the inadequacy of methods of imitation. Sheridan and Walker, whose methods are the earliest recorded in English elocution of any note, while they practically taught by imitation, each earnestly sought for a method which would be independent of imitation, and would more adequately meet the needs of delivery. So far as we are able to judge, Sheridan first began the struggle for such a method. His first book, published in 1759, in which he merely discusses general principles, is the best. The second, about fifteen years later, shows a departure in a more artificial direction. He entirely misconceived the nature of inflection, and so his work is confined to arranging a lot of rules for pauses and punctuation. He bewailed the fact that we have not, in English, a uniform method of accentuation with marks printed as a part of the language as clearly defined and as unchangeable as words. He contended that the glory of the Greek language was in its accents, entirely over-looking the fact that these accents were added in the Grammarian's Period — a period which marks the decline of Greek literature.

Sheridan and Walker are not literally followed by any one at the present time, so their methods belong to the history of elocution and not to the present survey.

About 1805, Austin published his "Chironomia," a book on gesture, which has had great influence on what might be called the Declamatory School or Gesture School. The whole method is one of aggregation; little attention is paid to the expression of the face or body, but nearly the whole book is devoted to the arms. Little or no attention was given positions and attitudes, the most fundamental and important part of Pantomime, but all was made to center in motions or gestures. As has been shown, it was an endeavor to transplant the Greek and Roman methods upon English soil. The whole work is in the spirit of Greek and Roman art rather than Christian ; hence nearly all expression is confined to the limbs. If one were to deliver one of the passages analyzed and illustrated as marked, "The Miser," for example, and then deliver it according to the simpler methods of the best work of the present time, the contrast would be won-derful. As Sheridan and Walker had bewailed the need of mechanical marks, and had endeavored to arrange them for vocal expression so as to furnish, so to speak, a score like music, so Austin prided himself upon having discovered a system for the notation of gesture ; what to move, and when to move, being indicated by letters. It is astonishing how long such a mechanical and artificial system has lived. The evils of his work are still found in school exhibitions when boys are seen to give wide, swinging gestures with full arm but without a particle of facial expression, even in the rendering of the most subtle poems.

Mechanical elocution was carried further, or as some of the leading advocates of the mechanical method contend, to the highest possible perfection, by Dr. James Rush, whose "Philosophy of the Human Voice" was published in 1828. He analyzed inflection into a radical element and a "vanish", and showed the meaning of the length of inflection. Another element which is probably the most fundamental of his system, is his idea of stress. He imagines that every passion has a particular stress, and divides these into radical, medium, intermittent, compound and the like. Walker had said respecting the expression of feeling, that "The tones of the passions or emotions mean only that quality of sound that indicates the feelings of the speaker, without any reference to the pitch or loudness of his voice; and it is in being easily susceptible of every passion and emotion that presents itself, and being able to express them with that peculiar quality of sound which belongs to them, that the great art of reading and speaking consists." But Rush contended that the qualities of the voice, as well as the stresses and inflections, could be so regulated by rule, that the expression of every passion could be indicated definitely, and even printed as a score like music.

Rush divided all qualities into orotund, pure tone, aspirate quality and the tremor. Sorrow is expressed with aspirate quality, joy with pure quality, noble emotion in what he calls "an artificial and improved quality" —the orotund. Grief is given with tremor. This system contends further, that each feeling and passion is to be rendered by inflection of a given length, stress of a given character, as well as by tones of a special quality. The teachers who have followed Rush have laid down rules for the use of all these. Here is an example literally copied from a lesson given by a teacher: *"Sorrow:* to be rendered by low pitch, long quantity, aspirate quality and slow time. *Joy:* rendered by high pitch, short quantity, pure tone and quick time," etc., etc. Any one in his senses who will observe nature, can see that sorrow is given in all pitches, and that joy is not confined to a high pitch. Such statements are preposterous, for these are mere accidental facts which are occasionally true, but so rarely true that to make them the rule is to superficialize and pervert nature, and, in fact, to become absolutely absurd.

For fifty years our elocution has therefore been chiefly concerned with the acquirement of an artificial tone — called so by the teachers themselves, and claimed as an improvement upon natural tone — known as the orotund, with certain modifications, such as aspirate orotund, pure orotund, and the like. A vast number of selections have been marked *ad nauseam*, with the statement at the beginning of what tone they are to be read in, what kind of stress and what pitch, and even how long the inflections must be made. One of the most important questions asked students by the teachers of such a method is, "What tone should such and such a piece be read in?" The highest power of elocutionists has been considered to be due to a knowledge of these "signs of emotion," and the ability to apply them with skill according to the nature of the extract. Lest this may seem exaggerated, let us open at random a book published in 1880 by a professor in one of our leading colleges. Before an extract, this is the analysis: "Predominating time, *slow;* pitch, *low;* force, *moderate, effusive* and *expulsive;* stress, *median,* and in strong passages, *terminal;* quality, *orotund.*"

Mr. Murdoch is the best representative of this school, and as his work has been published within a very few years, and with the professed object of justifying Rush, it may be taken as the latest expression of the system. Only a few quotations will be selected at random. After showing the importance of mastering the tremors of various kinds, he says, "The semitonic tremor is heard in the following, where we apply this movement to the word *all,* although the other words, or accented syllables, of the entire quotation would be given with the tremor and semitone:

> "'Oh, I have lost you all!
> Parents, and home, and friends.'"

He also says that the passional outpouring of the soul of the son in Jean Ingelow's "High Tide," "Oh, come in life or come in death," etc., should be given with semitonic tremor. By reading it this way the great struggle of the man to bear up under his great sorrow, is entirely lost. All becomes a mere weak whine. There is no manliness, no intensity of passion, no control of breath, and above all, none of that subtle color or modulation of resonance which is the result of passional modulation of the texture of the muscles of the body. A mere artificial expedient is introduced as a substitute for nature, and not only so, but a substitute that entirely overlooks the writer's introductory words, "yet he moaned beneath his breath," and perverts the spirit breathed into the poem, substituting weakness for strength. The "agonized supplication" of Enoch Arden is another illustration:

> "Too hard to bear; why did they take me thence?
> O God almighty, blessed Saviour, Thou
> That didst uphold me on my lonely isle,

Uphold me, Father, in my loneliness
A little longer; aid me, give me strength
Not to tell her, never to let her know."

This must be given with "aspirated quality, weeping utterance, waves and chromatic thirds and fifths."

This system makes no distinction between normal and abnormal qualities of the voice. Whatever is found in nature is to be practiced and mastered, whether it be normal or abnormal, strong or weak. Imagine Shakespeare's powerful, intense and dignified queen expressing her indignation and contempt by declaiming in "orotund quality and changing to a guttural", "Thou little valiant, great in villainy, hast thou not spoke like thunder on my side?" That the full force of this may be seen let us note what he means by this guttural: "The mechanism of the harsh quality of voice known as the guttural, or throaty voice, should be well considered and thoroughly understood. It is an element of speech of a strongly marked and expressive nature, partaking of the same kind though differing in degree, from that peculiar effect known as aspirated vocality. They both play a prominent part in the offices of spoken language, being inseparable from its expressive functions; and thus *defects* of voice produce *effects*. But, on the contrary, such qualities of voice are repugnant to the principles underlying the structure of song. Therefore, the guttural and aspirated voices should be familiar to the speaker and singer, in order that the former should use them as effective agents in his art, and the latter learn how to avoid them as damaging elements in singing. The one may be said to resemble the growl of a dog, while the other his snarl. The guttural is produced by a suffocation of the voice, which is crushed and squeezed, as it were, between the roots of the tongue and the sides of the pharynx.   This action, when deep-seated, causes that grating or rubbing which is the marked characteristic of this quality.   While the more aspirated, rasping, hissing form of aspiration is produced by a lighter pressure of the same parts, and near approach to the soft palate or uvula."   Think of Miss Terry, Mrs. Kendall, or any artist of the present time upon the stage applying such a system.   With such suggestions it is no wonder that elocutionary study often causes sore throats.   To master this guttural, a long list of individual words, such as "revenge" is laid down for the student to practice.

Again, note the mechanical rules in inflection.   "Come back, come back, Horatius," must be rendered "with a rising, discreet third."   The sentence might be read in fifty different ways, but, of all, the one chosen seems to be the most foreign to the true situation.   It could only be read so when a man is trying to carry out a "system," which is to him greater than nature.

All these may be regarded as mere questions of taste, but not so; they are the result of an endeavor to apply a system which is claimed to be better than nature herself. It seems wonderful that men, with all nature before them, with instincts stirring in their breasts, should endeavor to obey such mechanical rules; above all, that they should endeavor to force such rules upon other men.   It is inconceivable that nature should be so studied as to make no distinction between weakness and strength, that all attention should be given to mere accidents, which if made the rule, would destroy all variety, beauty and strength of expression.   It is strange that such superficial facts should be elevated to the dignity of great principles which form "the most complete system ever offered to a student of elocution," a system which "must be accepted in its entirety," a system which is held up as the standard of all advance, a failure to accept which explains "why there has been, thus far, no uniform elocutionary development from a source which bears within itself all the essential elements for the accomplishment of that result, and why there is, as yet, no established artistic standard of excellence and taste in elocutionary study and execution, which would be the natural outcome of such development."

The best teachers of singing have taught for years that all noble emotion should be rendered by pure tone. The Rush system entirely overlooks the subtle modulations of pure tone by emotion, which is the fundamental characteristic of the best expression. To render sorrow with an aspirate quality of voice is to degrade it. A strong character ever renders sorrow with a modulation and softening of pure tone, caused by the modulation of the texture of the muscles, by the diffusion of emotion. This is the method followed by all the best actors of our time. The Rush system has come to be known as elocution and has made the name synonymous with the substitution of artificial tricks for nature. Such a system makes the whole art of expression a mere matter of mechanical stresses, waves, semitones and tremors, and a reading by this system is little more than an exhibition of mechanical actions, miscalled "signs of emotion."

The greatest evil, however, of the whole system, is that it introduces mere rules, founded upon a mechanical mode of procedure. The whole action of the mind is focused upon the modes of execution by the voice, and not upon the successive ideas. There is thus a violation of the great law of nature which was formulated by Comenius, "from within, out." Such a method perverts the whole action of the soul. Instead of the mind being focused upon successive ideas and reproducing them, all is centered upon the performance of successive signs. This, any one can see, is a violation of Pestalozzi's principle — "the thing, not its sign," and, in fact, of every principle of true education. Such a method violates the principles of nature, which were found in the second part of this work. What is meant to be unconscious by nature is made conscious. What is meant to be spontaneous is made deliberative. What is merely accidental is placed for what is fundamental, and the fundamental is subordinated and forgotten. The whole mind is uncentered, unbalanced. Genuine, truthful emotion is impossible. Even natural thinking is not developed. A proof of the inadequacy of the method is found in the fact that it is condemned by all the best speakers and actors of our day.

Such a course is not in accord with the action of the mind in conversation. If a man in conversation is ever conscious of the inflections, stresses and above all, of the color of his voice, it is in a very secondary way, and is generally caused by ill-health or some misuse of the mechanism. Normally the mind must ever be centered upon its train of ideas, and any art that prevents this is false to nature and will end in superficiality.

Any one can see that such a system is in direct antagonism to the method which has been unfolded in this investigation. The mind is centered upon the mechanism. Every analysis and every rule laid down, tends to develop this. There is an endeavor, in studying literature, to adapt a piece to a certain tone, a certain mode of delivery. The mode of delivery is studied as a thing in itself, independent of the thought of the passage. The mind is centered upon manner, rather than upon matter; upon the means, and not upon the substance; upon the effect, and not upon the cause.

In the method contended for here the mind is to be centered upon the idea as the fundamental cause, the voice and body are to be put in tune by training, so that they will spontaneously respond to the conceptions of the mind and the emotions of the soul. In this way only will the fundamental actions of nature be rendered spontaneous, according to her own intention. While there must be a perfect knowledge of the normal and abnormal methods of expression in nature and perfect skill in execution, still the mind must ever be taken up with fundamentals, not with accidentals. There must be no artificial system of the "signs of emotion," elevated to something greater than the substance itself. While a man becomes conscious of himself and enters into possession of himself, he does not interfere with the unconscious and spontaneous tendencies of his nature. If all is made conscious, all will be unreal and superficial, and the great depths of the soul can not be revealed or the highest possibilities of expression realized. True expression does not depend upon a few artificial conditions of pitch and stress and inflection, but upon an infinite complexity of modulations which can never be completely reproduced by any conscious or deliberative process. The highest art is indirect, whatever is meant by nature to be conscious and whatever is meant by nature to be unconscious must be developed according to their fundamental impulse; the perfect man and the perfect artist ever being one who co-ordinates conscious direction with the unconscious and spontaneous impulses of his nature. The idea itself must be present before the mind and held as a stimulus to expression rather than any mere mode of mechanical execution or knowledge of so-called "signs."

Thus, even if the "signs of emotion" could be found, this method would be wrong. But the true signs of emotion have not been given in the Rush system. There is no distinction between weakness and strength. Whole classes of expressive actions like tone-color are forgotten. Everything is artificialized. It is a system that is the arrangement of a few facts and rules which are to be practiced, and in whose narrow circle every piece of literature must be confined. Faults have not been traced to their causes. The seat of all faults is supposed to be in the ignorance of the reader in regard to proper rules for inflection, or for stress, or for emphasis. There is little or no tracing of such faults to incorrect mental action.

Hence, the correction of faults has not been radical. Some have not even deigned to notice faults; considering them part of the art, and even to be practiced. In a higher form of the school there has been local study of faults and application of local remedies; but this does not go deep enough — does not reach the cause. Even so far as the physical is concerned, there has been in every case, a study of some expedient by which each fault can be corrected directly; for example, when the voice is metallic, the pillars of the soft palate are found to be too near together, and the correction of this defect has been merely to get control of these pillars, and to directly hold them apart in speech, until such action becomes habitual. Nasality is caused, according to these teachers, by sluggishness of the soft palate, and so the remedy has been to get control of the soft palate. Thus, whenever there is an imperfection, there has been an endeavor to apply some local remedy for its correction. In fact, it has been contended by many writers that all faults of speech are merely local, and the correction, a simple thing, merely a matter of securing control over these specific actions or local parts occasioning the fault. Thus, there has been continual emphasis of the idea that elocution is a mechanical thing and that all faults have their centre in some incorrect action of the agents.

Again, there has been in the mechanical school, great emphasis of accidentals rather than of fundamentals. For example, a certain pitch is given for each emotion. Any one who will think and observe nature, will find that pitch is a purely accidental thing; it is not an essential element in the expression of emotion. Joy, for example, may be given on a high pitch or a low pitch. It is, in fact, a very essential element in true expression, that there shall be ability to secure control of the expression of each emotion upon any pitch. In place of this, note the analysis of an emotion by one of our elocutionists, as already given: "*Joy*, high pitch, pure quality, short quantity, quick time." Not a solitary one of these is necessarily expressive of joy, nor with all of them combined will we necessarily express joy. We may, in fact, express the highest displeasure. All these means are the most external, the most superficial of all the actions which are expressive of the various emotions. Three fourths of the time they are not present at all, and if a student tries to execute them, in obedience to rules founded upon such incidental facts, he becomes in the highest degree, mechanical and artificial. By such a course, the attention of the whole mind is decentralized and placed upon mere accidentals.

Again, our elocution has been too much upon the plane of representation. There is too much imitation. There is no appreciation or understanding of the nature of manifestation. There is no conception that true delivery is ever in the highest sense governed by the laws of music. There is no understanding of revelation. All pantomime is merely gesture. There is no recognition of attitude, which is fundamental and of more importance.

Besides, even the gesture is of the lowest order, being entirely descriptive.

Another illustration is the fact that students are made to stand in artificial attitudes, are told just where to place their feet, the distance apart, the angle of the one with the other, thus to take attitudes independent of emotion, and fix themselves in positions that will resist the domination of the body by emotion, which is the fundamental principle in all expression. However beautiful the attitude may be, the very fact that it is assumed, prevents the emotion of the man from dominating the body, makes the man rigid rather than flexible, and substitutes an artificial action for a natural one.

Again, all our elocution has tended too much to a mere establishing of rules. While there has been an endeavor to found rules upon a study of principles, the principles themselves are too often related merely to the mechanism. The action of the mind and many of the most important phases in delivery, have been entirely ignored.

Here is a rule which is given in one of the latest books on elocution: "A question beginning with a verb must have a rising inflection." Any one can see that this is not true one half the time. Such slavish obedience to rule leads to a mannerism, leads to doing things in one way, makes a free art an artificial art. All delivery is like the growth of a tree. It has no external fixture, it is the direct unfoldment of the life within, under the dominion of the environment without.

Thus in inflections, stresses and pitches of voice, such rules are laid down. There is a clear indication of just how everything is to be done, so that the free, living action of the voice, which ought to be as unfettered as the slender reed playing in the wind, which is intended by the Creator to be swayed before the breath of passion, as the leaves of the tree are swayed by the breezes of Heaven, must be made to conform completely to narrow rules. Low pitch for sorrow, high pitch for joy, aspirate quality for sorrow, orotund for grandeur. There is to be always median stress for grief, which, though sometimes true, if elevated to a universal rule, would limit and fetter all spontaneity, all vigor in the action of the mind. Pauses are not explained as the gaps in vocal expression, caused by the action of the mind, but are said to be simply due to grammatical structure, their number and length being due to mechanical reasons.

Mechanical elocution is thus naturally led to take its place on the very lowest plane of art. It is these methods of instruction which have caused elocutionary art to be taken up with mere objective representation. It has become a mere show. Readers do not select the best literature, they choose those pieces which are capable of verbal quibbles, of verbal imitation and objective representation. The great point is to be representative, not manifestive, often not even expressive. The great central feeling, the great central thought, is sacrificed for externals. Elocution, instead of being as it should be, the freest of arts, has become the most conventional. There has been an endeavor too often to substitute the conventional for the natural.

As a proof that mechanical elocution has not met the requirements of the problem, it has been rejected by many of our greatest public speakers as useless. In the courses of lectures given at the Yale Divinity School by the leading clergymen of the country, only a few have approved of elocution.

Again, in characterization, elocution has been overthrown and rejected by actors, because of its absolute artificiality. Some of our public readers in giving Macbeth or Shylock or the Weird Sisters, merely cramp the throat and give an artificial, constricted tone. As we look at the face there is no sign of mental assimilation of the character; there is no sign of dramatic instinct, all is the product of a mere elocutionary trick, a trick of the throat, which is, nine tenths of the time, untrue to nature, unlike anything on earth. Stage art may be upon a low plane, but it can not endure such perversion as this.

The Rush School is not the only mechanical school. It is only chosen as the leading one. A book by one of the leading teachers of Boston — just issued from the press — contains extracts marked in the most mechanical way for students to follow. Nothing is left to difference of personality or the unconscious or spontaneous impulse of the soul. All must not only be conscious and deliberative, but must be given by every person in the same way. Lest this be thought an exaggeration, let the book be opened at random and extracts marked in this way will be found:

"Can't you be cool like me? What good can pâssion do? Passion is of no service, you impudent, insolent reprobate. Màrk! I give you six hours and a hàlf to consider this; if you then agree, without any condition to do everything on eàrth that I choose, why — confound you, I may in time forgîve you."

Such marks might be occasionally used to train the ear of a student, but even then it is always better to have some extract done in a variety of ways. The way such marked extracts are usually taught degrades all expression to the plane of a mechanical art.

The popularity of the mechanical method, and especially the Rush system, is strange. It is probably owing to two reasons. It is rather flattering to a man to tell him that his thought is great, that he has imagination and passion and all the requisites of a great speaker. He only needs a few rules to execute certain vocal actions and he will be all right. A man often takes it personal to be spoken to in regard to the action of his mind. The second reason is the longing on the part of elocutionists to find a scientific basis for their instruction. The mechanical system seemed to get at some definite facts upon which a system could be built.

There is no doubt a truth in the mechanical school. It shows the importance of thorough scientific knowledge of the exact difficulty in the technical action of the voice. A debt must always be due to Rush for his service to the science of the speaking voice, while he himself was not a teacher. One half of the things he contended for were useless, on account of the fact that he made no distinction whatever between the normal and the abnormal in nature, between the expression of weakness and strength, between the ideal intentions of nature and what is merely due to bad habit and perversion. Still, he did analyze correctly the length of inflections, and while his "shock of the glottis" is wrong and has been given up by the best teachers, yet that there is a stress in the speaking voice, a radical and a vanish different from the singing voice, was clearly shown by him. Teaching, as he did, the importance of analyzing into its fundamental nature the speaking voice, the special incorrect physical action in faults has been found and a more radical treatment of defects made possible. The elements of melody having been partly explained, men have been set to observe more carefully the phenomena of speech; so that Rush's system has indirectly rendered important service in unfolding knowledge which must be understood in improving delivery.

XIX

THE IMPULSIVE SCHOOL.

All art must be preceded by a certain mechanical expertness. — *Goethe.*

THE reaction against such mechanical methods must have begun early. Criticisms and condemnations of elocution have been growing more and more common for the past hundred years. The critics, however, are usually so general, so vague and indefinite, that it is hardly possible to present their arguments in a systematic or adequate manner. No criticism of any consequence appeared or was put into any definite form until Archbishop Whately published his Rhetoric, in 1825. The fourth part of this work is devoted entirely to the subject of elocution. The Rhetoric appeared a very short time before Rush's book, but, evidently, neither ever saw the other's work. Whately's criticisms are chiefly directed against Sheridan, but Sheridan was only selected as a type and was probably chosen because he was the best and most illustrious of all the teachers of elocution, and as Whately himself says, all his criticisms apply with equal force to Walker or other teachers of elocution, and as has often been recognized, they apply with especial force to Rush. That this is true is shown by the fact that so many of Rush's successors have taken it upon themselves to answer the arguments of Whately.

The influence, direct and indirect, of this discussion by Whately has been very great. Since his book, no work upon rhetoric has given any attention whatever to delivery, while before his Rhetoric was published, delivery was considered an essential part of rhetoric. The widely extended opposition to elocution among scholars has been directly or indirectly colored by Whately's views. Any review, therefore, of the subject would be incomplete without a consideration of Whately's criticisms.

Whately not only criticised elocution, but professed to present an original method or system of dealing with the difficulty; but his criticisms were far more effective than his construction of a better method. In fact, he did not show any adequate remedy, and has founded what some have called systems of "no elocution" which, for the sake of a convenient term we will call the impulsive school. Treating the errors of mechanical elocution, as I think, clearly, and himself furnishing no remedy, many came to believe that there was no such thing as a true elocutionary method. His discussion is very broad and recognizes many of the fundamental elements of the great problems of delivery, and no teacher of elocution has ever spoken more earnestly upon the importance of a good delivery and of the imperfect character of modern oratory in this respect, than this greatest critic of the prevailing methods. "On the importance of this branch," he says, "it is hardly necessary to offer any remark. Few need to be told that the effect of the most perfect composition may be entirely destroyed, even by a delivery which does not render it unintelligible; that one, which is inferior both in matter and style, may produce, if better spoken, a more powerful effect than another which surpasses it in both these points; and that even such an elocution as does not spoil the effect of what is said, may yet fall far short of doing full justice to it." He says that, while he opposes artificial systems he must not be understood as advocating no system at all.

He shows, however, that although the subject has engaged so much attention, and though it has been confessed that the delivery of the modern orator is more imperfect than any other part of his function, yet that hitherto all efforts to develop delivery have failed. "Probably not a single instance could be found of any one who has attained by the study of any system of instruction that has appeared, a really good delivery; but there are many, probably nearly as many as have fully tried the experiment, who have by this means been totally spoiled — who have fallen irrecoverably into an affected style of spouting, worse, in many respects, than their original mode of delivery. Many accordingly have, not unreasonably, conceived a disgust for the subject altogether; considering it hopeless that Elocution should be taught by any rules, and acquiescing in the conclusion that it is to be regarded entirely as a gift of nature, or an accidental acquirement of practice." He proceeds then to criticise the systems of elocution and to point out the causes of their failure. "There is," he says, "one principle running through all their precepts, which being, according to my views, radically erroneous, must — if those views be correct — vitiate every system founded on it. The principle I mean is, that in order to acquire the best style of delivery, it is requisite to study analytically the emphases, tones, pauses, degrees of loudness, etc., which give the proper effect to each passage that is well delivered — to frame rules founded on the observation of these — and then, in practice, deliberately and carefully to conform the utterance to these rules, so as to form a complete artificial system of elocution."

Whately goes on to show why a speaker's conscious presentation of arguments was justifiable and consciousness of delivery was unjustifiable. The speaker must be conscious of his arguments because the chief aim of his discourse is to convince, while his delivery, being only a means to an end, should not seem to call attention to itself.

His fundamental objection to Sheridan is that this writer adopts a peculiar set of marks for denoting the different pauses, emphases, etc., and applies these, with accompanying explanatory observations, to the greater part of the Liturgy, and to an essay subjoined; recommending that the habit should be formed of modulating the voice by his marks; and that afterward readers should "write out such parts as they want to deliver properly, without any of the usual stops; and, after having considered them well, mark the pauses and emphases by the new signs which have been annexed to them, according to the best of their judgment."

The summary of his criticism will be best presented in his own words: "First, such a system must necessarily be imperfect, because, though the emphatic word in each sentence may easily be pointed out in writing, no variety of marks, that could be invented — not even musical notation — would suffice to indicate the different tones in which the different emphatic words should be pronounced; though on this depends frequently the whole force, and even sense of the expression. Secondly: But were it even possible to bring to the highest perfection the proposed system of marks, it would still be a circuitous road to the desired end. Suppose it could be completely indicated to the eye in what tone each word and sentence should be pronounced according to the several occasions, the learner might ask, 'But why should this tone suit the awful — this, the pathetic — this, the narrative style? Why is this mode of delivery adopted for a command — this, for exhortation — this, for a supplication?' etc. The only answer that could be given is, that these tones, emphases, etc., are a part of the language;

that nature, or custom, which is a second nature, suggest spontaneously these different modes of giving expression to the different thoughts, feelings and designs, which are present to the mind of any one, without study, speaking in earnest his own sentiments. Then, if this be the case, why not leave nature to do her own work? Impress but the mind fully with the sentiments, etc., to be uttered; withdraw the attention from the sound, and fix it on the sense, and nature, or habit, will spontaneously suggest the proper delivery.

"That this will be the case is not only true, but this is the very supposition on which the artificial system depends; for it professes to teach the mode of delivery naturally adapted to each occasion. It is surely, therefore, a circuitous path that is proposed, when the learner is directed, first to consider how each passage ought to be read; *i. e.*, what mode of delivering each part of it would spontaneously occur to him, if he were attending exclusively to the matter of it; then, to observe all the modulations, etc., of voice, which take place in such a delivery; then, to note these down, by establishing marks, in writing; and lastly, to pronounce according to these marks. This seems like recommending, for the purpose of raising the hand to the mouth, that he should first observe, when performing the action without thought of anything else, what muscles are contracted — in what degrees — and in what order; then, that he should note down these observations; and lastly that he should, in conformity with these notes, contract each muscle in due degree, and in proper order; to the end that he may be enabled, after all, to lift his hand to his mouth; which, by supposition he had already done.

"Lastly, waiving both the above objections, if a person could learn thus to speak, as it were, by note, with the same fluency and accuracy as are attainable in the case of singing, still the desired object of a perfectly natural as well as correct elocution, would never be in this way attained. The reader's attention being fixed on his own voice — which in singing, and there only, is allowed and expected — the inevitable consequence would be that he would betray, more or less, his studied and artificial delivery ; and would, in the same degree, manifest an offensive affectation."

He then proceeds to unfold his own method, which is to avoid the evils unfolded in these criticisms, and says that "The practical rule, then, to be adopted in conformity with the principles here maintained is, not only to pay no studied attention to the voice, but studiously to withdraw the thoughts from it, and to dwell as intently as possible on the sense, trusting to nature to suggest spontaneously the proper emphases and tones. He who not only understands fully what he is reading, but is earnestly occupying his mind with the matter of it, will be likely to read as if he understood it, and thus to make others understand it ; and in like manner, with a view to the impressiveness of the delivery, he who not only feels it, but is exclusively absorbed with that feeling, will be likely to read as if he felt it, and to communicate the impression to his hearers. But this can not be the case if he is occupied with the thought of what their opinion will be of his reading, and how his voice ought to be regulated — if, in short, he is thinking of himself, and, of course, in the same degree abstracting his attention from that which ought to occupy it exclusively."

The system proposed by Whately has often been shown to be inadequate. It would have been far better if Whately had left the problem untouched, unless he could have devoted more attention to it. He did not penetrate to the fundamental need in developing delivery. He furnished no solution of the problem.

Many persons acknowledge, says Whately, that it is a great fault of a speaker to be too much occupied with thoughts respecting his own voice and delivery, but there may be some attention ; but he says there is no middle ground, that a middle course entirely nullifies the advantages of his system, that the reader will be sure to pay too much attention if he pays any at all, or if he does not strenuously withdraw his attention from it.

Many have been the answers given to this criticism upon elocution ; George Vandenhoff, Zachos and others have endeavored to answer the criticisms. They contend that there must be attention direct at the time, that the consciousness of the man must be upon delivery, and endeavor to answer Whately by turning upon him his own arguments from logic and rhetoric, entirely ignoring his anticipation of this argument.

None of the answers have, in my judgment, been effective ; and hence, it is not wonderful that a custom of absolute neglect of delivery has arisen. Many views follow, consciously or unconsciously, in the path of Whately, without going to the depth of the subject. It might be well to discuss the subordinate divisions into different forms of this school. One might be named the homiletic. The homiletic method consists in having the students speak with very long criticisms upon their needs, that they may know their faults so as to think of them at the time of delivery and correct them by conscious avoidance, the criticism being taken up with certain points which are entirely external. This method, though possibly founded upon Whately, is in contradiction to his suggestions, as it is the most direct method of calling "attention to modes of delivery at the time of speaking."

Another form might be called the sentimental. One prominent teacher says that "all vocal technique is a necessary poison." Students are recommended by the advocates of this method to come into class and sit and meditate over certain great themes, and absorb the spirit of delivery; they say it will come to them unconsciously, that there is no need of work upon modes of execution. In the foremost institution which follows this method there are never any examinations. Again and again students are received with the understanding that they are to do no work at all, but simply to sit and listen and absorb. And such students go away with a degree conferred upon them, it is understood, by the authority of some great state. Such views are too ridiculous to need any discussion. Of course this is an exceptional case, but it shows the ridiculous extent to which sentimentality in educating delivery can be carried.

The truth which is emphasized by the impulsive school is that the problem is not a mechanical one. "It is the soul that speaks," and not the mere body. The soul must be studied as well as the body. No set of marks must come between the soul and its mode of manifestation. Its weakness is, that it overlooks the nature of art which demands technical skill as well as impulse. It overlooks habit. There is no conception of training as a method of correcting abnormal conditions. The statement that if a man has the thought and is stirred by the feeling he will be likely to say it right, is true, if the man were normal, if all the channels of expression were open and if the man were free from bad habits. But to give no attention to habit or right and wrong modes of execution, to have no regard for unbalanced emotional conditions or perverted channels of expression, is to abandon men to all sorts of wild impulses and to reduce all oratorical delivery to chaos. This has been the result of Whately's work. During the last fifty years less and less attention has been given to delivery, until now men stand up before audiences with their hands in their pockets, and with scarcely a movement of the body or modulation of the voice, give thought with no relation to experience.

The indirect results of Whately's work have been helpful. The emphasis of the importance of not placing the mind upon mere modes of delivery has prevented, in many cases, artificial results which naturally follow from the mechanical school. While it has caused absolute distrust of the mechanical school among the best scholars it has left many with a firm belief that something must be done for delivery; and while elocution is condemned, yet many have been heard to say, "It seems to me there must be a science of voice that can save us from wasting our energy." The spirit of Whately was so fair, his emphasis of the importance of developing delivery, and his endeavor himself to formulate a kind of system, as well as his qualifications in his foot-notes of his criticism, make us feel that he himself did not have a complete grasp of the problem with which he was dealing.

XX.

THE SPECULATIVE SCHOOL.

It seems to me the danger in teaching elocution, although I do not claim to be an authority, is that some formal and artificial method should supersede nature.
—Henry Irving.

ANOTHER method introduced within the last twenty-five years must be discussed in this place. The so-called Delsarte system has already taken many forms, owing to its being grafted upon old systems.

Delsarte never published any thing himself. His supposed writings were bought by three Americans, but they were sorely disappointed at the few relics that came into their possession. After his death, a priest, who had studied with Delsarte, published without any authority whatever, the notes he had taken of his lessons. The little book was published in Paris for fifty cents, but even at this price, the small first edition was not sold; a poor translation, however, by one who knew nothing of Delsarte, was published in America, and sold at two dollars a volume, greatly to the financial gain of its publisher. The book was universally condemned by every one who knew any thing of Delsarte, both in France and in this country. It was crude, and misrepresented his method. It has hurt Delsarte wherever it has been published, and robbed Madame Delsarte of any money she might have gained from gathering and publishing her husband's notes in a complete and unperverted form

Thus, the history of the work of Delsarte is very curious. In France, the birthplace of the system, though many teachers can be found who studied with Delsarte, yet not one of them teaches in accordance with his methods, but in this country it has been almost universally accepted. One cause of its being received so enthusiast-ically, was no doubt the almost universal dissatisfaction with the mechanical methods. Teachers were eager for any thing that might give promise of a philosophical basis for a better method. Another cause was the able lectures delivered by Delsarte's favorite pupil, Mr. Steele Mackaye, in different cities of the United States, during the winters of 1869–'70 and '72–'73. The wonderful control of his body illustrated the power of the master's training, in most complex movements. Still another cause was the exaggerated claims that the system con-tained a key, not only to all the difficulties of delivery, but to all art and to the whole universe. Some teachers claimed to have wonderful notes which they had secured. There was a universal longing for some adequate method, and as there was no distinct explanation of this system, the imagination of men elevated it to a fanciful height. All this encouraged the wildest pretensions.

So exaggerated are the claims which have been made for the system of Delsarte, that all French acting has been held up in this country as the fruit of the work of Delsarte. As a matter of fact, the work of Delsarte was almost completely discarded by the French people. He himself said to Madam Pasca, "Your greatest hindrance will be your teacher." He was appointed at one time an instructor in the National Opera, but the artists went to the directors inside of a month and declared that they would resign if he was not sent away.

I regret very much that it is necessary to review the system before there is any adequate publication of the elements of the method from one who has followed it and who believes in it. I have studied it for many years, but a part of it I never believed and I have grown further and further away from the part I did believe, with every year of increased experience and study of nature. Besides, I received all my knowledge second hand. I have studied with every known pupil of Delsarte, but I never saw the master himself.

Mr. Steele Mackaye is thoroughly competent to give the world an outline of the system of Delsarte, but he has allowed himself to be engrossed with other things, and neglected to give the world an adequate presentation of the method of the master who so loved and honored him. Much of the work which is popularly known as Delsarte in this country is an absolute perversion, or at least, does not faithfully represent the work of the master. It represents the mechanical, the weak side of the work, more than the strong side. The great principles of training which Delsarte originated, are entirely forgotten, while only his *system* has been promulgated and held up before us as Delsarte. This system, to the best French minds, who saw its results, was the worst type of a mechanical system.

Thus, it can be seen that it will be very difficult to give an outline of his work. In the work on the history of elocution there will be an endeavor to bring out its weak and strong sides, but this work would be incomplete without an outline of that which is popularly known as *Delsartism*, that it may be compared with the other leading methods.

It may be well to state that the old master disliked the word "system". He contended that his was simply a philosophy of nature, and that his teaching, like that of all great teachers of song, was simply a method; but his so-called philosophy is most emphatically a system, and, as will be shown, a very artificial one at that.

The fundamental idea of the system, according to the so-called Delsartians, is that every thing in its elements is a trinity. Different teachers have presented the system in different ways. Professor Monroe and his pupils began with God; God's fundamental attributes, love, wisdom and power, being the first trinity. God, man and the world form another trinity. Man himself, has soul, mind and life. The body of man is composed of torso, head and limbs. Each agent in man's body has a center, a summit and a base. All these, with innumerable others, passing through every thing, even down to a stick with its two ends and a middle, are in correspondence. The system seems to be founded upon the doctrine of correspondences in Swedenborg, and some have said that Delsarte was a very earnest student of Swedenborg's writings, though we have no absolute testimony on this head; but Professor Monroe, who worked out a similar system before he knew of Delsarte, obtained his trinities from Swedenborg.

Others still begin with "the outside of the universe," time, space and motion. One of the leading advocates of the system once gave a course of lectures upon it. He began with a point, as this is the simplest object of nature, and could not be conceived without giving it cosmic existence — without giving it length, breadth and thickness — so every thing, he argued, must be a trinity when traced to its fundamental elements. I have heard Mr. Mackaye start an explanation of the system from many different points of view. However, the beginning may be made, the conclusion is the same that every thing is based on this idea of a trinity, and that if we do not conceive it as such, we do not have complete grasp of the truth. The applications of this to expression were manifold. One point is the significance of each agent of the body. The head for example, is mental, the limbs are vital, the torso is affectional in significance. The arms denote sensibility, the shoulder is the thermometer of passion, the wrist and hand the thermometer of mental activity, the elbow the thermometer of the moral, and so on through every part of the body.

Every phase of being and body, of thought and language, must be divided according to this system of threes. In reading a selection, or studying a part, the great question is whether it is predominately moral, predominately vital or predominately mental.

Delsarte endeavored to construct a chart of the whole universe in accordance with this artificial principle. Many years ago three different copies of this chart of man, which was a part of his chart of the universe, fell into my hands. As neither of these has ever been published, to my knowledge, I will print one of them here as the best means of presenting in a few words the system. These three charts evidently belong to three different periods of his life. I choose the one belonging to the middle period as the one most free from mistakes.

The lower half of the chart relates to organs, or agents of the body concerned in expression, and to their use as languages; all above this is supposed to show the faculties of man's psychic nature. It was Delsarte's belief that the Psychic and Organic were in perfect correspondence. Speech is the manifestation of mind or man's reason; pantomime, of the soul or the spiritual nature, and tone, of the vital nature; each principle of being having thus a special language in manifestation. The chart is an endeavor to cramp the Psychic faculties and their characteristics into agreement with the organic agents, or to show the agents and the faculties in exact correspondence.

Great ingenuity was shown on the part of Delsarte in his explanations of the terms in his chart, and his little

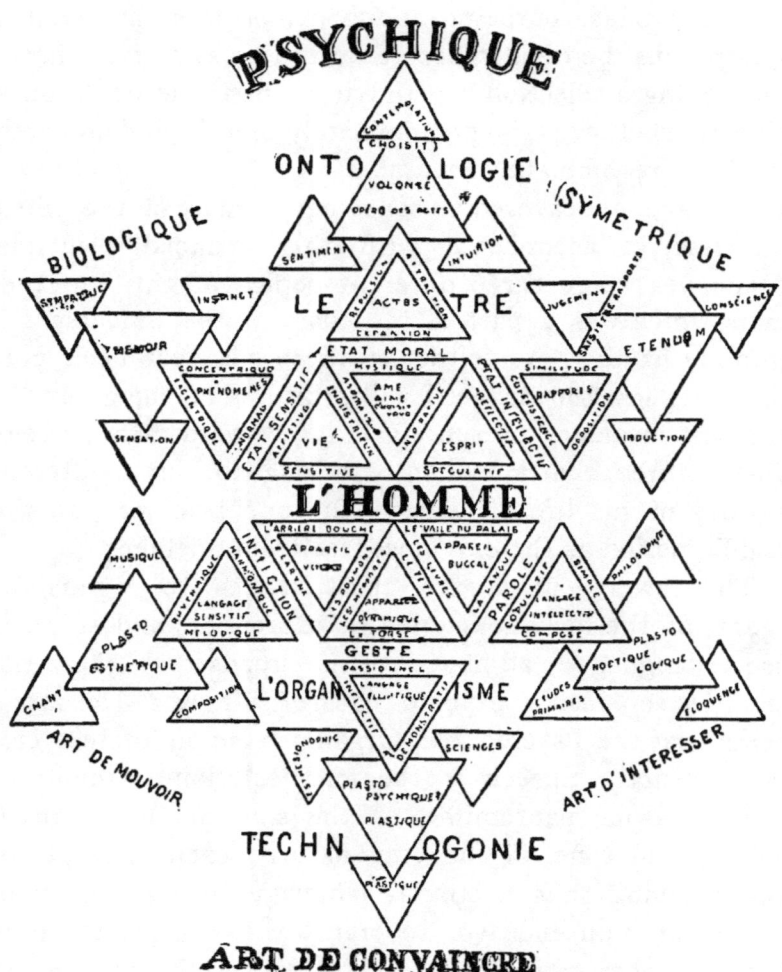

audiences, we read in the French papers, were accustomed to applaud the new definitions. The definitions were attractive to some because they were so novel and so ingenious, and also because they were so wrought out in a mechanical or crystalline form that they could be easily comprehended.

Many of Delsarte's definitions are lost. It may be well to enumerate a few that have come down to us. "Life expands." "Mind contracts." "Soul modulates." "Life joins. Mind separates. Soul re-unites." "Life acts fatally. Mind acts disinterestedly. The soul acts freely." "There are three forms of variation from the normal — by depression, by exuberance and by displacement of center." "Beauty charms, truth illumines, the good perfects." "The artist is one who has knowledge, possession and the free direction of the full apparatus by means of which the life, the mind and the soul reveal themselves." "Knowledge alone makes the critic; possession added makes the connoisseur." "It is only when we have the free direction that we have the artist." "There are three elemental modes of measure — by number, by volume and by weight. Number is a rational, volume is a vital, weight is a moral mode of estimating value," etc.

Another fundamental idea in the system is a combination of these three with each other, which has been called Delsarte's "law of the nine-fold accord," that is to say, whenever we have three, we must necessarily have nine in the elemental combination. According to this law of combination, the human being composed of three elements, was divided into nine elemental faculties. The analysis of the mind may be taken as the best means of illustrating the system.

The three elements of the human being according to

Delsarte, are life, mind and soul. These elements, called "principles of Being", combining with each other give rise to the following nine "faculties":

Life of the Mind.	Soul of the Mind.	Mind of the Mind.	HEAD
Life of the Soul.	Soul of the Soul.	Mind of the Soul.	TORSO
Life of the Life.	Soul of the Life.	Mind of the Life.	LIMBS
LIMBS.	TORSO.	HEAD (of the Animal).	

of Man.

Some, drawing their inference from a more universal trinity—God, man, cosmos—use the words human, divine and animal. The combination will be as follows:

Animal-Human.	Divine-Human.	Human-Human.	HEAD
Animal-Divine.	Divine-Divine.	Human-Divine.	TORSO
Animal-Animal.	Divine-Animal.	Human-Animal.	LIMBS
LIMBS.	TORSO.	HEAD (of the Animal).	

of Man.

Now, what are the names commonly given to these faculties?

I have had many explanations of these faculties, and as all essentially agree, they may be understood to be really from Delsarte; although there are in some of the explanations, especially in those of Mr. Mackaye, many additions. I will cling, however, as far as possible to the exposition given by Professor Monroe; as his was the earliest I had, it became very firmly fixed in my mind.

A square divided into nine smaller squares was drawn upon the board and a representation of a man upright was drawn on one side while an animal horizontal was outlined below. "Man has all in him that there is in the animal, though the animal does not possess all that there is in man."

The question would be asked, "What is the most fundamental faculty or power of the soul or affectional principle of being?" Delsarte is said to have placed love, reverence, contemplation; the last being the true one. This, therefore, is supposed to be the most fundamental spiritual characteristic or power of man. The next question would be, "What is the most fundamental characteristic of animal life?" Students in the tread of the system could easily begin for themselves to catch the right word. All would put "sensation". The next question was, "What is the most fundamental faculty of the intellect?" The answer on the part of some would be "deduction," some "reason," but Delsarte's word was induction, as that which furnishes the most fundamental characteristic. Thus, we have the three most essential characteristics of the three fundamental principles of being. The next question is to fill the other six places with combinations. Taking the lower and the base line, the question would be asked, "What is the mind of the life?" and the answer given was "instinct". Then the question would arise, "What is the soul of the animal?" The answer given would be that it was "sympathy". In this way would be found out the soul of the mind to be conscience; the life of the mind, judgment; the mind of the soul, intuition; and the life of the soul, sentiment or human love. When completed we had the following as the elemental faculties* of the psychic nature of man:

Judgment.	Conscience.	Induction.	MIND	
Sentiment.	Contemplation.	Intuition.	SOUL	of Man.
Sensation.	Sympathy.	Instinct.	LIFE	
MIND.	SOUL.	LIFE	(of the Animal).	

The form of this last chart was used by Delsarte as a means of recording the expression of all the agents — the attitudes, functions or gestures of the hand, the feet, the head; in fact, all the actions of every agent in the body. The various expressions of every language of man must fit into these squares. For example, the whole body may be divided by the law of "the nine-fold accord", or "law of intertwining" (*circumintercession*), according to the significance of each part in expression. Each of these is also a zone of expression, so that when the hand rests upon any of these it indicates the principle of being "predominating in activity at the time". Thus, too, when the gesture of the hand or arm starts from any part, "the point of departure indicates the principle of being, whose predominating activity causes the gesture."

There are three kinds of motion — toward a center, from a center, and about a center; motion toward a

---

* These faculties are the same as those at the extreme triangles, page 40.

center is rational ; from a center is passional ; and about a center is affectional in significance. So we come, by the combination of the three into nine, naming these accentric toward a center, eccentric from a center, and normal or concentric with or about a center; by combination, we have accentro-accentric, normo-accentric, eccentro-accentric, accentro-eccentric, normo-eccentric, eccentro-eccentric, accentro-normal, eccentro-normal, normo-normal. Marks were also arranged to represent these : \ stood for accentric, mental ; / for eccentric, passional ; | for normal in man, and — for normal in animal, moral in significance. A chart of the significance of all parts of the body may serve as an illustration of the innumerable applications of this manifold division.

Vito-mental. Mouth. Base of Brain.	Moro-mental. Nose. Top of Head.	Mento-mental. Region of Eyes. Side of Head.	MIND \
Vito-moral. Abdomen.	Moro-moral. Region of Heart.	Mento-moral. Chest.	SOUL |
Vito-vital. Shoulders. Hips.	Moro-vital. Elbows. Knees.	Mento-vital. Wrists. Hands.	LIFE /

MIND. /	SOUL. —	LIFE (of the Animal). \

MIND \ SOUL | LIFE / } of Man.

It must seem to most minds that this is the result of ingenuity, and that the aim is chiefly to fill the squares rather than to get at the truth. This is usually the result of such a method upon the student. The greatest struggle is to find nine kinds of emphasis or nine gestures or nine different attitudes such as will fit the squares. But to the Delsartian, it means more. As

every thing is upon the basis of the trinity in the foundation of things, so this nine-fold accord is the test of truth.
Whatever fits the three is true, and whatever fits the
nine is true. If we do not get the three and the nine,
we have not yet the essential elements of the truth.
The whole universe, when science and investigation shall
have discovered the whole truth, will be found to be built
upon the basis of these threes and combinations of
threes.

It would seem to any one with any experience in the
observation of nature that such a system as this would at
once be rejected, but to many minds it has a very great
fascination. I wish, therefore, to show carefully some of
its leading evils.

In the first place, it is artificial. Things are measured
by an artificial standard. The mind, the body and nature
are searched, not for truth, but for something to fit into
an ingenious and artificial mould. One of the best
teachers I have ever been privileged to be under, again
and again said, when two things were presented to him,
that we did not know the real truth or we would have
three; we must lay them aside until we can further
investigate. This same teacher in dividing sunlight into
its elements, said that it was composed of an illuminating
principle, heat, and a third element, which he thought
would be found to be electricity, stating, that "here
philosophy was ahead of science". Hence, it can be seen
at once that while there is a seeming comprehension of
the whole universe, really there is included only one class
of facts, namely, those where there are three elements.
There is more or less truth in many of the things which
Delsarte said; but the effect is to blind men to the truth.
The eye is not equally open to observe all the facts of
nature. The human mind can be made one-sided.

Every man sees things, not so much for what they are, as for what he is himself. If two men should pass along the same path up a mountain side, the one a botanist and the other a geologist, and if each should give an account of what he has seen, the difference would be marvelous. The attention of each man has been trained to look at different classes of things, and so it is in respect to such a system or method as this. Men, as Mr. Irving indicated, are in great danger in elocution of substituting an artificial system for nature. Mr. Jevons well says: "Nothing is more important in observation and experiment than to be uninfluenced by any prejudice or theory in correctly recording the facts observed, and allowing to them their proper weight. He who does not do so will almost always be able to obtain facts in support of an opinion, however erroneous."

There is as much difference between this artificial system and the real facts of expression as between the shrubbery in the gardens at Versailles, trimmed into artificial shapes in imitation and for the remembrance of the folly of an evil age in landscape gardening, and the great trees growing in all the freedom and spontaneity of nature. The one is artificial and stiff, and has a very unpleasant effect upon any one trained to observe the freedom of nature, and can only give delight to an uneducated and unobserving mind.

In the second place, it is a *system*, although the author may have disclaimed the word. There is a good sense in which the word "system" is used, but when it is applied to an art, especially to a method of training, it becomes mechanical. In fact, a system in this sense is a series of facts built upon a mechanical plan. Nature was never built in such a mechanical way. A machine can be arranged and regulated by figures, but no tree ever grows, no volcano ever upheaves to flow along a mechanically-laid track; each obeys a mighty impulse of central force. The tree grows from within out, as has been proved. Its limbs are not built by mechanical rule, but unfolded freely, in proportion to the impulse within, the soil, the heat and the moisture.

The great teachers of the world have ever called their modes of work methods, not systems. A method, as the etymology of the word shows, is only a mode of accomplishing a result, but a system is the placing together of things by the mind. A method is founded upon the study of nature; a system is apt to be founded upon an orderly arrangement of facts to suit the convenience and purpose of man. The great vocal trainer despises the word system. A method he has, but in his use of the word he implies a reverence for nature — a reverence for the basis of things with the arrangement of which he has had nothing to do.

The danger of a system, especially in art, is to substitute the individual's conception as the great center around which all is arranged. A system in training causes a man to prejudge faults, absolutely unfits him for criticism, gives him an artificial ideal, causes him to lose sight of the great universal types of nature, and especially the individual powers and peculiarities of the student. In spite of all that may be done, a system tends to make every one alike. The mind is hindered in its discovery of fundamental needs, and is prejudiced against some of the great facts of nature which do not happen to fit his little model.

One of the chief proofs that the work of Delsarte was a system, is that the real points in which he made advance have been entirely forgotten by nearly all his followers, and only the mechanical system has gone abroad and has made the terms Delsartian and Delsart-ism, by-words among the best histrionic artists and teach-ers of the country.

In the third place, that there are an infinite number of threes no one can doubt, but the system is not founded upon truth; it is not true that everything is fundament-ally a trinity. If the universe were built upon this plan, it ought to be apparent in those sciences which, more than any others, have gone to fundamental depths. Of all sciences that have gone to the foundation of things, chemistry is one of the most important. If the Delsarte principle was true, we must expect that everything should be built upon a basis of three, and that the nine-fold accord would be found everywhere as the elemental mode of nature's combination. According to this, water ought not to be composed of oxygen and hydrogen, but of three elements. According to the Delsarte method of pro-cedure, we must throw away oxygen and hydrogen as mere illusive phantasms, because we can not find that water is composed of three elements. Now we very well know that in all the substances in nature, when tested by chemistry, there is no such mechanical arrangement. Nature is not built upon threes, nor upon any series of combinations in a "nine-fold accord".

Even granting that man has three natures, and a correspondence in his body with this triple being, and granting that this brings us to many facts, yet to make it a universal criterion is false to nature. But even in the human body itself it is not true. If we take, for example, the hand, how can its multiplex actions be arranged in multiples of three? It so happens by accident that a man can stand upon both feet, a forward foot and a back foot, but when we come to the gestures of the arm, what folly to stop when we have nine and congratulate ourselves that we have the whole truth, or later, when we have twenty-seven or eighty-one.

One chief reason for the popularity of the Delsarte system is, that it is artificial and by rule. It is as mechanical in relation to gesture as the Rush System is in relation to the voice. The better portion of the work of Delsarte — that relating to training — has been forgotten, while the artificial elements have been grafted upon the old mechanical school. When one who really knows the best work of Delsarte sees the work commonly done under that name and hears the terms employed and the explanations given, he feels at once that the hand is that of Esau but the voice is that of Jacob.

Just as Rush's system tended to center all consciousness upon the voice, its stresses and inflections, so the Delsarte system tends to center all consciousness upon pantomime. The man must be able to think in pantomime. If the pantomime is right the voice will be right. This system is a mechanical pantomimic system, as Rush's was a mechanical vocal one, and the same arguments will apply to both. Pantomime is as spontaneous and natural a language as vocal expression. They must bear the same relation to consciousness. Mr. Murdoch holds that pantomime must be completely in the background for the voice. Delsarte held that all attention should be given to pantomime and that vocal expression should result from it. Neither is right. The great center of consciousness must be upon the thought and action of the mind, and these two natural languages having a great element of spontaneity, must not be brought too much into the foreground of consciousness.

Thus the Delsarte system practically belongs to the mechanical school. All spontaneity is simply skill. Spontaneity, for example, in pantomime, is the same as with the player upon the piano. We must first get a knowledge of the language of all the agents in the body, ·even of the nose and the eyes; secondly, acquire skill to play upon them until the pantomimic actions become as easy as the use of the keys to a player upon a piano. There is, of course, an element of truth in this, but the hand, unlike a musical instrument, has a physiological and an organic connection with the soul of the artist. Besides, it overlooks the fact that nature meant some forms of expression to be unconscious and only voluntary in the sense of being co-ordinated with other agents. So far is this carried, that Delsarte is credited with saying that a man without any emotion whatever can be trained to make a motion that will raise the hair upon another's head, and that the ability to do this makes the man an artist. One of the greatest advocates and teachers of Delsarte's method says, that an actor must have only what he calls "symptomatic emotion·". For example, "a man can twist his face into such an action that goose-flesh will rise upon his back." This is not emotion, but simply a symptom of emotion.

Much, therefore, of the work of Delsarte is built upon the views of Diderot; nearly all the so-called Delsartians naturally hold Diderot's mechanical view, discussed in Chapter V. Many of the advocates have been chiefly characterized by an admiration for beautiful attitudes and beautiful motions. Passing along Broadway once with a prominent teacher who believes in this system, looking over a number of photographs of actors and actresses, he asked if I could "pick out the Delsartians". Pointing to one prominent actress, whose stilted and artificial attitudes were photographed in all conceivable ways, he asked if I saw "the Delsartian attitudes". Thus, many people have grown to regard Delsarte's work as a display of motions and attitudes, and to believe that these are synonymous with expression. This is not wholly fair to Delsarte, but there must be some cause for its wide-spread diffusion.

Still another criticism is the exaggerated estimate placed upon pantomime. "If pantomime is right, the voice must be right." When I once asked M. Regnier, the great teacher at the *Conservatoir*, and leading actor for forty years at the *Theatre Français*, about Delsarte, he said, "He was a very good singer, but his gestures were all too labored. He did not have the simplicity of nature in his movements." This same criticism can be made upon every real follower of the system, whom I have ever seen except, possibly, Madame Pasca of the *Gymnase-dramatique*.

Thus we can see that the Delsarte system is worthy of the name applied to it, namely, that it is a speculative system ; that it is not founded upon a true observation of nature, but is an endeavor to place upon nature a pre-conceived artificial conception.

Delsarte made all training and all practice of expression too much an end, and not a means. Every thing had to be consciously directed. The action of the agent was to be brought into consciousness and done deliberatively. Nothing was left to spontaneity. There was no recognition of the unconscious actions, such as has been contended for in this work. Nor did Delsarte carefully distinguish between preparatory actions and expressive actions.

Notwithstanding these severe criticisms, Delsarte was the most original investigator in the department of delivery of any teacher or writer during the present century.

Among the special points in which he made advance over all before him may be mentioned, first, the importance of the preliminary training or the attuning of the whole body. This was, of course, universally followed among the Greeks, and had been practiced in relation to the voice by the teachers of song for hundreds of years, but in the realm of histrionic expression and in the use of the voice in speech had been almost completely neglected. Delsarte did not stand wholly alone in his discovery of this point, but he gave it peculiar emphasis, such as it had never before received.

Again, an important point in Delsarte is his emphasis of what may be called fundamentals. He taught that beneath all accidental actions and combinations, there were fundamental actions which, if they could be made right, would not only correct faults, but develop power. He earnestly taught that if exercises were merely accidental actions, mediocre results would always follow, but if exercises were given upon fundamental actions, strength and power would be achieved. None of the methods, either by imitation or by mechanical analysis, recognize this principle. Imitation always proceeds from mere accidental elements. In this respect, Delsarte was in advance of Rush. Dr. Rush was not an artist. He treated every thing as a scientist. Hence, all qualities of the voice were alike important to him. His guttural qualities, his husky and tremulous qualities, though recommended to be used, are absolute faults, and the mechanical school founded by him has never conceived the idea of distinguishing between what is fundamental and what is accidental.

It may be well to illustrate what Delsarte meant by fundamentals. The ordinary method of developing a proper position was to have the student place his feet at a certain angle, a certain distance apart and the body erect. One of the leading teachers made this angle always thirty degrees, and the distance apart the length of the foot. The man directs his will to hold himself in just such a position. The tendency of all such directions is to limit and fetter the man ; to fix the body and to prevent its modulation by passion, which is the fundamental element of all expression. The angle of the feet and the distance apart are mere accidental facts, which vary according to temperament, and according to the intensity of emotion dominating the man. Delsarte would say, a good position is an important thing; but there is something fundamental to position, that is, poise. So, instead of limiting a man and trying to give him a position, the body must be so centered or poised that the position will be fundamentally correct, while all its accidents must be free to be dominated by emotion and passion. Poise, thus, is fundamental to position. Poise is something unchangeable ; position is something that changes with every passion. Thus, work upon accidentals limits man's freedom. Work upon fundamentals develops power.

Again, to improve a man's pantomime, Delsarte would not give a vast number of positions and motions to practice, but he would give the student a *series*, which he considered fundamental to all pantomime. Instead of literally practicing a great many gestures he would work, it is said, for as much as three weeks upon one of the steps of his series, the successive unfoldment of the parts of the arm, because this is fundamental to all gesture. Unless a man develops the fundamental after he has made one gesture right, he must repeat the process for all the others, but with the fundamentals correct, the whole gesticulation of the agent is normally developed for all forms of expression. Delsarte contended that work upon fundamentals also developed precision. If we take the elemental actions of the head, for example, and study them, we become conscious of the tendencies to mix the actions of the head. It is this clearness and purity of movement which was one of the most important results of his training.

The great characteristic, therefore, of his training was a study into the fundamental "norm" of the whole body, and each agent in particular. The few elemental actions of each agent, absolutely simple and unmixed with any other, were the points to which training must be directed to develop power in expression. To one who has never studied into this nor seen the wonderful variety and power that such training gives to the human body, there will be no conception of the wonderful results accomplished. Just as in chemistry, there must be pure elements to accomplish results in the laboratory, so a man's power, his grace of movement, and all the effectiveness of his expression, in pantomime especially, is dependent upon the distinctiveness of elemental actions.

Of all Delsarte's pupils with whom I have studied, I have had this explained by but two, and by one of these only partially and vaguely, and by the other too much as a theory; but to me it is the most important point in which he made advance, and in this he must be followed if true grace and power of expression is ever developed in the whole man.

The so-called Delsarte system of training which is every where spoken of, contains nothing of this idea; in fact, it does not come from Delsarte or from Mackaye. It is a perversion of some of the exercises mixed with the common calisthenic movements; in some cases even musical accompaniment to the exercises has been added which was entirely foreign to Delsarte. It is more frequently governed by sentimental considerations than by any principle ever obtained from Delsarte. The attitudinizing and *pose* positions which are so commonly practiced, are in direct antagonism to his method of training. These so-called Æsthetic Gymnastics do not bring grace, but affectation ; they do not develop control over body as an agent of the mind, but artificiality; they do not secure power, but engender weakness.

To show how Delsarte's trainings can be perverted, a lady has arranged an exercise which she calls "get up drunk". Her young lady pupils with dreamy eyes fall on the floor and stagger up in the most irregular way possible, the torso and upper part of the body completely abandoned. She says in explanation that this exercise is to enable students to stand with the least possible expenditure of energy. As if the mast of a ship made greater strain upon the ropes when in the perpendicular than when swaying to and fro at random. Such results as these are to be expected when it is remembered that many who teach Delsarte, have secured their knowledge by merely copying notes without ever going to the source of information and without ever mastering a solitary exercise or even understanding the principle underlying any step. Before I studied with Mr. Mackaye, the most important exercises were given me entirely at random, without any explanation of their purposes, or the principles underlying them. Of all the pupils of Delsarte with whom I have studied or teachers who teach this system, who have not been pupils, he was the only one from whom I could secure any explanation of the purposes of the exercises, and who could direct me carefully in mastering their subtleties or understanding their true character.

The greatest cause of perversion of the exercises and training is that superficial students, without any thorough understanding or preparation and without any permission whatever, have published notes, copied in some cases directly from Mr. Mackaye, but perverted or explained so as to lead students to misconceive their true character. The superficial presentation of exercises has in many cases completely vitiated their aim.

Another point in which Delsarte made advance is, that pantomime belongs to the whole body. To him every part of the body had a language of its own, and the language of each part was different from the language of every other. All true expression requires the cultivation in diverse directions of each agency.

There has been a tendency in all English elocution, to over-estimate the motions of the arms. The face and the rest of the body have been almost entirely neglected. Visit some school "exhibition" and notice how the motions of the arms are entirely separate from all expression in the face. Hence, all pantomime has been called gesture. Delsarte showed that in any part of the body a motion was meaningless unless it came from and ended in an attitude. For example, a gesture of the arm, unless it ends in a distinct attitude of the hand, is a mere meaningless nervous movement. In fact, the spirit of his whole method was to show men that the attitudes of a man should transcend his motions.

Delsarte showed the great influence of pantomime over the voice, and that the voice can not be thoroughly trained to the highest realization of its possibilities without attention to pantomime. This was, in a great measure, the discovery of an old teacher before him. Delsarte carried the thought entirely too far. It is not true that, "If the body is right, the voice will be right," but that there is here a great truth and the key to a vast number of difficulties in the voice, is never questioned by one who has investigated the voice from such a point of view. The color of the voice, to use one fact as an example, is caused by the modulation of the texture of the muscles, and hence when the texture is hard the voice must more or less partake of the same quality, To correct many defects of the voice, such as weakness and one-sidedness, the muscular texture of the body must be improved in its tone. That pantomime should precede speech is a very old discovery, but that pantomime precedes speech and is a part of nature's mode of determining the quality of the voice and giving it its color and texture, was discovered by him, or at least his principle has led to its discovery. Delsarte also emphasized strongly the unity of all the languages of man. While laying too much stress upon pantomime, and while he himself lost the true unity in expression, yet he aided in an advance. The reason for his lack of unity was the focusing of his mind upon the pantomime and not upon his ideas, and endeavoring to secure unity mechanically and deliberately and not from the spontaneous diffusion of emotion and the centralization of the impulses of the soul.

While Delsarte's idea that everything is, in its elements, a trinity, is untrue, yet holding that "a trinity is the union of three co-essential, co-penetrant and co-extensive elements," he emphasized the fact that every product is complex. Dropping his idea of the trinity, we can say that every product or act of expression is the unity of many co-existent and co-essential elements, and we have a great truth which is entirely overlooked in ordinary elocution.

Again, while Delsarte discovered the true elementals in only a few directions, while he was misled by his theory that the fundamentals of everything were a trinity, yet he has indirectly led men to search for the true elements of expression. In fact, the chief advantages of his work have been indirect, and while we feel that he engaged in many foolish undertakings, and like Madame Arnaud, we can not follow him with his trinities "to the angels", yet all must acknowledge that he widened the field of investigation; that he led men to study the whole man in expression; that he has gathered — or has been the means of awakening others to gather — an infinite number of facts regarding pantomime; that while his philosophy was wrong, yet in order to fit out his system, he traced certain lines in pantomime which opened new avenues of information. Many a theory in the history of the world that has been false, like the theory of epicycles, has been the means of leading to great discoveries. The theories about alchemy led to the discovery of the science of chemistry.

Again, Delsarte has indirectly aided in the rejection of some of the mechanical views of delivery. He has indirectly and unconsciously led men to study the mind and to study nature. While failing himself to get the true psychic action, yet he caused men to study the psychic action, and sooner or later this will lead to the discovery of the fundamental elements of all expression.

Thus, the Delsarte system is built upon a series of trinities, beginning with the Universe as composed of God, consciousness, cosmos; God as love, wisdom and power; Man as soul, mind and life; and the organism or physiognomic man, as torso, head and limbs, each in correspondence as to significance, the first term of each group being spiritual, the second rational, and the third passional or vital. Each trinity gives rise to a series of "nines," as the immediate combination of the three elements with each other. Then there are three kinds of motions: about a center, toward a center and from a center; also, with corresponding significance, which can be applied to all the agents of the body and to their actions. This, in a word, is the Delsarte system, artificial and untrue, bringing narrowness, one-sided views of nature and perversion, to any one who gets within its constricting grasp. Back of this system there was a method of training which is entirely forgotten by nearly all teachers. The facts of the system so preponderate that the few strong, original elements of training are completely buried or so mixed with the system as to be almost entirely perverted.

XXI

THE ADVANCE NEEDED.

It is a natural thing that man should speak ;
But whether this or that way, nature leaves
To your selection, as it pleases you. — *Dante.*

THERE are, of course, an infinite number of methods
for the development of delivery. Each teacher will
develop, more or less, a method of his own ; and many
teachers combine elements from several systems, but all
the leading methods of the present time will fall under
these four schools.

It must be remembered that there is truth in every
one of these methods. The truth in imitation is, that
impulses toward art, and especially toward expression,
are awakened from observing expression in others. We
are sympathetic beings, and, while many will not go
so far as a distinguished clergyman of a most conservative denomination, who, when he wished to preach upon
a great theme, went the night before to see Hamlet
acted by Booth, yet any one who will study the nature
of man, can realize the great inspiration that came to
him. He did not go in order to preach upon Hamlet,
or to express any thing as Booth did ; he went that the
fountains of feeling might be stirred, and that every fibre
of his being might be made to quiver with life. This, of
course, was not imitation. It was inspiration from actual
contact with the expression of great thought and feeling.
No great art can ever advance without continual observation and study of the living action of great artists.
Clergymen who never hear any speakers except those of
their own denomination, are nearly always manneristic and

faulty in delivery. All good teaching requires examples, and of all teaching, the development of delivery requires the teacher to be alive in every fibre of his being, and able to illustrate every phase of his work.

Assimilation ever plays an unconscious role in expression. Hence, the teacher must so plan his work that students may come in contact with the greatest varieties of delivery in forms of expression as different as possible from their own, thus to avoid the evils of imitation, and yet secure the advantages of sympathetic contact.

The truth in the mechanical method is, that the elemental vocal actions must be studied, that there must be analysis of the mechanism of speech. The mechanical nature of faults must be understood. The ear of the teacher must be quick to note the specific form of every fault, and able to meet the fault directly and indirectly mechanically, when necessary, as well as from the eradication of its causes.

The truth in the impulsive method is, that nothing must ever be a substitute for the practice of expression under the dictates of emotion. Every soul has impulses within it toward expression, which must be obeyed and developed by practice. The deep, unconscious impulses of the human soul are as potent in expression as conscious actions. All mechanical work must be subsidiary to this. The dictates of instinct — instinct refined by thorough knowledge and cultivation — must ever be the final law.

The great progress made by Delsarte can hardly be estimated from the perverted methods which pass under his name. His emphasis of fundamentals, the necessity of the co-operation of the whole man in unity for perfect expression, the preparatory development of the whole body, the influence of the body as a whole upon the voice, and the study of the laws of universal art are all of the highest importance.

But have any of these four methods met the great needs of the problem? If so, why do so many leading actors discard elocution as something artificial, and as having failed to develop delivery? Why do so many able speakers regard it as useless?

If we recall some of the aspects of the problem which have been unfolded, we can see that many of the most important points are not touched by any of these methods. Instead of paying attention to the fundamental elements of the problem, the tendency in elocution has been to devote itself to the outside. There has been little or no study into the fundamental causes of faults in delivery. Elocutionary teachers, again and again, have sneered at the idea of the mind having any thing to do with the subject, contending that delivery is wholly a physical thing. The almost universal custom has been simply to study the effects and to secure the performance of certain mechanical actions, which are directly concerned with effects. Rarely do we find any tracing of faults to psychic causes.

Again, elocution has been taken up too much with some special phase of the problem. Everywhere we have some kind of a system. Nearly every elocutionist who has not copied his method from another, has built up his system upon his success in meeting some special fault in delivery. To one it is matter of inflections, to another, the whole need is mere stresses, to nearly all, the problem of elocution is confined to the external signs of emotion. Delsarte is almost entirely taken up with his speculations about trinities or with pantomime, saying that if this is right, all must be right. Thus, all systems have been one-sided. Each is founded upon merely one aspect of expression.

Again, instead of a thorough method of training, all has been devoted to a mere study of faults and their external correction by expedients. If all the faulty elements of delivery were removed, there would be little left. There is no such thing as a mechanically perfect product in nature. The study of mechanical imperfections as a basis of developing delivery fundamentally, violates the characteristics of nature and every principle of modern art. Such a method substitutes mechanical art for free art. In mechanical art external, mechanical perfection is the fundamental aim; but in every fine art the aim is the revelation of the soul. Faults must be removed, but imperfections of a plant are not removed as those of a machine. "To err is human," is a saying as old as Sophocles. So long as work upon delivery is merely to point out defects or endeavor to mechanically correct faults, the deeper needs of the man can not be met, and there will be a strong tendency to affectation. Training must be such as to meet the fundamental needs of delivery. The latent powers of a man must be awakened, and all imperfections as far as possible, must be corrected from within. Whatever does not correct the causes of faults can not be an adequate remedy.

Again, elocution has not been studied in accordance with the fundamental principles of art. It has been regarded as if it were a department of mechanical art. The best art is never founded upon the mere study of outside mechanism. While all art has a technique, yet that art which has nothing but technique, is purely mechanical, and will ever be concerned with accidents rather than with fundamental causes, and will substitute weakness for strength. That there is a mechanical side, all can see at once, but any one who has looked into the depths of the problem of delivery must see that this mechanical side can not be disconnected from the mind of the speaker. Delivery is not a mere physical action; the fundamental causes of all faults are in the mind. Every one of these methods has overlooked this fact.

In the face of all this, what advance is needed? If we can get into the innermost instincts and ideals of the best artists and teachers, what would be the concurrent feeling as to the need of advance?

As we review all the facts placed before us, we can see at once that it is first necessary to a good method for the development of delivery, that the whole man and all the fundamental needs of expression and not a mere part, shall be considered. A mechanical school of elocution not only fails to consider the whole man, but especially fails to consider the action of the faculties of the soul upon which all expression fundamentally depends, and also fails to study all the languages of man, ignoring almost wholly if not perverting attitude, the most fundamental form of pantomime, but also ignoring some of the most important and highest modes of expression peculiar to the voice, such as tone-color.

The so-called Delsarte method, while analyzing the faculties of the soul, yet in the practical work of expression almost if not entirely ignores the action of the mind as the cause of expression. But it also gives us little if any attention to the voice, and concerns itself almost entirely with pantomime. As has been shown, delivery is the revelation of the whole man. The human body is an organism; the voice and body are most intimately associated with being, and each of these has a multitude of languages which are directly revelatory of the powers of the soul. In the work of developing delivery, therefore, no one of these facts must be ignored or unduly subordinated or exaggerated. All the systems have been one-sided, mechanical arrangements, and in the hands of many teachers have become substitutes for nature. They have been founded not upon the study of nature, but upon a conventional system or authority. In the practical working of all these methods, the action of the mind is almost if not entirely ignored.

But these systems also give very little if any attention to the preparatory training of the voice, and concern themselves almost entirely with pantomime, as with certain artificial vocal actions.

Any artificial method like Rush's system, which endeavors to exaggerate some one little peculiarity of the voice, even though it may be true to the expression or execution of one man in one peculiar emotion, by being made a rule for all emotions and all other actions of the voice, which are intended by nature to be different, can only end in making all one-sided and artificial. In fact, this has too often been the result of the so-called elocution ; for it has looked only at one phase of expression. It has looked merely at the effect, and has little or nothing to do with the fundamental cause of expression, but simply aims to secure means to accomplish the effect. This violates the most elemental principle of nature which has been considered a fundamental law of education from the time of Comenius.

Again, attention must be given to all the facts. Any adequate method of training must not be founded upon a hobby, must not consider merely one side or one language. Every part of man is linguistic. Every part has a role to play in expression, and all success in the development of delivery must depend upon developing each role and bringing all into harmony.

The voice and the body must be thoroughly trained and prepared for their work, and the action of the mind in expression must be developed properly, and a technical execution unfolded in connection with the action of the mind. There must be a study of all phases of expression, co-ordination of all to the exclusion of none; a study of delivery as the expression of the entire man; the manifestation of the whole soul with all its faculties and powers through the whole vocal and physical organism, with all their various agents and actions; a discrimination between what was meant to be conscious and what was meant to be unconscious, and such training should be adopted as will not aim to make all conscious. Every faculty and power, every agent and every language, must be developed according to its own inherent nature.

There is also needed a deeper study into the fundamental principles of nature, and an obedience to laws, and not to rules. William Russell, the father — as he was called by Prof. Monroe — of American elocution, said in the preface of his leading work, that if elocution could not be taught by rule, it could not be taught at all. But this is an entire misconception, not only of the subject of delivery, but of all art. It is only a mechanical art that can be taught by rule. A house may be built by rule, a mechanical structure can be executed by rule, but a work of art is an embodiment of the fundamental principles of nature. It must spring from creative instinct. No mere mechanical rule can furnish any substitute for nature's methods. Nature does not grow or produce her effects according to rule. All is free and spontaneous. To act by rule causes everything to be made alike. The one is a mere copy, and a copy can be produced by rule. Human expression is not an imitative work. It is not a mechanical production. Every man's delivery must be the revelation of his own character, must be the manifestation of his own personality. Every idea in the soul of a man, every emotion and experience, must necessarily have a shade of difference from all others, and that difference must be seen in expression.

Again, while all art is founded upon the study of nature, the work of expression requires the most intimate and constant study of nature. Some say it is nature herself, rather than art. Whenever things are arranged by rule, the fundamental principles of nature are ignored. If the feet are arranged at a certain angle, if the thumb is to be fixed at a certain point, then all is stiff, and expression is limited and fettered; in fact, there is no realm of art where rules must be so absolutely ignored, as in the realm of expression. So general is the action of being upon body, that at times there may be a direct reverse of action to produce the same effect. For example, under the effect of surprise, whether you pass backward or forward depends entirely upon circumstances. For example, you may be looking out upon an imaginary rider, your whole attention eagerly absorbed and your body advanced; if you see him suddenly fall, then you will naturally recoil. Again, you may be standing on the back foot gazing upon the same rider, the whole body extended with exultation and excitement, but with reposeful confidence; now when you see the sudden fall, the body will more naturally advance. Either of these expressions would be satisfactory to an audience, and very effective because the body would show movement which would indicate the change in the mind.

Let it not be considered, however, that a principle is necessarily vague and indefinite, and that a rule is exact and definite. He who has the grasp of a broad and deep principle, has something that is unchangeable. Nature ever has a stable center and a variable surface. He who works by rule is to him who works by principle as he who makes leaves by machinery is to the one who plants and stimulates the growth of a tree. No man who works by rule can get nature upon his side. All spontaneity is fettered and excluded. The great impulse of nature is destroyed. Expression is a co-ordination of the conscious with the unconscious. Too great conscious obedience to rule will be injurious. In all true expression, nine tenths of the acts must seem to be done for the speaker, the same as in all great art.

There is also needed a broader and more careful study of art. All artists have one aim and one principle, though they may have varying methods and modes. Hence, for any advance in a specific art, there must be comparative study of all art. If all dramatic art is simply a mirror held up to nature, which shows "the very age and body of the time, its form and pressure," and if the histrionic phase is still more merely the reflection of the particular condition and artistic conception of an age, then in order to improve it, to elevate it, there must be thorough study of the artistic conception of the time. Histrionic expression, if it is to "show virtue its own feature, and scorn its own image", ought to be in advance rather than behind the other arts; lacking the permanence of other arts it ought to compensate by the greater intensity, by greater inspiration and by being more full of the spirit of progress. Hence, the greater insight and recognition of the highest artistic conception of any age, ought to be shown in histrionic art. Where histrionic expression is behind other forms of art, it cannot be advanced without a study of this artistic spirit as seen and felt in other arts. And at all times it must be compared and tested by the standards of these arts that are objective and permanent. Study of art quickens a teacher's insight. All art is a revelation of the soul. It is the most ideal form of expression. Therefore the study of art is a source of inspiration to the student of expression that must not be neglected.

Elocution has been regarded, as has been already shown, as a mere representative or even imitative art. The pure and simple manifestation, or revelatory elements in it, have been almost entirely ignored. One of the most important advances needed in the development of expression is a recognition of the real philosophical principles underlying music as the art most akin to delivery. It can be seen at once that the conception of the relation of expression to art greatly affects methods of developing expression. Rush's mechanical signs of emotion are inadequate, when we look at the manifestive elements in expression, and until we do so, we are very apt to overlook their artificial and superficial character. If expression is regarded as merely representative, we are apt to exaggerate mechanical elements. Working upon them so exclusively, the manifestive elements are destroyed. On the contrary, if expression is chiefly manifestive, the principles that have been laid down as to training the mind and the training of the voice and body, can be seen to be necessary, and the whole work is changed.

Again, there should be a more thorough study of the results of modern science, a scientific as well as artistic study of nature. In the midst of the deeper insight into the processes of nature, into the laws of evolution and growth, which have been gained during the last fifty years, it is wonderful that there has been so little study into the principles of training. There has been some study of the physiological aspects of the problem, but the deeper and broader aspects of training are wholly unstudied, or at any rate, as yet unrecognized by scientific men. A science of training becomes absolutely necessary when a teacher comes face to face with an awkward man without any control of his limbs, whom he desires to elevate along the lines of nature's intention, or in contact with a voice constricted and hard, nasal and throaty, which he must improve. Mere hap-hazard practice has unfortunately been the custom or practice in elocution in accordance with some mechanical and artificial system, but neither of these have ever been adequate. The voice is not a machine and cannot be built. It is a part of nature, and must be developed in accordance with her laws.

There is a tendency at the present time to consider the word training as having reference to athletics, and the development of great and unusual strength for the accomplishment of specific feats. But a true science of training must secure control over voice and body, must bring man's organism under control of his being, must develop both ease and strength, grace and power, beauty and health, and not affectation or external and superficial modulation, but skill in revelation of the mind and soul. There is also great need for specific application of a scientific method to all the work of expression. The great discoveries in science since the time of Newton have resulted from a specific method as has been shown by Mr. Jevons. A union of induction with deduction has been the method followed by every discoverer since Sir Isaac Newton.

The true scientific method is first the formation of a hypothesis from insight into a few facts, and then a long course of experiment and observation for the establishment or disapproval of the hypothesis. Then and then only, can we arrive at a conclusion. All the work in expression is dependent upon discoveries. The work of training the voice and body, methods for the development of the action of the mind, and in fact, every case requires such a course to arrive at the real needs. This, however, is not always consciously the case, because the best critics and teachers in work of this kind often criticise from direct instinct. But the greatest problems and difficulties have to be met by most careful and definite observation. Every teacher in every department of study must have a good method, but a good method is absolutely necessary in such subjective work as the development of expression, because there is greater danger of going astray than in any other department of education.

Again, one of the greatest needs of work of this kind is co-operation. In all the great sciences the great results have been obtained not merely by one man but by the co-operation of a great number. Even the great law of gravitation was not established by Newton alone, and it is doubtful whether Newton could ever have conceived his hypothesis and got a clue to the course of reasoning that established it, had it not been for Keppler and others; and the calculations to verify his law have been made and are still being made in every observatory in the world. The isolation of teachers of voice, both in music and the speaking voice, is greatly to be regretted. It has not been possible thus far, for these teachers to support periodicals such as would offer them a means of co-operating with each other in the investigation of the great problems of their work. All such periodicals have been in the hands of speculators. It is to be doubted whether, except among a few teachers, the sense of professional honor toward each other is the same as among lawyers and physicians.

Again, there is needed a more definite and careful study of man, not merely of psychology or of physiology, but of the latest phases of physiological-psychology, and not only all these but a deeper and broader study of man as an artistic being. A study, not only of the mind and body, but of the actions of the one upon the other; not only of the imagination, but of the means of developing it, and of its relation to human emotion and of its modes of manifestation. There must be such a study of the whole man as will enable the teacher to recognize both the conscious and the unconscious elements and the relation of these elements to each other, so as to enable him to adopt such methods as will secure harmonious co-ordination of every faculty of the mind and agent of the body concerned in expression.

There is need for more thorough study of the great fundamental principles and laws of education. All the reforms in education for the past two hundred years have been in the direction of expression. All perversions in education have violated the fundamental principles of true expression. Often there has been an acquirement of dry, dead facts, resulting in a mere book-worm; or on the other hand, education has aimed to secure ornamental adornment. To harmonize the education of the mind with the education of the body, to co-ordinate the power of thinking, and the power of feeling, and to harmonize all the faculties of the mind, has furnished the greatest problem of education from the days of Pythagoras, and as we have found, the highest test of this is furnished in the study of expression.

For example, let us note some of the lessons which have been furnished to expression, through the reforms in education in modern times. The lesson we learn from Rousseau in the Emile is, that education can not be the result of conventional rules or authority. The final appeal must ever be to nature and to spontaneous impulse.

All must not be conscious or deliberative. All must not be the result of rules and authority. A great majority of the work in education must be through spontaneity, or the unconscious unfoldment of nature. Nature must be trusted, nature's way is right.

While Rousseau may possibly have gone too far, yet in expression no great results can be achieved without reverence for nature's methods and nature's impulses. Any means of training must be simply the direct and greater stimulation of nature's processes, without any reversal or perversion of them. They can be directed, they can never be reversed. In all development and training it is necessary for us to feel what Browning has said in "By the Fire-side":

> "How the world is made for each of us;
>   How all we perceive and know in it
> Tends to some moment's product thus,
>   When a soul declares itself — to wit,
> By its fruit, the thing it does:
>
> Be hate that fruit, or love that fruit,
>   It forwards the general deed of man,
> And each of the many helps to recruit
>   The life of the race by a general plan;
> Each living his own, to boot."

By wrong choice and use, nature's help may be made a means of perversion. The foundation of all training, if not of all education, is the study of nature's elemental tendencies, impulses and modes of working; and any method must seek to co-ordinate conscious choice with the spontaneous impulses, to develop unity in the mind and body by exercise, to bring such objects before the mind as will stimulate and direct the tendencies of nature to the highest efficiency. Rousseau practically taught that nature was always right and art always wrong, and failed to see that true education is a balance of the two.

But the world had neglected nature more, and this is the case with present elocutionary methods, so that his exaggerations can be easily seen, while his lesson is the most important that needs to be learned.

Again, what lessons can be learned from Comenius! The great principle that education must be from within out, has already been applied to expression in this work. The writer thought at first that the principle was original, but found it was unfolded by Comenius in relation to all education. As we proceed in the study of Comenius we find the lessons so numerous that they can not be enumerated. All the principles unfolded by Comenius, such as, that "nature never makes any leaps", apply directly to the development of expression.

Again, Pestalozzi and Froebel furnish innumerable principles of like application. Nature must be observed. "Such objects must be brought before the mind as to stimulate spontaneous activity." "Things rather than their signs must be studied."

One of the most marvelous things is, that such teachers as William Russell, who had himself so many advanced ideas upon education, could not see that the mechanical suggestions of Rush were in direct violation of all the great laws and reforms in education.

Yet, however much elocution, as it is so commonly taught, may be found to violate the great principles of advanced education, one thing must ever be said, that many elocutionary teachers for the past one hundred and fifty years have been reformers in education. They have rendered the most important service in advancing the study of English. Sheridan outlined a system of education which came very near being adopted. Had it been established as he planned, the beneficial results would have been very great indeed. It was Walker, with all

his artificial rules about inflection who wrote the dictionary of the language which has been the foundation of the
subsequent works and is still quoted as an authority. It
was Professor Russell and Professor Monroe who materially aided in the establishment of those wonderful
methods in the Boston primary schools, which have been
in recent years put forth as some great original principle,
and called by a new name.

These facts show on the one hand that all the best
teachers of elocution have ever made a thorough study of
education, and that they were in accordance with the most
advanced ideas of their time. On the other hand, these
facts show that the most advanced methods of education have ever had direct application to a better use of
English. As the President of Harvard University is said
to have remarked, "The highest aim in education must
ever be to enable men to have a better mastery of their
native tongue." Does not the same principle apply to
the natural languages, for these are more native to his
soul? They are the direct agents of personality, and if a
correct use of words is "an aid to thought", then correct expression of any kind is an aid to the development
of personality.

Another advance needed in the study of delivery is,
that expression must be founded in a more thorough and
practical study of literature. Literature is itself in all its
forms but a different phase of expression. Much literature is written especially in reference to being histrion-
ically rendered. Browning's monologues, for example, and
Shakespeare's plays must be conceived in relation to
expression, if not as delivered orally. Difficulties in
Shakespeare vanish at once when a sympathetic mind
thoroughly understands, and renders them in accordance
with the intention for which they were written; while

the book-worm student, dreaming alone in his study chair, reads difficulties into the play, and makes mountains of mole hills, which one with the least dramatic instinct can see at once. Of course all Shakespearean criticism is not of this kind, but there are many difficulties which would vanish with a mere reference to delivery, and the elemental principles of histrionic expression. The same is true of Browning. Many of his monologues were evidently meant by the poet to be rendered. They are elliptic and obscure, but many of these obscurities disappear in the hands of one who has the dramatic insight or instinct to render them according to their intention. They never were meant for the sofa, they were meant to be thoroughly studied. They never were meant for thought or feeling alone, but for both. They were meant to be studied and felt by the whole man.

On the other hand, the power to render a beautiful little lyric of the language without declamation, without rant, is one of the rarest and one of the most important attainments. It must ever be a fundamental step in the development of any kind of delivery. And yet, strange to say, in reading-books few lyrics can be found. Most of the selections or so-called Readings contain the very poorest of literature. The reason for this is, that elocution has been concerned with the mere study of external, mechanical action, and not with the spirit. A lyric is subjective and ordinary elocution is objective. It has been concerned with the body of language, and not with the soul. Histrionic art is ever supposed to be the chief aid for the interpretation of the best literature. What a miserable failure it becomes when devoted to the poorest and weakest. The contempt which has been heaped upon it of late is no more than just. Elocutionary rendering of any kind, when concerned with the weakest in literature, becomes insipid, enervates the mind and taste of reader and hearer. The function of reproductive art is to make clear, and to extend the influence of the greatest, the most difficult and the most misunderstood and the most original art of a given age. Where reproductive art is concerned with the lowest, it is one of the worst of all servants of a vitiated taste and is a curse to any community.

But, expression is not a mere reproductive art. There are some thimgs in connection with expression which require original work. A true reproductive artist of any kind seeks continually to produce original results; otherwise he becomes weaker and weaker; at any rate, the reproductive artist ever seeks to keep himself in sympathy with the very highest and best creative art. There is ever danger of a reproductive art becoming artificial and mechanical; and this tendency is ever most manifest where reproductive art allies itself with what is lowest, and does not continually seek to keep abreast with the best and most creative art of the time.

The study of expression and the study of literature must ever go hand in hand. The literature needs the expression to interpret it to the common mind, and expression needs the literature to give it subject and inspiration.

The study of literature and the study of expression together, furnish the most profound study of man. A study of literature alone may help a man wonderfully, improve his taste and his judgment; but to get the best results out of literature, we must ever follow the law advanced by Comenius, that, "if we wish to learn anything we must do it". It may not be necessary for us to write another play in order to appreciate one of Shakespeare's, but we must be able to give a beauty to one that is already written; we may execute it according to his ideals in another sphere of language.

Above all, the work of educating the powers of expression needs assistance. How little encouragement is given to teachers in this department of education. There are few colleges or educational institutions where teachers in this department stand side by side with the professors of other subjects. In all other departments of study men are given large salaries and every seventh year allowed to go to Europe for further study. Often before he begins his work he is sent away for a year or more of special preparation. But the poor elocutionist must piece out a small salary by private lessons, and deny himself every comfort to steal away to study for greater advance in his work. In fact, as we look at the past hundred years and remember the temptation to make all elocution merely an amusement, when we remember, also, all the sneers that have been thrown at it, the fact that speakers with wretched delivery excuse themselves by reproaching elocution, we wonder at the advance that it has made.

As we look over the whole field of delivery, examine all the methods and hear all the criticism, we find that the word elocution has come to be used as a term belonging only to the mere mechanism of speech. One of our leading dramatic critics stated that Bernhardt's elocution was absolutely perfect, but he proceeded to criticize her acting. In fact, the term elocution has long since become limited to the mere mechanical actions of speech, or to the mechanical method of developing delivery.

If elocution, therefore, has come to mean only the physical side of delivery or to refer only to the technical modes of execution, implying that the problem is merely a mechanical one, is it not well that another word should be used to express this broader and deeper method of developing delivery which we have found to be necessary?

A leading college president once said, "You must redeem the word elocution from the mechanical views concerning it, instead of calling your work by a new name." But words have a history, and it is very hard to interfere with the tendencies of words to certain meanings. The word elocution has come to be so universally applied to mechanical methods, that it seems impossible to make it mean anything else to the minds of the majority. A new thing, a new mode or method is ever expected to have a new name. Let us therefore call the method here advocated, expression. Then those who believe in the one-sided and merely mechanical method can call their work by their own beloved name, elocution; and those who believe in the deeper and broader work, including training for cause, means and effect in delivery, can be known as teachers of expression.

The difference, then, between the two systems will be clearly drawn. Elocution will mean the mechanical actions of speech or the mode of developing delivery by working merely upon technical effects. While on the other hand, expression will mean the study of causes and means as well as effects, and tracing faults to the action of the mind, securing control over the body and all its agents and actions as a means of revealing the man's thought and manifesting the deepest emotions of his soul. While the one method will consider a part of the facts of delivery, the other will study the whole man and will ever contend that it is the "soul that must speak".

Elocution will be considered as a representative art, while expression will be regarded as both representative and manifestive, with the manifestive ever transcendent in proportion to the ideal character of the art. Elocution will be concerned merely with the signs of emotion, will seek to make all conscious and deliberative, and will be represented by such teachers as the one who said that unless a student got "a certain inflection for a certain sentence in a certain way he should not speak at commencement". Or by a teacher who has a student sit without making a tone and merely thinking an imaginary tone in the top of the head. Expression will deal with the action of the mind, will strive to get men to think, will endeavor to arouse an idea in the soul which shall stimulate emotion and the fundamental causes which will spontaneously manifest experience with all the plenitude of nature. While one will endeavor to make all deliberative, and make all knowledge center upon the proper modes of delivery, the other will train and attune the body, will study the great principles of universal art and of nature, and will endeavor to translate all knowledge into instinct, that the man in all good speaking may be free from the mechanical shackles of artificial rules. One art will be seen to grow more and more conventional, more and more governed by mere authority; the other will be seen to partake of the elements of all the other forms of art and keep pace with their highest advances.

The one will endeavor to form rules which will be consciously obeyed; the other will seek into the great processes of nature for universal laws that a trained body and soul ever unconsciously obey. The one will be concerned with technical expedients; the other will be concerned with the whole mind and body of the human being. The one will ever be plucking away that which is imperfect; the other will be ever endeavoring to quicken the spirit that lies beneath and causes all external modes of manifestation. In other words, a teacher of the one art will be ever seeking to find faults and to adopt such expedients as will correct these faults. A teacher of the other will ever be seeking to find the fundamental needs of the man, to train the voice and body and all the powers of the soul into harmonious co-ordination — will ever seek to trace the fault to the fundamental cause, and will labor consciously and unconsciously to remove that cause. The key-note of one method will be training, that of the other mechanical rules. The one will endeavor to secure consciousness of detail and so displace consciousness from its normal center; the other will be ever endeavoring to center the consciousness of the man upon his ideas and thought, upon the images of his soul which are intended by nature to furnish the stimulus to every emotion. One method will endeavor to make all voluntary and conscious; the other will endeavor to apply such exercises as will co-ordinate the unconscious with the conscious, the involuntary with the voluntary. The one will be concerned with what is external and accidental, will ever make this an end; while the other will use exercises and training as a means to attune body and soul to the end of manifesting the activity of the soul.

Expression will ever be found saying that all passion, at least all noble passion, can be manifested by modulation of pure tone; while elocution will be contending for throatiness, huskiness and all the train of vocal imperfections as a means of manifesting the deeper and even the nobler thoughts of literature; and while thus making no distinction between the abnormal and the normal, will be found to degrade the art more and more to a rendering of the poorest and worst literature. Expression will ever be found studying the great laws of education, the fundamental principles that develop all a man's faculties, and will endeavor to seek to understand the fundamental excellences of every method of training and mode of advancing the human being; while the other, ever blinded by merely looking at the outside, will gauge all by a little, narrow system, and will tend to dwarf the infinite variety of nature to a dreary monotony by a mechanical and artificial mode of rendering.

If the problem of delivery and the hints that nature furnishes as to methods of meeting it, is compared with the traditional elocutionary systems, we find that the methods usually adopted are one-sided, mechanical and artificial. They have only dealt with external faults and not with the deeper and the real needs of delivery. Each system has been built upon some one fact and exaggerated in one direction, to the exclusion of other truths equally important. The advance that needs to be made is the application of the broadest scientific method to the observation of the facts, a higher study of the relation of expression to art, and above all, a deeper study of the action of the mind in expression, that the most fundamental causes of faults may be corrected, and the highest laws of education be obeyed. The facts of the body and the voice must also be carefully investigated, and a science of training formulated, with thorough methods for the development of every part of the organism to the highest efficiency. Attention to artificial expedients to the neglect of true training, must be corrected, and a thorough study given to all the elements of expression, so as to secure a broader and more harmonious development of the whole man.

There must especially be more attention to the normal actions of man's faculties and powers, and greater reverence for nature. The almost universal tendency in elocution to change unconscious actions to conscious, or to neglect them altogether, needs reform. What nature meant to be conscious and what she intended to be unconscious, must each be developed according to its peculiar nature. The true elements of expression in the human being must also be studied, and the subjective or manifestive which have been entirely overlooked must be developed. The whole artistic nature as revealed in all forms of art must be understood by the teacher, that he may feel their relations to the most fundamental and natural modes of expression, so as to develop delivery to the highest possible efficiency.

IV.

Some Applications.

" . . . . Instinctive art,
Must fumble for the whole, once fixing on a part,
However poor surpass the fragment, and aspire
To reconstruct the ultimate entire."

— Browning.

"Art is nature made by man
To man the interpreter of God."

—Owen Meredith.

XXII

FUNCTION OF EXPRESSION IN EDUCATION.

To know the truth it is necessary to do the truth. — *Maudsley*.

HAS the development of expression anything to do with general education, or is it merely for the training of speakers, readers or actors? Is it merely for the purpose of developing an ornamental accomplishment, or is it a vital part of the development of the faculties and powers of the human soul?

In a practical age like this, however clearly we may unfold theories and principles, men will still ask, "What is the use? Granting that such results can be attained, what advantage are they to the race?" There is a common idea that such work is only for a few specialists. When a man is going to be an actor or a public reader, then it is well enough for him to pay attention to such studies and enter into such training. Possibly, also, if a man wishes to become a public speaker a very little time might be devoted to it in order to enable him to understand his faults; but such studies form no part of general education. According to this view they are only an ornamental branch, like dancing, or possibly they form a very unworthy part of physical training. The aim of training is to develop health and strength; but to improve the voice is of no earthly value, except, possibly, to a singer or to one who wishes to make an exhibition of himself. Possibly, also, it might be well for consumptives to engage in such work so as to develop their lungs to counteract the disease, but the work is essentially physical, and has nothing to do with the mind.

A few years ago, a petition for vocal training, signed by many teachers in the public schools of Boston, was before the Legislature of Massachusetts, and one of our learned mis-representatives spoke against it. He said that vocal training or elocution was a mere ornamental branch of education, and should not be introduced into our public schools ; that it stood in the same relation to schools as dancing, and that while it might be a very good thing to have all our teachers taught to dance, yet such accomplishments were foreign to education ; and the training of the voices of teachers and children belonged to exactly the same category, and had nothing to do with true development.

While it may be granted that work in expression has a relationship to art and that there is a professional training connected with it of very great importance, yet such work is not a mere ornamental accomplishment, but belongs to universal education. It has an application to all life and the development of all character. It has a vital relation to the harmonious growth of the soul and is vitally necessary to happiness and must be a part of the development of the powers of every human being.

Whatever may be our understanding of the nature of education, whether as the "actualization of an ideal", as the "development of the possibilities of the race in the individual", as the "process of bringing such objects before the mind as will stimulate spontaneous activity", as the "discipline of man's powers and the attainment of skill in execution", or "as the development of character" or even the very lowest conception, namely, "the acquire- of knowledge", expression must play a most essential part. Education may be considered as having two sides ; all man's faculties are concerned with taking or giving, or both. The greatness of the human soul is seen in its possibility of reception and the possibility of revealing its possessions to others.

Few would say at the present time that the mere acquirement of knowledge can achieve the ends of education. Although in all our schools much of the time is devoted to this end, and an exaggerated estimate placed upon getting information, when we come to consider the discipline of the powers of man, we find that the taking of truth, the comprehension of truth, when not followed by an endeavor to manifest the truth, does not train these powers to their greatest efficiency. Expression is absolutely necessary to the proper development of the new education. It is one of the most important characteristics. "It is more blessed to give than to receive," and more difficult. It requires a different action of the faculties of the mind. The action of the mind in receiving truth may be merely analytical, the giving of truth requires a more or less perfect co-ordination and co-operation of all the powers of the mind. Consequently, while an endeavor to comprehend truth may discipline the powers, may quicken the activity of the individual faculties, expression brings these powers and faculties into harmonious co-operation with each other. A mind that merely receives becomes a kind of educational sponge, a Dominie Sampson, a useless appendage to society. Expression naturally follows impression. Exhalation of breath after inhalation is not more necessary to life than the endeavor of the mind to give what it receives, is necessary to vigor of mind. The whole process of education is concerned with the development or co-ordination of these two processes.

Men, according to their different views of education, emphasize either one or the other of these two processes. Carlyle said that all education was learning to read.

Taken in its broadest sense this is true. An educated man is known by his power to glean most quickly the fundamental ideas of books. Carlyle himself is said to have averaged eight volumes a day. Shakespeare was great because he was preëminently able to read the depths of the human soul. He had the power of insight into the motives and dispositions of men as no one has ever had before or since. Wordsworth was great because of his power to read nature, his insight into her most delicate beauty. He was not one to whom "A primrose by the river's brim, a yellow primrose was to him, and it was nothing more"; but to him "A violet by a mossy stone, half hidden from the eye," was "fair as a star when only one is shining in the sky." Everywhere he shows to us a power of penetration into the most delicate elements of nature's loveliness and beauty. Browning, of all the poets of our present age is the one who has been able to see deepest into the essential elements and fundamental needs of our life, and for this power of insight he is loved and honored as the poet who makes us think. Thus, insight, the power to receive, the power to penetrate and take from the things about us, the books, the men, the trees, the rocks and hills, is the glory of the artist, the orator or the man. But what men see, even what the greatest soul may conceive, is useless unless put into form. The ideas are mere visions without local habitation or a name, unless they can be embodied in some form of expression.

Thus there is something more. Shakespeare is not only great for his insight, but on account of his art. Wordsworth's insight into the delicacy and simplicity of nature led him to adopt simple words for the manifestation of that insight. There is not only impression as a process of education, but expression. The soul is not only disciplined by taking, but disciplined also by giving. If all education is primarily dependent upon exercising the human powers, then it can be seen at once that these two phases of education are complementary. Thus the soul must not only be disciplined to take but to give. "Reading makes the full man, conversation the ready man and writing the correct man," said Bacon. Taking these three aims as Bacon's ideal of education, we find that the first, which refers to the reception of truth, is universally recognized, but the other two, which refer to expression, are almost entirely neglected.

Besides, acquirement may not of itself discipline men's faculties. Expression requires more active use of man's powers. At least, it is as much concerned with the discipline of man's powers as reception. Men can not become fully cultured, can not become practical, can not use their knowledge for the proper influencing of their fellow-men without discipline of the powers of expression as well as the powers of reception.

Emphasis of practical execution in education has grown more and more marked in modern days. Emerson called attention to the subject fifty years ago, and caused a great change in the education of our country, and has more or less opened the way for the manual schools of our day. Mere reception of information by the mind without execution is not the highest aim of education; man's mind may grow, but his character does not. "To know may be first, but it is only by doing," that is, by execution according to knowledge that knowledge comes into being and character is developed. Just here is the evil tendency in education against which all great reforms have been directed. Breadth of grasp, skill in execution, harmony of the faculties of the man, such as will make him master of all the situations of life, and not mere acquirement of information has been the motto of every reformer for three hundred years.

There has been much discussion in recent years on the comparative merits of literary and scientific training. Mr. Huxley has discussed the advantages of science and Mr. Matthew Arnold fought for literature and literary training. But is not the problem a deeper one? Is not the real antithesis between scientific education and artistic education; between the training of individual faculties in the development of specialists and the harmonious development of all the faculties of the mind in their normal relation to each other, and in response to the spontaneous desire for creative activity generated by the true assimilation of knowledge; between the discipline to the mind received from the acquirement of knowledge of the laws and principles of nature and the development received from the endeavor to embody the conceptions of the human mind in accordance with the processes of nature in some form of art? Even granting that the artistic has to do merely with enjoyment and happiness, still it is man's duty to be happy. But this is too low an estimate of the functions of art. It has been well said that we do not see things as they are, but as we are ourselves. Every man looks through the eyes of his prejudices, of his preconceived notions. Hence, it is the most difficult thing in the world to broaden a man so that he will realize truth as other men see it. Breadth of view is ever one result of artistic training. Without the spirit of art, men are narrow and prejudiced; each one works on in his own narrow groove. It is the function of art and of the artistic in education to furnish man a means by which he can see the embodiment of what other men conceive to be the truth of life and nature. As a man looks at a landscape it may or may not leave any vivid impression of its beauty, but let him look at a painter's interpretation of it, and he is led to wonder if that is the artist's understanding of the scene. He goes back to nature with quickened attention and a wider view. So also, the ideal in every man's heart of the Christ is elevated and quickened by the struggle of great artists to embody their conceptions of the Master. Art is thus, a means of communion, deeper and more adequate than language; for art may "do the thing shall breed the thought, nor wrong the thought missing the mediate word."

The artistic faculties of man need, then, to be trained to awaken deeper love for nature and human character, and to stimulate and strengthen the higher and nobler emotions of the soul and to make the man happier and better. But this is not all; the artistic faculties of man need to be developed to make him practical rather than theoretical; to give him the power of execution, because until he is able to execute in some form what he sees and feels, however carefully he may be taught, "The truth by when it reaches him looks false nor recognized by whom it left." Thus artistic training is not concerned merely with the emotions and emotional powers, but is of vital importance in quickening those powers which are most intimately concerned with the adequate comprehension of the fundamental facts of nature and human life, and the ability to realize truth. It is, of course, not meant that artistic education should supersede the scientific; the two are, in fact, co-ordinate; one without the other will ever be incomplete; but the tendency at the present time in the education of the child is to neglect the artistic element.

The most effective mode of cultivating the artistic faculty is through expression. Art, as we have seen, is ever directly derived from vocal and pantomimic expression, or, at least, is very intimately connected with the natural languages. Expression is, in fact, the most direct work of these faculties and powers. If they are to be put into action this is the simplest and most direct mode of exercising them; it does not consist in the use of a mechanical chisel, brush or instrument, but in the proper use of the man's own body for the revelation of his soul.

Froebel said that all education was emancipation; if so, a study of expression affords one of the most effective means of removing all repression. In some of our schools there is an entire repression of all emotion. In studying literature the suggestion is given not to have any emotion but simply to bring out the thought. The effect of such repression is to cause one-sidedness and constriction. It might as well be said that one side of a tree could be completely fettered, tied up and kept from growing, and that the tree would grow symmetrically. Thought and emotion are two phases of man's nature. They are co-essential parts of human experience. The whole soul is a unity and must unfold in all directions.

Expression tests whether the whole man acts in unity or not. A man may be very one-sided and be a great scientist, but expression more than any other aspect of education requires harmony of all the powers of the man, and tests their unity of action. The creative energies of the man, especially the imaginative, the instincts and intuitions are quickened into life. The sympathies, emotions and passions are awakened and brought into unity and harmony, co-ordinated under proper control of will. Besides, work in expression tests the normal action of all the faculties and powers of the man, and brings to the surface one-sidedness in all psychic action and the effects of evil habits. To develop the highest power in expression abnormal traits of character must be corrected, and all the powers be brought into simultaneous co-operation. Wherever one faculty or power has an exaggerated action the effect will be seen at once in expression. Thus if harmony is the highest aim of education, an idea which is as old as Protagoras, if not older, any one can see that in an act of true expression, the faculties of the mind are brought into more direct co-ordination than in any other educative exercise. There can be no perfect expression without the co-ordination of the most antithetic powers, such as those of thought and passion; no form of education demands more powers and agents to be brought under control of will. Hegel defined a perfect man as one whose emotion and thought are balanced by will; the power of expression not only develops the power to think and to think more logically, and to think upon the feet, to create a living picture and scene, and to feel a response in the depths of our nature, but such exercise causes a union of this thought and feeling, and develops control over all.

Work in expression disciplines man's will. It aids in bringing all emotion and passion, every faculty and agent, under control. Knowledge may be in possession of memory, understanding or will. Knowledge is not truly in possession of man until it is under control of his will. Expression gives man power, not only to understand truth but to wield truth; not merely to apprehend, but to use knowledge. It not only quickens the power of subjective apprehension, but enables the man to reveal thought and emotion so as to move his fellow-man. In the work of acquiring knowledge a single power or faculty of the mind may be unduly exercised and the man may become more or less unbalanced. But expression calls for a co-ordination of all the faculties and powers of the mind. It is the most adequate test of one-sidedness in the power of man; for it must cause each and every faculty to act, to act decidedly, to act vigorously, and all to act in co-operation with each other toward the accomplishment of a common end.

Training for expression must, therefore, form a part of education, for true work in expression is the most direct means of accomplishing some of the highest aims of human development. That work in expression belongs to education, is thus proved by the nature of education itself. Not only does expression belong to education but all progress and reform in education from time immemorial, directly or indirectly, have lain along the line of expression, from Rousseau's emphasis of nature as opposed to conventionality, Comenius' founding all education upon the processes of nature's growth, Pestalozzi's "things, not their signs," Froebel's principle of using objects to "arouse the faculties of the mind to spontaneous activity," down to the natural methods of teaching language and the principles contended for in our manual schools. The development of expression gives man possession of his faculties and powers, enables him to discharge his functions more effectively in relation to his fellow-men, and in every way makes him more of a man.

It is not meant, of course, to include in work for the development of delivery, all the executive or practical side of education. There are other means of manifestation, such as manual dexterity and writing; but it can be seen that expression is one of the most fundamental, that it begins in earliest childhood, in the very first efforts of the mind to act, and that it ceases only with life; that it extends through all stages of education, from the cradle to the college, from the Kindergarten to the professional school. Not only so, it furnishes also a practical means which is most simple and most fundamental for developing the faculties and powers of the mind, which lie at the basis of all literary training.

To enter into a more specific study of the function that expression discharges in education, it develops faculties too often neglected. In all our common methods of education there is a universal tendency to neglect the imagination. This faculty, which is most alive in the little child, in our ordinary schools is often dwarfed and fettered. Expression when rightly studied, from the very first day that the child enters school until the young man leaves college, is the most important means of stimulating this faculty. Imagination is the fundamental element of dramatic instinct or power to see into the souls of other men, to look through other eyes upon nature and man ; to see things as a Greek, as a German sees them, a power that enables the soul to rise out of a narrow groove to the highest standpoint of the race, a power which is the basis of success in nearly all occupations.

Again, the work in expression develops sympathy and the feelings. It is a strange fact that the power of passion is despised and its training ignored, and yet the impulses and motives of human life, all its happiness, depend upon the relation of emotion and passion to the will. In the struggle to manifest the spirit of the best literature, the feelings and passions common to human nature are trained to respond to intelligent purpose and developed out of the domain of the appetites.

Again, it is the most direct and immediate mode of stimulating taste, especially taste for literature, for poetry, for that which is most delicate and beautiful in art and nature. It is true a taste for the poorest in literature has often been fostered, but the power of bad training to pervert is only a proof of the power of the right kind of training to ennoble and elevate. This perversion shows how closely connected expression is with the emotions and artistic faculties, the source and fountain-head of taste and even moral character. This has been more or less acknowledged in all time from Quintillian, who defined oratory as "the good man speaking well", to Dr. Phillips Brooks, who defines speaking as the "presentation of truth by personality".

Again, it secures the development of philosophic memory rather than mere verbal memory. Of all the faults in education the mere training of verbal memory is one of the worst. When the intellect merely apprehends the signs of things rather than the things themselves, the whole mind is superficialized, and the deeper powers of feeling and imaginative activity which assimilate truth, are rendered dormant, and no co-ordinate experience is awakened. But that there can be no expression from mere words or parrot-like repetition of signs can be seen at once. The fundamental characteristic of all noble expression is that the mind must realize ideas. Thought must ever be united to experience, or the voice will be cold and hard in spite of all elocutionary tricks. Expression is only a process of thinking aloud and a lack of feeling, a lack of co-ordination of all the faculties of the mind in expression reveal in many ways the mere repetition of words. Thus the teacher has a perfect clue by which he can distinguish the mere memory of words and signs from the true memory of ideas. In fact, vocal expression furnishes the most perfect training for the imagination and philosophic memory.

Again, expression educates the intuitive action of the mind. It stimulates conception, and the power of creation causes the student to trust his instincts, centers his consciousness in relation to all knowledge and to all nature ; makes him feel that his own soul is the center of feeling, thought and light. Such study awakens reverence in the soul for its own nature.

The greatest need at the present time is assimilation ; books are multiplied by the million, newspapers are infinite, people are continually reading, skimming over facts ; there is, however, little assimilation. We no longer take the advice of great thinkers who tell us that "we must eat a book," not merely taste it, but "eat and digest it". Men skim over great poems, and if the thought is too deep, as in Browning, to be taken at a glance by shallow, superficial attention, the newspaper, where one idea is extended over a column, is taken up in preference. The poem is pronounced dull and without meaning. To render a poem according to the true principles of art, means to give its emotions, to render its thought, to render its fundamental idea and its spirit. To give a student a poem to study without any explanations regarding it, and so compel him to struggle to find the logical continuity of ideas, to realize the associated experience and to give its emotion, will train his taste and insight into the best artistic spirit, better than a long course of lectures upon English literature, and will furnish a means of testing, if not of developing, the mind's power of assimilating truth.

Such work furnishes the teacher indirectly the best means of judging the real personality of his pupils, the real relationship of the student toward truth. The great need of education, then, is not merely to acquire knowledge, but to cause that knowledge to be assimilated, to carry it into the depths of man's experience and character and to help the student into a right relation to truth. With all our public speakers this assimilation of knowledge by the personality of the man is the chief difficulty.

The knowledge of the man is too often a mere aggregation. It has not been assimilated by experience. As his thought comes to us it does not come from the circulation and life-blood of the soul. The study of expression provides a remedy.

Here we have the solution of the great problem of the study of English in our schools. The common methods of studying English are too verbal. Many of our authors are studied as dry fossils. The plays of Shakespeare are dissected, analyzed and studied as words and forms. This process may be of some advantage in studying language, but it is not studying Shakespeare; it is not studying art; above all, such work never develops the artistic faculties of the man, nor does it create a love of literature in the minds of students.

What needs to be done in the study of English is to rouse the faculties of the mind which are concerned in literary production. The imagination and the sympathies need to be awakened, all the creative faculties of the mind must be quickened and put into action. All this can be done in the study of expression.

Of course, some teachers of rhetoric will laugh at the idea of vocal expression as a means of developing style, but such results have been accomplished again and again. The whole artistic delivery, flexibility of the voice and ease of body, and even style in the verbal sense have not only been improved, but developed and even completely reformed, by the true study and rendering of the best authors and the speaking necessary in expressive training. The reason for this is plain. In the study of expression according to the method outlined, the mind is trained to vividly realize ideas and to view them successively in logical order. It has been shown by Mr. Walter Pater in his essay on Style that it is the very first principle of all true style that the words used shall be in correspondence with the picture of the mind. The method here evolved for the development of vocal expression is founded upon the same principle. All delivery is traced to the pictures in the mind as the stimulus and impulse which is to determine everything. To render the best literature according to this method develops the power to use any means of manifestation, whether tones or words, because it develops the instinct of correspondence between the pictures of the mind and any mode of expression. In mere writing it is rather more difficult for a teacher to see into the action of the mind and test the correspondence of the expression to the pictures; but in vocal expression, where the means used are natural rather than conventional, and respond spontaneously to the mental picture, when properly trained, it becomes very easy. A dull imagination can be most directly quickened by such a course. And not only so, but a study of the action of the mind leads to a rejection of mere useless words. It develops insight into fundamentals. The requisite of all oratory, all writing of every kind, is this power of insight into essential elements. No speaker is a speaker without it, no writer is a writer without it. Here is the primal source of all artistic power in every sphere.

In short, as has been maintained again and again in these pages, expression carries the human mind to the fountain-head of artistic endeavor. In expression we have the earliest struggle for art whether in the race or in the individual, and it furnishes the most immediate transparency of the action of the artistic faculties, or of all the faculties of the mind acting in an artistic direction. Thus we can see that the use of his native tongue by any man is closely connected with his dramatic instinct.

Hence, histrionic expression, the most immediate and direct application of the endeavor to make form correspond with a picture of the mind, is fundamentally necessary to the development and education of the human being. Literature is a department of art and all the work for the mastery of one's own native tongue, if done rightly, is according to the principles of expression, and these principles are most easily understood in their simplest and most natural embodiment — vocal expression. Each art ought ever to be studied by going to the fountain-head of all art for a mastery of the principles. All the faculties concerned in creating must be brought into exercise before any art can awaken interest and love. Contemplation of any art tends to do this of itself, but active execution leads to a deeper understanding and appreciation of subtle beauties. The proper rendering of the best literature in vocal expression is one of the most fundamental means of discovering the beauties of an author.

The study of literature and so-called English according to the ordinary methods is among the most mechanical of all work in education. Mere rules are laid down, and practice, so far as any is found, is mechanical and perfunctory. Instead of the mind of the student being trained to find the real spirit, instead of the imagination being stimulated to create vivid pictures of the scenes and to render the feeling of authors, all attention is devoted to cold analysis, which dulls all feeling and spontaneous love of the author. Rhetoric is studied as a collection of facts and rules. There is little or no endeavor to stimulate the creative faculties of the man. The whole subject of rhetoric is presented objectively, language and figures are considered as mere objects of knowledge. In fact, in taking up the subject of invention

even here mere forms are studied and there is no indication of stimulating the man from within, in a suggestion of a trained personality using form freely, but
with exact truth and correspondence with the thought.
Instead of endeavoring to stimulate the action of the
faculties which cause figurative language, instead of
securing imaginative action of the mind, figures are
named and examples more or less hackneyed are given
for analysis. Such work discourages rather than stimulates the student to write. This explains why some of
the best teachers of English discard a theoretic study of
rhetoric altogether. The true method of training in
written expression, as in vocal, must be to stimulate from
within. The creative faculties must themselves be
aroused and forms compared with the figures existing in
the mind. If a young student is made to recite from a
great author he is made to think over again the successive ideas in relation to expression; his imagination is
thus quickened and his power of discriminating as to the
power of words is unconsciously stimulated. He is thus
trained to carry a succession of ideas in relation to the
tones that manifest them. This, of course, cannot compensate for a higher and more analytic study of language
and choice of words. There must be technical work in
every art. But it is a beginning and a beginning in accordance with the methods of the most artistic of all peoples,
the Greeks. It is a beginning in accordance with the
great laws of education. The mind that thinks and feels
must be awakened, the impulse to write must be stimulated. This must ever be the first step. The imagination that paints must ever be stimulated before there is
a more objective study of figurative language. There
were figures long before they were named, and a mere
study of figures will never stimulate the faculties for

their production except in the most mechanical and artificial way. Thus, a proper study and stimulation of the right action of the mind in reading and speaking will lead to a correct action of the mind in writing. As a child learns to talk before it can read or write, so it should be in the process of education. There must be an improvement in the child's conversational powers, before there can be improvement in its power to write. A child talks not for the sake of using words, but to say something. Of course, when the man chooses to become a speaker or a writer, then there must be greater work to attain special skill in the use of the special forms of language, but for the general purposes of education to prepare the man for success in either, attention must be given to both. Even he who is to become a speaker or a public reader or an actor will receive great assistance from the habit of close analysis secured in efforts to express thought in written form. In fact, it is absolutely necessary for the highest success. There are a few forms of art so near to the soul that a certain mastery of them is demanded for the development of the soul.

The time may come when rhetoric and delivery will be studied as fundamentally connected as they were in the days of the Greeks, when true artistic results were accomplished by educational processes. Our great artists, writers and speakers at the present day became such in spite of their education in English, not by its aid.

Expression trains the power to see into the needs of other men, to be able to understand and appreciate the motives and actions of others. Some one has said that this is the fundamental need of every soul. The man who is able to help his fellow-men is he who is able to enter into the spirit and motives of his kind, who has, as it has been called, the dramatic instinct. How can this be educated without a direct study into the nature of the human heart, without a direct rendering in expression of the emotions and experience belonging to man? A theoretic study of the great dramatic poets will do much, but can really only give a start. The necessity for this dramatic training is seen in every profession. The teacher must have it or he will not understand his pupil, the speaker must have it or he will never be able to understand his audience, and adapt his truth toward moulding them to nobler ideals.

The study of expression gives men an understanding of human character, it gives a man an understanding of himself, it reveals to him the possibilities of his own nature, it stimulates and brings all his powers into simultaneous and harmonious activity. It stimulates the ideal, it develops the taste and ennobles the imagination and all the artistic faculties.

The study of expression develops simplicity and naturalness. It corrects and prevents all affectation on the part of students. It has been charged that the study of elocution is the most direct and effective means of developing affectation. This is no doubt true when the method is a mechanical or an artificial one, when it is a mere study of signs independent of the action of the mind; but the true study of expression not only does not develop affectation, but is the most effective means of eradicating it. Men are often affected without knowing it, and the true study of expression is the most effective means of revealing this fact to the man.

Again, the study of expression removes self-consciousness, whether that self-consciousness be an egotistic one or a self-depreciating one. It gives the over-confident student a truer understanding of himself, it gives the timid one a power to centralize the mind upon ideas and removes confusion and embarrassment and gives him confidence to face his fellow-men.

Expression develops careful observation of nature, leads the mind to study fundamentals, and brings the soul directly into contact with elemental truth. Every argument for manual schools, all the arguments for practical education, apply to the fact that expression should have a place in universal education.

Again, there are two recognized methods of studying the mind: by self-analysis or conventional authority as some think the method has become, and by the modern physiological method. Both are inadequate. Here we add a third, not as a substitute, but as a co-ordinate form to aid in practically testing the truth of the others. In fact, it is almost the only method of studying the faculties of the mind in action. Expression shows the workings of the human mind. We can render through the voice more emotions than are named in psychology.

Expressive training serves as an aid to the practical application of the best methods of education. Great teachers make students work, they do not give them opinions. Expression can thus be used as a test of harmonious growth. It tests evil tendencies in students; some students will be found to be reading one class of works, others another. One man will read only scientific works until his mind becomes cold and abstract; he has no appreciation of poetry. The moment he tries to render some form of literature this can be seen, and the teacher can prescribe works on imagination and poetry. Another reads only the superficial and sentimental poets, and he loses the logical faculty and becomes a dreamer. Such a student is utterly unable to read and manifest the antithetic power of Macaulay, he needs a good, strong diet of Carlyle and the great essayists, that the logical power of his mind may be strengthened and vigorous thinking awakened. As Bacon has said "Every defect of the mind may have a special receipt".

Thus, laying aside the great importance of expressive training in its own particular sphere, such as the softening and training of the American voice, the development of the art of oratory, to serve as the guardian of liberty or as the means of advancing every great reform, of elevating the arts of entertainment, we find that it has a vital relationship to the great problem of universal education, and is necessary to the development of the highest possibilities of the human being. We see this from the nature of education itself, from the nature of the human mind, from the relationship which it bears to artistic training; we see it from the fact that it develops those faculties and powers which are most concerned with the happiness and success of the individual. We see that it is of importance indirectly or as an assistant in other departments of education. We can see that a teacher through expression will be enabled to test the harmonious development of students. It tests whether students have a possession of mere words or a grasp of essential ideas; whether they have mere command of accidentals, or whether they have a possession of the fundamental elements of truth. It aids also the student himself in that it develops philosophic memory rather than a mere verbal memory. It trains the logical faculties of the mind, it trains the imagination and creative faculties of the man so that his thoughts and ideas will not be uncertain and confused, but clear, distinct and adequate.

XXIII.

OFFICE OF A TEACHER OF EXPRESSION.

We ought to inculcate all we possibly can by actions, and to say only what we cannot do. — *Rousseau.*

IT has now been shown that expression should form a part of universal education. No matter what profession a man may intend to follow, some form of expression is necessary to develop his faculties, especially his imagination, and to bring all of his powers into harmony with each other; to stimulate his appreciation of nature, literature and art, and to give him insight into human nature and into his own life and character. It has also been shown that all reforms in education have a direct or an indirect relation to expression. In the development of every one such work is necessary to prevent mere aggregation or lack of assimilation, one-sidedness and a long train of imperfections.

The question now arises whether this is the whole work of expression. If expression is so vital a part of universal education, then should it simply form a part of other studies, or should there be special attention to expression as a separate department of human development? In other words is it simply a phase, or is it a department of education? Is there any use of a special teacher? Every teacher, if he is a true teacher, will know something of expression, and will be able to assist in this work. Many think, therefore, that it is simply a vital part of a general teacher's office, and that special teachers are only a hindrance. The reason assigned is, that they develop artificiality. Devoting themselves entirely to this specialty, they look more for special tact or skill, some mode of execution or power of imitation, and will place this as the fundamental element of expression before all acquisition of knowledge or experience. Studying only manner, they forget the true nature of manner, and make it an end in itself. Devoting themselves especially to delivery, they ignore all thinking and come to consider all delivery as a mere matter of the body and forget that it is as fundamentally an act of mind as is the reception of truth.

There is an important element of truth in all these supposed objections, but if we examine more closely we find that the work of expression is both a phase and a department of education. So far as the simple development of the soul in childhood is concerned it belongs to the function of every teacher, but viewed in a professional aspect in relation to the development of speakers and special teachers of expression, and the training of public readers and actors, or the eradication of special defects or even in advanced education of any kind, it is a special department of education demanding a special teacher specially trained in a special professional school with special equipment, peculiarly constructed buildings and adequate endowment.

In the first place, such a specialization is along the line of progress in education. A division of labor is now made in education as well as in business. In the work of education in the higher schools and colleges, it is necessary, if each teacher is to do his best work, that he should do a certain kind of work. There is little trouble, in a college course in the co-ordination of a vast number of subjects, each under the direction of a specialist. If this is true in other departments of education, it must certainly hold good in the work of expression.

In expression, of all departments of education, a teacher must have special technical training. While his work is more general than any other in all education, yet it is also the most special. The voice as a physical instrument is the most delicate and the most difficult to train of any of the organs of the body. Diseases of the vocal organs are among the most subtle and the most difficult to deal with, and a great number of specialists in throat diseases are to be found in every city. So vocal training is the most difficult of all education. It is a notorious fact that there are fewer good teachers of voice than in any other department. In either the singing or the speaking voice this is true. Mistakes are made continually; voices are ruined every year. Faults of voice are so extremely subtle, that there must not only be a physiological and anatomical diagnosis; there must also be deeper search into the emotions and conditions of the soul. The fundamental causes of faults of voice are found in the action of the mind upon the body. A wide experience, constant attention specially directed to a great variety of actions and conditions is necessary to enable the teacher to penetrate into the causes of the most common faults of voice.

It is universally recognized that the physician needs long years of careful training, and in most States special laws are enacted to prevent one who has had no such training from setting himself up as qualified to treat diseases. And yet, strange to say, there is not the least hesitation on the part of the most ignorant, with little or no special preparation, to undertake to train the most subtle organism belonging to man, where there is greatest danger of malpractice; and people make no objection. In fact, in some parts of the country, a student who has taken a prize at some contest is often at once considered fit to teach elocution without any further preparation. In many advanced schools and colleges teachers who have failed in other departments are given elocution as a last resort, as that is not considered as requiring any special training. Some think they can attend a summer school for a few weeks or take a short course of private lessons and at once set themselves up as being able to teach.

But if the principles unfolded in the present work are true, if such is the nature of delivery, if such are the dangers that meet the teacher on every side, it is absolutely necessary that there shall be thorough technical training, that the subject shall be taught by those who are specially and thoroughly prepared to meet the needs of the case. Unless this is done such work will be neglected and despised. Besides, more than in other studies, students must be inspired with its importance. Incompetent students may fail in written examinations in other studies, but such tests are almost entirely wanting in the subject of expression. If a student takes no interest in his work he will do poorly in any department, but he will make an absolute failure in expression. Effective practice must proceed from love of the work, and this can be inspired only by a teacher who himself loves the work, who can see to the depths of the minds of men and can make them realize their needs and possibilities.

Again, expression should form a distinct department in advanced education, because it has a special function to discharge. It is entirely different from other departments of education. Work in mathematics, work in the languages, work in psychology and in the sciences are all analytic or scientific in character. For this reason they are antithetic to work in expression, which is essentially synthethic and artistic. Work in scientific subjects calls for attention of the mind — calls simply for careful and exact thinking. Its highest end is nearly always reached when the student understands the principles involved. But expression starts from this point. Knowledge of a subject is pre-supposed in expression. It is not only necessary to know; expression calls for doing.

For this reason this work must be arranged at a special time entirely distinct from scientific work. The class attitude must be different. The atmosphere in the class must be different from the atmosphere in a scientific class. A teacher must learn the art of awakening interest, arousing enthusiasm and stimulating emotion. He must have an atmosphere where feeling will be possible, and not be considered a disgrace.

This same argument ought to apply to the study of all literature and English, and the failure to have adequate methods in teaching these is a proof of the principles involved. Students are often made to study English — a play of Shakespeare, for example — as if it were a mere stone or shell. No feeling is allowed. There is a continual digging into the roots of all the words, until the student, when he gets through with the play, has no love for it. I have heard many students express a dislike for plays studied in this way at school.

Again, this department is the best for the development of the imagination. Its very connection with other subjects, especially with English and with rhetoric, as has been shown, is a proof that it needs special emphasis. Every true teacher of English and every true teacher of rhetoric ought to recognize at once the truth that it is necessary to train the faculties that create figures, rather than to acquire a mere technical knowledge of figures; that those powers which appreciate literature must be awakened before a genuine love can be born. Expression rightly taught more than all else, will awaken these faculties.

Another very important argument is, that the work belongs to no other department of education. Among the Greeks it belonged to rhetorical study, but it has, in these days, become entirely divorced from that department of education. It would seem at first that it ought to be a part of the study of English, but it is found to be separate from that department. The study of literature is conducted mainly for the acquirement of facts; for an understanding of etymology and the growth of English, and to acquire a vocabulary. This is very important, but it needs, as a complement, the work of expression.

To illustrate, therefore, the function of a teacher of expression in a college: He is, first of all, a representative of the importance of doing, as well as of acquiring; of execution, rather than the mere development of the understanding; of expression, as well as of impression. He must arouse the creative faculties of the mind. By having students speak extemporaneously, by having them recite, by having them read and by other exercises necessary to the work of expression he will be enabled to study the real possibilities of each member of his class. Hence, he will or should know their practical possibilities better than any other teacher in the college. Other teachers are engaged more upon specialties. They test a student's knowledge, they study subjects; but the teacher of expression studies the *man.* By virtue of the very nature of his work he is brought face to face with personality. More than any other instructor he can find whether knowledge is merely taken into the head — merely taken into the memory. He can see whether the student has merely crammed, and can thus easily write out answers to questions and pass his examinations, or whether he has really assimilated and entered into positive possession of knowledge; whether he has merely grown in knowledge of facts, or whether his personality is growing by the truth it feeds upon.

More than any other teacher will a true teacher of expression be enabled to see the advancement and harmonious growth of a student. He will be prepared, therefore, to give advice, and if he is the man he should be, his advice will be sought regarding lines of reading. When a student has no love for poetry, his imagination, however strong naturally, is slumbering. Every man needs this faculty, no matter in what department he is to labor or what profession he is to follow.

Again, a teacher of expression can see whether a man is merely sentimental or emotional without thought; whether he reads only emotional literature and has an utter lack of logic, or whether he has no feeling and emotion. Any such one-sidedness will be seen at once by the teacher of expression. And not only so, but he will trace such imperfections to their causes, and by suggestions and often by direct prescription of work he can furnish an adequate remedy, sometimes in his own department, often by recommending attention to studies in other departments. He can show the student by special criticism the causes of his failures, analyzing his mind and indicating the lack of harmony in his development. The teacher of expression has definitely in his department the problem of harmony. The teacher of mathematics tries to emphasize his own department and exaggerates knowledge of mathematics. The teacher of Greek feels it his special duty to emphasize its importance, to make it interesting to students and to be sure that they are thoroughly posted in that language. But the teacher of expression looks at the man in his assimilation of all his studies, calls upon him to manifest his own personality, and looking at him in the act of production, in the act of thinking aloud, more than any other he is able to judge of the student's imperfections — of his departure from the normal — and more than any one else will be competent to advise the student in the arrangement of his electives for another year so as to emphasize those things which are especially needful.

Thus a teacher of expression has an important indirect function to discharge. He will make the student more alive to the broader needs of culture. His influence will be felt by the student when reciting Latin, when demonstrating his problem in mathematics. The whole bearing of students toward each other, toward their class, toward their teachers, in all discussions will be affected by such a teacher. He will save students unconsciously and indirectly from falling into extravagant errors. The voices of college students are often hard. In fact, the class attitude and class tone in all our institutions of learning is very apt to be cold and without resonance. In a college where there is a teacher of expression, teachers in other departments can remind students that they seem to need vocal training when they can not be heard in class or make an egregious blunder in pronunciation or are awkward in bearing. Thus such a department tends to bring an atmosphere into the institution favorable to graceful bearing and artistic culture.

Again, a teacher of expression, while his department is not directly connected with physical training, will yet be enabled to see by means of the revelations of the voice and body, the conditions of health. As is well known to all physicians, the voice is most sympathetically related to vitality. The moment any abnormal physical condition is present, the moment disease makes any attack, the voice will show it. The condition of the muscles, even of those far removed from the parts specially concerned in the production of voice, has an influence over the tone, and one who has been thoroughly trained feels the whole man revealed in that tone, not only as to the harmony of mind, but as to harmony of body and the condition of vitality.

Again, a vast number of students, the very best students, are nervous and embarrassed. It is a notorious fact that some students who stood highest in their classes do not stand highest in the actual world. Some have, therefore, falsely concluded that their education was of little use to them. But the fault here was not that they studied too hard, but on account of one-sidedness, of too great subjectivity, or it may be, because the artistic execution in their education did not keep pace with the accumulation of knowledge by the mind. As the lungs not only need to take in air, but to give it out, so the healthful mind must present truth, must manifest its relations to personality as well as secure information. The growth of the plant is not due merely to the amount of material that is heaped about it; but depends upon the harmonious co-operation and assimilation of light, heat, soil, moisture and air. So the soul must grow from the co-ordination of all its elemental acts. Nay, further, as the soil may be made so rich as to kill the plant, so the mind by mere work in the aggregation of facts may stifle its own life and become dwarfed into a Toots or a Dominie Sampson.

The progress in all education has ever been toward more work in practical execution. Even in the technical schools there is now less theory and more practical work, in chemistry less mere reading and more work in the laboratory, and everywhere less speculation and theorizing and more experiment and earnest endeavors to learn from objects themselves.

Some of the functions of such a teacher, aside from what will be considered his real office, are the training of the voice, the development of grace and ease in the body, the removal of all awkwardness and stiffness, the development of a man's power to think upon his feet as well as at his desk; in short, the improvement of the use of his whole speech and bearing in public and in private. But there are more general functions of as great importance. Studying the student in active execution, in a unity of his personality with his knowledge, he sees revealed before him all the peculiarities and necessities of the man's nature. Hence, his function is lifted in dignity above that of a mere specialist.

If such is the function to be performed, what are some of the qualifications of a man to fill such an office? It would seem at once, from the nature of the case, that he should be a broadly educated man, that, of all teachers in an institution, he should be selected with the most care; and yet, what are the facts? One college president says he only wants to hear a man read to know whether he will be a good teacher of elocution or not. When I once asked one of the most prominent college presidents if it was true, as reported, that his university employed the poorest man they could find to teach elocution in order to throw a slur upon the whole subject, he turned the question off with the remark, " We spend very little money upon it, at any rate." In short, the ordinary opinion regarding a teacher in this department is, that he need not be a thoroughly educated man; he only needs a little technical skill, "a little ingenuity and artifice," as Mrs. Malaprop would say, to do such work even in a college. Again, persons planning to become teachers think very little study is necessary to prepare them for such an important work. A short course of lessons, in their opinion, is sufficient. Some even look with contempt upon broader subjects and their connection with expression, when such are placed in the course of study to prepare them for the discharge of such an important office in human education.

Again, while it is known that in such a subject as this personality is brought into more intimate contact with personality than in any other department of education, and that there is thus, consciously or unconsciously, a greater influence wielded for good or for ill, yet there is a common opinion that in elocution you may expect a little departure from conventional standards. Nay, even more; little attention was formerly paid to character in the selection of teachers.

A teacher of expression must be a thoroughly developed and widely-educated man — a man not only widely informed, but of true and deep instincts, because the subject he comes to teach is the most difficult of all. It is so many-sided, so tempting to a hobbyist. He is required to have a deeper insight into personality, a more profound knowledge of human nature and a broader understanding of the educational value of every subject in relation to personality. He must especially be thoroughly posted in all advanced methods of education.

Again, a teacher of expression must be an educated man because he must be able to penetrate into the deepest needs of students. He must know something, therefore, of all departments of knowledge, especially in their relation to education, that is to say, he must understand the effect upon personality of all subjects. If in conducting a class, for example, in extemporaneous speaking, he has a student who is illogical, who presents his thought at hap-hazard and without method, the teacher must be able to prescribe for this special need. Unless he, himself, has a thorough knowledge of the practical application of logic, how can he make an intelligent criticism ? How can he give the proper logical prescription, so to speak, for the need before him ?

This breadth of culture, however, must be of a practical kind. It must be artistic and literary, as well as scientific. There must be insight and true love for all literature and art. It has been shown that delivery is essentially a department of art. Without such a love of art and literature he can never love this work, he can never inspire students, he can never awaken the creative faculties of their minds. More than any other teacher, his knowledge needs to be translated into instinct. All his knowledge needs to be assimilated. He must have perfect control over himself. He has to give illustrations of all kinds, not that he is to teach by imitation, but he must lead ; he must illustrate faults, he must illustrate differences between excellences and faults. He must stir up the artistic natures of men, and this can only be done, in many instances, by art. He must be enveloped by an artistic atmosphere ; he needs not mere critical knowledge, but thoroughly trained artistic power for execution.

His powers of observation must be most thoroughly and carefully developed ; as the student stands before him to speak there will be a thousand aspects from which he can be viewed. He must have his faculties and sensibilities so trained, his dramatic instinct so developed, that he can see the subject exactly as the student sees it. He must not frame an ideal of his own and place it as a standard for another, but he must penetrate into the ideal of another. No man can succeed in such work as this without great dramatic instinct and broad sympathies. He comes more closely, probably, to the soul-life of students than any other teacher. The very nature of his work, if it is successful, requires this. It is for this reason that there must be time for his work; he must meet students a sufficient amount of time to be enabled to understand them and for them to understand him. He must also be a man of great magnetism.

"Know thyself," was carved upon the ancient temple, and self-knowledge has been considered from the time of Socrates as the fundamental requisite of education, yet the fact remains that study of ourselves is the least interesting of all studies; and especially that artistic work with our own poor voices and our own poor bodies as the technical means requires most resolution. A teacher who can make a class study themselves, who can stand before them not with a subject, but with personal specific criticism, that goes to the very depths of their nature and penetrates to their ideals, must have great imagination, sympathies and insight.

So subtle and delicate is the work to be accomplished, that he must be a man of patience and perseverance. There is no mechanical instrument concerned, there is no mere building to be constructed or reconstructed, but all must be dependent upon nature's processes of growth.

Of his special technical training, his thorough understanding of the many habits of men — and this not only in their nature, their physiology, but in their possibilities and the principles underlying methods of training them, his thorough understanding of what is natural and what is unnatural, and of the peculiar nature of mannerisms it is not necessary to speak.

If the function of a teacher is so important, we must at once recognize the importance of his preparation. How shall this preparation be given? It is of such a nature that it demands a preservation of traditions, a continuous history, a progressive development from age to age, constantly renewed study of the problem by a union of leading specialists. This can only be done through a special professional school for such teachers.

The great cause of the lack of progress in this work, the cause of its failure to keep pace with the needs of the problem, has been the fact that there has been no such school where the best traditions could be preserved, and where the discoveries, the successive advances made by different teachers, could be given "a local habitation and name", where they could be tested and tried by experience and by the co-ordination of many minds.

There can be no important growth or advancement in any science or art that does not take place by means of a co-ordination of many minds. The human being has this peculiarity: he can communicate with his kind. But for this, probably the human mind would be completely locked in a subjective dungeon. It is only when an idea of one mind is brought in contact with another that it grows and strengthens, and whenever we have a form of work, a department of science, which is isolated from others, its advancement is very slow, if it improves at all; but where an individual is working alone, his methods die with him and always become abnormal without a co-operation of other minds. This is exactly what has taken place in elocution. Books have been written, and men have studied with individual teachers to receive their traditions, and in this way, as has been shown, there has been some growth; but this has not been accelerated or assisted by specially-organized schools, by any association of men, as has been the case in other departments of knowledge.

There are many reasons why such a special school should be established. The work is so peculiar, so different from all other phases of human education, that it will be overlooked unless there is such a school for technical preparation. The teacher often thinks he needs only the common preparation of every teacher, but while the teacher of expression needs the preparation of the ordinary teacher, he needs something more. He needs technical training, technical knowledge, technical skill.

It may be very well to ask why there should be a special school in any province of knowledge. A special school should be organized either on account of the peculiar nature of the work, the peculiar character of the training, on account of its definite relation to some profession, or to give emphasis to some neglected phase of education. A special school of law is necessary because the aim is to prepare members for a specific profession. The same is true of a school of theology. The doctor is not only prepared for a special profession, but, in the very nature of the case, he needs peculiar and special information regarding a definite field of knowledge. A clergyman has often risen to great power without the theological school, with merely a college course and his own study into the needs of men, but the doctor, either in the regular medical school or as the private pupil of some physician, absolutely requires a special preparation. The technical schools and the manual schools, especially the latter, are organized to emphasize a definite phase of education.

Teachers of expression have a peculiar work different from that of all other teachers, who need special technical training. The knowledge that is to be attained and the skill that is to be acquired is almost, if not quite, as peculiar as that of the doctor. The technical skill and execution required is almost, if not quite, as special and peculiar as that needed by the musician. If there are to be special schools of music on account of the peculiar training that is required and the technical skill that must be mastered, then the same must be held true of work in expression. Just as there is a little music which belongs to all education, so there is a certain amount of expression which belongs to all education, but as it is absolutely necessary that a teacher of singing, to be effective, should have special training in order to give his work in the public schools, so it is with expression. There is a certain amount and form of it belonging to the development of every man, as has been shown, but the teacher who does this general amount of expression requires a place at which he can secure definite and special training so that he will be able to meet the needs of those committed to his charge.

There are, in the case of such a school, peculiar and special dangers. Being a study to a great extent of manner, there is a danger that it should become superficial, as has been shown. Besides, since it is a subjective work, it especially favors pretensions and extravagant claims. It is very liable to end in mere show. There is more danger of superficiality and conventionality than in any other form of education. There is also danger of merely working for money. Being an art that when popular brings the greatest financial reward of almost any, there is great temptation to sacrifice true artistic work for what is merely popular, if not degrading. Being an art which is not reined up by open criticisms as other forms of art, being an art that is completely passing, and having no permanent body by which it can be criticised and its weaknesses held up to ridicule, it is especially liable to aim for the popular and temporary rather than the artistic and eternal. By teachers and schools holding out exaggerated hopes to incompetent persons, by flattering the inexperienced and the ignorant, much money can be made, and there is a constant temptation in this direction.

For this reason such a school needs to be endowed and established upon a most solid foundation and in the care of trustees who love the work, who understand its needs, its possibilities and its dangers, and who can place both school and teachers beyond temptation.

Again, such a school, while it should be special, while it has peculiar and special training, ought to belong to some great university where it will continually be inspired with a spirit of scholarship, and not be isolated and the more endangered on account of being separated from universal education. Such work, in fact, demands a more intimate connection with the university than even the other professional schools. Otherwise it will become merely technical, or tend to become so, and will become a mere matter of manner and the thorough discipline of the faculties will be lost sight of. Such work, in fact, while needing separate attention, should be as far as possible associated with other forms of education. It has been shown that it lies along the line of advanced education in all departments. Without advanced methods in education, other subjects may advance to some extent, but the development of delivery will be absolutely perverted.

XXIV.

THE SPECIAL ARTS OF EXPRESSION.

"Education is the development of all the powers of man to the culminating point of action—action in art."

IT may be well still further to illustrate the application of expression to education and to discuss some of the special professions for which such training is necessary. Let us first of all consider its service to teachers, not merely to technical teachers of expression, but to all instructors. Work in expression is necessary to these on account of the general reasons already given, but more especially because every teacher must use his voice. He must present the truth, and his manner of presenting the truth is vitally important. If his voice is cold and hard, he will weary his students. If he is monotonous he will fail to awaken or at least to sustain interest.

Many failures among teachers may be traced directly to a misuse of the voice. Teachers in our public schools are continually breaking down from sore throats and ill health of various kinds. Many suffer continually who say nothing about it, lest they should lose their positions. What is the cause of this? Most teachers have to speak in large rooms to forty or fifty children, some even to sixty or seventy. Very frequently the rooms are in a noisy part of a city and teachers have great difficulty in making themselves heard. The result is, they begin to strain the voice, not knowing how to use it, and a sore throat is the inevitable consequence. Many not knowing how to breathe, cramp the lungs and strain the throat, so that the whole nervous system becomes broken down and the organs of the body ready for disease.

That something destroys the health of teachers has been recognized for some time; and physical culture has been brought forward the last few years as the remedy. This is very important, but it does not go to the root of the evil. Nine tenths of the time bad health is due to a misuse of the voice and the organs of expression.

When we come to think of the teacher's function, of the influence of tone upon children, when we see what unconscious imitators children are, we feel at once the great importance of having teachers trained in the use of their voices. Teachers must present the truth. Children often get more from their teachers unconsciously than they do consciously. If a teacher has a cold, hard voice, the children will be affected unconsciously. For these, and other reasons, we can realize at once the importance of special training of all instructors in the use of their voices.

Again, it is universally recognized that our American voice is growing hard and unpleasant. Much of this is due simply to neglect of vocal culture; there is none of it in the home, little or none of it in the school. But the chief cause is either the bad example or the bad methods of teachers. For instance, the common methods for the development of articulation constrict the throat and harden the voice. In reading there is little or no study of the qualities of the voice. The right attention to the use of the voice is more universally needed to-day by teachers than any form of training or subject of study.

Again, parents justly complain of the lack of general culture among teachers. The mother goes to see the teacher to whom she is to commit her child, and finds one who is thoroughly posted in the methods of the Normal School, but whose voice is cold and harsh and whose imagination and taste are crude and undisciplined. She goes home feeling discouraged. There are many such; but unfortunately there are more who pay no attention to the matter at all, who commit their children to any-body, trusting entirely to the school committee. The result, especially upon the voice, and often upon the health, is very bad.

Teachers need culture, literary culture, culture of the voice and culture for grace and bearing of the body. The teacher must have imagination and insight into human nature. Expression furnishes almost the only effective means to enable the teacher to secure the breadth of culture that is needed. Not only is express-ive training needed by teachers for the sake of their health, for their direct and indirect influence over chil-dren, but for other reasons. They must have the power to adapt truth to others. A knowledge of expression aids them in a knowledge of human nature. Their insight into the needs of children is quickened, and they are enabled to be far better judges of the children's growth and harmonious development.

One of the most important applications of expressive training, must be the development of public speakers, the improvement of the art of oratory. However beautiful a method for the development of expression may seem, if it fails to develop public speakers, it must be funda-mentally wrong, for oratory, as the world has ever held, is the highest of all the vocal arts, if not the highest of all the arts. When we think of Greece we think of the climax of her art in Demosthenes. Although many relics of her sculpture and architecture have come down to us, although we can still gaze with enraptured vision upon the relics of the Parthenon, upon the Hermes, the Theseus and the Venus de Milo; yet, while we have only the bare words of the Oration on the Crown, and the music of the voice that poured forth the passion and patriotism has long been silent, still it is considered as one of the highest flights of human genius. It is this phase of expression which is held by the world to be more sacred than any other, the divinest mode of conveying truth. Whenever soul faces soul, all other forms of art seem cold and lifeless. Whenever a man has been on trial for his life or has sought to awaken the patriotism or quicken the life of his race, the means that has always been adopted has been oratory. No reform has ever been propagated without its aid. The Goddess of Liberty has ever held her sister Eloquence by the hand. Discourse is the crowning achievement of the human mind, without which freedom, benevolence and progress have ever slumbered. "No free country has ever existed that has not erected its altar to persuasion."

Men have said that oratory belonged only to ages of ignorance and unlettered peoples; that it is displaced now by the printing-press; he who has anything to say must now say it through the medium of newspapers or books. But while the press as a method of communication has become more and more influential, still whenever there is a political campaign, whenever there is public agitation on any great subject, that printing has not displaced oratory, must be clear to the most skeptical. So long as the world stands, there will be an art of oratory, and in some form or other it will be found to grow and advance. While its form may change, its spirit will remain.

Nothing is more universally acknowledged than the fact that modern methods of education do not develop, or at least are unfavorable to the development of public speaking. There are many reasons for this. The modern tendencies have been toward science and material advancement, or toward those arts which are associated especially with decoration and ornamentation.

Besides, modern education pays very little attention to literary and artistic training of any kind. Scientific culture and the utilitarian or business education in our modern days have, in a great measure, supplanted artistic development. Even in art work students are made critics rather than artists. The creative faculties are not awakened; the imagination is not stirred; the emotions and passions of the man are either repressed and killed, or perverted; there is no discipline, no great endeavor in education to co-ordinate, to harmonize and unite passion and thought, a co-ordination of which must ever be the fundamental requisite of oratory.

If modern education has failed to develop orators, certainly elocution has made a still worse failure. As was shown by Whately many years ago, more speakers have been spoiled than have been made by the old artificial methods.

One main reason for this, probably, is on account of the tendency to develop self-consciousness. Elocution contending that the speaker must understand and hold every thing in his mind and obey consciously-prescribed rules for every vocal modulation or physical action, the oratoric instinct is perverted, all is made artificial, and the death of true oratory naturally follows.

Let us look for a moment carefully at the problem of public speaking. Judging from the nature of the case, what needs to be done? First of all, the speaker must have great powers of mind. It is the soul that must speak. Accordingly a speaker must be trained to think; but this is general and applies to preparation for any profession. There is, however, in speaking a special kind of thinking. The speaker must have deep power of insight into fundamentals. It is not the number of thoughts that a speaker utters, but their character that accomplishes the end. His power depends upon his grasp of what lies at the foundation. A speaker must say the right thing. He must therefore of all men, have insight into human character — into human knowledge — into human motives. He speaks to awaken thought in others. So important is suggestion in oratory that the speaker's chief power is to know what not to say..

Again, his imagination must be thoroughly trained. He must not only have power to think, but his thought must be living. It must breathe and move in noble form and vivid color. A mere abstract thinker can never make an orator.

Again, an orator must be a man of feeling. Magnetism is simply the result of passion, united to thought. It results from sympathy of the man with his kind. The greatest orators in all ages have been men of strong, deep emotion. And not only so, the emotion and thought of the man must be co-ordinated by will. Feeling without thought is sentimental and vain ; thought without feeling is cold and dead, and both without will are weak. The orator, before all men, must co-ordinate the primary acts of his soul ; these must be united in one strong impulse.

Thus we can see that it is not merely the acquisition of knowledge that makes the speaker. While knowledge is power, knowledge alone will never constitute oratoric power. The power of an orator is measured by his assimilation of knowledge : knowledge that has become a part of him ; that is not merely in the memory, but in the life-blood of the soul.

But the orator is also dependent upon expression. He must have a vocabulary. He must have command of words, command of voice and of body. He must command all the languages of his nature. As many a speaker has only one emotion and never makes a strong effect upon his fellow-men and needs to have developed a broader and greater gamut of passion, so it is with his languages or modes of expression. A man with only one gesture, with only one tone, with only one inflection, with only one color to his voice, can never make an orator. He must have command of all the languages which belong to man.

Again, he must not only have the power to create a vivid idea; he must not only have command of all the languages that manifest this idea; but he must have power to abandon himself to the idea. Eloquence is the result of the domination of the human soul by an idea. The great unconscious forces of the man must be aroused and stirred. If oratory is the presentation of truth by personality, the deep, unconscious powers of the man which constitute the greatest element of personality must be awake.

There must, therefore, be absence of self-consciousness. While there must be an extension of consciousness — while the man must be more or less conscious of his whole body, of his audience, of his modes of expression, especially as to whether he is saying the right thing or not, still the unconscious forces of his nature must be roused and their involuntary modes of manifestation developed. He must lose consciousness and care for the opinion of men. He must, as Edward Everett Hale has said, be willing "to make himself a fool for his subject." No man who is not willing to do so has ever made an orator. He must not be too conscious of mere conventional propriety. The voluntary and involuntary parts of his nature must both be awake. There must, in fact, be a co-ordination and union of the conscious and unconscious to such an extent that he can hardly draw the line between the two. He is both conscious and unconscious of his voice, and of his body, and of his audience; he is both conscious and unconscious of his feeling; but he is directly conscious of the great ideas upon which his whole soul is concentrated.

He must thus be trained to think upon his feet. Without power of extemporaneous speaking, there can be no growth in the orator. While recitation may be important, while every great orator has loved and studied the poets, especially the dramatic poets, while every great orator in all time has devoted much time to recitation, yet the one exercise which is absolutely necessary is found in the various forms of speaking itself, and especially in extemporaneous speaking.

Thus, all training to improve the orator must develop his power of putting thought and passion together; must develop his power to bring the grandest thought and the highest abstraction into the realm of the imagination. A vague and indefinite truth must be assimilated and realized by the man. Every faculty and power of his nature must be aroused. Above all, training to develop an orator must give him control of his voice and his body, of every agent and of every language, as well as of every faculty of the soul.

If we compare this ideal with the principles unfolded for the development of expression, we find that true work for expression will develop all these powers and agents and languages, and secure all these actions. The fundamental requisite of all expression has been shown to be a harmonious co-operation of all the powers of the man. The unconscious impulses of the man can be trained. It has been shown that not only can education affect the faculties by bringing them into consciousness, but that it can also affect the faculties without bringing them abnormally into consciousness. The spontaneous and deliberative impulses of the soul, as intended by nature, can be made stronger and co-ordinated into greater unity for the highest art. The development of the powers of expression does not require that the consciousness of the man shall be placed merely upon language or upon the agents of the body or their motions, but can be kept centered upon his ideas. The train of ideas which passes through his soul furnishes the key to the nature of all expression. Even faults of breathing, faults of voice, can be traced to the action of the mind. It has been shown that the whole power of the man can be con-centrated upon these ideas, that they can stimulate the passion and impulses of the soul. The speaker can abandon himself to the dominion of these ideas, and they will stimulate and co-ordinate all the spontaneous impulses of his nature when rightly seen and rightly produced. The orator, therefore, can be developed without being made self-conscious. He can secure self-control without developing affectation. He can develop power to aban-don himself to passion and thought without losing control of the fundamental poise of his nature. He can develop power without abnormal extravagance, and control with-out repression.

The speaker can acquire a facility of expression by personal contact with literature, by a thorough study of the best authors. He can become master of the art of putting thought into words. No mere scientific course of training or mere acquisition of knowledge can ever develop a speaker. Of course scientific training is very important. A certain amount of it is the very best train-ing that can be secured to develop powers of observation or the logical faculties of the man ; but it can never alone make a speaker. The place of literary training can never be filled by scientific training in the development of any artist.

In the application of methods for the development of delivery to public speakers, a vast number of difficulties are encountered. For example, in the theological school expressive training is so absolutely different in method and nature from the other studies in the school, that students of such schools are very difficult to teach ; besides, elocution has been so often condemned by great preachers of the century, that many students look at it with suspicion. For these and many other reasons, it often takes time to make students realize their needs and understand in the smallest degree, the true course which they must take in order to secure possession of them-selves, and achieve their ideals. Yet of all men at the present time, theological students have most need for the development of delivery, and when once they are awak-ened, there is no class of men who realize the importance of such training more than clergymen.

There is a universal consciousness that there is some-thing radically wrong in the methods of developing the delivery of clergymen. Students themselves have often felt it. The lay members of the church have, however, felt it most, and the adequate training of clergymen as manifest in their delivery, their general culture as shown in the use of their voice, are among the most important of the elements that weigh in the selection of pastors. Good delivery is accounted one of the most fundamental requisites, but one of the rarest attainments.

What is needed to-day in the education of the speaker and especially of the clergyman is an application to the whole subject of delivery, of the true principles governing natural methods in education such as have been applied even to the study of Hebrew. In short, there is needed an application of a careful method of observation, a thorough study of nature in the light of modern science and the most advanced methods of education. The needs of the preacher are the needs of all our schools and professions at the present time, only more accentuated. There is no place in all education where there is greater need of the application of the principles advocated in this book, than in the training of preachers. Elocution has proved inadequate because it has been too narrow, it has not gone to the depths of the problem, it has left untouched many of the most important elements of expression. Clergymen need to be shown the artistic phase of education. Many of their faults can never be eradicated without a more thorough and radical development of their imagination, of their literary taste, of their dramatic instincts and their creative faculties. The same applies to all speakers. In fact, careful study of delivery and thorough training according to the principles here advocated should be applied, if public speaking of any kind is to be improved.

Oratory is an art that aims to present the truth for the conscious and direct persuasion of men. But there are other arts of expression which reach their results indirectly; though not consciously or directly persuading, yet they move the soul as potently by unconscious influence as oratory. Man is so constructed that he is influenced both consciously and unconsciously. Conscious influence is worth but little without unconscious influence. Just as expression itself is composed of a co-ordination of conscious and unconscious elements, so the arts of expression have a corresponding complexity. All great art chiefly depends upon reaching men uncon-

sciously and indirectly. A great painting does not consciously preach, but it does influence men. A sermon
upon the conscience is very important ; but Shakespeare's
art in Macbeth accomplishes the results indirectly. Here
the thing is done that breeds the thought. There is no
conscious and direct preaching, but two souls are portrayed under the influence of conscience ; right is made to
triumph according to the law of all great art. Shakespeare taken as the type of all great artists never tries to
justify wrong or right, but each is painted in its own
native colors. Nature, the highest artist, causes her sun
to rise on the evil and the good, but seeks ever to awaken
the impulses of the soul. As the aim of art is usually
considered to be indirect, mystic or unconscious, some
deny that oratory is an art at all. True art, however, is
the co-ordination of conscious and unconscious elements,
and the highest oratory is not direct exhortation, but
approaches the subject indirectly and awakens unconscious as well as conscious motives. As a man becomes
eloquent, spontaneous elements become predominant.
The difference between the two, therefore, is one of
degree rather than kind. Oratory has more conscious,
histrionic expression, more unconscious elements.

Some regard art as simply "delight in God's works."
Others regard it as a means of telling the truth. However art may be regarded, its power to elevate or degrade
men can not be ignored. The effect of art upon men,
whether conscious or unconscious, direct or indirect, may
be explained on this ground. Art itself being the
actualization of an ideal, we can see its kinship to human
life. Life itself is a realization of an ideal. Every man
has consciously or unconsciously an ideal within him,
and character and all human life is the actualization of
this ideal. Browning has said that the ideal of the worst

man in the world is higher than the actual life of the best man in the world.

Now, when art is presented to the human soul it appeals to this ideal, and will, of course, elevate or lower it. However comic, however temporary or transient the art may be, it will have an effect upon man's ideal. Man can be pleased above or below the plane of his ordinary feeling. However low the tone of a man's mind may be, he can be pleased in the direction of still lower tendencies. This, of course, will degrade the man. But whenever a man is pleased above the ordinary plane of his emotions he is elevated, his ideal is quickened, and his emotions and impulses toward reaching his ideal are stimulated.

Shakespeare's art has always a most healthful moral effect upon us. He does not preach, but however low the character he portrays, it is related directly or indirectly to an ideal. All is permeated with the moral spirit inherent in the human soul. One who makes a study of Shakespeare or lives with such art as Walter Scott's novels, receives unconsciously a great influence into his life. The especial function of fiction and dramatic art in the general education of the race is to awaken ideal conceptions of manhood and womanhood, to show men the different points of view among men, and to stimulate dramatic insight into human character. The parable falling from the most sacred lips is a recognition of the necessity of teaching men through the medium of art. The deepest lessons must be given to men indirectly and unconsciously as well as directly and deliberatively.

It has been shown again and again that histrionic art broadens and expands the human soul more directly than any form or art. Men's views of human life would be narrow and one-sided without the assistance of dramatic art. Art does more than merely stimulate an ideal and please, it enables men to look at truth from different points of view.

No greater mistake has ever been made than to leave dramatic art to hap-hazard study, to the vicious and the ignorant, and never to consider it as in any way belonging to education or as deserving any attention or regulation.

How do the principles governing methods apply to the development of histrionic expression?

What are some of the methods usually employed for the development of the histrionic artist? The one most commonly in use is that of simple dramatic rehearsal. The student who desires to prepare for the stage is first employed at the theater as a "supernumerary." He does "utility business". He receives no instruction except occasionally something to do upon the stage. He is employed with a large number of others as a mere figure-head in some scene.

In this way he is supposed to absorb the principles of the art. Some studious aspirants observe the acting of the ablest "star", and endeavor to imitate all his peculiar movements and expressions. Many such aspirants do nothing at all. Of course only one in a thousand ever succeeds; only one in ten thousand ever reaches artistic prominence. The method is vicious. All attention is directed to imitation. Brought before an audience before any self-control has been secured, brought into positions by some mechanical direction, and made to think of business and nothing else, all expression becomes artificial and stilted.

There is no more effective way to destroy the student's ideal of the true artistic nature of expression, no worse way to fetter the imagination and stifle the whole artistic nature. True expression must ever begin with the study of ideas and the awakening of emotion. The artistic instinct must first of all be stimulated and the individual secure control of his own power of rendering, before he is worked into a scene to co-operate with others for a simultaneous and co-ordinate manifestation, such as is called for in histrionic expression.

Another method is the "Amateur Company". This is worse still. The student is not brought in contact with art nor with any standard of true criticism. Many who attend an amateur performance are there to laugh at the egotism and the unconscious blunders of the performers. An audience often laughs in the most serious scene, because the actor is making such a ludicrous figure, of which he is wholly unconscious. Amateurs fall into the habit of mouthing and rant. Everything is made stilted, and all ease and simplicity are destroyed. Everything is the result of aggregation and extravagance. An amateur is easily known. He has no expression in the face, all subtilty of nature is lost and his every action is stilted and labored. There are, of course, a few exceptions, but they are extremely rare. The few who succeed either by this, or the first course, do so by accident. They never can rise to the height of art that would be possible with a more adequate method.

The third method adopted is the elocutionary one. This has also failed. It is almost universally condemned by the best actors. The ordinary work of elocution is too mechanical and artificial. The few who have studied elocution before going upon the stage, have afterward said that they had to forget all that they had learned. Mechanical elocution causes self-consciousness, substitutes tricks for natural expression, trains the student to obey rules rather than natural impulses of the heart, makes him distrust himself and nature, and trust entirely to some mechanical or artificial mode of procedure.

All these modes have been proved to be inadequate. They all result in artificiality and mechanical modes of expression. There is to-day very little dramatic instinct upon the stage. The methods for the development of actors, the nature of many of the plays which are produced, call for mere mechanical performance and not for artistic acting. Many times a man is chosen for the part of a Frenchman, for example, simply because he has a French brogue and can walk through the part without any mechanical offense. Women are chosen for parts simply because they are beautiful and have a fine form. The whole art of acting is looked at from an external aspect and not in reference to the true principles of art or the real nature of the human soul.

Everything upon the stage is looked at from the point of view of representation, and nothing from the standpoint of manifestation. As has already been shown, true dramatic art is a co-ordination of manifestation with representation. Accordingly, modern acting is all tending to farce and the comic opera. Appealing to a depraved taste which it stimulates more and more, the educated classes almost universally remain at home. Instead of endeavoring to awaken in an audience a love of true art, of the action of the soul, of dramatic instinct, of the manifestation of the noblest feelings and ideals, the appeal is more and more to the eye. Expression is confounded with exhibition and oddities and characteristics substituted for character.

One who wishes to make a success in dramatic expression needs to obey the principles here unfolded, to secure control over voice and body, to develop the artistic faculties, to stimulate the imagination and the sympathies, to develop ideals of art from the depths of his own soul and from an ideal study of the best possible art of every form. Then, and not till then, he should begin to study the business of his art; otherwise he will be more conscious of the external than of the internal, he will all his life lack control of his voice and of his body, which should have been attained as the most preliminary step in his training.

The actor is more conscious of the manifestation through every part of his body, of the various modes and languages of each agency, than the speaker, but in general the same principles apply. The more eloquent a speaker is the more the spontaneous element predominates. Every step we have attained, every principle of nature unfolded, applies with equal force to every application of expression. The unconscious as well as the conscious use of the faculties must be stimulated. Expression of whatever form when it rises to its highest aspect is a revelation of the whole man. The orator is called upon to discharge a conscious process of thinking and to form his ideas into words, but the true actor also has to *think* his part, and while he does not choose his own words, still he must carry all the languages to a much further height, must use a greater number, and bring them all into a greater and more absolute unity, so that every power of his nature must be awake.

Another important phase of histrionic art is public reading. It is essentially different from acting. It is more subjective, more manifestive. Good acting, as has been shown, is both representative and manifestive, but on account of the presence of scenery and the fact that an actor confines himself to one part, there is a tendency to exaggerate the representative element; but public reading must first of all be manifestive. The representative element can only be delicately suggested. The representative element must in nearly all cases be subordinated to the manifestive element. Another difference is, that public reading must be more dramatic than acting. Of course many will laugh at this, but a little investigation will prove it to be true. A good reader must give in co-operation a great many characters, while the actor gives but one. The actor by make-up can substitute some physical characteristic, even some oddity of dress, for true dramatic instinct, but as a rule true and noble public reading calls for the mental difference of characters. When Mr. Irving acts in Hamlet the audience sees his conception of one part, but when he reads the play he furnishes a conception for every part. He must suggest by more subtle means the real nature of Hamlet, must suggest the fundamental elements not only of this, but of every character in the play. His instinct as to the relation of these characters and the blending of all into unity, must be seen and felt. In this case he reveals the play of his soul in more aspects, in more relations than is possible in any other form of dramatic art.

Endeavors have been made in all ages of the world to keep the theater upon the plane of art, but it ever tends to sink to spectacular shows. It has ever been more or less in the hands of money-makers.

There is, however, no desire to disparage theatric art, but only to say a word in behalf of a neglected and despised phase of dramatic art which is worthy of the highest claims and which the sneers of self-styled dramatic critics have never been able to kill. It is older than the art of the theater. The art of the theater came only, strictly speaking, when Æschylus introduced a second actor. Stage art is, strictly speaking, a phase of recitation rather than public reading, a phase of theatric art. The world must and will have sóme form of dramatic art. That which can be easiest regulated, that which can be preserved most inviolate, that which can be made a subject of artistic criticism, that which can be made to respond most sensitively to human nature, that which can be held up most easily as a mirror "to show virtue its own feature, scorn its own image," is public reading.

Professor Murdoch has shown that there never was a time when there were such great spectacular shows as in the time of Shakespeare. The exhibitions given by Leicester at Kenilworth for Queen Elizabeth were beyond modern imagination. Scott has endeavored to paint them in his novel, but he has hardly exaggerated them. And yet notwithstanding this, Shakespeare rejected them and produced his dramas with little of the splendor of modern productions and did not have the real candles upon the altars, the gorgeous scenery with which his plays have since been produced, though he could have had them. The acting of his plays was more like public reading than modern dramatic acting. Theatric art in our time, with some noble exceptions, is a means of exhibiting ten thousand dollar Paris wardrobes and gorgeous displays of scenery. Of course all lovers of the drama regret this and condemn it; yet the Jockey Club is ever ready to hiss down a Wagner who refuses to insert a ballet dance in one of his great musical dramas, and introduces instead a most delicate and original presentation of artistic music. It does not do merely to sneer at Paris for doing this; the spirit is in the modern theater and its patrons, and it must be recognized.

One remedy, as it seems to me, is to build up a co-ordinate art, to foster it, to encourage it, to recognize it by special criticism, to feed and encourage the deep and most profound and most necessary dramatic instinct of the race which is being stifled by the modern theater. It may thus react and furnish one lever to assist in elevating its more representative sister.

The art of reading, denied the adjuncts of make-up and scenery, must be more suggestive, it must appeal more to the mind than to the eye ; there must be a series of hints and intimations to awaken thinking and to stimulate the imagination and feeling of an audience.

If all this is true, public reading must be inherently a higher art than acting. It has greater possibilities in its application to a greater variety of literature. It can be applied to lyrics, to ballads, to the monologue, to short stories and to the novel, while acting can only be applied to one particular form of literature. If the monologue is one of the latest and most important forms of dramatic literature, then the rendering of these must be one of the highest forms of histrionic expression.

On the other hand public reading as an art is on a lower plane of development than acting. The reason for this is, that public reading has been more in bondage to mechanical elocution than acting. Again, the public reader having a very difficult task to perform in contrasting characters, has been led to adopt extravagant tricks in order to make his contrasts emphatic. He has adopted tricks of body, tricks with the face and tricks with the voice, and he has even adopted the worst faults of voice for the purpose of interpreting character. Public reading has in fact in many cases become an art of caricature rather than of characterization. Besides, public reading has tended to confine itself to the lower and farcical class of literature. The beautiful lyrics of the language, for example, have not been considered proper subjects for public reading. Again, in public reading the arrangement or the abridgment of literature for the purpose of reading has often destroyed the highest qualities of that literature. A novel, for example, like David Copperfield or the play which was founded upon it, in being arranged for reading has been completely spoiled. One of the most prominent readers of the country in his rendering of this work practically obliterates all the normal characters. There is nothing left but " Micawber " and " Uriah Heep." Even poor old " Peggotty " is cramped and dwarfed and has dwindled into an abnormal specimen of humanity. Another whom I taught in Nicholas Nickleby, in spite of all that was said and urged, makes Nicholas weak. As Nicholas was natural he could not see that this character needed more work than Squeers or Mrs. Squeers. Normal parts raise no laugh, so they are to be slighted. Often, however, neglect of such parts is merely unconscious, but it shows the condition of the art.

Such readers, or impersonators, as they like to call themselves, entirely overlook the principles of literary art. They entirely forget that we take no interest in an abnormal character in true dramatic art, or in the true novel, or in any high art work, except as it is contrasted with a normal one. Dickens is always true to this principle in all his novels. David Copperfield is rightly named. It is the noble character of David that is felt from first to last. Nicholas Nickleby is the central figure in our minds from first to last as we read the novel. Shakespeare more perfectly than any dramatic poet obeys this principle. To cut out the normal characters in " Twelfth Night ", as is so often done, is to turn this noble comedy into a farce. " Twelfth Night," " Much Ado About Nothing " and the " Merchant of Venice " are not farces, they are comedies; wherever we have only abnormal characters we have a farce. The form in which these plays are read by our public readers destroys their high literary art by a violation of the principles which Shakespeare always obeys, of introducing the comic and abnormal characters and humorous situations in direct contrast with normal ones, to heighten the effect. Dicken's great novel of David Copperfield can never be made out of "Uriah Heep" and "Micawber". True art uses the abnormal and the normal to accentuate each other by contrast.

This same principle applies to the arrangement of programs in miscellaneous readings, and is always obeyed by Prof. J. W. Churchill. This eminent artist ever seeks to arrange his readings with great contrasts and also with great variety in the contrasts during the same evening.

The best of our readers excuse themselves for not reading a better class of literature on the ground that audiences do not appreciate the best literature, and that they are compelled to read the worst form, otherwise they would not be appreciated at all; but in this I think that public readers are mistaken, for though the ordinary audience that now gathers to hear public readings might not receive it, yet if better literature was rendered a better audience would be attracted who would like it, and not only so, but that audience would be an ever increasing one, and the whole art would be advanced and elevated.

Professor Monroe used to tell a story of a committee from a New England town who wrote to him to give them a public reading; they specially requested as is unfortunately common with such committees, that the readings should be comic, and stated that they did not wish any Shakespeare or anything serious. At Professor Monroe's earnest request he was allowed to read a selection from Hamlet. It was this particular reading for which he was most highly complimented, and which pleased the audience universally more than any other.

This and hundreds of other instances could be shown to prove that such committees know little about art and often under-estimate the taste of an audience. Being so anxious to make their readings popular, and knowing that almost anybody can read a comic piece to please, they make their demands. They also make a mistake in failing to see that even the comic parts of a program lose their highest effect when they are not alternated with something which is ideal and serious.

Public reading has itself to blame that only those who love the lower class of literature go to hear readings. This particular taste has been fed. The best people, who wish to hear the best literature, do not go to public readings because they know that they will be disappointed. Wherever any great artist will pay the price he will receive a reward. The public reader himself seeks too often merely to raise a laugh. Henry Ward Beecher said that if he could get an audience to laugh he could make them shed tears in a few minutes. The great aim of histrionic art of the highest kind is to sway an audience. If an audience laughs and nothing else all is one-sided, the audience is not truly moved. Shakespeare makes an audience laugh in all his highest tragedies, but he also makes them weep more than any other writer. The last act of Hamlet is introduced by grave-diggers and a very comic situation, but in that very comic situation a grave is being dug, and in a few moments the audience is swayed to another extreme. Shakespeare has dared violent contrasts just as the greatest musician dares to introduce the greatest dissonances. The true impersonator or public reader, if he does not wish his art

2

48 *Application.*

to become degraded and fall into mere farce, must obey
the same principle in arranging his readings and in
abridging his selections. There must be a study of the
principle which is entirely over-looked in much of the
public reading, and the characters and situation contrasted
according to the principle of the best art.

Besides, such committees and the lower class of readers
over-estimate a laugh. They think that they have moved
an audience when they have caused an external demon-
stration. This was not the opinion of the great actor,
Betterton. He was never pleased with the clapping of an
audience. He said that any fool could raise a laugh or
cause tremendous noise, but it took an artist to awe an
audience into silence.

Nearly all our public readers, as is the case with many
of our actors, make some little success, and they proceed
ever afterward to imitate themselves. They get into a
specialty and are continually striving to find something
similar so that they can reproduce the effect to an audience. A painter, a poet, an artist of any kind, has fallen
into a very bad way when he endeavors to imitate himself.

What public reading to-day needs as an art is great
mastery of voice and body, no less than the technical
work which is now practiced by the best readers. Simultaneously there must be improvement in literary taste, a
development of the imagination, the dramatic and the
assimilative instincts and artistic insight, that public
reading may be made a servant, not of the lowest, but of
the highest literature, a means not of degrading but of
elevating public taste, to show the world beauties in the
highest literature which they have entirely over looked.

A great opportunity is open to one who is willing to
work for years and pay the price, who would be willing
to do his very best artistic work to a "fit audience,

though few." At first the audience might be small, but it would grow. The struggle itself would make such a reader grow, and his circle would widen and his art be lifted to higher heights. Every man must do something for his art as well as for the audience to which he reads, and such unselfish work, soon or late has ever met with its reward. The greatest artist has ever had to pay his price and wait long for his reward, but that reward when it comes is greater and higher and more satisfying to the artistic soul.

One of the great needs of public reading is the application of dramatic criticism. The stage has made most wonderful advance since the introduction into the best class of periodicals of dramatic criticism, but no one has yet dared to do this in relation to public reading. This is a great loss, as the public reader, even more than the actor, is tempted to extravagance, tempted to mannerism, tempted to do everything his own way, and therefore needs another artistic mind to mirror his endeavors, his successes and his failures. It is this lack of proper criticism, the silence of so many persons competent to speak on such a subject, that causes public reading to be where it is. Public sentiment needs expression. There can be no advance without it. The expression of public sentiment, the expression of the feelings of the one who is sincere, outweighs a whole theater of others. The voice of the ideal which is found in every heart, must be expressed through the critic as well as through the artists, to enable even the artist himself to grow.

Public reading, combining as it does every element of expression, is one of the highest forms of histrionic art, and its proper development is very important. As we look at an ideal of the art in comparison with the principles unfolded which govern the development of expres-

sion, we feel more than ever their truth, their importance
and their adequacy to meet all the great problems.
There is needed a development of the unconscious as
well as the conscious, the awakening of the most profound depths of the dramatic instinct, the development
of the whole artistic nature, a development of the manifestive as well as the representative elements, so that
public reading may include the most delicate lyrics and
give them the most truthful rendering as well as the
strongest and most passionate scenes.   The most careful
training of the voice and body, the highest development
of each agency and the highest mastery of the languages
belonging to man, the development of the imagination
and of the powers of emotion ; in short, versatility of
mind, agility of voice and flexibility of body, will find a
means for the highest and most ideal and artistic use in
the sphere of rendering the noblest literature through the
various forms and modes of public reading.   '

There has been an endeavor to glance over the whole
field of human delivery so as to form a more adequate
conception of its general character, to aid in unfolding
more adequate methods for its development.   This general study has enabled us to form certain hypotheses
which will assist us in an investigation of each specific
phase of the problem.   While difficult and more or less
uninteresting may be the task of such general discussions,
yet they are absolutely necessary in such a complex and
misconceived problem as human delivery.   Without these
a teacher may take up vocal training or some one phase
of expression, and seeing its wonderful character come to
feel that it is the whole secret of delivery.
We have found that the act of expression is complex,
that it can never be made completely and solely a prod-

uct of will. Its improvement can not, therefore, be taught by rule; it is more connected with the soul than any other art, and its improvement demands the stimulation of the faculties and impulses that express.

We have found also that expression belongs to the very fountain-head of all art, that all art is a mode of expression or mode of recording expression, and that all art as an objective embodiment of expression, must be studied as the most adequate mirror to reflect the needs, nature, exaltation or degradation of expression.

We have found more especially that there are two great modes of expression: a process of representation and a process of manifestation; that the latter being more mystic and subjective and not subject to rule, has been neglected. Expression appeals to both eye and ear, it is extremely complex and calls for elements as widely apart as a tone and a motion of the hand. These elements can be divided into three classes, words, tones and actions. Each of these discharges a specific function, in fact, every part of the body plays a distinct role in expression.

Expression is so complex that every phase of the human soul can be manifested, directly or indirectly, by one language or by a combination of languages. The nature of expression shows that thought and emotion must both be revealed; tone and action, especially their manifestive forms are primarily intended to express feeling, and this presupposes that feeling must be truly and adequately expressed. The acts of nature, therefore, must be studied and modes of procedure must be obeyed in order to improve expression. We find in the study of nature, that expression is a universal characteristic of all life. We find that nature proceeds from center to surface spontaneously, simply with ease, unity, harmony and freedom. We find that man is a more complex being than any other, but that the same laws apply, that his whole nature must act in true expression and that this is the basis of spontaneity.

As a result of the study of nature, we find that expression must be improved by stimulating its impulse, by opening its channels of revelation and by securing skill in the execution of its manifestive actions. Expression being naturally an effect, must be improved by stimulating its cause, securing the proper condition and control of its organic means, a thorough knowledge of right and wrong, strong and weak modes of execution. The action of the mind is the key to faults, and all the psychic actions concerned in expression must first of all, be studied and properly disciplined. The voice and body must be more adequately trained, the principles of nature investigated so that there may be a science of training evolved for the development of the organs. To improve expression, insight of one human being into the process of the nature of another must be developed; the most difficult form of criticism is found in the endeavor to improve the living man, to show a man wherein he does not fulfill the possibilities of his own nature.

In comparing the development of expression with all education, we find that it is vitally connected with the creative aspect of human development, and that it holds a vital relationship to all phases of artistic training, and on account of its importance it needs to be taught by those who are thoroughly and adequately prepared.

Expression furnishes the basis of the great art of entertainment, it is the basis of power in the orator. Since dramatic instinct is one of the most universal in the human heart, it is of vital moment that expression should be elevated to its proper place.

INDEX.